THE BISHOP'S WIFE

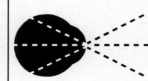

This Large Print Book carries the
Seal of Approval of N.A.V.H.

THE BISHOP'S WIFE

METTE IVIE HARRISON

THORNDIKE PRESS
A part of Gale, Cengage Learning

GALE
CENGAGE Learning·

Farmington Hills, Mich • San Francisco • New York • Waterville, Maine
Meriden, Conn • Mason, Ohio • Chicago

GALE
CENGAGE Learning·

LIBRARY OF CONGRESS CATALOGING-IN-PUBLICATION DATA

Harrison, Mette Ivie, 1970–
    The bishop's wife / by Mette Ivie Harrison. — Large print edition.
      pages cm. — (Thorndike Press large print reviewers' choice)
    ISBN 978-1-4104-7796-5 (hardcover) — ISBN 1-4104-7796-7 (hardcover)
    1. Mormons—Fiction. 2. Missing persons—Fiction. 3. Draper (Utah)—
Fiction. 4. Large type books. I. Title.
PS3608.A783578B57 2015
813'.6—dc23   2014047312

Published in 2015 by arrangement with Soho Press, Inc.

Printed in Mexico
1 2 3 4 5 6 7 19 18 17 16 15

For Sue Gong,
who is the best and most devout part of
Linda Wallheim — I hope she, and
I, will always have your blessing.

CHAPTER 1

Mormon bishop's wife isn't an official call-ing. "Bishop's wife" isn't a position listed on ward documents; there's no ceremonial laying-on of hands or pronounced blessings from on high. But if the bishop is the father of the ward, the bishop's wife is the mother, and that meant there were five hundred people who were under my care. I was used to the phone calls in the middle of the night, to the doorbell ringing far too late and far too early. I was used to being looked past, because I was never the person that they were there to see.

This morning at the six thirty doorbell, I shook Kurt. "They'll be wanting the bishop," I said. I was already out of bed and putting on my robe.

"I'll be there as soon as I can, Linda," he said sleepily. He hadn't been to bed before midnight last night, I was sure. I hurried downstairs, sure that something terrible had happened. It was late January in Draper, Utah, and as picturesque as the snow on the mountains was, it did not mix well with our modern lifestyle. My fear as I stood hesitating at the door was that someone was here to tell us that a teenager from the ward had skidded off the road and was on his way to the hospital. The doorbell rang again, and then the door was knocked on, impatiently.

When I finally opened the door, I saw Jared Helm, one of the newer members of the ward, carrying his five-year-old daughter, Kelly. She had curly blonde hair that always seemed messy, no matter how often it was combed. The remains of breakfast (oatmeal) were all over her chin. She was still in her pajamas, but she'd been bundled into an inside-out snowsuit. How her father had figured out how to get the zipper up without putting it on the right way around, I didn't know.

"Can I see Bishop Wallheim?" asked Jared.

Not an accident, then, I thought with relief. "Come in from the cold. He's awake, and he'll be down in a minute," I assured Jared. So would Samuel, the youngest of my five sons, who was a senior in high school; I could hear his alarm going off upstairs and knew he'd be rushing out the door soon.

I led Jared and Kelly to the front room, where my neglected piano waited for me to practice. Mostly, the room was used now for people waiting to go into Kurt's office.

Jared Helm looked terribly strained, though he was well-kempt. His hair was darker than his daughter's, but it was clear where she got the messy mop. His was wet now, the curls ruthlessly combed around a side part. He was dressed in a button-down striped shirt, cable sweater, and neatly pressed khakis. I wondered if his wife did that pressing or if he did it himself.

I wished I knew the Helms better, but I had only a general impression that he and his wife were unhappy, although devoted parents to Kelly, and that they were struggling financially, as a lot of people in the ward were currently. Maybe he was here because he was in money trouble? Kurt could send him to the bishop's storehouse for some basic food supplies, but many people were unwilling to take that kind of help. The stigma wasn't insignificant. More often, people wanted Kurt to write them a check.

I got out a toy for Kelly to play with, but she held it limply in her hands, uninterested. They were all trucks and building toys,

9

things my sons had enjoyed. I'd never had a chance to build a collection of toys for girls, though I sometimes imagined what I would have bought for a daughter. Dolls? Faux cooking supplies and a tiny stove?

I found a picture book and read it quietly to her, but after several pages I put it down. Kelly's eyes were wandering all over the room. I finally sat her on my lap and let her plunk on the piano keys, which she seemed to enjoy. None of my boys had been interested at this age, except for Samuel.

But after a few minutes, Kelly's piano playing earned the attention of her father, who had been staring silently at his lap. "Stop that noise," he snapped. "You know how to behave better than that." He didn't seem to see me at all.

The little girl immediately went still and folded her hands together. The moment Jared looked away, Kelly slipped her thumb into her mouth, her eyes intent on her father, and I had the sense that she would be in trouble if he caught her doing that, too.

I moved slightly to the side, protecting Kelly from her father's critical gaze with my body, and I thought, as I so often did, about the daughter I had lost. Too often, I knew I judged other parents for not treating a daughter as I imagined I would have treated mine, had she lived.

I could hear Kurt's feet thumping on the floor of the bathroom. He was out of the shower. "The bishop will be down in just a minute, I'm sure," I said again to Jared. It wouldn't take Kurt long to dress. He had become quite efficient at putting on his daily suit. He didn't used to wear one to work every day, but since he became bishop last year, it had seemed that there was no time when he could wear casual clothes.

Samuel rushed past Jared Helm and out the front door, hair still wet, a piece of bread between his teeth. "Love you, Mom," he mumbled as he headed out to the bus stop.

"Love you," I said, still seated with Kelly on my lap. I gave up on the hope of giving my son a hug and kiss goodbye this morning. He wasn't exactly unwelcoming if I was waiting by the door and it was easy for him to stoop over me, but he wouldn't kiss or hug me back.

After Samuel had gone, I noticed that Jared was wiping tears from his eyes. He was in distress, that much was obvious. Where was his wife? If this was a financial problem, as I had first thought, why weren't they here together? I had seen Carrie Helm last Sunday at church and she had been sit-

11

ting a clear distance from her husband, with Kelly between them. It had been obvious that they were in the midst of an argument, but I hadn't thought much of it at the time. Married couples fight.

Carrie Helm was one of the voices I most enjoyed in Relief Society, the church women's group. Carrie was intelligent and she wasn't afraid of saying something that might sound controversial. She was earnest about what she said, too, and didn't do it purely for the sake of causing a stir. But I'd always had the feeling her husband's viewpoints were more conservative than hers, and had wondered how that affected their marriage.

Last week in Sunday School, with Jared sitting beside her, Carrie had made a comment about the priesthood not belonging to men, but rather being God's power that men had access to. Jared's expression was livid. He'd leaned over and whispered something to her, and after that, I saw her flinch when he tried to touch her. Four days later, and apparently Jared Helm had still not apologized to her sufficiently.

And now he sat here crying silently in the hall at 6:50 on a Thursday morning. "Are you hungry?" I asked. "I can get you something to eat." Food is the first thing we Mormons tend to offer. Sometimes it helps and sometimes it doesn't, but the offer is a way of showing concern, at least.

"No, thank you," said Jared, clearing his throat. "I'm fine."

"I'm hungry," said Kelly, taking her thumb out of her mouth.

"You don't need to eat again. I already fed you breakfast at home."

Kelly looked at her thumb and said nothing.

"Growing children are always hungry," I said. "I don't mind fixing her something. It will make me feel useful." I put Kelly down, covering up the hand with the damp thumb as I led her into the kitchen.

"Behave yourself, Kelly," said Jared.

I wasn't sure if he was always like this with her or if he was simply overly anxious about being in someone else's home. I hoped it was the latter, and I could show him that I didn't mind the trouble.

In the kitchen, I set Kelly on a stool by the counter and set out six separate jams for her to choose from as I made toast. A few minutes later, I heard Kurt come downstairs. He spoke briefly to Jared in the front room, then invited him into his office. I breathed relief and focused my attention on Kelly. After she had chosen a separate jam for each slice of toast and worked through three full pieces, the little girl drank a glass of milk and burped.

"Are you too hot? Maybe I could help you get that snowsuit off," I offered.

"Daddy put it on wrong," said Kelly, glancing in the direction her father had gone, as if she wanted to make sure he couldn't hear her.

"I can see that," I said, fighting a smile.

"Mommy never puts it on wrong, but Daddy always does."

I smiled at the echo of Carrie's spunky attitude. "Daddies are sometimes good at other things," I said.

"I know. But Daddy says Mommy is bad," said Kelly. Her lips quivered. "He says that I shouldn't want her."

"But all little girls want their mothers," I said. "Of course they do." Was Kelly telling me that her mother had left them? I supposed this was the answer to the question of why Jared was here. Poor Jared. Poor Carrie. But most of all, poor Kelly. The children were the ones who always suffered the most when parents had problems. "Your daddy loves you very much," I said.

Kelly put her hands to her hair. "He forgot to brush me," she said.

"Well, let's deal with that right now," I said, and led Kelly to the upstairs bathroom.

I didn't have any ribbons or hair elastics suitable for a young girl, but I used what I could. In the end, the hair was well brushed, and I had a few tiny braids in it that were holding. By the time her father came out of Kurt's office downstairs, Kelly was giggling and making faces at herself in the mirror.

But then Jared called for his daughter and Kelly tensed, all the happiness erased from her face. Just like her mother at church last week. What was going on here? I'd thought it was simply a case of an unhappy marriage, but was it more serious than that?

"I have to obey Daddy," said Kelly.

"Yes," I said, and led her downstairs to her father's arms.

Jared didn't say a word to her or to me, simply took his daughter and left.

Kurt closed the door behind them.

"Can you tell me anything?" I asked. Most of the secrets Kurt found out were to be held in confidence, but there isn't the same kind of strictness in a Mormon bishop's counseling session as there is with Catholic confession.

Kurt shrugged. "It will come out soon enough. Carrie has left him."

"Last night? Did they have an argument? Why didn't he come then?"

"Apparently she left him in the night. He

woke up and found her gone. She left a note saying she wasn't coming back."

"I'm surprised she left Kelly," I said. I was more than surprised. I was in knots about it. A mother leaving a child, it was — unfathomable to me. What pain had she been in? What had she been thinking? It was one thing to file for divorce and to ask your husband to leave the house. Or even to take your daughter and find an apartment. To leave her behind, and in the middle of the night without a proper goodbye . . . I shivered.

"It's hard to know what goes on in the mind of a woman," said Kurt.

I hated when Kurt said things like that. "It is not that hard. Women are just as sensible as men," I said. "If you understand what their lives are like."

"Then how could she leave her daughter? I never would have thought it of Carrie Helm, of all people. She loved that little girl so much."

Yes, she had. She had always walked Kelly to Primary and made sure she had a big hug. "She might not have felt she had any choice." It was the only answer I could think of. Kurt, as bishop, was the one who should know more of the inner workings of their relationship than I did. But then again, Carrie and Jared had never come to see him together, so now all he would have was Jared's side of the story. Jared had a calling as an instructor in the elders quorum and fulfilled it faithfully every month. As far as Kurt was concerned, he was the one who was reliable and trustworthy.

"I asked him if there was any hope they might still reconcile. I wish they had come to see me earlier. I might have been able to help." He looked toward the kitchen, the smell of toast and jam drawing him, and we moved in that direction. I put new toast in the toaster and he got out a plate.

Along with his big appetite, Kurt had enormous faith in the power of prayer. He thought any marriage could be saved with enough work and help from God. I am sad to say I am not as believing. Some marriages aren't meant to last, and it was quite possible that Jared and Carrie Helm's was one of these. They did not seem like a particularly good match. There were marriages that worked despite disparities in character, but not many.

"He said she was very final about it. She said she was never coming back. He thinks there may be another man involved."

"I see," I said. If Carrie Helm had realized how mismatched she and Jared were, and

17

she'd found someone who was less of a mismatch — well, it almost explained things. It was selfish, but people are sometimes selfish. Sometimes even mothers. Perhaps mothers especially, since they spent so much time being unselfish.

"He's going to have to deal with divorce papers and child-care issues, along with custody agreements," Kurt was saying as he opened his favorite jam jars and began to stir the contents. Why he did that, I never knew. "But he wasn't up for talking about any of that. He just wanted to hear me say that he wasn't to blame for what had happened, and that God still had good things for his future."

Well, I was glad that Kurt hadn't insisted on reconciliation, as most bishops would have felt obliged to do to keep the family together. "Poor Kelly," I said.

"The whole ward will have to band together to help Jared and Kelly. She'll need a lot of substitute mothers." Kurt was looking at me then. I would do what I could, of course, but I wasn't sure I knew what Kelly needed.

"I'd like to talk to Carrie. Do you think Jared might have a number for her?" I asked.

Kurt shook his head. "He said she didn't leave any way of contacting her. We'll have to wait and see what happens in the next few days." He stopped short of saying he hoped that she came back, and that all of this could still be fixed.

"Carrie is a good woman," I said, hoping it was true. I had thought I knew her, but obviously I had not known her well enough.

"Well, I suppose God can find good in any of us," said Kurt. That was as close as he came to saying he considered this situation to be Carrie's fault.

Didn't he remember those years when I had been at home with all five boys, Adam, Joseph, Kenneth, Zachary, and baby Samuel? I had never said it aloud, but there were times when I had had fantasies of walking away, going out and getting a job, finding a life of my own again, where I wasn't on call twenty-four hours a day and responsible for tiny lives. It was too much for any one person. Maybe more so for someone who had reconciled herself to not being married and never having children. And then Kurt had come along and changed all my plans, made me believe again I could have the whole Mormon dream. Husband. Children. Temple sealing. And all that went with it. We lived in a city that had once been known for the state prison at the point of the mountain and was now known for the

Mormon temple that had just been built. But it seemed that the Mormon plan of happiness with a perfect family full of forgiveness hadn't worked out as well for Carrie Helm.

CHAPTER 2

Cheri Tate's second daughter was to be married the next day at the church. Kurt would be there to officiate, but Cheri needed support. She was Relief Society president, and very good at that job. Give her a list and she checked off every item on it. She was in charge of making sure the bishop knew about the practical needs of all the women of the ward. No one who had a baby or was in the hospital ever went without a week's worth of hot homemade meals delivered by the Relief Society sisters, all coordinated by Cheri Tate.

Her children were younger than mine, and I had married later in life, so I suspected I was nearly fifteen years older than she was. That made me feel a little maternal toward her. I could see her flaws, but I could also see her attempts to grow. She wasn't a listener and she had no sympathy for whining, but at least she was not a hypocrite.

She wasn't whining about her daughter's wedding. She was just doing what had to be done.

The wedding colors were gold and silver, which I thought was a little over the top, but I had seen worse. I went early in the morning to help with the decorations. The wedding and reception would both be held in what was called the "cultural hall," but it looked more like a gym than anything else. It had hardwood floors and was polished every year so that now the polish was as thick as the wood itself. It was also painted with basketball lines underneath all the polish, and there were hoops overhead.

The cultural hall was behind the chapel in the standardized, streamlined church design that allowed three different wards to share the same building for Sunday and weekday meetings. Around those two central large rooms were hallways that led to a ring of smaller classrooms and the offices for the bishopric, Stake Presidency, and High Council. There was also a kitchen — only to be used for warming up food, since no one in the ward had a state food preparation license — on the side of the building, so it could be ventilated easily if something burned.

I found Cheri in that kitchen, with her

22

daughter, Perdita, who was wearing jeans and an old T-shirt. Obviously she hadn't headed off yet to have her hair and makeup done at a salon.

"How can I help?" I asked.

"Oh, Sister Wallheim! I'm so glad you're here. The gazebo isn't set up yet, but the pieces are in the gym," said Cheri. "Do you think you can manage it? I asked my husband to come, but he can't get here until four and we'll only have two hours until the wedding then."

"I'll see what I can do," I said.

There would be no elaborate dinner, nor even a luncheon for this. The reception was after the wedding itself, starting at seven, just as it had stated on the original invitations.

Perdita, who was eighteen, and her fiancé, Jonathan, had been dating steadily since they were sixteen, despite Cheri's lectures. The Mormon church's rules on dating were clear. No dating at all before sixteen, and no steady dating until after a mission. But apparently Perdita always said she was going on group dates (which she was) and promised her mother that she and Jonathan weren't going to have sex before they married. Cheri thought that meant they'd wait until after Jonathan went on a mission, but

23

Perdita and Jonathan had declared they were too much in love to wait for two years.

They might still have been married in the temple without Jonathan going on a mission. But when it came to their premarital and temple recommend interview, it turned out that Perdita and Jonathan had come so close to having intercourse that Kurt told them they couldn't get married in the temple unless they waited another three months. And kept their hands off each other until then. Completely off. Kurt hadn't told me specifics about what they had and hadn't done, but it was his right as bishop to determine who was worthy for a temple recommend and who wasn't.

In the end, Perdita and Jonathan decided to go ahead with their original wedding date. They had already sent out the invitations. They would have had to send out a set of cancellations, and then new invitations several months later. It would have been confusing, and expensive. But most of all, it would have been embarrassing. The words "sealed in the Salt Lake Temple" were embossed in gold on the wedding invitations, but since only thirty or so people were allowed into the sealing room — the closest of family members with temple recommends themselves — few people would know about the canceled temple ceremony.

"It smells wonderful, by the way," I told Cheri and Perdita. The kitchen was filled with cinnamon, ginger, and allspice.

"It's a kind of post-Christmas theme," said Perdita. "I love gingerbread."

"Ah," I said. That explained it. I gestured at the twenty-gallon pot on the stove. "And that is?"

"Wassail," said Perdita. Nonalcoholic.

"It's pretty adventurous, doing it all yourself," I said. "You weren't tempted to get caterers?"

Perdita shrugged.

Cheri put in, "We told them that if they did it themselves, they would get the money we saved to live on."

"Do you know how much caterers cost, Sister Wallheim?" asked Perdita, her mouth open wide.

"Actually, I do." I had two married sons, and even if I'd never had to do as much work as the mothers of the brides, I had paid for half the catering to be fair. I also thought it was worth every penny. A wedding was stressful enough — all the family members coming in, the emotional difficulty of letting go. I didn't think anyone should have to put more on their plate.

Cheri, for instance, looked like she had

spent the last two weeks in a clothes dryer. Her hair was frizzled under the curlers she had in, and her skin was worse than the normal Utah winter desert crack.

"Well, we can live for three months on that, if we scrimp," said Perdita.

I glanced at Cheri, who looked away. I was more and more impressed with Perdita and her good sense. She might be just out of high school, but she knew who she wanted and she knew how to survive. That was more than I could say of myself at that age. I had been a disaster, and had spent six years figuring out how to move on with my life.

"I'll come back when I'm done with the gazebo," I said with a nod toward the cultural hall.

"Don't hurt yourself," said Cheri.

The gazebo wasn't heavy, but it was tricky to put together. I painstakingly put part A in slot B, then part C in slot D. And the gazebo went up. When it was taller than I was, I got some chairs to stand on. I heard a door open and saw an unfamiliar face bringing in flowers.

"The Tate wedding?" he asked.

"Yeah, that's here."

He nodded and carried in several boxes of flowers, then left again.

The silver and gold ribbons were wrapped around cardboard in a pile by the door. I got them out and tried twisting them together and arranging them on the gazebo. I wasn't an interior designer by any means, and my house was proof of that. But ribbons I thought I could manage. I poked around in the flower boxes and found some garlands to put over the top of the gazebo, as well. It wasn't going to look like a summer wedding, but it would be nice.

Just as I was finishing, Cheri came in and stared at the gazebo. "Thank you so much," she said. "I really didn't think that was going to get done. I was so worried."

"Now you can go home and take a nap before the wedding," I suggested.

She began to cry.

Cheri Tate. I had honestly never seen her cry before, not even when her older son was in the hospital with double broken arms from a skateboarding accident. She had mostly been angry then.

"It's all right," I said, moving closer to her. "It's going to be fine."

"I just — never thought that Perdita would be married like this. It feels so wrong. It should be at the temple. I talked to her all those years about being married in the temple. A white dress, a white tuxedo, and

27

pictures at the temple to put on her walls forever. And now this."

A church wedding also required the couple to make certain promises about their religious beliefs. But a temple wedding is the symbol of extreme righteousness. Perdita and Jonathan hadn't had any problems with the tithing, Word of Wisdom questions, or attending church every week and supporting their leaders. But the chastity outside of marriage question had been the stopper. I tried to make Cheri see the bright side in all of this. Her daughter was getting married and this should be a happy day. "She still has a beautiful white dress. And Jonathan seems like a nice young man. He loves her deeply and they seem sensible." Not that either of those qualities would make marriage easy. But at least they would get through the first few years, which could be the hardest.

"They won't be sealed for time and all eternity."

"But there's nothing to be ashamed of. They're marrying, not living together. They're still going to be good members of the church." Perdita and Jonathan's marriage would be for "time only," until they waited the requisite year to be sealed in the temple eternally. The year wait was supposed to make people more eager to marry in the temple in the first place, but it could feel like a punishment. I knew, because Kurt and I had been sealed a year and three days after our own church wedding. It wasn't something that Kurt brought up a lot, but a handful of people in the ward knew about it. "But what if something happens? What if one of them dies before the year is up?" asked Cheri.

"Come now," I said. "If one of them dies, you're going to be worried about whether they were married in the temple or not?" Surely there were more important things to deal with in those circumstances.

"Yes. It won't be binding in the afterlife."

"But you can have the sealing done after death," I said. Wasn't that what temples were all about? Doing vital ordinance work for those who couldn't do it themselves? "Or what if they leave the church, either of them? Then they won't be sealed, either."

"People leave the church who marry in the temple, too. It's not a guarantee. And the sealing is broken as soon as they disobey their covenants anyway."

"Maybe you're right and I'm worried over nothing," said Cheri. "I don't know." She wiped at her eyes. Then she glanced around to make sure that no one else was there.

Mothers never worry over nothing, but it is true that sometimes we worry over things we can't control. But I knew Cheri would never have had this conversation with me if I weren't with her here, in her time of need, and if I weren't the bishop's wife. "Is Perdita still in the kitchen?"

Cheri shook her head. "She went to get her hair done. Jonathan's sister is doing it."

"To save money again?"

Cheri nodded and wiped her hands on her apron, which was on top of a skirt and nice blouse. I had worn jeans and a T-shirt, anticipating hard work, but I think Cheri felt like she had to wear Sunday clothes every time she was inside the church. "But I feel like I'm walking around naked. Every-one in the ward knows every problem in my life. Every mistake I made in raising Perdita. Every time I indulged her when I should have been more strict — every time —"

I put a hand on her arm. "Stop," I said. "No one is looking at you like that. No one is judging you." I knew it was a lie. I knew there were plenty of people who were doing just what she was afraid of. Those same people had made judgments about me when I lost my daughter. They told me I hadn't chosen the right doctor, that I hadn't gone to the hospital soon enough, that I should

30

have taken better care of myself while pregnant. But I chose not to let them have power over me. And I didn't think Cheri should let them have power over her, either.

"But —"

"Perdita and Jonathan may end up as one of the best, most moral couples we have ever seen, deeply in love, and devoted to the church. How do you know they won't?"

"But this is such a bad beginning."

"It's not a bad beginning. It's just not the beginning you imagined." But of course, Mormons have to have absurdly high standards. Other people try not to drink to excess. Mormons refuse to drink at all. Other people cut back on their coffee at Lent. Mormons drink neither coffee nor tea, ever, and I know plenty of Mormons who think it is wrong to drink hot chocolate, or herbal tea, or decaffeinated coffee. Or anything that could be mistaken for tea at a casual glance. Or anything coffee-flavored. Or rum-flavored. Or even vanilla extract.

"What if they have children?" asked Cheri.

I thought of Kelly Helm. A temple marriage hadn't saved her parents' marriage, or her. What was sealed in heaven often didn't make a damn bit of difference on earth. "Let's focus on the good things right now," I said, "not all the bad things that might go wrong in the future. Perdita and Jonathan love each other. They're going to be happy together. They both have strong testimonies of the church. Do you believe that?"

Cheri nodded, then started to cry again.

"This is their wedding day. You're supposed to be happy for them," I reminded her.

She nodded again, and straightened. "You're right. I can't indulge myself. I have to put on the face they expect to see. All of them."

That wasn't precisely what I had meant, but I guess it would have the desired effect.

She started getting out the tables that were stored under the stage on the north side behind the basketball hoop. We set chairs around the tables, and I found the nice lace tablecloths in the Relief Society closet. Silver and gold horns, jewels, and links went on the center of every table, along with flowers in a silver and gold vase.

Other women came in then, and I excused myself. The plates would have to be set up, and the photographer would show up at some point. There would need to be signs on the through street outside directing people to the right building. In Draper, Utah, there were many Mormon churches, and they all were built on the same plan, so they looked nearly identical.

In the meantime, I went shopping, watched the news while I cleaned the house, and spent some time with a good book of the sort that Joseph Smith was thinking of when he said that "anything that is lovely, of good report or praiseworthy, we seek after these things." I attended the Relief Society monthly book club regularly, and we were frequently giving each other recommendations for books without bad language, bad moral values, or explicit sex.

I hadn't had a job since I was pregnant with my oldest son, and I kept myself busy. But lately, I had begun to wonder if I ought to be contributing to the world as more than a wife and mother. It wasn't that we needed the money, but with Samuel about to leave home, I would have more time on my hands.

Being a bishop's wife wasn't a full-time job and it certainly didn't pay. But then again, no calling in the Mormon church does. Bishops, stake presidents, and all the other leadership positions were unpaid. That meant if you were called to go on a mission, you had to pay for it yourself. The prophet and the apostles had their travel expenses paid for and were sometimes given a stipend, but usually not.

Kurt was as an accountant, and would

continue to work as one through his years as bishop and whatever came afterward. His life was particularly difficult during tax season, when he had to balance double business hours as well as his church work. We didn't see him for much of March and April. Kurt had been bishop through one tax season already, and that meant it would likely be four more until he was released as bishop and another man from the ward would take over.

I came back to the church with Kurt that evening for Perdita and Jonathan's ceremony. Kurt had put on a clean white shirt and tie and I was wearing one of my best dresses, a shell pink sheath that everyone said looked good on me. It made me slightly uncomfortable because pink had never been a color I liked much, but this was a wedding, and it was not about me being comfortable.

Inside the cultural hall, under the gazebo, Kurt waited for people to arrive (Mormon-standard time meant ten minutes after the wedding was supposed to begin). I sat quietly in the front row, listening to heels tapping and squeaking on hardwood. Tom deRyke and Karl Ashby, the first and second counselors in the bishopric, arrived next with their wives, Verity and Emma. I greeted them with a nod. More people arrived by the ten minute after mark, which was pretty typical of Mormon standard time.

Then Kurt brought the couple up to the front and gave them advice. This was the longest part of any Mormon wedding ceremony, in a church or in the temple.

"Jonathan, you need to think of Perdita as the most important person in your life now. You give her one hundred percent because no marriage works unless both people are giving all they can. And if it feels like Perdita isn't giving as much as you are, get on your knees right at that moment. Ask God to show you what you aren't seeing. Because we are all blind. We see what we sacrifice, but we take for granted what other people give up. And that is true nowhere more than in a marriage," said Kurt.

He turned to Perdita. "Perdita, Jonathan is your top priority now. I don't mean making him happy or pretending to agree with him." Kurt's eyes slid toward mine and I couldn't repress a slight smile. "I mean, his real well-being. If he is wrong, I don't want you to think that being a good wife means ignoring that. Being a good wife means telling him the truth as best you can. It means dealing with the hard stuff together. It

35

means having courage to face the world, and having even more courage to face God together."

I knew very well what Kurt was doing here. He hadn't said a word about the temple marriage ceremony or the secret endowment ceremony that these two would have gone to if they'd ended up marrying there. But his advice was filled with allusions to temple doctrine. The Adam and Eve story might be about women making the wrong choice in other religions, but in Mormonism, it is all about Eve making the right choice, even if it meant facing difficult consequences. She was the one who reminded Adam that they couldn't obey the commandment to multiply and replenish the earth unless they ate of the fruit, and Joseph Smith argued that she spent a thousand years thinking over the decision before she finally had the courage to face the consequences of being sent out of the Garden.

When Kurt was finished with his advice, the simple wedding ceremony was merely a question, at which Perdita and Jonathan agreed to marry each other with a single-word answer: "Yes."

They exchanged rings after the words were said, but it wasn't a necessary part of the ceremony.

The couple turned around to the family members watching from their chairs. There was some light applause as people tried to decide if it was appropriate or not. The couple kissed a second time, this time a lot longer. The photographer zoomed closer, but I had the sense that this was a real kiss, not one extended for show. It gave me a good feeling. I was glad to see that what I had told Cheri earlier wasn't a pleasant lie. These two had a better chance than most couples.

Cheri came forward and hugged her daughter and her new son-in-law. No tears in her eyes now.

More photographs of the extended family were taken. I watched with some satisfaction as they posed under the gazebo I had put together. It didn't fall on anyone.

Kurt came up behind me and put his arms around me. He leaned close and I could feel his breath in my ear.

"Happy memories?" he asked.

I was a little choked up. I nodded rather than trying to speak.

"I was a lucky man then. I am an even luckier man now."

"I frustrate you to no end sometimes," I

said. "And I have as loud a mouth as ever I did."

"I frustrate you, too," said Kurt. "And as for your mouth." He slid his arms around me, then kissed me gently. "I have always loved your mouth, open or closed, full of words, full of love, or full of sharp barbs. I love it all. I love all of you." We held hands for a little while, until he was called away.

I stayed through the end of the reception, and after the couple had gone, I helped Cheri clean up in the cultural hall, the halls around the church, and finally in the kitchen.

"Their car was kept safe?" I asked. That was one tradition I had never approved of.

"My husband had it in the garage. He came and brought it to them, so no one could cover it in slime."

"Good for him," I said. He was helping sweep the polished wooden floors of the gym.

I stared at the place and thought how strange it was that we could repurpose the same room for so many different things. This cultural hall would see everything in the course of its life. Funeral luncheons, weddings, basketball games, monthly Relief Society meetings, a Road Show or Stake Pageant, music practices, Sunday School,

Young Men's and Young Women's activities, Boy Scout meetings, and the overflow from sacrament meetings and stake conferences.

In many ways, this hall was the most Mormon place of them all. Didn't that make it holy in its own way? Maybe more holy than the quiet, white temple that was not part of our weekly worship?

This hall was where God came, if you believed in God.

And I did. After all this time and all my doubts, I did.

CHAPTER 3

Kurt went to church two hours early on Sundays, at six thirty. We shared our building with two other wards in the same neighborhood, and since we had the nine o'clock schedule this year — instead of the more envied eleven o'clock schedule or the nap-stealing one o'clock schedule — that meant his meetings with our other ward leaders were mighty early. He sometimes tried to get home for fifteen minutes before church started so he could spend time with the family and get some food.

I had started making breakfast when he called. I sighed, knowing the fact that he was calling meant he wouldn't make it home before church this week. It was likely he wouldn't be done meeting with members and giving callings until late afternoon. And he would have to go back in the evening for a fireside or other activity.

"Brother Rhodes called to ask me to talk

40

to him," he said.

Brother Rhodes wasn't an "official" member because he lived outside the ward boundaries. He had argued with his own bishop and thus had come to our ward as a kind of rogue member.

I made a small sound — not quite a groan. "You know he isn't your problem," I said.

"He feels like my problem," said Kurt.

"At some point, someone needs to tell him to go back to his own ward and mend fences."

"I tell him that every time he talks to me," said Kurt. "But he has some genuine grievances. You know he does."

Brother Rhodes was a stickler for historical fact. This did not always go over well in gospel doctrine classes, which were designed to give people a warm feeling about the church, and perhaps a bit of a kick in the pants to work harder and stop criticizing so much. But Brother Rhodes had a PhD in history and he could not bear inaccuracy. When polygamy came up, he had to explain every date in detail, every bad story about Joseph Smith that had been told, and what he thought was likely or unlikely about it. A number of ward members found these kinds of frank discussions about the founder and greatest prophet of Mormonism unsettling.

41

"I hope you take notes," I said. "I want to hear all the details of what we're doing wrong."

"I'll do my best to remember, but I don't want him to think that I'm taking notes for use in a church trial. You know he is paranoid about that."

"Ah, well," I said. A church trial is convened if membership privileges are at stake. It doesn't necessarily end in excommunication, but it is the church's only way to discipline its members.

I called Samuel downstairs, and he and I talked while we ate. Samuel wasn't in gospel doctrine class, which is for adults, but he knew Brother Rhodes from his testimonies. Testimony meeting came once a month. It could be dangerous, and Kurt had to sit on the edge of his seat, ready to interrupt if someone went too far astray.

"Is he going off on the Mountain Meadows Massacre again?" asked Samuel.

"No," I said.

"Must be polygamy, then," said Samuel.

"You know, we should all thank Brother Rhodes. He works as a wonderful inoculation against anything anti-Mormons might say about the church. No literature you read on your mission will compare to the real facts as he offers them, completely unvarnished."

"Yeah, but I think a lot of people just turn a blind eye to the problems in the church."

Samuel might get flak in church for expressing these views, but at home I didn't mind questions. I believe strongly that God wants us to learn and make our own decisions about our lives.

"Turning a blind eye can be dangerous," I said. I was thinking of Carrie and Jared Helm. It had been three days since Jared showed up on the doorstep, and so far, we'd learned nothing more about where Carrie had gone. Jared had taken several days off work, but how long that could continue, I didn't know. He would have to find at least part-time care for Kelly, who was only in half-day kindergarten.

"You know, Mom, I worried a little bit when Dad was called as bishop."

"I worried, too," I said.

"No, I worried about you. I thought you might go to another ward or something like Brother Rhodes." Samuel played with the curl over his left ear. He had lighter brown hair than Kurt and my other boys, but in every other way looked like his father's son. The same height — six foot — and the same rugged build with wide shoulders and chest. The same narrow, long face and thick nose.

But in other ways, I knew he was mine.

"I don't have a problem with your father as bishop, you know," I said. None of the other boys would have said something like this, and even if it made me a little uncomfortable, I didn't want to cut him off. "I would have thought you saw enough of our relationship to know I would support him in whatever he did."

"I thought maybe you wouldn't want to put him in a position where he had to tell you that you were wrong publicly."

"You mean, unlike all of the times when he has already done that?" I asked, smiling, thinking about how we had argued in front of the kids over politics. Kurt had voted for both Bushes. I had voted for Clinton and Obama and even for John Kerry. And at one point, Kurt had tried to tell me that my cooking wasn't good for his cholesterol, which I hadn't appreciated at all.

"It would be different with him as the bishop," said Samuel. "If he had to tell you that you were wrong in front of the whole ward."

"Ah," I said. I hadn't thought about that from Samuel's angle, but I could see now why he had worried. "Most people think I'm fairly conservative," I said. I didn't talk politics at church because I thought that was rude, and since I attended church and generally supported church activities, ward members probably thought I believed the same things they did.

Samuel rolled his eyes. "Most people are idiots," he said. Which was a direct quote from me, I think.

"I try not to make waves," I said.

"And you do a good job of it. It lets you see things that Dad doesn't. You understand people in so many ways. You don't judge them."

It was an unexpected compliment, the kind of thing you don't get often from a son, or from any child. I teared up a little, and then Samuel got embarrassed, and I knew that was the end of this conversation. Samuel might be more empathic than my other sons or than Kurt, but that didn't mean he wasn't a teenage male.

"Well," I said.

He stood up and put his dishes in the dishwasher, not the sink, then went to get his scriptures and his tie.

I helped him with his tie, not that he wasn't perfectly capable of doing it himself. I liked to remind him that I was still in his life, still watching out for him, even if he was nearly grown up.

We walked to church together, since it was

45

only three blocks away. Then he went off to his priesthood classes, and I went to Relief Society.

The lesson was on the priesthood, the power and authority from God that was bestowed on men of the right age and worthiness. It was not my favorite topic. If only Brother Rhodes ever came to Relief Society. I was sure he had lists of women who had been ordained to various offices of the priesthood in the old days of the church, or women who hadn't been ordained but had nonetheless called on the priesthood power from God to give blessings of healing, even using the holy, consecrated oils that their husbands had left behind.

But since Brother Rhodes wasn't here and I was biting my tongue as bishop's wife, I looked out over the women in the room and wondered how many of them were dealing with problems no one knew anything about. How many of the women were being abused? How many were having affairs? How many of them didn't know if they would have enough money to make a house payment next week or to buy medications they needed?

Midway through the lesson, I got up and went into the bathroom. I took my time about it, too, hoping the poor teacher hadn't been offended by my abrupt departure. It was while I was washing my hands that I saw Gwen Ferris step into the bathroom and slip into the first stall. She was red-faced and I could hear her breathing heavily through the stall door.

I turned off the water and got a paper towel for my hands. Then I sat there in the nursing mothers' chair, wiping at them for a long time to avoid going back to class.

Gwen came out of the stall and started washing her hands. She had thin, faintly curly dark hair and a perfectly heart-shaped face that made her pale, large eyes stand out even without makeup. She looked up at her reflection and seemed to consider the puffiness around her eyes. She turned to get a paper towel and then she saw me.

Her eyes immediately fell. "Excuse me," she said. She pulled off a towel, dipped it in the cold water, and pressed it onto her eyes. After a moment, she looked back at herself, and then at me.

"Am I in your way?" she asked, and stepped back from the sink.

I stood up and threw the ripped and worn paper towel away. "Not at all," I said. "I just wondered — if there was anything I could do to help. You seem upset. Was it something in the lesson?"

47

"I'm fine," said Gwen. She still hadn't met my eyes.

"Is it about women and the priesthood?" I asked. "Because —" I don't know what I was going to say, but Gwen interrupted me.

"No, not that. It's — everyone always talking about how it's a woman's true calling to be a mother. About how children are such a blessing. And that's just — some days it really gets to me."

I stared at her, cut at the reminder. Fertility problems can be very painful in a church that still believes in the commandment to multiply and replenish the earth and still promotes the idea that a woman's place is in the home. Gwen had a good job and she was moving up the corporate ladder, as far as I knew. Until now, I had assumed that was what she wanted.

"I'm sorry."

Gwen finally looked me in the eye. "It's not your fault."

I put an arm around her and felt rather awkward patting her nearly skeletal form.

"Thank you," she said afterward. The bell had rung, and soon there were going to be Primary children in here, with their curious eyes and ears.

"You can talk to me anytime," I said. "I don't mind."

"You must be so busy," she said.

"Maybe we were meant to see each other in here," I said. "Maybe you have as much to teach me as I have to teach you."

She ducked her head, and I couldn't tell if that meant she would talk to me again or not.

I had done what I could, I tried to tell myself.

Of course there was no way Jared Helm could know about the conversation I had had with Gwen Ferris, but as if to rub salt in the wound, he raised his hand in Sunday School to answer a question about Adam and Eve. His voice shaking, he talked about the importance of eternal marriage and having children.

"There is no reason to put off having children, not for financial reasons or for emotional ones. God will bless you if you follow His commandments. We need to rely on Him more to support us through whatever difficulties may come as we obey His every word," he said.

I looked back and saw Gwen Ferris get up again and leave the room, her husband looking after her, but not following.

I stayed where I was and made a note to talk to Kurt about the Ferrises.

It was Fast Sunday, a monthly Mormon

tradition of going without food for twenty-four hours (or less for younger people and pregnant women) and then giving the money saved from not eating to the poor. It is also thought to be a way to gain spiritual closeness to God through denying the body and seeking spiritual strength instead. The fasting ends with a group meeting where people share their experiences either about the fasting or other things that happened during the month. People simply stand to give testimony as "moved on by the Spirit." Though occasionally bishops have to step in and ask people to sit down, or are prompted to remind members of the guidelines that testimonies are to be largely focused on Christ.

Brother Rhodes got up to bear his testimony after a few other speakers. He tended to be long-winded, and I didn't know if I was glad about that or not. Sometimes, instead of Brother Rhodes we have a line of small children whose "testimonies" are whispered into their ears by older children. I disapprove of this practice, and there are times when church leaders send letters out to wards also discouraging it, but it never seems to stop for long. Parents are too enthused about the cuteness of young children on the stand, their testimony "as pure as the angels."

Finally, Brother Rhodes sat down, and I thought that would be the end of today's fast and testimony meeting. But little Kelly Helm leaped out of her seat and streaked to the front of the chapel before Kurt could close the meeting and announce the final song and prayer.

She grabbed the stool that was off to the side and jumped onto it. I stared at Kurt, wondering if he was afraid she would say something about her mother leaving, announcing private information to the whole ward. But how long was it going to stay private?

I tensed as she began to speak. It was an ordinary child's testimony, full of thanks for her many blessings, her food and her house, to be a member of the church, and to have the Book of Mormon. Then she got to her family. "I'm thankful for my daddy and my grandpa. And I'm thankful that my mommy is my mommy forever and that she will love me forever and that God will make us be together forever. Amen."

I muttered an "Amen," not sure if that was agreement or simply relief that Kelly was on her way back to her father's place in the congregation.

Kurt closed the meeting and we sang "God Be with You Till We Meet Again."

CHAPTER 4

On Monday morning when he went into his accounting office, Kurt put a note up on the fridge. It said Anna Torstensen.

I knew what it meant. He was worried about Anna Torstensen, possibly because of thoughts that had come to him during prayer the night before, possibly because of something mentioned in all the church meetings he had gone to on Sunday. He wasn't allowed to tell me why, and he was at work all day today, but he was hoping I might have a chance to go see her.

Sometimes weeks went by without a note left on the fridge and sometimes there were several names all at once. I didn't always have time to see to everyone the day the name went on the fridge, but I did my best. I knew that Tobias Torstensen was ill, and that at his age, any illness was something to take very seriously. Other than that, I wasn't sure what Kurt thought Anna might need.

I did the dishes from Sunday evening (I always wish in the mornings that I was one of those women who couldn't go to bed with dirty dishes in the sink — but of course, the night before, I am always glad I am one of those women who can go to bed with dirty dishes in the sink). After that, I took a shower. I was tempted to go out walking first, but I didn't want to keep putting off something Kurt had thought was important.

I made up a quick batch of cinnamon rolls. After they had baked, I left one pan cooling on the stove, then covered the other in aluminum foil to take with me. As I stepped outside, I glanced at the Helm house just below our hill. The yard was still covered in snow, but Kelly and Jared were out playing on a sled. Jared was dragging Kelly along with a rope around his chest. Apparently she was in afternoon kindergarten.

I waved as I walked by. Up the street, the Torstensens had a large lawn that in summer was beautifully kept. Even now, in winter, three bushes with red berries on them decorated the edges of the yard. Seeing them made me shake my head at our rather dull yard. I could blame it on Kurt's being too busy these days to devote himself to yard work — not that I was willing to give up my books or cooking to pull weeds, either. But even before Kurt was called as bishop, he had preferred to spend his Saturdays with the boys, playing football in the backyard or working on Boy Scout projects. All five of my sons were Eagle Scouts, and I was proud of that, not just for their sakes, but for mine and Kurt's. We'd done plenty of work to earn those badges, too.

I went up the steps and rang the doorbell.

"Sister Wallheim, good of you to come by." Anna Torstensen was tall and fit with thick, bluntly cut dark hair. She was one of the few women in the ward who had a graduate degree, and she had worked full time as a banker before she had married Tobias Torstensen. They had never had children of their own together and I didn't know if that had been a choice or not. But Anna had helped Tobias raise his two sons from his first marriage.

Now he was retired and she had worked part-time intermittently when she chose. She had an independence, financially and emotionally, that I admired enormously. It seemed she had been able to manage all the things women are told they can't juggle at once: job, marriage, children. She was what

I wished I could be like when my sons were all gone from the house and raising their own children. She didn't seem lonely at all. She seemed full of energy and sure of herself.

I suppose I had been intimidated by her for most of the time I had been in the ward and had never spent much time talking to her other than in passing. But I should have. I knew it the moment I saw her. I could have learned from her.

I handed her the cinnamon rolls. It felt like a gimmick, the traditional Mormon woman offering homemade food.

"Thank you," she said. "But I'm afraid I don't have time for a chat." She put a hand on the door to close it again.

"Is it Tobias? Can I do anything to help?" I asked, a little hurt at the rejection, as though I were one of those missionaries who had just tried to place a Book of Mormon. I fully expected the door to continue closing. I was already rehearsing explaining to Kurt that I had failed.

But Anna's hand dropped, and I saw a look of fear passing over her eyes. "He won't let me take him to the hospital, but he's so pale and he's wheezing, as if he can't get in enough air." She took a breath and hesitated. "Would you come look at him and tell me what you think? Try to convince him to go in if you think he should. He won't listen to me, but if it's someone else's opinion, it might help."

"Of course," I said. I knew all too well that men sometimes have to be coaxed along to seek medical attention. Just last year, Kurt had ended up with pneumonia after tax season. I had told him again and again that he needed to cancel meetings and stay home in bed. He wouldn't listen to me. And then one morning, he simply could not get out of bed. He said he felt like there was an elephant on his chest. I'd had to have Samuel help me get him into the car, and I drove him to the hospital in a dripping sweat of anxiety. The doctors told him he might have died if he hadn't come in for another day, so I felt a little vindicated.

But then Kurt had taken calls as bishop right in the hospital, counseling other people until I went behind his back and told people that Kurt might die if he wasn't given peace. I won't say everyone listened to me, but it helped.

Such delicate creatures men are, I thought. With their pride.

I went upstairs to the Torstensens' master bedroom. It was very clean and rather sparse, with few feminine touches. Was it because Anna was not typically feminine? Or because she had felt constrained not to change the way things had been when she came into a family already formed? I had never considered how hard it must have been for her to step into another woman's shoes.

But as soon as I saw Tobias, my thoughts about Anna were pushed to the side. He looked fragile indeed. There was a smell in the room, some combination of sweat and medicine, that felt wrong. Kurt had been right to put Anna's name on the fridge.

I moved closer to the bed and stood over Tobias. His hair was very dark, obviously dyed, the roots pure white around the crown of his head. He still had a full head of hair, though, which was more than Kurt could say, and Tobias had to be in his seventies.

"How are you today, Tobias?" I asked.

The old man's hands were shaking, and he seemed to have difficulty focusing. But he said in a strong voice, "I'm fine. I don't need any help. You can tell Anna she doesn't need to watch over me like a mother hen."

Anna Torstensen? A mother hen?

"She's only worried about you," I said softly. I didn't want to chide him about his attitude. I was more concerned about his health. "Can you tell me what happened?"

This seemed far beyond the cold or flu I'd assumed he had.

"Nothing happened. I'm only getting old," said Tobias.

"He was out in the garden," said Anna. "And he fell. I didn't see him until I got home in the evening. I can't find any sign of a broken bone, but it's been three days."

And neither of them had come to church yesterday, which had signaled something in Kurt's subconscious. Or maybe it was the Spirit whispering to him, depending on your view of the world. Anna came to church tirelessly. I should have noticed she was missing in Relief Society. I might have, if I hadn't been preoccupied with Gwen Ferris.

I leaned closer to Tobias. I could see a purple bruise on his right wrist and arm, presumably from the fall. But I could see no sign of a break. Still, at his age, it was worrisome.

"He should get an X-ray," I said.

"I don't need an X-ray," said Tobias sharply. "Nothing is broken. I can move my arm perfectly well. If it were broken, it would be swollen."

"It could be a hairline fracture," said Anna.

"And what would they do for that? Nothing at all. I just need a little rest, and then

I'll go back out to the garden and finish what I was doing," said Tobias, waving his hands as if to grip something and lever himself out of bed. He gave up and lay back.

"But it's winter," I said. "What are you doing out there at this time of year?"

"Says someone who knows nothing about gardening," said Tobias.

I tried not to be stung by this. He was understandably irritable, and I wasn't a gardener. I didn't even try to grow vegetables, despite the frequent reminders in General Conference that we should grow as much of our own food as we could.

"I told him that we could hire someone else to do it for him, but he won't hear of it," said Anna.

Tobias made a face at Anna's words. He was clearly not in a mood to listen to me or Anna. Which meant this was something for Kurt to deal with, I thought. Man to man. "It would make Anna feel better if you saw a doctor, you know," I tried again. "She's very worried about you."

"Well, it wouldn't make me feel better," said Tobias, waving me off again. "It would make me feel worse. I hate doctors. All they do is tell you what you already know. You're too old. You're too thin. You're too tired."

"It's good to have someone remind us of

what we know, don't you think?" I said, turning to see Anna's face sink in despair.

"No, I don't," said Tobias.

"So you don't care what Anna thinks or feels?" I said, trying one last time.

Tobias's demeanor changed for a moment. "Of course I care what Anna feels. I love Anna more than — more than life itself." Tears suddenly appeared in his eyes, and even if he didn't shed them, I was touched. His first wife had died of cancer, very young, as I recalled. His relationship with Anna had always seemed a little businesslike, but that might be Anna's doing as much as it was his.

"Then wouldn't you want to help set her mind at ease? If you don't want to drive all the way to the hospital, Kurt might be able to find someone in the stake who could come see you at home."

Tobias looked away. "I saw a doctor two weeks ago, Anna," he said, his voice low and gravelly and almost ashamed.

Two weeks ago? Then whatever was making him unwell had nothing to do with his fall in the garden.

Anna picked up Tobias's hand and held it to her cheek as if she were a young bride again, desperately in love. "What did he say, then? Why didn't you tell me?"

61

Suddenly, I felt as if I were intruding. I withdrew a little, moving to the door, but I did not leave the room — partly because that might have been even more disruptive than staying, but also partly, I admitted to myself, because I was curious about what the doctor had said. I had always been curious as a child, and growing older had not cured me of it. It was why I was a news junkie, switching back and forth through all the commercials to get as much information as possible.

"It's my heart," said Tobias at last. "He gave it a fancy name. But if I wanted him to translate what's wrong with me into Latin, I'd get out my dictionary."

Anna smiled valiantly at this. "Your heart? Go on."

"The point is that my heart is failing. It's just spent too long beating and it wants a rest. The final rest," he said, his impatience returning.

"But can't they do anything?" said Anna, leaning over him, the picture of devotion.

"They can put me on a monitor, but as far as I can tell, all that will do is make it more clear how close to the end I am. He can give me something to help me feel better, but nothing that will make me live any longer."

"But what about a transplant? Can't they get you a new heart?" asked Anna.

"I'm too old. No one wants to put a new heart in this body." Tobias gestured down at himself. "Save it for someone who has more of a chance at life."

"Then you —" Anna began, pressing her hand to her mouth.

"I'm dying," said Tobias. "And not very slowly anymore."

A sound like a cry. "Why didn't you tell me?" Her head sunk to his shoulder, and he patted her back ineffectually.

It was one of the sweetest things I had ever seen. Their marriage might not be a typical one, at least not in Utah, but this was true love. I felt a tiny prick of jealousy for them, then reminded myself that I loved Kurt, too. He put up with all my failings and I put up with his, and we had five sons together. We were very happy, in our own way. I didn't need to see Kurt close to death to remember how much I loved him.

"I'm not going to give up working in the garden," said Tobias when Anna pulled back from him. "Even if that doctor did say that it might give me a few more weeks."

Anna laughed shakily, wiping at her face. "I don't expect the impossible."

I stepped out the bedroom door at that.

Anna met me in the front room after a while.

"Thank you," she said. Her face was streaked with tears. I realized I didn't think of her as any less strong because of that. Maybe I thought of her as stronger, because she felt no need to hide her emotions. She was honest and open, and that was something I had always admired.

She sat down on the tan couch, and I finally felt able to sit as well. My legs ached.

"I'll tell Kurt," I said. He would want to alert the high priests group, the most senior men in the ward, so that they could check in on Tobias regularly. And the Relief Society would need to prepare to deal with a funeral and the aftermath for Anna. "Do you need anything? Meals?" I asked. Food again. It probably wasn't what Anna really needed, but it might make her feel connected and cared for. But Anna shook her head. "We're fine. I think we'll take it one day at a time. I like cooking these days. Though Tobias used to be the cook in the family. He complained about my cooking more, too. I'm not sure if I've actually gotten better or if he just can't taste the difference anymore."

"We'll assume it's not because he's simply mellowed out and doesn't complain about the little things," I said, smiling and thinking about what he'd said about doctors.

Anna let out a brief laugh. "No, that's not it," she said.

I stood up, preparing to leave. I had surely outstayed the minimal welcome I had expected. "I'll come back to check on you in a few days, if that's all right," I said, and not only because Kurt would want me to. It was only now that I was leaving that I realized how much I wanted to stay and talk to Anna.

"Oh, you don't need to do that," said Anna.

"Would you prefer I didn't?" I asked bluntly. "Do I bore you?" It was absolutely the wrong thing to say, and I wished I hadn't as soon as it was out. But I realized I cared about her opinion. She had done so much more with her life than I had with mine. I always excused myself because I got started so late, but that hadn't stopped her.

"Not at all," said Anna. "I didn't mean that. I only meant that I'm sure you have a lot of other important things to do, as the bishop's wife. You don't need to come play nursemaid to me. I'm perfectly capable of managing things on my own."

"I know that," I said. In for a penny, in for a pound, I thought. "And that is precisely why I'd like to know you better." I felt dizzy as I said the whole truth, and hoped it didn't come back to hurt me.

"If you want to, then," said Anna. I wasn't sure if she was trying to be kind, or if she just had other things to think about. But I would stop thinking about myself, now. There would be plenty of time for us to become better acquainted.

She stood and moved to the door with me. Her eyes seemed distant. "I think his wife died of a heart condition," she said. "His first wife."

I put my hand on the doorknob, then turned back. "I thought she died of cancer." I tried to remember where I'd heard that.

"No. It was her heart. The boys speak of it frequently. I don't know if it's irony or some kind of cosmic justice, but . . . when his heart fails as well, he will return to her in heaven. Do you know, we were never married in the temple? He feels he is still bound to her, though he and I have been married five times as long."

"He has his sons with her, I suppose," I said, opening the door and stepping out onto the porch. Did this bureaucratic detail bother her? If anyone questioned the nitty-gritty details of who would be with whom in the afterlife, we were told that God would work it out, and that there was the whole millennium for church work and temple sealings to be finished while Christ Himself would be leading the church. But why had Tobias not had the sealing done here and now? The Mormon church didn't allow living widowed women to be sealed again to a second husband, though men had a different rule. A man who had been a widower could be married to a second wife so long as she hadn't been sealed before. And if his second wife died, even a third wife could be sealed to him while he was still living. If he was divorced, that was a different story completely, and he'd have to have special permission for a sealing to be canceled by the First Presidency before he married again.

I wondered if Kurt even knew that Anna was not sealed to Tobias. "You can always be sealed now," I said.

Anna shook her head. She was leaning against the door, holding it open now, though before she had nearly closed it on me. "He won't do it. I always thought he would change his mind. He said that he never would. At least he warned me. He is one of the most truthful people I know. His truth may hurt, but at least he does not hide it."

"Yes, I prefer the truth, as well. Might as well get it over with from the first." I felt a surge of sympathy for Anna once more. Why had I never gotten to know her better? Fear of not being good enough had kept me from someone who might have been a dear friend.

I told her I would come see her again soon, then went home and read an old Agatha Christie novel, one of my favorites, *One, Two, Buckle My Shoe.* I had always liked mysteries.

Samuel came home in the afternoon, and he mentioned he was trying to decide between two girls to ask to a dance at school.

"You should go with the person you want to go with," I said, thinking it was a simple choice. I didn't remember any of my other sons having this problem.

"But how do I know who I want to go with?" he asked, looking genuinely confused.

"I thought you said there was a girl you wanted to spend more time with?"

"There is," said Samuel. "But she isn't — I don't think she feels like that for me."

Like that? I suppose he didn't want to go into more detail with his mother. "And another girl does feel like that for you?" I asked.

Samuel squirmed, which looked very odd at his height. A giant child-man. "But I don't feel like that for her, and I worry if I ask her out, she might think . . ." He trailed off.

Samuel thought I understood what he was talking about. He was supposed to suppress sexual feelings as if they were wrong. I supposed there were advantages to this indoctrination. At least the church taught clearly that it was not his right to satisfy sexual urges on any girl he thought was pretty.

"I wish we could put aside the whole dating thing and just go out as friends. Not pair up or anything, just be a big group," said Samuel.

Again, I thought how different he was from my other sons, who had complained that they wished there weren't so many strict rules on where you could touch a girl, how you could look at her, and how long you could kiss. "Well, eventually, you'll be thinking about getting married, you know. You might as well practice spending one-on-one time now."

Samuel made a face, but he didn't say anything more, just loped upstairs to do his homework. He was such an easy kid in so many ways. He'd always been obedient. He was kind and gentle and he understood feelings in a way that even teenage girls struggled to do. But there were these weird areas that he didn't manage, like dating. It seemed like it should have been so natural, especially for someone like Samuel, who socialized easily. But it wasn't, and that was just one of the mysteries of my life, I suppose.

Kurt came home at six, the usual time for dinner. We sat and ate, the three of us. It was good family time, with inside jokes Samuel then texted to Joseph and Adam to make them laugh.

After dinner, when Samuel had gone back upstairs, I found a moment to talk to Kurt as we worked together on the dishes. I told him about Tobias Torstensen's heart, and about the fact that he had never been sealed to Anna.

"He's been a wonderful ward member. We'll be sad to lose him," said Kurt, handing me plates. "But there's nothing I can do about his choice not to be sealed to Anna, you know. That's a personal decision between him and God. And his first wife, of course."

I felt a pang for Anna. Would she be alone in the eternities? The church taught that everyone who was in the celestial kingdom had to be in a marriage — marriage was the

70

highest law of the gospel — but that didn't mean she had to be married to Tobias. In the old days, people would say worthy single women were lucky because they'd be married to Joseph Smith or Brigham Young in the afterlife. But people didn't say that anymore since anything but historical polygamy had been scripted out of the mainstream Mormon church. Who would all the worthy single women marry, then? The boys who died young and were supposed to be "perfect" because they hadn't had a chance to sin before the age of eight, the age of accountability?

"What about his first wife?" I asked Kurt. "Do you know how she died? Anna said it was her heart, but I always thought it was cancer." I didn't even know her name, I realized. I was rinsing dishes in the sink. You were supposed to save water in Utah and let the dishwasher rinse, but it never worked that way in my experience, no matter how new the dishwasher was.

Kurt thought for a long moment. "You know, for some reason, I thought she had died in a car accident, but I can't remember who told me that. It was years before we moved in."

How strange that Tobias would never speak about her, especially now that I knew he wanted to stay sealed to her and only her. "Does anyone know the real story?" I asked.

"Well, Tobias," said Kurt. "You'll have to ask him, I suppose."

If I decided ancient history was important enough to bother a dying man, I would.

CHAPTER 5

I spent all Tuesday reading, but had been bored by it more than usual. It made me wonder what was wrong with me. This was the life every stay-at-home mother eventually worked her way towards. After all those twenty-four-hour days with kids scraping their knees, making messes, vomiting and needing constant baths, to have some hours of peace and quiet should have felt like a blessing. But I was itchy for more occupation. Maybe I should join the PTA, although it was a little late for that with Samuel a senior. I should be content with being bishop's wife.

The doorbell rang that evening just after I'd served dinner. "I'll get it," said Kurt, staring at his plate then taking one last, large bite of his potatoes.

"I'll put your plate in the fridge," I said, and stood up with him.

"Poor Dad, always on call like a doctor,"

said Samuel, as he watched his father walk to the front door and open it.

I heard both a male and a female voice, but I didn't recognize either of them. I put the dinner in the fridge to wait for Kurt's return and felt only slightly guilty continuing to eat without him.

"Linda, do you mind coming into the office?" Kurt called out a few minutes later.

I was startled and stared down at my own plate.

"I'll put it in the fridge," said Samuel, with a bit of a grin.

"Thank you," I said and went into the office to discover an older man and woman I had never met before. "Are you new to the ward?" I asked. There were still a lot of new homes being built in the area, though I couldn't think of anyone moving out.

"No," said the man. He had a large, Roman nose and a strong jawline. He also had an amazing head of hair for a man his age, which I guessed was about sixty. It was all black, and it looked natural, unlike Tobias Torstensen's. He had eyebrows that looked like they should have been combed — or cut back like an overgrown hedge. There was something about him that made me think I should remember him. Was he an old high school friend who had come to

74

look me up? Or someone I'd only seen in pictures in Kurt's yearbook?

The woman was greying gracefully, her hair long and thick. She wore little makeup, and had one of those pleasantly round figures. She dressed for comfort rather than fashion: a cotton floral patterned skirt that nearly touched the floor, and under it had on a pair of flat tan shoes. When I looked into her face, she met my gaze with piercing blue eyes and I suddenly knew who she was before the words came from her husband's mouth. She was her daughter's mother.

I felt an old, familiar flicker of irrational anger at that — this woman had a daughter, had been able to raise that daughter to adulthood — and tamped it down. I wondered how often that interrupted my relationships with other women.

"We are Carrie Helm's parents, Judy and Aaron Weston," the older man said, standing up in the now rather crowded room. Kurt's office was filled with two bookshelves of church books, and Kurt had read most of them. There were two paintings of Christ, one from the story in the Book of Mormon, of him blessing the Lamanite children during the visit to America after his death, and the other of Christ in Gethsemane with Michael the archangel behind him, giving him strength. There was also a drawing of the First Presidency, which I always thought was an odd image. To me, it looked like the three men — the president and his two elected apostle-counselors — had one neck with three heads coming out of it.

"Down from Sandy," added Aaron Weston.

That was about twenty minutes from Draper. I'd had no idea Carrie Helm's parents lived so close. I had never heard her talk about them. But then again, why would I?

"Oh. I see," I said, even though I wasn't sure that I did. I glanced up at Kurt, who was behind his desk.

"They are here because they have not heard from their daughter since she left her family here, and they are concerned about her," said Kurt.

"We are more than concerned about her. We are overcome with worry," her father said. He spoke eloquently, and with deep emotion.

"Please, sit down," said Kurt, nodding to the couch. He got out a folding chair for me, and we all sat. I felt as if the room became less crowded, which made no sense. It was something about Aaron Weston sitting down. He felt less — overwhelming in size and personality.

"I don't know what Jared has told you about Carrie, but there is no way she would leave Kelly like that," said Aaron Weston. He gripped his wife's shoulder, his knuckles white, and she nodded, a look of desperation on her face. I noticed, though, that her hands were folded neatly in front of her.

"I'm sure that she will get in contact with you soon. Maybe she'll decide she's made a mistake and want to come —" Kurt began.

Aaron Weston cut him off abruptly with, "The only mistake my daughter made was in marrying Jared Helm. He is a tyrant and a bully and quite possibly insane. Have you heard him talk about his political views? Or his religious beliefs? He is rigid and self-righteous and he actually thinks that the lost tribes of Israel are frozen under the ice at the North Pole."

If we kicked people out of the Mormon church for believing crazy things like that, we would lose half the people on the rolls. I'd heard the lost tribes under the North Pole thing at least a half dozen times before, though it was usually a couple of generations removed from Jared Helm's age group.

Aaron continued, "I have talked to my daughter on numerous occasions about leaving her husband. I wouldn't care if she

77

did that. But she always made the plans with Kelly included. How could she leave her daughter with such a man?"

There was a long silence. I couldn't help but think of the way that Carrie had hugged Kelly when she left her in Primary. Aaron Weston was right. Carrie leaving her daughter behind struck me as wrong. How could any mother do that? My throat tightened.

"I've never heard anything against Jared Helm, not from your daughter or anyone else," said Kurt. "Not about him being dangerous, in any case." Just a bit right-wing; we'd both heard him in church meetings call homosexuality and universal health care "signs of the end times."

"Did you ever talk to Carrie about him in private?" Aaron Weston said. "She is afraid of him. She would never say anything close to the truth when he was around." He pounded a fist into his hand when he said the word "never." I was somewhat taken aback by his size and the strength of his body language. "But if you have not noticed the look of unhappiness in her eyes, the way that she edges away from him if she can, the way she stands between him and Kelly whenever she can, you have seen nothing at all. How can you be a bishop without looking past the most obvious of pretenses?"

Kurt looked at me. I did not know what to say. He was a man who tended to assume that the obvious was true. It was one of the reasons I loved him. He appreciated honesty rather than subtlety. He did not enjoy the games men and women often play with each other. When I said I wanted one thing, he did not think that it must mean I wanted the opposite. But at times this habit did not serve him well.

"I've noticed that she seemed unhappy," I said. "And lonely. She didn't make many friends in the ward. I wondered why." Now that I thought about it, I only remembered her sitting next to Gwen Ferris, but Gwen was a bit of an outsider herself. It occurred to me that the scene in the bathroom with Gwen crying might at least in part have been precipitated by Carrie Helm's absence. She and Gwen had always sat together in Relief Society and must have helped keep each other sane when stupid things were said, from remarks about depression being the work of the devil to God showing His love by making the righteous wealthy.

"Jared was careful not to leave any marks on her," Aaron Weston told me. "He threatened her. He told her that he would kill her if she ever tried to leave him, and he would make sure that Kelly never heard of her again. He whispered to her at night. Sometimes he woke her up to tell her that God would judge her if she didn't obey her husband's every word, or give details on how God would torment the wicked in the afterlife."

I blanched at this. That was not only directly against the doctrine of the church, but it was monstrous. No wonder Carrie had kept to herself. She must have been terrified every moment of her life. How could I not have seen that in the small rebellions she tried to make in public at church on Sundays? I had let her walk around with no allies to turn to. I wasn't the bishop and I couldn't call her husband into repentance, but the bishop's wife was the unofficial mother of the ward. She — I — was supposed to comfort and help and, well, see things!

"If you knew all this, then why didn't you do something?" asked Kurt. "Why didn't you call the police?"

"She begged us not to. He told her that if the police ever came to the house, he would make sure that they saw the perfect husband. Also, he had a notebook of mistakes she had made, with all the proof and photographs to show if there was ever an occasion that he needed them." He paused and sighed.

"What kind of mistakes?" I asked, though I realized as soon as I said it that it was probably too intrusive a question to ask parents.

Aaron Weston gestured to his wife, who finally spoke. "Things like taking money out of her daughter's college funds so that she could buy food," said Judy Weston. "Or not taking Kelly to the doctor after she had fallen and cut open her cheek."

I wasn't sure either of those constituted the kind of mistake that could make Carrie Helm look bad in court, if it came to that. But what mattered was probably what she believed, not what was really dangerous.

"I think more than anything she was ashamed she had married him in the first place." Aaron Weston added, "She made a mistake and she felt bound to him forever. She didn't know what to do, with her daughter eternally sealed to him." He interlocked his hands in a gesture of sealing that looked more like prison.

The doctrine of temple sealing was supposed to make families feel more secure, and to offer peace to those who had lost children or spouses. But there were times when it shackled a woman to a man who had become a tyrant, simply because of a ceremony performed and because of children created together.

"That is not what an eternal sealing means," said Kurt, as I'd heard him say on more than one occasion. "If Jared Helm was not living according to the laws of righteousness, the sealing was already broken."

Did that mean Carrie was free of him now? And what of Kelly, whom she had left behind? Whatever the church liked to say about broken sealings, genetics and the law of the land were not broken so easily.

Before Aaron Weston had the chance to say anything further about Jared Helm's righteousness, Kurt asked, "When did she tell you about all of this? How recently?" He wasn't taking notes during the conversation, but he kept glancing at the notepad on his desk. He never put anything on the computer, but he did take notes after an interview was finished. To keep things fresh in his mind when he prayed, he said. Suddenly, I wondered if he was doing it for legal reasons. Would Kurt be called to testify if this came to court?

"We knew something was wrong shortly after they got married," Aaron Weston said. "We tried to get her alone to talk about it openly, but it was difficult. It took months.

Jared would not let her meet anyone privately, not even us, her parents. Even when we thought we had made arrangements to talk to her alone, he would appear halfway through, or we would find out that he was eavesdropping. She was never able to talk candidly about why exactly she was not happy." At this point, Aaron nodded to prompt his wife again.

"I thought he had certain appetites," said Judy. She left the rest unsaid. Sexual appetites, obviously. But we Mormons never speak about that.

I hated the feeling of helplessness that seeped into my bones like cold. What I wanted to do most was go to Jared Helm's house and take Kelly home with me. That little girl, who had sat on my lap and tried to plunk out notes on the piano before her father stopped her, had settled into my heart. The power struggle between Carrie's father and her husband was of little interest to me, two men strutting about and comparing their size to each other. Judy Weston had barely said a word, and only when prompted by her husband.

"And when did you hear the rest of it?" asked Kurt.

"She wrote a letter to us only the day before she disappeared," said Aaron Wes-

83

ton. "She said that she was tired of living with Jared's outbursts and his judgments, and that she was going to run away. With Kelly, of course. She said that she was leaving Jared and that she hoped we would protect her confidence as long as we could. And she warned us that she would not be able to communicate with us for some time. She told us to pray for her and for Kelly to be safe." He turned to his wife.

She opened her purse and took out a letter. I didn't know anything about Carrie's handwriting, but it was a real letter, written by hand, not emailed. Email would be too easy for Jared Helm to read.

Kurt read it, and I stood up and moved so I could look over his shoulder. Aaron Weston had summarized it adequately. My stomach twisted at the strange ideas that Carrie listed that Jared believed in. Polygamy for one, which some Mormons still thought might be reinstituted, in the afterlife. But Jared Helm took it further, according to Carrie. He thought that he could make a list of women who would be his in the afterlife.

He also thought women were born evil, more worldly minded, and that he had a duty to "tame" his wife and his daughter, whatever that meant. He went on tirades about the clothing Carrie wore because it was not modest enough, nor was the clothing she bought their daughter. But I had never seen Carrie Helm wear anything that was remotely immodest. She had always seemed well dressed, but a little formal for a woman her age. Now I suppose I knew why.

"You have gone to the police then?" said Kurt.

I was still standing, feeling too much negative energy to sit back down. I wanted to scream and kick and tear at things. Instead, I clenched my fists.

"We did. But she has not been gone long enough for them to declare her missing. And there is no evidence of any foul play. They say that a letter alone is not enough to pursue Jared criminally. They need more than that. They need some proof that she has been harmed and isn't just a troubled woman who left her husband and daughter." This last Aaron Weston got out with difficulty, each word thrust out from behind his teeth.

"And what would you like me to do?" asked Kurt.

I wanted him to look at me so he could see the fury in my eyes. If I could have reached his hand, I would have gripped it so hard he could not possibly have ignored me. Something had to be done. When Jared Helm had brought Kelly here, Kurt had believed his story, had thought of him as the wronged husband. Somehow, as the bishop, Kurt should have known the truth behind Jared Helm's lies. It made me angry at God somehow that he hadn't.

"Find her," said Judy Weston, but to me, not to Kurt. "Please, find her." She was gasping, but she was not weeping. Her face was clear and insistent.

One mother who was desperate for her daughter's return to another mother who would never have hers back.

"You think that she has been harmed?" asked Kurt.

"There is no other reason she would leave her daughter. She has to have been hurt. Possibly —" Aaron Weston didn't finish.

But if Carrie Helm was dead, then I had no more chance to help her. I would have to admit I had failed her. I could not do that.

If she had lived, my daughter would have been in her twenties now, only a few years younger than Carrie Helm. She had been born between Joseph and Kenneth, but we had never brought her home from the hospital. My doctor at the time had said anything might have caused my daughter's death, maybe my taking cold medicine before I knew I was pregnant, or letting my body temperature get too high in a hot tub when Kurt and I were on vacation for a week when I first found out I was expecting. I had no way of knowing if it was my fault or not, or if I would ever see that daughter again in the afterlife.

She had died before she was born, and that left her in a kind of limbo in terms of Mormon doctrine. Stillborn children are sometimes listed as members of the family and sealed to their parents, but sometimes they are not. Some Mormons firmly believe a stillborn child is only a body, and that if there was once a spirit attached to it, it has gone to another body, to other parents.

Joseph Smith had given a famous funeral speech for a young child, claiming that children who died before the age of eight were automatically taken into the celestial kingdom and that mothers would there be allowed the privilege of raising their children to adulthood if they had missed the chance in this life. Still, I didn't like the idea that a child was waiting all those years for me to die before she was allowed to grow up.

I hoped fervently that the Westons were blowing the potential danger to Carrie out of proportion, and for the first time I hoped that Jared Helm's story was true and Carrie had just abandoned her family. Now, having read her letter, I began to understand why the young mother might make that choice. If Jared had made her believe she was a bad mother, she might have become convinced Kelly was better off without her. I could sympathize with Carrie Helm in ways that her parents and even Kurt probably could never understand.

"If you could talk to Jared," Judy was saying, turning away from her husband and appealing to Kurt now. "Maybe he would tell you where she is. She did not simply disappear. She would not do that. She would not leave Kelly with him."

"There might be some other explanation for all of this," said Kurt. He always wanted there to be an explanation.

But sometimes the explanation was that men took advantage of the power they had over their wives, in society and in the church. Even the kindest men in the church had no idea of the many ways in which they made their wives and daughters into lesser persons than their sons and fellow male church members. "I wouldn't be where I am today without my wife," they say in testimony meetings. But what they are also saying is that their wives have given up their personal ambitions in favor of the ambitions of their husbands. Mormon men protect their daughters, but they encourage and cheer on their sons. And I, who had never had a daughter, and had so few female friends still in the church, had done little more than any of the men had to help the women around me. But that had to change. I had to change first, and make the church and culture change around me. First came speaking the truth.

"You need to get the press involved," I said, thinking of the news stories I had seen that week on television. The missing persons cases with the best publicity always get solved the fastest. "If the police won't act, then we need some help. Some people out there, looking for her. People who might have seen Jared the night Carrie disappeared." This was what I had learned in my years of watching missing persons cases on TV, not anything official, but I believed it.

"Press?" said Kurt in a choked tone.

But Judy Weston nodded. "That is a good idea. I know a writer for the local paper." She glanced at her husband.

"But he isn't anyone important," said Aaron Weston. "I have some friends who work at KSL, members of the church I've come in contact with in my leadership positions."

I disliked the way that he dismissed Judy's suggestion and had to put his own ideas first, but I wanted this done more than I wanted to argue about who should lead it. "Start with any local connections you have," I said. "But national coverage would be better. We want to force the police to pay attention. The longer they wait before acting, the less chance there is of . . ." I couldn't allow myself to believe that she was dead. Carrie Helm had to be alive.

Aaron Weston was nodding vigorously. He could agree with me, if not with his own wife, it seemed. "Good," he said, putting a hand to his heart. "The Spirit is speaking to me right now, telling me this is the right path. We'll go and get started. Thank you so much. We'll be in touch with you again soon about the results."

I nodded, feeling alive in a way I hadn't for years. My fingers were tingling and I could feel the beat of blood in my neck. Other bishop's wives didn't get involved in personal crusades, but I couldn't turn this one aside. I owed it to Carrie Helm, after all the time I'd neglected her.

"I knew this was the right place to come,"

said Judy Weston softly. She stood up and came toward me, hugging me gently despite my stiffness. I was going to have to learn sometime, I told myself. This was how women interacted with each other.

Holding her husband's hand as they walked to the front door, Judy Weston said, "I am sure that God is watching over Carrie even now."

I watched them leave and then Kurt gestured me back to his office. "If Jared Helm is innocent, you have just put him into an impossible situation," he said sternly.

"Do you really still think that is likely?" I said, annoyed with him. "You read that letter Carrie Helm wrote. It sounded pretty bad to me."

"I admit, it was disturbing, but it seems unfair to paint Jared Helm as an abuser. Or a possible murderer. That letter isn't proof of anything other than the fact that Carrie and Jared had a troubled marriage, and we knew that already."

"Carrie Helm is gone and no one has heard from her. She might well be dead. I think the possibility of that outweighs Jared Helm's need for privacy," I said. But I thought, please, don't be dead, please don't be dead. It was the same mantra I had repeated that night so many years ago, when

Kurt drove me to the hospital.

Samuel was waiting for me and Kurt at the bottom of the stairs. He told us he had decided to go to the dance with the girl he was comfortable with and seemed relieved at the choice. I was relieved that he was going to the dance at all. I slipped out of bed late at night to go downstairs and watch the news. But there was nothing about Carrie Helm. Yet.

CHAPTER 6

The press conference with the Westons appeared on local television (on Mormon church-owned KSL, of all stations) at noon the next day. The two parents stood together in a picture of marital harmony in front of their local church, which looked much the same as ours. Aaron Weston did most of the speaking, as he had at our house. Kurt was at work, and I was sure he was fielding plenty of calls there, but within minutes of the end of the conference, I had to deal with the frightened women of the ward who suddenly thought Jared Helm was a danger to them.

The truth was, Jared Helm wasn't a danger to anyone anymore, except perhaps his own daughter. The real danger to the women in the ward was the same danger they had faced yesterday and the day before that, and ever since they were married: their own husbands.

I am a happily married woman myself, but I acknowledge marriage can be a dangerous covenant. When both people are honest and good, it is still difficult to live together so intimately, day in and day out. But no one is perfectly good or honest. And so marriage becomes a dance over hot coals and metal spikes. We contort ourselves trying to disguise one habit or another, trying to pretend to love one part or another of our partner's that we don't. All so that we can get along.

Privacy cannot exist in a marriage, even when it should, even when it is healthy. And just as dangerous is the legal bind we are in. Shared finances may be fine when people have similar habits, but when they do not? And none of this begins to address the difficulty that is expounded when a marriage produces a family.

I know from personal experience that marriage can be a holy institution, blessed by God. I have felt moments of perfect bliss and contentment with my husband. I have been expanded in many ways by being yoked to someone who is so different, and I am glad for those chances. But there are twice as many occasions when I shake my head and wonder if we would be happier if we could only live together as friends. Or be business partners. Or share parental responsibilities. Does it always have to be marriage — everything shared and stirred together?

On television, Aaron Weston had said, "My daughter is missing. Her husband claims she disappeared in the middle of the night, leaving her five-year-old daughter behind. This husband claims that my daughter left no address for anyone to contact her. He claims that she took nothing with her, not a car, not her coat or purse, not even money from her checking account. I do not believe him, but the police refuse to do anything unless there is some evidence of foul play. My daughter may be in danger. She may be out of money, without food. She may be dead or lying badly beaten in a ditch. I need your help to help her."

I found myself clenching my fists when he said the word "dead." But it might bring more attention to the case, which could only do good.

The camera panned to Judy Weston, who was wearing a tailored pink wool suit and frilly white blouse, and far more makeup than she had the last time I had seen her. I wondered if she had chosen that herself, or if the television people had suggested it. Or if Aaron had.

She was looking down at a piece of paper

in her hands. Aaron moved to the side so she could lean over the microphone. She read from Carrie's letter.

"Jared told me that my daughter was his by blood and by right. He said that he could replace me as a mother if I left him. He said that Kelly would not remember my name or my face, that she would have a new mother, a better mother. He said that God would seal his new wife to him and to Kelly and would rip me from them, that I would live in the hell prepared for women who do not love their daughters and husbands naturally. He said that the whole world would remember me as a crazy woman and him as the wronged man. He said that he would be purified by any hurt I did to his heart, and that he would think of me as a trial that God had given him to prove himself."

Then Judy looked up at the camera. Her face had blotches on it, clear marks of tears, but she wasn't crying now. She had masked her pain so that she could do what had to be done. I felt like I was looking in a mirror. There was no peace in her expression, only terror of judgment. If she believed in God or in His mercy, she didn't look like it now.

"That sounds very ominous," said the

newscaster, a woman in a bright royal blue suit. "Have the police seen that letter?"

"They've seen it and they said that it didn't change their procedure," said Aaron, moving in front of the cameras again. "If she had filed a police report or asked for a restraining order, that would be something else. But she was terrified of contacting the police. She only wrote this to us a few days ago, when she was so afraid that something would happen to her anyway that she didn't think it added any risk."

"And you, Mrs. Weston? Do you have anything you'd like to say to the police?" asked the newscaster.

Aaron put his arm around his wife's shoulder, guiding her toward the microphone. Her voice sounded a little shaky now, as she moved off of a memorized speech.

"This is my daughter, my little girl. And she has been hurt by the very person she ought to have been able to trust the most, her husband. It is beyond my comprehension, beyond my ability to imagine —" She put her hands over her face, unable to continue.

Aaron spoke next, as if finishing what his wife had meant to say. His voice was more firm, and his expression vengeful rather than

97

sad. "If she is dead, then Jared Helm must be forced to own up to his crime. He cannot be allowed a free pass. He cannot be allowed to raise my granddaughter as a prize for his reprehensible actions in his marriage to my daughter."

"What would you like our viewers to do?" asked the newscaster.

"I want them to call the police and demand that they look into this case. And tell everyone you know to do the same."

"What about volunteers to help search for your daughter?"

After Elizabeth Smart, this was a common question asked about missing children. The Mormon church could mobilize thousands of volunteers in a couple of hours if necessary. But a search was not often organized for a missing adult. The question set my mind running through possible scenarios. What if Jared Helm hadn't killed Carrie, but was holding her somewhere against her will, punishing her for thinking of leaving? But where? How would he get to her, to bring food? After this publicity, he wouldn't be able to leave his house. And that was my fault.

"That is a secondary concern," Aaron Weston was saying. "If we can't get the police to act, then I will ask for volunteers to search for any sign of her. But first, let's get the official channels working." He looked directly at the screen. "If it were your daughter in this situation, what would you want the police to do?"

The newscaster let the moment draw out. Then she said, "And what do you say in response to your son-in-law's comment, which he sent to our station early this morning when we asked for his response?" She looked down at a paper in her hands. "Jared Helm says that his wife was 'sadly deluded and possibly mentally ill at the time that she wrote that letter. I hoped to get care for her and had asked her to see a psychiatrist on numerous occasions. She would not. Nor would she take the depression medication that our family doctor had prescribed for her. The records of that appointment are enclosed. She disappeared because she could not deal with the responsibilities of an adult life as a wife and mother. I pity her, and I hope the best for her, but I cannot allow her back into my life or my daughter's.' "

The newscaster paused and the camera zoomed in on the Westons. I stared at Aaron Weston's face and thought I saw a hint of anger, but he did not show any embarrassment or distress. His tone was precisely clipped when he spoke, however.

"And when his wife is missing, all my son-in-law thinks about is how it will look to the press, and making sure that he is protected legally? If my daughter did see a doctor about depression, it was depression he caused. And if she refused to take medication, it was because she was more concerned about her daughter than she was about herself. Taking pills when you are with an abuser is not a solution to the problem and may blind you to the real effects of the abuse. My daughter likely knew that." He gestured emphatically at the end of each sentence, and I had the impression of a man who knew how to use force when he wanted to.

The camera turned to the newscaster. "Well, we thank you for your time. And viewers, if you feel strongly about this, we urge you to contact the number on the screen below. You can also give us feedback at our website, on Facebook, or on Twitter." She smiled and I winced.

When Samuel came home, I asked him if he had heard anything. He shrugged and said that they had watched the news at school in his journalism class.

"What do you think happened to Carrie Helm, Mom?" he asked.

"I think she's in danger," I said carefully.

"Do you think she's dead?" he said.

"I hope she isn't dead," I said. Samuel was old enough to hear the truth. "But I'm very much afraid she is."

Samuel was in the kitchen, where he had started to get a snack. He stood in front of the pantry, frozen. "Then you think we have a murderer in our ward? Shouldn't someone have seen the signs of something going wrong? What about her visiting teachers?" With each question, Samuel's voice rose. "What about Dad?" he finished.

Samuel had every right to be angry at all of us. We told him that God would protect the righteous by warning us of danger, and then this happened.

"I wish someone had seen something. I wish I had," I said, unwilling to point the finger at other people when I held equal responsibility.

"Is Jared Helm going to be excommunicated?" Samuel asked. "Or on a church trial or something?" This was more than just idle curiosity on his part, I sensed. But why was he asking the question? We hadn't had a church disciplinary court in the year since Kurt had been bishop.

"I'm more concerned about whether Jared Helm goes to jail or not." His eternal welfare, God could figure out later. "But first the police need to figure out what really happened."

Samuel thumped the counter in frustration. "It's not enough," he said.

"Listen, why don't we go visit Adam and Marie?" I said.

Adam, our oldest at twenty-six, had been married several years ago, and he and Marie lived south of us, in Provo, where they were both still going to college at Brigham Young University. They came up for our monthly family dinners, and they called occasionally, but we didn't see them as often as I wished we could.

"Okay," said Samuel.

"All right, I'll call. Do you want to see Zachary while we're there, too?" I asked. Zachary, twenty-one, had returned home from his mission a few months ago and was also at BYU. Joseph, twenty-four, our second oldest, lived in Ogden with his wife, Willow. He hadn't gone on a mission, despite the cultural pressure. It had been a struggle for Kurt to deal with, but he hadn't been bishop then, and we all made it through. Less than half of eligible young men go on missions, and the pressure to do so has decreased. Not everyone is ready to serve, and it can cause problems if young

men go on missions when they are still dealing with problems socially, physically, or
religiously.

Kenneth, at twenty-three, lived in Salt
Lake City, where he enjoyed the city life.
He had gone on a mission, but I wasn't sure
of his church activity since then. I saw him
becoming distant from the church and had
no idea what to do about it. I didn't think
Kurt had noticed yet, but he would, in time.

We drove the half hour down to Provo and
caught up with Adam and Marie for a few
minutes before they had to go to work and
to study at the library, and then we stopped
in and took Zachary out for some burgers.
He told us about his latest prank on his
roommates, which had been to switch the
wiring in the apartment so that the hot
water in the shower only worked when the
kitchen sink light was on, and the freezer
began defrosting as soon as anyone turned
on the dishwasher.

Zachary had always been a terror when he
lived at home. I hadn't been afraid he would
kill himself by accident, but I wasn't so sure
about the rest of us. He was studying
engineering now, but it only seemed to give
him better ideas for bigger pranks.

On the drive home to Draper, Samuel
turned off the radio for a moment and said,

"Thanks, Mom. I feel better."

"Good," I said. I felt the same.

CHAPTER 7

By the day after the Westons had appeared on television, the whole neighborhood had changed. There were news vans constantly in front of Jared Helm's house and he could not go out to the grocery store without being mobbed by reporters. It was enough to make me feel sorry for him.

Jared tried to come to church the following Sunday, but by the time he got there, the news vans had all moved into the parking lot. It was impossible for anyone to get into the building without being asked to speak on camera and give an opinion about Jared and Carrie Helm.

Kurt ended up tapping Jared on the shoulder during priesthood class and taking him into his office on the other side of the building. I heard about this after the fact, as I left the sacrament meeting, from one of the women in the ward whose husband had been there.

"So, what did you say to him?" Samuel asked when Kurt came home from the last of his Sunday meetings at eight o'clock.

Kurt was sitting at the kitchen table while I warmed up yet another meal Samuel and I had eaten without him. He sighed and bowed his head until it was resting on the wood, as if it was too heavy for him. Then he raised it and met Samuel's eyes. "I asked him if I could send the deacons to give him the Sacrament in his home, and if he could read the lessons online and talk to his home teachers about them without the disruptions to the whole ward." It was clear that Kurt had not been satisfied about this solution to the problem.

He took a bite of food and chewed at it unhappily. The number of times he had skipped dinner completely since he became bishop was larger than anyone would guess. It was a good thing stress makes a person hold onto calories or he might have shrunk entirely away.

I sat next to him, my shoulder touching his in hopes that he would feel the physical sense of support. I could understand his conflicted feelings when it came to Jared Helm's attending church. After all, a bishop was in the business of making sure people came to church. Obviously, there were times when exceptions could be made, but those exceptions are supposed to happen only in cases like natural disaster.

"And what did he say?" asked Samuel.

"He didn't say anything really. He just nodded a lot and then he went to get Kelly from the Primary," Kurt said.

So Kelly would not be at church, either. That bothered me. The little girl needed some contact with people who were not her father, I felt strongly. He already had so much power over her, now that her mother was gone. But how would she get it now that his house had become practically a prison?

"But the news reporters didn't come into the church building, did they? It's private property," said Samuel.

Kurt's mouth twitched at that. "It's private property, but the signs say ALL WELCOME. We don't want to give the impression that you have to be a member to attend services. So that means we can't really keep reporters out, either."

I was astonished at the gall of anyone coming into a religious meeting to insist on interviews. But then again, this was their job, Mormons or not.

"Were they bothering Kelly at all?" I asked. "Trying to get her to talk on camera?" The idea of making that little girl's life worse than it already was made me want to hunt down every reporter there and make them vacuum up Cheerios for the next ten years of their lives.

Kurt said, "They were trying to get anyone on camera they could. The Primary Presidency, Kelly's classmates, even the deacons who eventually went to give the Helms Sacrament at home."

"The deacons?" said Samuel. "Why? What would they know?"

"I don't think they knew anything, but they're the youngest and most vulnerable. They look like church leaders on camera to some extent, in ties and white shirts and suits. I told them not to speak to any reporters," said Kurt. "I gave them strict instructions before they left the church."

"I saw at least one of them on camera," I said. Maybe it wasn't keeping the Sabbath holy to watch the news, but I often did anyway.

Samuel made a face. "I bet I can guess which one, too."

Samuel did not always get along with the other young men in the ward, though it was often for reasons that I sympathized with. There are certain teenage boys who are forces of nature, and it is only going on a

108

mission that tames them. Though heaven help the mission president who ends up with them on his roster.

"You could make sure he regrets it," Samuel offered with a smile. "He could get called into the priests quorum. Or be called as one of the young men who help the Cub Scouts. Or he could be asked to organize a special service project."

"Thanks for the ideas," said Kurt. "But I think I will let the Lord offer suggestions instead, Samuel." He pushed his plate away. I had made a fine dinner of chicken fettuccine with fresh rosemary in the sauce and tiny peas on the side, but I didn't think it mattered how well I cooked now that Kurt was bishop and had other things on his mind. "Isn't it time for you to be in bed?" Kurt said to Samuel. "It's a school night."

"It's not even nine," said Samuel. "And I'm not a little kid anymore. I know when I need to go to sleep."

"Bedroom, then. Quiet time," said Kurt.

When Kurt and I were left in the kitchen, I said, "You're worried about something else."

Kurt stood and bused his dish. "If Jared and Kelly Helm can't come to church, I feel like they might slip through the cracks." He stared at the refrigerator as if he expected a note about Jared and Kelly Helm to magically appear there.

"You mean, no one from the ward will be able to check on them."

"Yes." Kurt looked up at me and I realized he was thinking something he couldn't say. I was worried about Kelly, but Kurt's mind was hierarchical.

"You think Jared might do something?" I asked. "To himself?" Jared Helm hadn't struck me as the kind of man who would easily become despondent. But with his wife gone, his daughter entirely dependent on him, his job slipping away, and now being trapped in his house by the news reporters outside — I had not considered any of this when I told the Westons to go to the press about Carrie.

When the Westons came to talk to us in Kurt's office, I had been so sure that Jared had killed Carrie. But since then, I'd developed doubts. I'd seen that Jared Helm was controlling, and I believed he had whacky political ideas. He was inflexible and arrogant, as I'd had plenty of chances to see in church. But that didn't necessarily mean he was a murderer. Whatever Carrie's letter had said, it wasn't proof of anything but her state of mind. She had been afraid of him, but had she believed he would kill her? And

110

even if she'd believed it, did that make it true?

If he was innocent, then I had caused a lot of problems for a man who was trying to be a good father in the way he knew how. I had ultimately created a situation where Kelly could not go to church.

"I don't know what to think," said Kurt. "But I know that we're in a ward so we can look out for each other, and now I've asked Jared Helm to sacrifice his fellowship in the ward for the sake of the rest of us. Now, when he might need us the most. I feel terrible about it."

Kurt felt like anything that happened on his watch was his burden to bear, not only in this life but in the one to come. Priesthood authority had that disadvantage. God expects an accounting for those under your care, and so Kurt would never blame me for what I had done, since he had stood by and let me do it. I was his wife and if he could not use gentle persuasion to convince me he was right, it was his problem.

"I could bring him a homemade loaf of bread," I suggested, and wrote Jared Helm on a note to put on the fridge myself. "That might at least get me in the door."

"Thank you," said Kurt, closing his hand around mine as I put a magnet in place.

I was more concerned about Kelly than Jared, but isolation wasn't going to make him a better father. "Are you sure you don't want to go see him yourself?"

Kurt shook his head. "If it's a visit from the bishop, it's official. He'd be on guard. But you have a much better chance of seeing what is actually going on there."

I would be all but invisible to Jared Helm, who wouldn't respect me enough to imagine I had any ulterior motive. Kurt was telling me quite clearly that he, Kurt, did respect me as his partner in this, that he valued and relied on my abilities. My husband knew exactly how to push my buttons.

"So you're starting to think he might have done something to Carrie?" I asked after a moment.

He sighed. "I don't know what to think, honestly."

"Whatever the truth is, by refusing to speak to the police, Jared isn't acting like an innocent man," I said. The public response to the Westons' televised appeal had been enough for Carrie Helm's disappearance to be upgraded to "suspicious" and for there to be an official investigation opened.

"He's angry and he feels betrayed," said Kurt. "He might act like that even if everything he says about Carrie's disappearance is true."

"Hmm. I hope that if I disappeared you would be out there with the searchers, looking for me in fields and mountains, not telling people that I must have left you and my children because I was crazy."

Kurt smiled at that. "Luckily, I am not afraid of that happening."

"Because you think I'm too much in love with you to ever leave?" I asked, eyebrows raised.

"Because you would make sure everyone heard about all my faults if you decided to leave me," said Kurt. He paused. "And if you were kidnapped, you would do a 'Ransom of Red Chief' on them. They'd regret it and bring you back as soon as they could."

I let out a laugh. "I hope so. But you may be the only one who knows what a pain I can be. Lucky you."

"And the boys," said Kurt. "And some of the teachers at the school that you've wrangled with on the boys' behalf. But just because your strength isn't always visible doesn't mean it isn't powerful. In fact, I have often thought the reverse is true."

"Bonus husband points," I told him, leaning closer.

"Ooh. You know how much I try to earn those," he said with a smile. He kissed me and then nuzzled my neck. For a moment, I thought it was going to turn into more than that. Kurt was good in bed, even if he didn't have time for it very often anymore. That was one of the things that the stake president didn't talk about when he asked you about supporting your husband in being the bishop. Long hours was one thing, but when it was compounded by lack of sleep and the distraction of other people's problems, it did not make for a high libido. When Kurt was released in four years, I wondered how long it would take him to recover. I was looking forward to finding out.

But the doorbell rang, rupturing the moment. "Who could that be?" I said, barely restraining myself from cursing.

"Oh, I know who it is," said Kurt.

"On a Sunday night? Don't they know you've spent all day at church already?"

Kurt shrugged. "It was the only time that fit into their schedule and it was important. Really important. They are struggling, Linda. I know you'd want me to help a young couple struggling." He kissed me again, less passionately this time. What had he been thinking, to kiss me like that before, when he knew we would be interrupted?

Kurt opened the door. To my surprise, Gwen Ferris and her husband, Brad, were standing there waiting. They were holding hands, but Gwen seemed nervous. She glanced past Kurt at me, and then looked away again.

"Come into my office," said Kurt, and he closed the front door and gestured them in.

Gwen moved awkwardly and nearly fell into a houseplant that was on the floor by the office door. Brad grabbed her and steadied her.

"Did I hurt it?" she asked, patting at the leaves.

The plant had survived five teenage boys careening by it every day, so it was unlikely that one grown woman was going to bother it. "I'm sure it's fine," I said, still curiously watching Gwen. The fact that she was here with her husband seemed to indicate they were coming for marital counseling. I knew there was trouble having children, but was there more? Gwen's eyes were puffy and red. Her whole demeanor suggested shame and discomfort. She moved into the office with her shoulders hunched, as if trying to make herself smaller.

Gwen's husband had always seemed such a nice man to me. He had one of those baby faces that made you think he would always look young. Could he possibly have abused her? An extreme conclusion to jump to, but

115

I suppose after everything we'd heard about Jared and Carrie Helm, I was anticipating abuse everywhere.

"Go on in," said Kurt in a cheerful voice. He waited until they were inside to turn back to me.

Samuel was already in bed, but I went into the kitchen and made some more fresh cinnamon rolls. There was a batch waiting in a take-away tin for the Ferrises when they came out of Kurt's office at about one o'clock. I read in the front room, waiting for my husband. Once I had offered the rolls and the Ferrises were gone, I climbed the stairs slowly at Kurt's side.

"You too tired?" asked Kurt, massaging my back.

"Definitely not," I said.

CHAPTER 8

Monday morning, I couldn't sleep in, despite how tired I felt. I went into the kitchen and worked on some homemade wheat bread in the empty house. For some reason, the only recipe I knew how to make was for eight loaves. I had an oven large enough to fit them all at once, but after I'd pulled them out, I still had to wait until one of them was cool enough to wrap in plastic. Then I looked around for a bow that didn't look too holiday-specific. A plain gold one would do, yes.

And because I couldn't help myself, I cut into one of the loaves fresh out of the oven, burned my tongue on the first bite, and then blew out while taking the next three bites. The wonderful thing about hot bread is that you can't tell how much butter is melting into the dense, moist crust. I always put on as much as the bread can hold.

I cleaned myself up, put on a coat and

walked over to Jared Helm's house. The news vans were still there; a head peeked out of one of the windows as I passed.

"Who are you?" a voice called out.

"The bishop's wife," I called back, and that was that. They didn't need any more information from me, it seemed. I tried not to be annoyed that my presence was taken for granted; my invisibility was an advantage.

I rang the doorbell and waited patiently for several minutes. I could hear someone behind the door, looking through the peephole. I held out the bread. "Bringing a gift," I said.

Finally, the door opened.

Jared Helm looked as if he had been exercising. He was wet with sweat and his hair was standing on end. He must have run his fingers through it a hundred times. "Sister Wallheim, come in," he said.

"I thought you could use some home-baked bread," I said. I couldn't find it in myself to offer him verbal sympathy.

He took it from my hands. "Thank you so much. It feels warm still."

"Just out of the oven." I tried not to be too obvious about looking for Kelly behind him.

"It's so nice to know that there are people

118

out there on my side," he said, and caught a sob. And that was all it took — the next thing I knew he leaned forward and put his head on my shoulder. I felt awkward and tried to remind myself that I was the mother of the ward, and that included Jared Helm, guilty or not. We are all sinners, aren't we?

He took a deep breath. I closed my eyes for a moment and thought of Samuel with his head on my shoulder. It helped.

Then I heard a voice. "Daddy, can I come downstairs? It smells good."

Jared pulled away from me and wiped at his face. "Come on, Kelly," he said, beckoning to her.

She skipped down to him, and threw her arms around him. Her hair had been combed and pulled into a ponytail, but it was already looking a little matted at the back, and curls were poking out around her ears. Her outfit was horribly mismatched, pink polka-dotted leggings with a plaid flannel shirt. She had big pink pig slippers on, as well, which looked as if they had passed their best days. I didn't know if her father had allowed her to dress herself or if this was his idea of appropriate clothing, but it was hardly evidence of abuse. Or neglect, for that matter. For the moment, he seemed

119

an ordinary father with a daughter he adored.

He carried her into the kitchen and set her on the counter. The cabinets were white-painted wood that looked as if it had been done recently, with the stencils that are so popular as lessons at Relief Society meetings. Likely Carrie had done them herself. The floor was spotless, and the dishes were all in the dishwasher. There were no high-priced, flashy appliances, but it looked like a kitchen that was used often.

Jared Helm opened the bread bag and cut a big slice for Kelly.

"Can I have butter and jam, Daddy?" she asked.

"Butter and jam," he said, and went to the refrigerator. He gave her a portion of butter that was nearly equal to my own, then jam as well, and handed her the dessert.

She ate it happily, getting jam all over her face.

He watched her and seemed in no hurry to clean her up.

I couldn't help but think that this could be a performance, designed specifically for me. I thought of how tightly wound and controlling he had been the last time I'd seen him; this seemed like a different man.

Had it been the stress of Carrie's departure that made him so short that morning when he'd come to see Kurt? Had he been broken by the publicity? Or was this tender father act just that? But Kelly was only five years old. It wasn't an act on her part.

I considered the possibility that Jared Helm was telling the truth about his wife. What if he were the injured husband and she psychologically unstable? It wouldn't be the first time a woman had made up stories about abuse. "Is there anything I can do to help you?" I asked.

He looked at me like I was offering him a lifeline. "Do you know, you are the first person who has asked me that. Every other person who has called to talk to me has wanted to ask me questions about my life. They want to make judgments about me. Or they ask about Kelly, as if they think I don't know how to take care of her. If she is eating enough. If I need some help finding her games or giving her a bath. As if I haven't had anything to do with my daughter for the last four years of her life."

The very questions I had wanted to ask but had held back.

"I'm five years old, Daddy," said Kelly, wiping her face off on her father's shirt.

He looked down at the mess, and sighed.

Then he ran a hand down her hair and kissed her cheek. "Of course you are." He looked back at me. "They're almost as bad as the reporters who want to interview me. They're vultures, feeding off a carcass."

"I'm sure some of them are just trying to help. Sometimes people don't know how to ask or what to say." I knew that as well as anyone.

"Well, I'm the one who has suffered a tragedy. Why do I have to make excuses for them?"

"Because it's the human condition, being stupid," I said. "We all have to make excuses for each other or we would never survive."

He let out a short breath, then nodded. "True," he said. "Thank you. For treating me normally."

"You're welcome," I said. I wasn't sure I had treated him normally, but he was clearly a devoted father and that meant a lot to me.

I stood up, ready to leave. I didn't want him to think I was staying too long, and I had found out what I wanted to know about Kelly. Whether or not Jared was guilty of abusing his wife wasn't yet clear to me, but Kelly was well enough. For now.

"If you really want to help me, there is something you could do," he said.

I turned back. "Yes?"

"I'd like to write a statement for the press. I'm working on it already, actually. I'm wondering if you would look it over, tell me what you think. Maybe the bishop could look at it, too? I would really appreciate it if he could add a statement of support or faith in me. Anything, really. I don't want to talk to the press, but I feel like I need to say something. I'm innocent, and I need to start looking like I am."

"Of course," I said, though my mind was spinning. So he was planning to go to the press, but not to the police? It was what the Westons had done.

"Can I email it to you?" he asked. "The address on the church website is good, isn't it?"

I nodded and moved to the door.

"Thank you so much, again. Kelly, tell Sister Wallheim thank you for the bread."

Kelly chimed in behind me, and I was outside again, staring at the news vans. I hurried home and checked my email. In the time it had taken to cross the half block between us, Jared Helm had already sent his email. But the statement to the press made me go cold.

I am enormously saddened by the decision my wife has taken to leave our marriage and our daughter. She has often been troubled and ill during the years we have been together, but I always supported her and gave her all the help she asked for. I do not understand why she could not have trusted me to continue to do so. I have always been a loving father and husband, and will continue to do what I can to protect my young daughter now that she has been made so much more vulnerable to pain at her mother's departure.

I do not know where Carrie has gone. She did not tell me, and she left no hints in the things that remain in our home. I hope that she is well, but I do not spend my time worrying about her. I do not think that she deserves that, after the choices she has made. She is a selfish woman, and I suspect that wherever she is, she will continue to make immoral, selfish decisions that may offer her momentary pleasures but will never bring back the happiness she has lost by turning her back on her eternal family.

If anyone has seen her, I urge those people to contact the police immediately, so that they can be assured that there is no need for a criminal investigation. I also ask the media to leave me and my daughter in peace. We have a difficult enough road ahead of us without having added complications. Kelly needs to have as normal a life as possible as we move into the future, and I need to be able to father her, which will include returning to work and earning a living. I thank all of those people who are out there, wishing me the best. You know who you are, and that you are true Christians and true Saints in the best senses of the words.

It was all about him. A few words about Kelly. But nothing conciliatory about his wife or sympathetic about his wife's family and the distress they were going through.

I shouldn't jump to conclusions. He was in a terrible position. Someone who had just suffered a loss wasn't always thinking clearly. And selfishness was a natural reaction to pain.

Jared needed to say something about his wife if he wanted to make himself look better to the press, but I wasn't sure if I wanted to help him. I read a book and tried to distract myself with thoughts about going back to school. I had gotten a degree years ago in philosophy, of all things. Useless for getting a job, though I had found it interesting in other ways. I was beginning to wonder if I had too much time on my hands. If I had more things to do on my own time, maybe I would be less sucked into responsibilities as a bishop's wife.

I also went through our finances, which was something that Kurt used to do before he became bishop. Then I cleaned the house rather more thoroughly than I normally bothered to do. It was something to keep my mind and hands busy.

When Kurt got home, I pulled him into his office so that Samuel didn't overhear us, then asked him if he wanted to see the statement Jared Helm had prepared for the press.

"I got it, too," he said, settling into the chair behind the desk.

"And what did you think?" I refused to sit on the couch, and perched myself next to him on the desk.

Kurt shrugged. "I already emailed him back and said that he didn't need to respond to the press at all. He should focus on Kelly and himself and staying healthy and strong for her."

"And is that what you really think he should do? Or did you say that because you didn't want to say anything else?"

Kurt shook his head. "Honestly, I think I need more information. I feel like I don't know him as well as I should."

Which was what I felt, too. But how could we ever know anyone well enough to know what to do in a situation like this?

"I told him that I'd like him to come over and talk to me sometime," said Kurt, "if he could manage it. I wanted to give him comfort and advice officially, if I could. I told him that he could bring Kelly and you would watch her, if he needed help." He wasn't making eye contact, which was odd, since he had more or less just volunteered me for something.

"And what did he say?" I was willing to watch Kelly, for whatever reason.

Kurt stood up and started moving papers around his desk. "He demanded that I promise that his parents-in-law would not be here."

It was the wrong thing to say to Kurt, who was losing patience with Jared Helm's attitude at last, I thought. "You think he might be guilty now?" I asked.

"I don't want to think the worst of him, but he's making it difficult." He sighed, and kept at his organizing.

For whatever reason, Kurt and I both tended to clean when we got upset. It made for a very clean house when we were having extended arguments.

"Maybe he's just a jerk," I said, trying to

ease Kurt's mind. "Maybe he's a bad husband, but not a murderer. He seemed so devoted to Kelly when I brought the bread over."

"If he's just a jerk, then where is Carrie?"

It was the million-dollar question, wasn't it?

"What about his job?" I asked. "He can't be earning money if he's at home all day."

"I asked him about that several days ago, if he needed any church assistance. He said that he could work from home for a while and promised he would tell me if he got into any financial trouble. Apparently he works for his father's business, and it's all programming stuff that he can do remotely."

"Well, it can't stay like this forever, with all those news vans. The story is going to get old and they'll go home," I said.

"And what does that mean for the chance of finding Carrie Helm?" said Kurt. His desk was now clean. If he wanted to do more cleaning, we'd have to move someplace else. Unless he wanted to get out the vacuum.

"If she's dead, they will have to find her eventually. Bodies don't just disappear," I said.

"This is Utah," said Kurt. "Do you know how many millions of acres of untouched land there are in this state?"

I felt sick at the thought that Kurt on some level had come to the same conclusion I had, that Jared Helm had killed Carrie and then disposed of the body somewhere. I kept questioning my first instinct on this, but what if I had been right from the beginning? What if the Spirit had been speaking to me and telling me what to think about Jared? What if Kurt was finally feeling the same spiritual impression?

"There would have to be evidence somewhere," I said. "Some video camera at a gas station. Someone who saw him buying something at a store." I was trying to think like a detective, like a professional, and not just a bishop's wife.

Kurt folded his hands together, as if coming to a decision. "But in any case, that's something for the police to deal with," said Kurt. "I'm in charge of Jared and Kelly's spiritual welfare."

"Not Carrie's?" I asked.

Kurt flushed. "Carrie has left the ward, so no, I'm not her bishop now. Unless she comes back."

That seemed rather cold. Though technically, it was true. Kurt's obligation was to a specific geographical flock. "And if she's dead? And died while in our ward?"

"Then God will take care of her better than I could. I deal with the living," said Kurt. "We all have our roles, and we should stick to them."

We moved back to the kitchen and called Samuel for dinner. But as they chattered about school and Samuel's upcoming dance, I could not help but think about Carrie and what my obligation to her was. I had felt that immediate protectiveness toward Kelly, in part because she was so young, but did we simply give up on Carrie? Did we turn our backs on those who left the church, even if they remained in need?

Kurt liked coloring inside the lines. It had worked well for him his whole life. And generally, I'd done the same. But it didn't feel right in this instance.

CHAPTER 9

Cheri Tate called me on Wednesday to tell me about her plans for the next weekday Relief Society meeting, which would be in March.

"You know you don't need my approval, right?" I asked. Even Kurt's approval was only a technicality. Woe betide any bishop who told the Relief Society president she couldn't do a meeting on the theme she had selected. She had been given the right to revelation for her specific needs when Kurt put his hands on her head and set her apart. Women don't have official authority in the Mormon church, but any man who ignores the real power of women in the church is an idiot. Kurt is not an idiot.

"I wasn't looking for approval. Just your opinion," said Cheri. "And maybe any advice you have to offer."

"Well, what do you want to do?"

"I'd like the topic to be about domestic

violence," she said quietly.

Ah. Now I understood her concern. That was a difficult topic, not the usual Relief Society meeting about Easter crafts or filling your lantern with the light of service. "It might be wise to wait until the Carrie Helm case has been resolved," I said.

"Yes," said Cheri. "It might be wiser. But then people would be less interested. We would get fewer women coming out, and the very people we are trying to protect might not hear the message."

Also a good point. "How can I help?" I asked. Cheri and I were not of one mind about many things, but I was impressed with her foresight here. Not to mention her courage.

"I'd like you to come speak, if you would."

"Me? I don't know anything about domestic violence."

"Well, that's what everyone is going to say, isn't it? I was hoping you could do some research and talk about some of the warning signs to look for when dating, or early on in marriage. I was going to talk about what to do if you're sure you are being abused. Hotline numbers to call, people to confide in, the steps to take to protect yourself, and how to make the final moves."

She was doing the heavy lifting. I could

do a little bit. "All right," I said.

"You'll do it?" she asked.

"I said I would."

She let out a long breath of relief. Had she been afraid I would say no?

"The women listen to you, you know."

"Because I'm the bishop's wife," I said.

"And because you don't speak often, and when you do, it is with carefully chosen words, meant to move people to action," said Cheri.

I was surprised into silence. "Thank you," I said at last.

"Do you think we need to bring up *Twilight*?" asked Cheri. "Meyer is a Mormon and so many people talk about that book in terms of abusive boyfriends."

"I think we can safely leave vampires out of this," I said. "Let's talk about real-life abuse cases. There are too many of those for us to ignore."

"There is one other thing," said Cheri. "I'd like to float it past you before I make a commitment."

"What's that?"

"I'd like to have one of our speakers be a woman from one of the shelters in the area. For victims of domestic violence. And I'd like her to come with a list of possible volunteer opportunities that we would sign people up for."

"I think that's a wonderful idea," I said.

"I worry it will make some women uncomfortable. Or afraid that it will bring abuse into their own lives."

I snorted, not delicately. Abuse wasn't catching like some kind of disease, no matter what our cultural tendencies to avoid the very mention of it might indicate.

"But I also feel strongly that we need to do real work, and see both the reality of sin and the redemption of it."

I wouldn't have put it that way, but I agreed wholeheartedly. "You are going to do great things, Cheri," I said.

"And if your husband asks you about it?"

Kurt was unlikely to, since he knew me too well to misunderstand what I would think of this. "I will tell him to get behind it," I said. "And get the men behind it as much as they can. Maybe you can have a flyer sent around to help men understand what warning signs are, as well?"

"Hmm," said Cheri. "I'll think about it."

There was a long pause. I was trying to think of something to say about her daughter's wedding that wouldn't be taken the wrong way.

"I also wonder if we should have a ward fast and prayer to help bring Carrie Helm back home to her daughter," Cheri said.

I held in a groan. Fasting and prayer were not the solution to a problem like this. God might intervene in extraordinary cases, but most of the time He expected us to fix things here on Earth ourselves. The scripture says, "Men should be anxiously engaged in a good cause, and do many things of their own free will." Which meant that if Carrie Helm chose to leave her daughter, we couldn't pray her back. God wouldn't help take away the free will of any of His children.

"And of course, to help Jared repent," Cheri was saying.

Repenting of domestic violence might be possible, but I didn't want to count on it. And I wasn't convinced yet that Jared either was ready to confess to such a sin or wanted to change that part of himself. It sounded to me like he still thought he had been right in every one of his actions toward Carrie.

"Well, thanks for your call, Cheri. I'll talk to Kurt about both ideas," I said.

I waited until that night to talk to Kurt. He got to hear my full opinion, and finally held up his hands and asked if he could go to bed already.

I let him, but I went downstairs and finished my thoughts on the computer, and emailed them for him to read the next day.

I was still thinking about Carrie Helm, free will, and patterns of abuse when Anna Torstensen called the next morning.

"Anna, I should have called you earlier this week. What can I do for you?" I asked, because her voice sounded thready and broke even when she said her name.

"It's Tobias," she said. "They've decided it's time for hospice care. The doctor has recommended a nurse to come in full time until — until —" She couldn't get the rest of it out.

Was it that far along already? It had been less than two weeks since I saw her last. "I'm so sorry," I said. I had said the same thing so many times before. It always felt inadequate, but we were supposed to mourn with people who mourned, weren't we?

"I don't know how I can get through this," said Anna. "I've lived all these years with him, loving him more and more. That's what you're supposed to do, isn't it? When you're married, you fall more in love. And then suddenly it's like my legs have been cut out from underneath me. I don't know how to stand on my own." The words sluiced out of her, tumbling over each other, almost incomprehensible.

"You're a strong woman. You're going to manage this. It will be terrible, but there will be a time in the future when you will be happy again, I promise it," I said. I wasn't sure I sounded convincing. I felt her pain so clearly. Had I become too involved in this?

Anna hiccoughed over a sob. "I'd rather die in his place than watch him go through this. Why can't I trade him? Why can't I go first?"

"I don't know," I said, though she was quite a bit younger than Tobias. And then I said, "I'm sorry," again.

There was a long pause. I could hear her weeping, then taking a breath and holding it, as if she were trying to get control of herself. And then she would fall apart again. I waited.

"They said I should call and make sure that you and the bishop knew. To make arrangements for the —"

"Funeral," I filled in softly. "I'll tell the Relief Society to prepare to do a luncheon. And I'll tell Kurt. I'm sure he'll want to come see you later tonight, if he can. And Tobias, too, of course." There is no such thing as last rites in the Mormon religion. There are rituals that are necessary to get into the highest level of heaven, of course,

137

but the more important changes are always in the heart.

"Will you come with him?" asked Anna. "Tonight?"

A part of me wanted to say no. Kurt could go and not fall apart. I couldn't. But instead I said, "Of course, if you want me to."

"I need to talk to a woman," said Anna. "Does that make any sense? Or maybe it's just you. I don't know."

I should have been honored that she wanted to connect with me. "I'll be there. And any time you need to talk to me, you call. Not just in the next week or so, but afterward, too. It doesn't have to be for any particular reason. You can call me if you want someone to go shopping with you. Or just sit with you and listen to music. It can be a lonely thing, grief."

"Thank you," said Anna. "I'll expect you tonight. Tobias might be asleep, but I'll wake him when you come."

"There's no need —" I started to say, but Anna had already hung up.

I called Kurt and told him about the hospice and about the promise to see Anna tonight. He sounded very cool about it, not emotional at all. When I asked why, he said, "Death is a natural part of life. We'll all go through it, and Tobias has had time to accept it. Besides, death doesn't mean the end of things. It just means a change from one side of the veil to the other."

"Easier to say than to believe," I said.

"But I do believe it. And so do you," said Kurt. "You believe your parents are waiting for you, behind the veil. And our baby daughter."

Some days I believed that more than others. I wasn't sure today was one of the better days. "I hate change," I said grumpily. I didn't talk about our daughter, not even with Kurt. Not casually like this.

"Yes, I've noticed that," said Kurt.

When Samuel came home, I found out that he had decided to join the new Gay-Straight Alliance at his school. It wasn't a popular thing in the Mormon world, coming out in defense of homosexuals, but there was a lot less talk about how evil it was, and even the apostles had begun to admit there was likely a genetic component that was not a lifestyle choice.

"You are so wonderful, Samuel. I want you to know how proud I am of you for standing up for people who are being hurt, ignored, and told they aren't worth being defended," I said, kissing him on the forehead.

He shrugged and moved away uncomfortably. "It's not that wonderful, you know."

"Of course it is. You just don't see how unusual you are."

I made a quick dinner, and after Kurt had finished some phone calls to the stake, he and I dressed in warm coats and walked over to the Torstensens. It was the only kind of "date" we had anymore, walking together arm in arm as he went to visits.

Anna opened the door. She was wearing far too much makeup, but even that couldn't disguise her red eyes or the puffiness around her cheeks.

"Thank you so much for coming," she said to Kurt.

"No trouble at all. Of course we want to be here for you. How is Tobias doing?" he asked.

She shook her head. "He's not always coherent, but he is upset about something. He keeps talking about a secret, but he won't tell me anything about it. He says that he'll only talk to you, Bishop Wallheim."

"Well, then, perhaps I should go see him privately and you and Linda can talk."

Anna nodded and watched Kurt go up the stairs. Her hands were tight little rocks.

We stood in the front room, with a view of the kitchen. "Have you eaten anything today?" I asked her.

"What? Oh. I think so."

"What did you have for dinner?"

She waved a hand. "I had some toast. I don't remember when. I'm not really hungry."

She needed to eat. She needed her strength. "Do you have some eggs? I could cook you up a couple. How do you like them?" I led her into the kitchen, which was very different from the Helms' kitchen, and from my own. It was smaller, but the wood of the cabinets was thick and the finish was buttery. Everything inside the kitchen looked sturdy and old, and there were very few of the everyday appliances that people seemed to use now. Anna sat at the small kitchen table, but she continued to protest. "I don't think I could eat anything now. It would just come back up. I haven't felt this nervous since the day I first met Tobias."

I rummaged around to find a pan in the cupboards and then eggs in the refrigerator and bread in the breadbox. There was butter covered on a ceramic plate, which was something else younger cooks didn't often do.

After a moment's pause, Anna said, "It was so long ago, when we met, but I remember it so clearly. I was sure he would never look at me again, that I'd have those few moments with him and then he'd be gone. I had one chance to say the perfect sentence, to make him pay attention. I could barely speak, I was so worried."

"What did you say, in the end?" I asked, curious about Anna and Tobias's courtship despite myself. Young couples were always talking about how they met, their first dates, their weddings, but the older we got, the less it felt like the people we had been at that age were the same ones we were now, after all the becoming that came with life. It was like thinking back to a book you read in high school, and then reading it again, only to realize it said things you had never understood, and that it didn't say any of the things you thought it had.

"I told him he had the prettiest ears I'd ever seen," said Anna, blushing even now.

"And that did it?" I asked, smiling.

"He said after we were married that he didn't remember what I said at all. He only remembered the way I looked at him."

"And his ears," I said, working from the table to the stove.

She let out a little laugh. "Yeah."

I finished making the eggs and put them on a plate. Anna sat down and started to pick at them.

"Is there anything I could do to help you?" I asked.

"I'm fine," she said automatically.

"No, think about it. People always say they're fine and they're not. You're obviously not fine, Anna. I could do laundry if you want. Or come in and help you clean. You want to spend what time you have left with Tobias, not doing meaningless chores around the house."

"I'm very particular about the laundry," said Anna. "I haven't let Tobias do it for years. I think it would only make me worry more about it if you did it."

"All right then. What about something outside? What about the chores that Tobias does — did — normally?"

"Oh!" Her eyes widened. "Well, the shed is a disaster. Tobias tried to keep up with his garden work through the fall, but I'm afraid he did a haphazard job when it came to organization. I could use some help there."

"Great!" I said. "That's exactly the kind of thing I'm happy to help with."

"But it's so cold," she said. "You might as well wait till spring."

"I've got a coat on. I'll go out right now and see what needs to be done. Then I can look at my schedule this week and see what

143

time I have." Of course there wasn't any reason the shed needed to be taken care of right now. It was the woman who disliked even the thought of the disorganized shed I was concerned about. If I could decrease her stress even the tiniest bit by helping with the shed, I'd have accomplished something.

I cleaned up in the kitchen, then trooped outside to the shed. Like the kitchen it was ancient; it wasn't the prefabricated kind that was delivered and set up on concrete blocks. This was made of aluminum and had been set up by Tobias, back in the day. The door was difficult to open, and when I stepped inside, I could see why. The floor was littered with tools and other equipment. I bent down and began to pick up flowerpots and half-empty bags of fertilizer. I stacked together things I thought should be thrown away, including several tools that looked rusted and ruined after sitting too long without being cleaned. It was a shame.

For a moment, I stood, arms wrapped around my coat-clad shoulders, and thought of the shed as Tobias himself, a man who had not even shared his life story with his wife of thirty years. How many things had he left inside himself to canker, because he thought he would get to them later? How many inner wounds were still oozing blood and pus? Was he ashamed of the truth of who he was? Did he close the door on his own past secrets to keep them hidden from other people? And what would happen when God opened the door at his death?

I swallowed what felt like a large piece of ice.

What did my own shed look like? I suppose we are all like Tobias, putting off things that we should take care of but which we are too tired or too ashamed to deal with. And someday, the end will come for all of us, and other people will root around in our things, finding out what we wish no one would ever know. It made me want to go home and clean my house, and then the garage.

But what was lurking inside of my heart? You hope that people remember the best parts of you at the end, and forgive the smaller darknesses. You hope, but how can you ever be sure?

Once the shed floor was clear, I nodded to myself with pride. I'd done something right here, at least. I checked my watch and realized I'd been out here for over an hour. Was Kurt still talking to Tobias? There was more to be done in the shed, and I thought of mentioning the ruined tools to Anna, then immediately decided against it. She didn't need more to do. I made a note on my shopping list to just buy new tools for her. I could bring them back with me after the funeral.

With that thought in mind, I looked through the cabinets, trying to make a list of other items I should buy to make spring cleanup in the yard easier. Fertilizers, of course, and fresh soil. Tobias had his own mulch pile that he turned periodically. I was probably not going to be able to do that well enough to make the mulch useful, so Anna would have to make do with a commercial product. The last cabinet I opened had some fabric in it. I assumed at first it was Tobias's work clothes, but when I pulled them out, I realized it was a dress. A knee-length pink floral dress that was dirty and so old the seams were coming apart.

I had no idea why it was out in the shed or what Anna would make of it, but I thought to return it to her, if only to solve a mystery for her. No doubt she'd been looking for it for years, and had given up ever finding it again.

I closed the door to the shed behind me, then went back inside. Kurt was with Anna in the front room, and he quirked an eyebrow at the pink dress I had brought in.

"He has lucid moments, and that's a good

thing. He told me how much he loves you and his boys. He asked if they would be here. I told him we would all do our best to make that happen," said Kurt to Anna.

"I've already called them. They're going to try to make it in time to see him, but they both have work projects they have to finish first," said Anna.

Work projects took precedence over their father's dying? It made me wonder about their relationship with Anna and their father.

But Kurt nodded. "Good. Then you're doing the things that need to be done. I know this is hard, but it will help to focus on what you can do, not what you can't. All right?" He patted her on the shoulder.

I had had to get used to Kurt touching other women. It still felt a little strange. I wondered sometimes if it would ever feel normal.

I offered the dress to Anna. "I found this out in the shed. I thought I would bring it in, just in case it disappeared a long time ago and you never knew where it went."

But she shook her head. "That's not mine. You found it in the shed?"

I unfolded it and shook it out. "Maybe it's something Tobias found discarded some-where and forgot about?" I said.

Anna touched it again. "That style is so

old. And the pattern. I wonder if it belonged to Tobias's first wife."

"Oh," I said, and wished that I hadn't brought the dress out. Clearly, Tobias had kept it in the shed after all those years because it reminded him of his first wife. He didn't want Anna to know about his souvenir, and now I had shown it to her.

"I suppose that's sweet of him, to keep it after all this time. Why he kept a dress, I don't know, but —" She shrugged.

"Shall I put it back in the shed?" I asked.

"I can't see what use that would be. You can just throw it in the garbage, I think. Tobias won't be needing it anymore to remind him of her. He'll be seeing her soon himself." She said it without wincing, but I couldn't help but think it must hurt her, on top of everything else she had to deal with, to realize that her husband had been so in love with his dead wife that during their whole marriage he had kept this secret token of his first love.

"I'll take care of it," I promised.

Kurt and I went home, and I put the pink dress in our garage. It was as I was folding it again that I realized there was a brown stain on the neckline. I stared at it and told myself that it was probably the reason that the first wife hadn't worn it anymore. But why had Tobias kept a ruined dress? And what was the stain?

It looked like blood, I suppose, but there could be a lot of reasons she might get blood on the back of a dress. I turned out of the garage with a shudder, wondering what was wrong with me, that I became suspicious of every neighbor in the ward. I saw blood everywhere, it seemed, and thought of all men as potential murderers. Was the problem me or was it them?

CHAPTER 10

The police served a warrant on the Helms' home Friday morning, after Kurt had gone to work. I got a panicked call from Jared and rushed over. There were a dozen policemen in uniforms already moving through the house. Jared was in the kitchen, holding Kelly in his arms. He was weeping again, and she looked like a scared rabbit.

"You can both come to our house. There's no reason you have to be here while the police search," I said. I looked around and found a plainclothes policeman who looked like he might be in charge. "Can he leave? Does he have to watch this?"

"As long as we know where he is, in case there are questions," was the answer.

I wondered if he meant in case they found evidence enough to arrest Jared on the spot.

"You take her," said Jared, standing up and pushing Kelly toward me. "I'll stay here."

I hesitated. "Are you sure?"

"I need to be here," he said. "This is our home. I'll stay here to watch over it. But Kelly shouldn't have to worry. Take good care of her?"

I nodded. "Of course I will. We'll have fun together, right, Kelly?"

She nodded at me, then tucked her head into my pant leg.

I took her hand and it felt so good, that tiny, warm bit of flesh and fingers, that I thought there was something wrong with me. How could I feel so right with this other girl who wasn't my daughter? But somehow I felt like she belonged with me, like she was my second chance.

As we walked back across and up the street, I noticed more than one curious neighbor poking a head out, taking in the police vehicles in the Helms' driveway and along the sidewalk. I felt a pang for Jared Helm. No matter what he had done, he was still a scared young man trying to do what was right for his daughter.

When I turned back at the front door of my own house, I could see several white-gloved policemen in the Helms' garage lifting the trunk of the family car.

Kelly caught a glimpse of this, too. "What are they doing? Are they going to take our

151

car away?" she asked.

"No," I assured her. "They're just looking for your mother."

"Why are they looking for her there?" said Kelly.

"They don't know where else to look for her," I said.

"But she's not there," said Kelly insistently. "She's gone away."

"Yes, sweetheart. But she didn't say goodbye to anyone, so they're worried about her. They want to talk to her and make sure she's all right."

"She said goodbye to me," said Kelly.

My heart nearly stopped at that. I pushed the door open and pulled Kelly inside. "Come on inside to the kitchen," I said. What did Kelly know about all of this? No one had ever thought to ask her this particular question before, it seemed. Or Kelly hadn't felt comfortable enough to answer.

"Why don't you tell me about your mommy?" I said, trying to move to the larger questions cautiously.

"Mommy used to make brownies with me when she was feeling sad," said Kelly.

"Oh? What else did she do when she was sad?" I asked. I set her on the bar to watch me.

Then I got out all the ingredients to make

brownies, hoping it would make Kelly feel more comfortable, and possibly jostle loose some memories. I felt like I was no better than the policemen who were even now poking into her underwear drawer, and her mother's, as well. Prying out secrets from a child — how low did that make me? But I wanted to know the truth.

"She loved me," said Kelly.

"Of course she did." I hugged the little girl hard and set the butter I'd softened in the microwave in front of her, along with the sugar and cocoa, and asked her to stir it. I figured I would have a mess to clean up afterward, but Kelly had been trained well. She dug in with the wooden spoon and stood on the chair I pulled up for her, using the full weight of her body to cream the ingredients.

"Mommy likes chocolate best. It makes her feel happy again. And she likes the kissing movies."

I smiled at that. "What kissing movies are her favorites?"

"The one with the movie star and the man who lives in the blue door. The one with the floppy hair," said Kelly.

"Notting Hill?" I asked. It was also one of my favorites. "What else? You said she said goodbye to you before she left?" I was tread-

ing on dangerous ground here. I casually cracked eggs into the brownie batter, but felt as if my own house was as fragile as the eggshells. What if Jared realized what Kelly might say and came rushing over to take her back with him?

"She came into my bedroom and kissed me goodnight. She said to be a good girl for Daddy," said Kelly.

But that could mean anything. "Well, I'm sure you are a good girl," I said, hoping for more.

Kelly looked down at the brownie batter. "Can I have a taste? Mommy always lets me have a taste," she said.

"With the eggs in it? That's not safe," I said. "Raw eggs can have bad bacteria in them."

"Is that what made Mommy go away? The bad bacteria? Because she ate brownies before they were cooked?" said Kelly, looking up at me, her messy, curly hair now also dusted in flour and cocoa.

"No, I don't think so," I assured her.

"I'm not going to run away like Mommy. Daddy says I have to promise not to run away."

"Your daddy is right about that, Kelly. You shouldn't run away. Did you see your mom packing anything before she left? Are you sure she ran away?"

"Daddy said she ran away," said Kelly. "But I only saw when she got out of the car."

"She got out of the car?" I echoed.

"Daddy thought I was asleep. He told me to go back to sleep in the car, but when it stopped, I woked up," said Kelly.

"And what happened then?" I said, stirring the brownie batter far past what it needed. This was not what Jared Helm had told me and Kurt that morning weeks ago, but I couldn't react angrily. I didn't want to lose the sense of ease that Kelly felt in this familiar rhythm.

"Mommy got out of the car. I heard her thump on the ground."

I went cold at the childish description. "Then what?" I asked.

"Then Daddy said goodbye to her, too, and he got back in the car," she said simply.

I felt terrible pumping information from a five-year-old child, especially this very vulnerable one. If the police had done it, someone would have cried foul. But I wasn't hurting her, was I? And I needed to know what she had heard exactly. "Where were you? Do you remember anything about the place where she got out of the car?"

"It was dark," said Kelly helpfully. "And cold."

"But were there any lights outside?"

"I don't think so," said Kelly.

"And your mother didn't kiss you good-bye in the car?" I asked.

Kelly shook her head. "I was trying to be asleep. Daddy said to sleep."

"Did you hear her say anything to your dad?"

"She was mad at him. She didn't talk to him when she was mad."

Yes, that would be a useful survival strategy for a woman who had been abused by her husband.

Or maybe Carrie didn't say anything to Kelly because she couldn't. I wondered if Carrie Helm had been alive during this car ride Jared hadn't mentioned to the police.

Clearly, Kelly wouldn't know, so the questioning was over.

I stopped stirring the brownie batter and reached for a teaspoon. I offered it to Kelly, feeling like the witch in Hansel and Gretel, luring children in with a treat that wasn't good for them. "Kelly, are you ever afraid of your daddy?" I asked quietly.

"He shouts sometimes," Kelly said, looking down at her hands. "Then I run and hide in my room. I don't like it when he

156

gets mad at me."

Too vague, too vague. If this were a detective novel, I'd be the prosecutor asking leading questions. Of a child. "But does he ever hurt you?"

"Once he spanked my hand," said Kelly. "Because I almost touched the stove with it and he said it would have gotten burnt."

"And what about your mom? Did you ever see him hurt her?"

Kelly stared up at me. "He took her pills once," she said. "And put them down the toilet. She hit him, and then he held her hands. Then she cried. But Mommy told me never to tell anyone. She said she was sorry and he was sorry. She said she was wrong and not to hit."

Pills? Birth control or her depression medication? It didn't matter. I had to go back to the question of whether or not Carrie had been alive in that car ride. "Did you see your mom in the car? Or after she was dropped off? Did you see her waving at you?"

"It was dark," said Kelly again. "I couldn't see her."

"And there were no lights? Why do you think she wanted to go to a place where there were no lights?"

"I don't know," said Kelly. "Sometimes

Mommy said she needed to rest her eyes and her head and she would go into her room and close the door and turn out the lights. She told me to be very quiet then."

Did I really think I could get all the information I needed out of a five-year-old girl in an hour? I should leave the detective work to the real detectives. Still, I was itching to go through the house, to see how Carrie had left it. Jared would have moved things by now, maybe enough things that I would never be able to piece the full story together. And the police were going through it right now. But there might be things neither he nor they understood the meaning of.

We poured the brownies into a greased pan and put them in the oven. Then I showed Kelly into the front room, and she looked through my children's books with a cry of delight. "This is Mommy's book," she said. "She used to read this to me every day." It was *Harry the Dirty Dog.* "I wish she didn't take it with her."

"She took this book with her when she left?" It seemed an odd thing for her to take, considering she had taken nothing else.

"I asked Daddy to read it the next day, after she was gone. Daddy said she took it with her. He said she didn't want me to

158

have it anymore."

I patted her head, doing my best to suppress my fury at Jared Helm, then gently settled her into my lap and read her the book. She fell asleep in my arms. While her breath softened to a steady, slow pace, my mind was spinning wildly. I didn't know if anything Kelly had told me would be useful, but the car ride seemed important, especially since Jared had so carefully concealed that information even from me and Kurt, who he must consider to be mostly on his side.

I hoped my worst fears — that Carrie's presence in the car had been as a corpse — were wrong. I tried to think of more innocent explanations of Jared's behavior. If he had dropped Carrie off somewhere, then he had been complicit in her escape, not surprised by it as he had pretended to be. But why would he drop her off somewhere completely dark, with no wallet or keys? The missing children's picture book might mean nothing at all, but it was interesting at least. If Carrie had taken it, why that one thing? And if she hadn't, why had Jared taken away a book that reminded his daughter of her mother? Was it pure pettiness?

My arms ached, then went numb, and still I sat there on the couch in the front room, the warm weight of Kelly in my arms. It had been a long time since Samuel was this age. My own daughter had never been this age. Maybe she never would be, even in the afterlife in the celestial kingdom that I hoped for. She might belong to another family entirely. Or she might be taken from me, if I had been the ultimate cause of her death. How could Kurt be so sure about seeing her again when we had never seen her really to begin with?

The doorbell rang, and I started. Kelly rubbed at her eyes and her face had a little red mark on it where she had collapsed over her arm.

I shifted her to the side onto the couch and got up to find Jared Helm at the door.

"They're finished," he said. "She can come home now."

I didn't ask him anything, but I walked back over to the Helms' house with Kelly and Jared. The last police car was still waiting. Jared had a form to sign, a document stating that nothing had been taken from the house except certain items on a list he had to check off.

Then the police car drove away, and Jared lifted Kelly into his arms. He stepped inside the house reluctantly.

"I could come in and help you clean up, if

160

you'd like," I offered. What was I doing? Going into a house alone with a man who might have killed his wife to try to find evidence against him? But I had been drawn into this and I was going to use all the skills I had to resolve it.

"No, thank you," he said. "I need some time to myself. Just me and Kelly."

I tensed. I had to go in there. The police were looking for signs of Carrie's death, but I wanted more information about everything leading up to her disappearance. I wanted to know who she had been, since I hadn't found it out while she was here.

I took a breath to steady myself. Unfortunately, this wasn't the moment. I needed to let Jared trust me.

But I wasn't giving up.

"Of course," I said, and let the door close.

The police made no official report of what they had — or had not — found in the Helm house. Saturday evening, they released a statement saying that Jared was not a suspect in his wife's disappearance, but that he was a "person of interest." Which meant the news vans were still camped outside his house, causing Jared and Kelly to live a strange life inside their bubble of home.

On Sunday, they stayed home from church again, and Kurt made sure to contact the Elders Quorum Presidency to ask that they visit Jared, and the Primary Presidency to do the same with Kelly. Kurt got the Young Women to offer to babysit Kelly if Jared wanted to attend the ward temple night this week, or if he needed to leave for a police interview or to go shopping.

Instead of having strange babysitters in his home, Jared made a list of things he needed from the store, and Cheri Tate went out shopping for him. Every purchase she made, it seemed, was then listed on the news that Sunday night.

Kurt shook his head over that. "It shouldn't happen like that. Did she talk to the reporters? I thought I made it clear she wasn't to do that."

"About what she bought at the grocery store? Don't give her a hard time about that, Kurt. She's doing her best in a difficult situation." I imagined the reporters following her through the store, asking clerks what she'd bought, or chasing down mislaid receipts.

There was only so much you could expect anyone to do to preserve another person's privacy. But I wondered if perhaps Cheri Tate had begun to suspect Jared Helm of criminal behavior toward his wife. A part of me liked that idea very much.

CHAPTER 11

Sunday evening, we had our monthly family dinner, and I tried to be happy with all the boys around, and the two daughters-in-law. After so many years of me alone in a household of men, it was wonderful to have other women around, even if sometimes I felt as if I had learned so well to relate to men that I didn't readily understand women. I admired my daughters-in-law so much.

Marie is studying nursing and is going to be a power to reckon with. And Joseph's wife, Willow, teaches ballet in Bountiful, after two years in New York as a professional. She hopes to open her own studio someday, and when she does, her students are going to be very lucky.

I watched them carefully, thinking about Carrie Helm. Suddenly, I found myself asking terrible questions about abuse. I knew I was being alarmist, seeing the worst everywhere I looked. Yet I wondered if it was possible my daughters-in-law were being abused by my own sons? Boys I had raised? Was I missing the clues I should have seen? If I had missed them with Carrie Helm, why not with other women? Kurt had thought so well of Jared Helm until recently, and even now he was torn between his priesthood connection to Jared and the darkness that was beginning to rise around him.

Marie seemed so strong and gave her opinion so openly. She had always impressed me as someone who would change the world because she wasn't afraid of anything. But could it be a mask she was putting on? Carrie Helm had seemed strong and articulate, as well, except when Jared squelched her opinion.

And Willow was so beautiful and looked so fragile in some ways. She laughed easily and often, sometimes at things I didn't think were funny at all. Was she pretending to be happier than she was, as Carrie surely must have done?

It was hard for me to imagine my daughter as a full-grown woman, since I had never seen her that way. I had only seen the still, smudged grey skin of her imperfect infant body. There were photographs somewhere. A woman from Share, a charity founded to help parents who lost pregnancies and infants, had come in to help us and she had insisted that we would want photographs someday, to remember our daughter. But I had never looked at the photographs after they had come in. They had seemed so terrible to me, a picture of death, of nothing good. Who keeps photographs of a body in a coffin? That's what my daughter was by the time I saw her.

I would have been a useless mother to a girl who wanted to be a dancer. I was all left feet and had lousy rhythm sense. I could play the piano, but rhythm had always been my bugaboo. Would I have helped her do her hair? Choose dresses? I felt so inadequate helping in girlish things, but was that habit or some inborn trait? I didn't know the difference anymore.

I went and played the piano when everyone was gone, head down, thoughts draining away.

Samuel sat on the couch in the front room and listened until I was finished.

"I like it when they are here," he said. "But I like when they're gone, too. I like the quiet."

"I like the quiet, too," I said.

Later that night, when we were settling into bed I asked Kurt what to do about the

166

information I'd learned from Kelly Helm. It was the first time we'd had a chance to talk since Friday. Kurt had had to go back to the church after dinner, but it was "Family Sabbath," which meant he had canceled most of his meetings and other obligations. He was all mine for now.

"She's five years old. Are you really sure she remembers what happened that night? She could have it confused with another night. It could be a dream she had." Kurt turned down the covers.

I stiffened at this. "She seems pretty clear to me."

"But you're not her mother," said Kurt. That stung, and he must have seen it on my face because he added, "I mean, you don't know her that well. I would think that Jared would be a better judge of whether Kelly knows anything here."

"Jared is the last person anyone can rely on to interpret Kelly's words. He might have every reason to distort her meaning." I sat in the bed, my arms crossed.

"I think that you're too involved in this," said Kurt, getting into the bed beside me. "This is a police investigation. It's not something for you to poke around in."

"That's ironic," I said, turning out the light.

"What's that supposed to mean?" asked Kurt.

"It means that you're the one who is always asking me to poke my nose into other people's business. Putting names on the refrigerator. And now you tell me I'm stepping outside of my role."

"When you start investigating a murder, I think that's a little different than helping out people in our ward," said Kurt.

The emotional temperature in the room was somewhere near absolute zero at this point.

"Maybe it isn't that different," I said. And maybe Kurt just didn't like the idea that I wasn't going to let him be in charge of the information I'd found out, nor tell me what my next step should be.

"Linda, you're the one who said he was dangerous to begin with. I'm just paying attention to you. Why would you get mad at me about that?" he asked.

"Because you're telling me what to do."

"God," Kurt muttered under his breath. He very rarely swore, and it made me flinch. "You always were the most stubborn woman I ever met."

"Hey!" I said, wounded. "The most stubborn person, man or woman, you mean."

There was a long silence between us. I

took a deep breath and tried to let go of the hurt. I knew Kurt loved me. I knew he trusted me. I had always depended on that trust. What was bothering me didn't really have to do with him, if I could only admit it to both of us.

"I need to find out what happened to Carrie Helm," I said, finally. "She is just the age —"

He let out a sigh. "I know," he said. "You throw yourself into things. It's one of the things I love about you. You don't think twice. You commit yourself and that's it. But in this case —"

"In this case, it really matters."

"Because you're still trying to make up for all the mistakes you think you made with our daughter?" asked Kurt. He had moved closer to me on the bed and his hand was searching for mine in the dark. I let him find it.

I couldn't remember the last time that he had mentioned her. "I want to do the right thing. I want to make sure I have no regrets." I felt tears prick at my eyes.

As soon as I woke up Monday morning, I started thinking about Tobias Torstensen and his first wife. It was early enough that Samuel wasn't up for school yet, and Kurt

169

was still asleep. I put on a robe against the cold, then I went out to the garage.

There was the pink dress, just where I'd left it on the wooden utility table where Kurt sanded and painted things, sometimes cut them with an electric saw blade. The table was dusty and spattered with colors. I picked up the dress and played with it, feeling the worn cotton against my hands, and the crusted, dried blood that interrupted the softness. It was fragile material. I shouldn't touch it too much.

The blood could mean nothing at all. Tobias might have bled on it by accident, felt bad about it and hidden it away and when his first wife died, he didn't know what to do with it, so he left it where it was. But for some reason, my mind had latched on to the proposition that Tobias, like Jared Helm, had killed his wife and disappeared her body. That would explain why there were competing stories about her death by car accident, heart attack, and cancer. Tobias had told different stories at different times and couldn't keep them straight.

Had he killed her because they fought? Because she threatened to take his sons away from him? It was hard to imagine Tobias Torstensen, such a gentle and intelligent man, hurting anyone, let alone his own wife. Much easier for me to believe Jared Helm guilty, since I disagreed with him on so many topics. But if one man could do it and believe he had the right within the Mormon church, could another?

I shook my head. It seemed too much to believe that there were two murders in my tiny little part of Draper, one ancient and one modern, and that I was placed just where I was to find out about both. Unless I believed that God had put me here to do precisely that, because He wanted me to use my insatiable curiosity for some good.

I wished I felt a burning within the bosom, as the scriptures say that we are supposed to get with the Spirit's direction. I just felt — cold.

I stared at the pink dress and then put it down. I told myself that I didn't know if anyone had been murdered in our ward or not, either Carrie Helm or Tobias's first wife. And it seemed rather ridiculously arrogant to think that I should have some special place in finding out the horrible truth about others.

I was a fifty-four-year-old woman, a stay-at-home mother of five boys, and a bishop's wife. I was not a detective. I was not a prophet. I didn't know what I was doing here. And it was time for me to give up the

171

idea that I had some special connection to Carrie Helm, or to any other woman in the ward. This had nothing to do with my daughter. This wasn't something God had called me to do. There wasn't even a connection here between these two women, except the connection I was imagining in my own mind.

I put the pink dress into a plastic garbage bag and tossed it into our big green garbage can. It fell short, landing on the garage floor, but I was suddenly too tired to go pick it up. I'd find it before I put the can out to be picked up on Friday.

And then I went back inside, feeling quite a bit smaller than when I had gone out.

Kurt was in the kitchen, drinking the last of the milk straight from the jug. He looked at me sheepishly. "It was almost gone anyway," he said.

"And what if Samuel had seen you?" I asked him, smiling faintly.

"Oh, I made sure he wasn't around," said Kurt. "I wouldn't want him to learn all my bad habits." He looked at me as if he was waiting to see if I was still angry about last night.

I sighed. "I won't poke in this anymore. I'll let the police do their job, and I will stick with doing mine. Making bread, going on visits with the bishop, and changing minds slowly." As I said the words, I felt keenly how small of a job it was.

"I'm not saying you shouldn't act if you're inspired to act," said Kurt.

"But you want me to wait for clear revelation?" I asked. As if revelation was ever clear.

"I want you to stop feeling guilty for things that aren't your fault. I want you to stop making up for things that are for God to reconcile," said Kurt.

"I'll try," I said.

"I guess that's as much as I can ask for," said Kurt, and he held me tight, his lips pressed to my forehead, until Samuel came in and left again with a disgusted sound.

CHAPTER 12

I went shopping that afternoon for tools to replace the ones that had rusted in Tobias Torstensen's shed. It was unlikely he would ever use them again, but I made the effort anyway, because it seemed the right thing to do, to leave things as they should be. And also because it was the only thing I could do.

I delivered the tools to Anna and she asked me to put them in the shed for her. I stayed for a few moments, but there was nothing new to see. No spiritual sense goaded me one way or the other. I had been an atheist for several years before Kurt and I married, and this was why. Other Mormons feel a constant sense of direction, even in the minutiae of their lives, but I never had. Often, I struggled to feel any clear spiritual feeling at all. But I came back to Mormonism — and to God — because even if what I felt was very little, it was better to search for more than give up on anything beyond the mundane. At least, it was for me.

Even when my daughter had died and I had been angry at God, I had still wanted Him to exist. Because if He didn't, then none of my pain mattered at all. None of it made any sense. It was just random chance that she had died, just animal reaction that I mourned her loss. I wanted my life — and hers — to mean more than that. I went inside and talked to Anna. She seemed very quiet, and I soon found out why. Tobias Torstensen was not expected to live more than a week, according to the startlingly frank reports by his hospice caregivers.

"I'm so sorry," I said. "How are you holding up?"

Anna bit her lower lip and shook her head. Her eyes were bright with tears, but she didn't let them fall. She was too strong for that. "I'll survive," she said.

"Is there anything I can do for you?" I could see already that the Relief Society had been here. There were several casserole dishes, cleaned and waiting on the kitchen table, with names written on masking tape. I wondered if Anna had eaten all of that food. Probably not. Had she had to figure out a way to store it or had she been sensible enough to simply throw out what she couldn't use?

"I'm fine," said Anna.

"But is there anything that would help you? Anything I could get for you at the store? Maybe a treat you don't usually buy for yourself? A special perfume, lotion, or bath salts that might lift your spirits?" I wanted to do something.

She shook her head. "I'm not really thinking about myself right now. But thank you so much for bringing those tools for Tobias."

"I know they don't matter," I said. He certainly wouldn't be using them.

"Tobias still worries about the garden, even now. I can tell him you bought new tools, and he'll be eased by the thought that everything is properly waiting in the shed for the spring."

"You aren't thinking about trying to keep up his garden work, are you?" I asked.

"I'm trying to concentrate on now," said Anna.

Of course she was. I patted her shoulder. "I wish I could do more," I said. "Call me, will you? Anytime, day or night."

"Thank you for coming," she said.

I went home and tried to do what she had said, focus on now. My now was Samuel going on a big group date on Friday and

Kurt needing me to fix his second-best pair of slacks, which he had split at work the day before. I asked him if we needed to buy a new suit in a new size, and he had given me such a look. He did not like to be reminded that he was losing weight as bishop.

"It's good for me," he said. "They say Americans are all too fat anyway."

"Yes, but you weren't. I'm afraid all you're losing is muscle."

"I'm gaining spiritual muscle," said Kurt.

"Well, that doesn't hold up your pants." I'd bought him several belts over the last year, and he kept tightening them, but the pants didn't hang quite right like that.

"I'm going to gain all that weight back. I'm planning it. The month after I'm released, you and I will eat out every night, and I will always get dessert."

"Unless you get called to be stake president," I said, teasing. It was the fate of many a competent bishop, being given a more difficult job as a reward for the years of service.

He shook his head and looked sternly at me. "Don't you say that. Don't you dare."

Kurt and I went to visit Tobias the next night, and I made Anna some tea and talked to her about a book I had been reading as we sat at the kitchen table, but after a few minutes, it felt like I was talking into a void. "I shouldn't be prattling on," I said.

"Oh, don't say that. I like your enthusiasm. And I'd like to borrow that book sometime. Later."

"Of course. I'll bring it by." Later, I thought.

We sat in silence for a while, listening to the susurrating sounds of Kurt and Tobias upstairs.

"Thank you again for coming," said Anna, when Kurt came out of the bedroom. "You made me forget myself for a little while and I appreciate that enormously."

Wednesday evening after his church meetings, Kurt suggested we go to visit the Torstensens. He had called earlier in the day to ask Anna if we could come by late. Tobias wasn't sleeping well, snatches here and there when the pain medication was working, but when it wasn't, there was nothing that could be done.

After one look at Tobias in his room, I reconsidered my position on euthanasia. He was skin and bones, a scrap of humanity that breathed in and out with great pain. He moaned with every breath, and the sound rattled out of him as if he were already a corpse. I had to bite my lower lip hard to keep myself from weeping aloud. Luckily, I didn't have to stay long with him. Kurt motioned me to take Anna out while he talked to Tobias.

"What can I do for you?" I asked, as we walked back down the stairs.

"We're fine. I'm just — waiting. It's a difficult time," said Anna. Her eyes were bright with tears and her words were a whisper.

I put a hand on her arm. "Please. Tell me something I can do to help." Maybe I needed it more than she did, but I asked anyway.

"Well," said Anna at last. "Tobias keeps talking about his first wife. He wants to see her grave, he says. But I don't know where it is. I could call the boys myself, but I just don't have the energy. Why aren't they here yet? What are they waiting for? He is dying, and he wants his sons here with him to find a little peace. I have the feeling he could talk to them about his first wife when he won't talk to me." She waved a hand impatiently.

I remembered the important "work projects" that both Liam and Tomas claimed they had to finish before they flew to see their father on his deathbed. Anna had told them Tobias was dying almost a week ago.

"I'll call your sons," I said, glad to do

something with my angry energy. I'd either get them out here tomorrow or get information out of them about their mother's grave that would help ease Tobias's mind. "Do you have their phone numbers?" She wrote them out for me on a scrap of paper. "Thank you," she said, and held my hands inside of hers. "You don't know how much this means to me."

"I'll take care of it. You don't need to worry," I said to her.

She nodded, then went to bring Tobias a glass of water. "I forgot this before. He needs to drink. He needs to keep his lips wet," she told me as I followed her back up to his room.

I stood in the doorway and heard only the last bit of conversation between Kurt and Tobias. "But —" Tobias was saying, then he looked up and saw us. He was startled into silence.

Kurt patted Tobias on the shoulder. "Don't worry about it now. You enjoy a bit of time with your wife. I'll come back to see you again tomorrow."

Kurt and I walked outside together.

"He has something weighing on his mind," said Kurt.

"Did he say anything to you about his first wife?"

"Not directly."

"Maybe he was trying not to be a bother," I said and explained to Kurt what Anna had told me about his desire to see his wife's grave. "Do you have any idea where she would be buried?"

Kurt rubbed at his face. "No, I don't. She died long before we were in the ward, and the records just list her death place as Draper, but she's not in the city cemetery."

How strange that the death place wasn't always recorded in Mormon genealogical records, I thought. Shouldn't death be holy? Shouldn't we see it as the moment when the soul is invited back into the presence of God?

"Do you think he is worried about whether he will be with Anna or with the other wife in the afterlife?" I asked. We were getting closer to home and walking more and more slowly.

"Surely God will make the choice, if one has to be made, that will bring the most happiness to all involved." Kurt was staring past me, and I realized he was looking at the temple set on the mountain so recently.

"He seemed upset when we came in. Did he tell you anything?"

Kurt hesitated, then shook his head. "Something about a sin, but he wouldn't

181

say what. And I couldn't tell you about it even if he did."

The temple was supposed to be our most holy place, where no one was allowed to go if they were touched by sin. But of course, that was impossible. The final question of the temple recommend interview — and in some ways, the most difficult — was, "Do you consider yourself worthy in every way to enter the House of the Lord?"

How could anyone be worthy in every way?

But I didn't know if Tobias's sin was big or small. Was he overly worried about a peccadillo, or might I be right about his first wife's death?

Thursday morning, I woke late, after Samuel and Kurt had both already left the house. I got dressed, ate breakfast, and then took a few quiet moments to prepare myself. Then I called the first number on the scrap of paper Anna had given me the night before. The elder son's name was Liam. The younger son was Tomas, without the *h,* some tip of the hat to the Scandinavian heritage, I supposed.

Tomas answered immediately. I explained who I was, and then he told me he had just arrived at the airport in Washington, and would be staying at a nearby Salt Lake City hotel that night rather than bother Anna to try to prepare a room for him. So he would be here soon enough to see Tobias still alive, I hoped. Some of my anger dissipated, but I still wanted to ask about his mother.

I said, "Your father has been asking to see your mother's grave. Anna wanted to know if you could go visit it for him, perhaps take a photo or a video, just to put his mind at rest. I know it seems silly, and you must have plenty to do already, but I thought I would ask, since you are in the area."

"I'm sorry, but I don't know where she is buried," said Tomas. "Dad would never talk about her death or her gravesite."

I said carefully, "So you don't know how she died?"

"He told us she died suddenly of a heart condition, but we never saw her body at a funeral that I recall." Tomas spoke evenly, no hint of fear or nervousness in his voice. "And when I had my own heart trouble, and wanted to see if there was a genetic link, Dad said there weren't any records for her."

"I didn't know you had heart problems. I'm sorry," I said.

"Oh, I've had surgery for it since to correct it. Just a little hole in the heart. But why there were no records of her heart

183

condition, I never knew. It made me wonder if —" He cut himself off.

"If what?" I asked.

"If she hadn't died of a heart condition, after all." His tone was musing, not suspicious.

"You think he lied to you? But why?" I asked. I should have dropped this, but no one could blame me when Tomas Torstensen brought it up himself, could they?

"I don't know. Maybe she had a drunken accident. Something he was embarrassed about," said Tomas. "But to answer your question, I don't know where the grave is. We never visited it as children and as far as I know, Dad never went to visit it on his own, either."

"Then you don't think Liam might know anything more?" I asked.

"No. He and I have talked about it. Numerous times." He sounded annoyed now, and why shouldn't he? I was asking him irrelevant details about the past when his father was dying. Finally, he added, "Liam says he thinks she was cremated. But I don't know where her ashes would be."

Cremation wasn't forbidden by the church, but it seemed — odd. Especially for a young wife. "But then, why would your father be asking to see her grave if she

184

wasn't buried?" I asked. I wasn't just being nosy. Anna had asked me to help her with this so Tobias could die in peace, knowing how his wife's grave would be cared for when he was gone.

"Maybe his mind is going. Maybe he can't remember what he did with her remains," said Tomas. "I can ask him about it when I get there tomorrow afternoon, if you'd like." Now he was ready to go. I had kept him too long.

"I wouldn't want to upset him," I said. But wasn't it Tobias who said he wanted to see his wife's grave? Why was he talking about it now after so many years of staying silent on the subject? It wasn't until after we'd hung up that I thought to tell Tomas about the pink dress I still had in the garage, rescued that morning from the plastic garbage bag and placed neatly folded on a shelf with our garden gloves, which were woefully unused of late.

I tried to call Liam multiple times that day, and only got his answering machine. I left two urgent messages on it for him to return my call, and hoped that he was on an airplane even then. I wished I had thought to ask Tomas about his brother's plans. It sounded as if the two of them

talked to each other a great deal more than
either of them talked to their parents.

CHAPTER 13

Breaking news Friday at noon on KSL was once more about Carrie Helm. A convenience store camera had footage of Jared Helm and Kelly stopping to get gas at 3:00 A.M., just hours before he had come to my house to tell Kurt that Carrie was missing. What was he doing outside at that time with his young daughter in the car? And why had he not told the police or me and Kurt anything about it?

I had told Kurt I wasn't going to involve myself with the Helms anymore. But as soon as the news was over, I turned off the television and began to work on another pan of brownies. Kelly hadn't gotten to eat the ones she had made before.

While I was waiting impatiently for the brownies to cook, Adam called me. "I heard about the new information in that case in your neighborhood," he said. "Is Dad going to have to talk to the news people, too?"

"So far, he hasn't had to," I said.

"He sounds . . . different when I talk to him. I'm worried. Somehow it sounds like he thinks it's all his fault."

Did he? And here Kurt had been telling me to stop thinking that everything was my fault. "We should have seen more," I said simply.

"Mom, you can't do everything, you know. You're trying to make sure Samuel gets through school and you've got other people in the ward to worry about."

"Being busy is never an excuse for not helping," I said. It was an old mantra of mine, whenever the boys complained about a service project while they had homework to do.

"Our grades suffered because of that rule sometimes, you know," said Adam. He was the oldest, and we had made him do countless service projects for the youth organizations, Eagle Scout projects, not to mention the canning, apple picking at the church farm, visiting the nearby retirement home to do sacrament meetings and weekday services, shoveling snow during the winter and weekly church cleanup. He had been a good sport about it. He never complained, just did the work. A good example to the younger boys, for whom he always tried to make it fun.

Adam was the kind of kid you never worried about when he was older, but it had been a wrench when he left home. I'd felt keenly the loss of his help in mobilizing the troops. Even simple things like dinnertime conversation had seemed more chaotic and less kind when he was gone. But of course, he needed to make the leap and start his own family.

Marie was good for him, energetic and intelligent. I didn't know why they hadn't started a family yet. It was likely something they felt pressure about from within the church. They'd been married for four years now, and I knew it was none of my business to ask about grandchildren. But after listening to Gwen Ferris, I wondered if there was more going on than just the two of them trying to finish school before they took on another financial responsibility like kids.

"Well, you still got into BYU," I said, "so I can't say I'm too sorry for you."

"Luckily, BYU cares as much about service to the church as they do about grades," said Adam.

He was being a little disingenuous there. He might not have had straight As, but he had a lot of them, and he had tested superbly well. He could have taken a full-ride scholarship offer to the University of Utah. He'd also been accepted to Stanford, but we couldn't afford it and BYU had always been Kurt's first choice for his sons, so Adam eventually accepted their offer.

"How is Marie?" I asked.

"Fine." The conversation devolved from there into a discussion of classes they were both taking. Adam was hoping to be an engineer, which meant most of his explanations of what he was studying were hard for me to follow. Marie's nursing course kept her studying until the wee hours. Maybe that was the real reason they hadn't had any children yet. No time to make them. But it wasn't my place to say that, either.

Finally, Adam ended the conversation with, "Mom, take care. Of yourself and Dad, all right? Not just Samuel."

"I'll do my best," I promised him, and hung up.

Then I cut up the brownies and wrapped them in plastic to take over to the Helms. I didn't need Kurt's permission. It was just something that needed to be done.

I was self-consciously aware of the fact that the news vans were filming me as I walked up to the door and rang the bell. That meant that not only Kurt but everyone else in the ward might know what I had

190

done by evening. Not that I was trying to hide anything. Or that I really knew that anything I did would end up making any difference at all.

Jared Helm opened the door eventually and hurried me inside. Cameras caught it all on tape, but I was hopeful that I wasn't about to become part of the nightly news segment. There was nothing interesting about a neighbor bringing some brownies over, surely.

"Is there something wrong, Sister Wallheim?" said Jared.

It was a ridiculous question, since there were so many things wrong. "I brought these for Kelly," I said instead. "She said she loves brownies."

"Carrie used to make them with her," Jared said. His face was tense and grey with exhaustion. Before he could call for the little girl, however, she came rushing down the stairs and threw herself at me. I had to take a step backward to keep from falling over.

"Mommy called!" she said. "She said she is bringing me some brownies."

I stared at Jared. "Did Carrie really call?" I asked. Because if she had, surely this was something the police should know about.

Could it be true — was she alive? Or was it just a delusion on Kelly's part? Children sometimes had such vivid imaginary lives. When Zachary was little, he had such difficulty telling the difference between dreams and reality.

"Can I have one? Can I? Can I?" Kelly asked, hopping up and down and looking at my plate of brownies.

"One," said Jared. "I don't want you to spoil your lunch." He took the brownies into the kitchen, where he gave Kelly a plate with one brownie on it. Then he rewrapped the plastic and put the plate on top of the refrigerator.

Kelly ate happily while I changed my focus to Jared. I tried my question again. "When did Carrie call?"

"This morning," said Jared shortly.

"Did you speak to her yourself?" I asked.

Jared nodded. "I wouldn't let Kelly answer the phone in these circumstances."

Of course. He must get a lot of calls from reporters.

"But I thought that her cell phone was still here, at home."

"It is," said Jared.

"Then how did you know it was her?"

"I didn't until I heard her voice," said Jared. "It wasn't a number that I recognized."

I stared at him in astonishment. "And so

you answered it anyway? It could have been a reporter."

"It was out of state," he said with a shrug. "I thought it was worth taking a chance, anyway. And I was right." He nodded to Kelly. "She heard her mother's voice and knows she's all right. That's all that matters to me."

"But — surely the police need to know this," I said. Whatever the phone number was, they could trace it and find Carrie.

Unless — a part of me felt cold and wondered how difficult it would be to convince a five-year-old girl that her mother was on the phone. How many details would someone have to get right? Not many, I thought. Kelly would be primed to want to hear her mother's voice, especially if her father told her who it was.

"I don't think the police would believe me," said Jared flatly. "They've already made up their minds about what happened and any evidence they get all points the same way." He hesitated and then met my eyes. "But if you called them for me, Sister Wallheim —"

Why me? Because I was the bishop's wife and therefore more likely to be believed? Because he didn't think he could carry the lie that far?

"Can I see the number?" I asked. I wanted some proof of my own before I delved into this.

Kelly hopped off her seat, brownie crumbs all over her face, and grabbed the phone. She knew exactly how to get the number to show up on the screen. I didn't recognize the area code, which meant it was probably a mobile number. "Have you tried calling it back?" I asked.

Jared shook his head.

"I'll call it back," said Kelly eagerly. And that is just what she did, before Jared or I had a chance to react and stop her.

Then she handed the phone to me.

I looked at Jared, who didn't seem alarmed. I listened to the sound of ringing in the background. After five rings, someone picked up on the other end. It was not a woman's voice.

"Hello?"

"Hello. My name is Linda Wallheim," I said, using the telephone etiquette my mother had taught me. "I'm calling because a woman called recently from this number and I wanted to talk to her."

"Oh, you mean Carrie."

I felt a jolt of electricity and nearly dropped the phone. My hand was shaking visibly, and I switched the receiver to the

194

other ear, as if keeping the sight of it from Jared made the conversation more private.

"Carrie Helm?" I said. Was this yet another person involved in Jared Helm's conspiracy to cover up his wife's disappearance? That seemed less and less likely.

"Yes, but she's not available right now. Can I have her call you back?"

"If she would, I would appreciate it. Can you ask her to call Linda Wallheim?" I rattled off my own cell phone number. "I desperately need to speak to her."

"I'll tell her."

Now came the difficult part. I didn't want to hang up yet. "Do you mind if I ask who you are and why she called on this phone?"

"She doesn't have her own cell phone, so she borrowed mine," the voice explained, his tone annoyed at the obvious.

"And who are you?" I asked.

He sighed. "My name is Will. I'm a friend of Carrie's."

"A friend of Carrie's? Where did you meet her? She's from Utah, isn't she? Where are you calling from?"

"Las Vegas. Carrie and I met when I was in Utah a few months ago. Why do you ask? Who are you?"

Who was I indeed? "A friend of Carrie's from her ward in Utah."

He hung up immediately.

I tried calling back as Jared asked, "What happened? Did he hang up? Why did he hang up?"

I shook my head and moved away from him so he couldn't take the phone. But Will, if that was really who the man on the other end of the line was, did not answer.

After three tries, I gave up trying to keep the phone from Jared and let him call the number back. He had no more luck than I did.

Jared slammed the phone down and cursed.

I expected Kelly to startle at the coarse word, but she didn't.

"What's wrong, Daddy?" asked Kelly.

"Nothing," said Jared.

"Can I have another brownie?" asked Kelly.

Little manipulator. She knew Jared had told her one brownie, and now that he was distracted, she was asking again. Where had she learned that trick?

I hated that I was so easily led to believe that Carrie Helm was cheating on her husband. It was exactly the kind of story the press would eat up and report on in the next news cycle. Everyone would breathe a sigh of relief and the footage with Jared in the family car in the middle of the night with his five-year-old daughter would become obsolete.

What did I believe? That Jared had concocted all of this as part of a plan to make himself appear innocent? Or that Carrie Helm had run away from her husband and daughter and had called more than two weeks later because she had felt a prick of loneliness for the first time since then?

Jared got Kelly another brownie from the top of the fridge, and then one for himself. He picked at it with a fork, still standing up.

"Did you talk to Carrie yourself?" I asked. "When she called for Kelly?"

"Just for a moment. She was very insistent that she wanted to talk to Kelly. I told her I wanted to talk to her afterward, but she didn't wait."

"What did she say? Did she say where she was or if she planned to come back?" If she was struggling with depression, then that was an excuse for leaving her daughter behind, I suppose. But at some point, wouldn't she want to come home?

"All she said was that she was fine and she wasn't hurt." Jared's fork was halfway to his mouth and he held it there for a long moment before putting it back to the plate.

"I want Mommy to come back," said Kelly. "Make her come back, Daddy."

Jared looked at me.

"You have to tell the police," I said. "Think of all the money and labor hours being spent on this case when they could be spent on another." How many days ago was it that I had convinced the Westons to go on television to make sure the whole world knew their daughter was mysteriously missing? And now what was I doing?

Jared swallowed hard and looked down at the plate.

Kelly was eyeing his brownie as if she were ready to plead for a third.

I reached over and swiftly lifted her father's plate from the counter to the sink, dumping the brownie and then rinsing it down the disposal.

Kelly looked sad for a moment, then brightened. "Will Mommy be coming home soon?" she asked.

Jared patted her fluffy head of hair, as messy as ever. "I hope so," he said.

Would he take back a wife who had run off with another man, if she came back and asked him to? The letter the Westons had read seemed to indicate not. "Do you want me to sit with Kelly while you talk to the police?" I asked.

"Yes, thank you," said Jared. "I'd appreciate that."

In the end, he didn't have me make the
call for him. Only five minutes after he'd
hung up, the doorbell rang. The real detectives had arrived.

Jared spoke quietly to the police in the
next room while Kelly and I played with
some toys she'd brought down to show me.
I murmured pleasant things to her while
trying to listen in on the other conversation.
I only caught occasional snatches and those
brought me no new information.

It wasn't until the police were nearly
finished that it occurred to me to follow up
with Kelly on what she had said about dropping her mother off in the car. If that car
ride had happened in the middle of the
night, as the gas station footage seemed to
suggest, then what did it mean that Carrie
had called Kelly this morning?

"Kelly, come here for a minute," I said,
and pulled her onto my lap. "Do you remember when you told me about saying
goodbye to your mommy?"

She nodded.

"Did she sound the same to you then as
she did today on the telephone?"

"She didn't talk before. She won't talk
when she's mad at Daddy," said Kelly.

"And today?" I asked.

"She was happy today," said Kelly. "She said she would come back, that she was bringing me a new doll, the one with the blue hair like I told her I wanted. But last time, she said I couldn't have it. She said she didn't want me to have a doll with a belly ring."

A crass way to buy forgiveness — if it really was Carrie Helm.

I concentrated once more on the footage of the family car at the gas station at 3:00 A.M. "Kelly, I want you to think hard about this. Why did your father take you in the car with him the morning your mother disappeared?"

"He didn't want to leave me home by myself," said Kelly. "Mommy leaves me sometimes by myself, but Daddy never does."

And now I wondered what kind of a mother Carrie Helm had been. "Where was your mother sitting?"

"In the front, by Daddy."

"Did you see her?" I asked.

Kelly thought for a long moment. She shook her head. "I was sleepy," she said.

"But you know she was there?"

Kelly nodded.

"How do you know that?"

"Daddy kept talking to her," she said.

"One last question, Kelly. Do you remember where your daddy drove to? Was it any place familiar?" The gas station he had stopped at had been several miles north of Draper, just off I-15, but that didn't say much. He could have been coming back and forth from almost anywhere north or west.

Kelly closed her eyes, thinking hard. "It was dark out," she said. "I sawed a big moon."

So that was that.

The police left a few minutes later and Jared came in to thank me for watching Kelly.

"What did they say?" I asked.

"That they would look into it. I can only hope they find her and this all ends." He gestured at the news vans outside.

"Do you want her to come back, then?" I asked.

"Of course I do. More than anything," said Jared. And of all the things he had said, this sounded the most true.

CHAPTER 14

It took two days for the police to find the cell phone that had called Kelly Helm from Las Vegas, but by the time they had tracked it, it had been thrown in the trash of a casino. There was no sign of Carrie Helm or the mysterious man named Will who had answered. The phone itself was prepaid and had been bought with cash in St. George, Utah, two weeks before Carrie's disappearance.

It seemed clear from the police statement to the press Monday morning that they were not reassured about Carrie Helm's well-being, either. They said there was no evidence that she had left her home in Utah of her own free will, and they still considered her a missing person in serious danger. What worried me most was that the cell phone had been purchased two weeks before Carrie had disappeared. It could mean nothing or it could mean that Carrie had known what she was going to do. Or that Jared Helm had planned all of this a long time ago, down to the smallest detail.

Meanwhile, there were plenty of other minor emergencies in the ward. The Torstensens' ordeal was only one of many. Sister Grange had lost her father to a home accident in the tub. The Ringels were reeling from layoffs on both sides. The Andrews' had all come down with whooping cough, despite the fact that they had all been vaccinated against it, and the Utah Health Department had become involved to make sure that the strain didn't spread to other vaccinated people. The ward wasn't even allowed to go into the home to bring aid. And if that weren't enough, three of the Derringers were in the hospital with broken bones after a skiing trip.

For Kurt, this meant an enormous amount of time spent comforting families and updating various organizational heads. Over the weekend, he had spent almost no time at home, and he had even taken Monday off work, mostly so he could sleep.

Kurt had asked me to check in with the Torstensens every day that week. Despite the predictions of the hospice service, Tobias had survived past the ten day mark. The hospice nurse insisted that it was the arrival of his sons that had buoyed his spirits but did not think this meant any change in his prognosis. Both Liam and Tomas had arrived on Friday, and had found a hotel in Draper to share a room in.

I went over Monday afternoon, and was worried that Anna had begun to talk about plans for the future, as if Tobias would recover.

"If he starts to fail again, I just want to be sure you're prepared for it," I said.

"He wants me to help him out to the garden tomorrow so Liam and Tomas can do some clearing to prepare for spring planting," she said as she sorted silverware from the dishwasher.

"What about his wife's grave?" I asked. "Did you find anything out about that from Liam or Tomas?"

"Oh, that. I think he must have been confused. He says that she was cremated, and so there isn't any grave."

It still seemed odd to me, but perhaps odd was not reason enough for suspicion. "Where are her ashes, then? Did he say? Maybe that was what he meant, that he wanted to go back to the place where her ashes were."

Anna shook her head. "He said he didn't keep the ashes. He didn't want such a morbid reminder of her death. He had the mortuary dispose of them." She had opened the dishwasher again and was looking inside it, as if to find more dishes that had appeared there.

"Anna." I wanted her to listen to me carefully. "Do you want Kurt to come talk to you and Tobias about having your marriage sealed in the temple?"

"That would be a lovely idea. You and Kurt could come and stand with us. Tobias always loves to go to the temple, and he looks so handsome in all that white," said Anna.

"Anna," I said gently, because she wasn't understanding the question. "I don't think Tobias is going to be well enough to get to the temple. I meant Kurt could talk to you about having the sealing done after Tobias is gone. If that is what both you and he wish." I wasn't one hundred percent sure on the details of all temple ordinances, but I didn't think it could happen until Anna was also dead.

Anna's mouth compressed. "He is doing so well right now."

"But this is important. This is about what happens after this life. Forever after."

Anna began to cry. I felt bad for bringing her to this point, but I also thought it was necessary. She had to face the truth about Tobias's death.

Her shoulders shook, and the sobs were soundless, as if she was worried Tobias would hear her, but tears dripped down her face. She tried to wipe at the counter, but I put an arm around her and she let herself fall against my chest. I could hear the muffled sounds of her gasping breaths and realized she was terrified. As if a train were coming directly at her and there was no way for her to get out of the way. Was that the way it would feel for me, if Kurt were to die? With my daughter, there had been no chance to feel the anticipation. It had already happened before I realized it and had to take it in.

"I'm sorry," Anna said, and pulled away from me. She wiped at her face with the same wet dishcloth she'd been using on the counter, then stared at it as if she didn't know where it had come from.

"You don't have to be sorry," I said. "I'm happy to help in any way I can."

She shook her head. "I shouldn't make you feel sad when you've done nothing but be helpful and so kind."

But feeling sad was what I was here for, to feel sad with her. "No one expects you to do this alone. Or without showing your real feelings," I said.

Anna looked closely at me then, as if seeing me for the first time. "Do you know, I always thought of you as rather emotionless. Controlled. In charge."

I had plenty of emotions. I just didn't let myself show them because they tended to get out of hand. "I'm not in charge," I said softly. I was the bishop's wife. I wasn't in charge of anything but making the bishop dinner, not officially.

"At church, you always sound so assured when you answer questions. I think the Sunday School teacher quakes in his boots, hoping you don't correct him. He thinks you have the whole Bible memorized."

"Well, I don't," I said, astonished. I had always thought that I was just on the border of heresy, and she seemed to think I was some sort of icon of Mormon womanhood.

"I thought you would quote Bruce R. McConkie at me and expect me to accept death with grace and courage. As a relief and a triumph."

Bruce R. McConkie, author of multiple volumes of the once-beloved *Mormon Doctrine,* had spoken at General Conference just days before his death from cancer in the 1980s. He had looked pale and gaunt, and his voice was one of those harsh whispers that made you stop and listen. He had stood on the pulpit and before the audience of millions of Mormons had declared that he knew Christ lived, and that even when he was dead, he would not know any better then than he knew now that Christ was real. No one who had heard the speech live would forget it.

I said, thinking of that certainty in the face of death, "It's nice to have grace and courage after the fact. But I'm afraid most of us are all too mortal and only find grace and courage in special moments. The rest of the time we're alternately angry or fiercely afraid."

"You — afraid?" said Anna.

There was a long moment when I didn't know if I could be honest enough to tell her the truth. My mouth opened, but the words wouldn't be pressed out. They were too big to fit through the sieve.

"I lost a daughter," I got out finally, the words hardly audible.

"What? I thought you had five sons."

"And one daughter," I said.

"But — what happened?" she asked.

I took a deep breath, and then another. We hadn't lived here then, so no one in the ward knew. We moved here two years later, after Kenneth was born. Samuel and Zachary were the only children born in our Draper house.

"I don't know," I said. "I don't know what happened and sometimes that is harder than anything else." This had nothing to do with Tobias and Anna. This wouldn't help her deal with her own difficulties. I told myself to be quiet, that she didn't need to hear the details. But it had been so long since I had spoken about it. I wasn't sure I ever really had. And so I kept talking.

"I was scheduled to be induced the next day. She was overdue and the doctor was tired of waiting, I think. He never saw any problems in the ultrasound. She was losing weight, though. He said that babies sometimes did that at the end. He said it was nothing to worry about."

I wanted to take the wet dishcloth from her and use it. I wanted to do something with my hands while I spoke, but instead, I just stared down at them.

"That night, I went to bed and slept well for the first time in months. When I woke up in the morning, I realized it was because she hadn't moved all night. Kurt came over to touch my belly because he said it looked different. And somehow, that moment, he knew. He started crying. I called the doctor and asked for an appointment. I went down and ate some breakfast. And read one of those pregnancy books, which reassured me that the baby might just be uncomfortable or asleep. I was so sure that the doctor would say everything was fine, and that Kurt was a crybaby for nothing." I smiled a little at that. Kurt was often more emotional than I was.

"But he was right. There was no heartbeat. They rushed me to the hospital and induced me right away. Even then, I kept thinking that if I delivered quickly enough, maybe they would be able to revive her." The sounds of my own breathing were so loud that they embarrassed me.

"I'm sorry. I never knew," said Anna.

I shook my head. I could feel tears falling, but they were cold by the time they landed on my cheeks. It was all so long ago. People talk about how you recover from tragedy. But it's more like scar tissue. It's always there; you just find a way to work around it.

Anna was staring at me.

I felt suddenly self-conscious. I'd spilled my soul, and now I felt exposed. "I'm sorry. I came here for you, to talk about your problems, not mine. Please forgive me. I must be very tired."

"No, don't apologize. Thank you. Thank you for telling me the truth."

Did she realize that she was the only person I'd opened up to about this? My face felt sticky from the tears. A part of me wished I hadn't said anything about my daughter, maybe a bit like someone who has a hangover and wishes she hadn't had anything to drink. The aftereffects are brutal, but at the moment, I couldn't have held back.

"I think I understand you a little better now. I never had a daughter. I never had sons, actually." Anna put her hand over mine on the countertop, and I realized she did know how rare this truth of mine was, and she was honoring it with her own painful truth. "Only Tobias's sons, but they were never fully mine, no matter how much I loved them. There was always a barrier with them. We decided not to have our own children because I needed to focus on Tomas and Liam, make sure they felt my complete love." Her voice was strained. "But there is a certain pain in not being a mother in your body. I have put that away for a long time, but it is still there." Her hand let go of mine and brushed against her stomach.

Yes. She understood. It was strange that a pain that was so different could be so much the same. We had both faced the loss of

211

what we had expected, deserved, and dreamed about. A loss of the imagination, which was worse in some ways from any other loss.

"At least you are sealed to her, though," said Anna.

I could quibble with the point, but I didn't. She definitely wasn't sealed to Tobias. "You should talk to him about it," I said, following her unspoken train of thought. "He might be able to put your mind at rest."

"What if Liam and Tomas object? What if they don't want me sealed to their father?"

I was a little startled by that possibility. Did she think so badly of her sons? "Trust Kurt," I said. "He will talk to them. He will make it come right."

She took a breath, dropped her eyes for a moment, then nodded. "All right. I'll speak to him."

I hoped that we had not left it too late.

CHAPTER 15

I was standing at the door, ready to open it to leave, when I heard two male voices shouting.

"That's Tomas and Liam," said Anna. She swayed a little and I grabbed her arm and pulled her to me for stability.

Liam thundered downstairs. He didn't look much like Tobias; his thinning hair that revealed the shape of his head to be quite square. But in his nose, chin, and hazel eyes, it was easy to see he was Tobias's son. His lips were trembling, sweat beading up along his crown. "He's gone," he said.

"What?" said Anna. Her eyes widened and I knew she was thinking the same thing that I was, that Tobias had died while she was away from him and she would never be able to ask him about the sealing, let alone say goodbye to him.

But Liam said, "Out of his bed. We turned around for a moment, talking to the nurse in the bathroom after she had helped him to the toilet. Then he was gone. I thought he would be down here with you. Did you see him?"

Anna looked at me. We had been so involved in our conversation — could we have missed him if he'd gone right by us quietly enough?

"He couldn't have —" Anna said.

"The back door is open!" shouted Tomas. "He's out in the garden."

Of course he was, out in the garden.

We all hurried outside to where Tobias knelt in the garden some distance away, on the middle of the three landscaped tiers. The moment felt as holy as being in the temple, the veil between worlds very thin.

The sun was bright overhead, part of a week-long thaw that had left the ground bare of snow for a while. Tobias's shoulders were shaking, as Liam's had been when he came downstairs, but there was nothing angry in Tobias's bearing. He had a hand to the ground, touching it, caressing it. He brought a finger to his lips and tasted it. I could see the change in his back, that he relaxed, as if suddenly in a familiar environment again.

Home.

The garden didn't look like much now, it

214

was true. There was mulch piled on top of most of it, and old tomato cages stacked together like Boy Scouts on parade. There was a grape arbor over the eastern side of the garden, a dry, bare winter skeleton of twisted brown vines.

The stepping-stones down to the first level of the garden from the back porch were tufted with natural Utah prairie grasses. I could see the indentations in the ground where the frames for the climbing beans had gone, and there were remnants of last year's kale and cabbage. The kale was still inky about a foot high, the outer leaves limp and laced with insect damage. There were a few green leaves valiantly trying to grow from the crown, hoping for an early spring.

When Tobias had come to speak to the Relief Society several years ago about gardening, he had discussed the passage from the book of Moses about all things being created spiritually first, and the fact that every plant, tree, every bit of dirt, every insect, and the earth itself had "living souls." He treated his own garden as reverently as he did his temple clothes.

Seeing him out there in his garden right now, I felt a pang for the ward that we would never hear another lesson on gardening from him. We would never stir at his descriptions of a garden in full bloom. I'd never again see him out puttering around in the front yard, not gardening so much as talking to his plants, being one with them. I was struck with the thought that Tobias out in his garden was as godlike as any person I had ever seen. He knew these plants. He knew them better than anyone else. And he loved them, just as they were. He wanted desperately to stay with them. Maybe more than he wanted to stay with his sons or his wife.

He raised his hands over his head and then knelt down.

Tomas and Liam were calling at him to come back, but he didn't seem to hear them.

He leaned forward, his hands still overhead as if in some strange yoga pose, and he let his face fall to the ground.

That was when Liam leaped down the porch steps and began running toward him.

Tobias's mouth was touching the dirt. I could see when Liam pulled his head up that his lips were black with rich soil. The old man spit out something that flew away on the wind — a leaf or some bit of branch.

I thought for a moment that he would come willingly, that he was too weak to fight. But as soon as Liam tried to pull his father to his feet, Tobias began to struggle. I could see their mouths moving, but I couldn't tell what they were saying. Whatever it was, it seemed to be very emotional, because both Liam and Tobias were red faced.

By then Tomas had caught up and joined them in the garden.

The hospice nurse came down to stand with me and Anna by the door. "What do they think they are doing?" she said.

"Bringing him back inside," I said.

"They could hurt him. They should leave him be. What is so terrible about him being in his garden?" said the nurse.

"They are worried he will die out there," I said. "And that would embarrass them." Male pride again.

"Or are they worried he will live out there?" said Anna. She stepped forward, and I held her back.

"If you get involved, it will only make it more difficult." As she had said herself, they were not her sons. And this was their father.

So we watched together as Tomas and Liam struggled with a recalcitrant man. He kept trying to swing his arms at them. Any impact would end up with fragile elderly bones breaking, and Tomas and Liam had to keep ducking, and shouting, and then at last I saw Tobias collapse. It was as sudden as if he were a puppet and the strings had been cut.

Liam caught his upper body and then Tomas gathered up his legs. They carried him through the dirt, into the house, and back upstairs.

"Careful, careful!" warned the nurse.

Tobias was filthy from his feet to his lips. Anna made a face as she saw black mulch falling into the carpet.

"Tobias always made sure he didn't get the carpet dirty after he worked in the garden," she said, more wistful than upset about the dirt.

"I'll clean it," I promised, and followed her upstairs, looking for any sign of a vacuum.

As soon as Tobias was back on the bed, the hospice nurse began taking his blood pressure and pulse. "He's very close to the end now," she said. "He exerted himself too much. I should have seen this coming, but perhaps it is for the best." She glanced up at Tomas and Liam.

"For the best," muttered Anna angrily. Not long before, when Liam had come down the stairs, she had believed that Tobias had died without her at his side. Now she was going to make sure that wasn't possible. She pushed the nurse aside and held

Tobias's hand. "Get out!" she shouted, the veins in her forehead red and protruding. "All of you, get out. I want to be alone with my husband now!"

I retreated first, strangely satisfied at her outburst. Shortly afterward, I heard the other three come down the stairs behind me.

The sons stared at me as we stood facing each other in the front room, but I was used to dealing with grown sons staring. I wasn't going to say anything contrary to Anna's request. She deserved this moment alone with her husband, and I was glad she had finally felt able to demand it. It must have been very difficult, having the nurse and her two stepsons in the house, even if she loved those sons as her own.

I asked about a vacuum and Tomas found it for me. I spent twenty minutes doing my best to erase any sign of garden dirt through the house while the sons talked quietly in the kitchen with the nurse. When I was done, I put the vacuum away and wandered to the back door, where Tobias had so recently been brought in.

A part of me was waiting because I didn't know if Anna would want me to be there when she came back down. But as I stood there looking at the garden, I caught a glimpse of something in the soil where Tobias had been, something that wasn't mulch, and wasn't dirt or plants.

I opened the door and stepped outside, thinking about Tobias's insistence on seeing his wife's grave. A little wind blew into my face, and I walked down the stepping stones and then up to the second level where Tobias had been.

In the summer, I would never have been able to see it. It would have been covered in plants. In the winter, it would have been covered in snow. And as soon as spring came, Tobias would have been out there, digging around, putting in wood chips or setting out the tomato cages and the climbing frames for the beans. But now, just now, because Tobias had not yet had a chance to go out, I could see the flat off-white stone, glittering with bits of silver like granite did. It was granite, I thought, even if it was uncut. It looked like a stone you might pick out at a stonemason's for a gravestone. It was flush with the ground here, nearly invisible. But this was where Tobias had come and knelt, his arms stretched out almost as if to cover the stone with his whole body. He had kissed the dirt with his lips. Or was it not the dirt he'd been kissing at all?

My mind whirled. Tobias said he hadn't

scattered his wife's ashes anywhere, but what if he had been lying? Or if he had forgotten? Could she be here?

It might even make sense that he would lie about it to Anna. Clearly, she was sensitive about the topic of her husband's first wife. It might bother her to think that all that time her husband spent in the garden was time spent with his first wife, in his heart.

Why wouldn't he tell his sons? Did he think they might judge him, think him morbid? Or even a little creepy?

I leaned over and saw there was something long and thin half-buried in the dirt near the stone. I dug at it, curious, and when I pulled it out, I realized it was a hammer, ancient enough that the wood was almost rotted through and the metal head was rusted.

Tobias had let other tools get rusted and ruined. I had already seen that in the shed. I suppose it was no stretch that he might leave tools out in the garden, as well. Was it an accident that it was here, left outside since the fall? I didn't know what he would use a hammer for in his garden, but that didn't mean anything.

I stood up and carried the hammer back into the shed. I began to wipe at it to get off the dirt, though I knew it made no sense. I should just throw it away. A large chunk of dirt fell off the hammer, and I bent down to pick it up off the floor I had spent so much time cleaning only a week ago. That was when I saw what was underneath the dirt. There was hair, matted together by something brown and flaking.

Could that be — blood?

And whose hair was it?

I dropped the hammer and heard it thunk against the garden detritus.

My heart was pounding and I felt like all the saliva in my mouth had suddenly disappeared.

The dress I had found in the shed, dotted with blood along the back of the neck. The stone that looked like it had been made to mark a grave. And now this.

A hammer with hair on it that suggested violence. A woman whose cause of death was rumored to be any of several different things, even among her immediate family. A woman who had died young, leaving her sons with her husband. A woman whose gravesite was unknown. I walked out of the shed and back inside the house. I pretended that everything was fine with Tomas and Liam, though Anna was still alone upstairs with Tobias. A man who might very well have murdered his first wife. Should I stay to tell her what I suspected? No. Not until I knew for certain. I could not add to her burdens, which were already considerable.

So I said I felt ill and needed to go home, and asked the boys to give their mother my regards.

For an hour or more, I waited on our front room couch for the bishop to come home. Then I asked if I could speak to him in his office.

His eyes flickered with surprise. "If you want."

I nodded. I felt like this should be official. Kurt had said he didn't want me to play detective, and I hadn't meant to. But now I had to tell someone. I had to know what to do, and I wanted Kurt, as the bishop, to tell me. I wanted this taken out of my hands.

He sat at his desk. I sat on the couch opposite. And I listed the facts I'd uncovered. The stone in the dirt in the garden that looked like a headstone. The hammer under the dirt by the headstone. The blood and hair on the hammer, and the pink, faded dress with its stain.

"How can you be sure it's blood this many years later? It could just be dirt that looks like dried blood," he began.

I glared at him.

He sighed. "And even if it is blood, it could be from an animal. Or . . ." He seemed unable to think up another explanation.

"Why would Tobias put the hammer near that headstone? Why doesn't anyone know what his wife really died of? Why doesn't anyone know where she is buried? Why is Tobias so desperate on his deathbed to see his wife's grave?"

"Maybe the hammer has nothing to do with the headstone," said Kurt. He waved a hand, dismissive enough to make my fear simmer into anger. "Maybe it's not a headstone, anyway. It could be a decorative stone."

"Kurt, his garden is carefully groomed. Everything has a place. The decorative stones all match. This headstone doesn't."

"It could still have another, perfectly innocuous explanation," he said. But he didn't suggest one.

"Kurt, if there is a human being buried in his garden, don't you think we should find out who it is?"

"You think it's his dead first wife there," said Kurt.

I shrugged. Who else was it likely to be? And with all the different versions of what happened to her, it almost made sense. But now that I was away from the garden, away from the sight of Tobias kissing the winter dirt, I was starting to reconsider my own conclusions. Tobias Torstensen, a killer? He was the nicest man. Could he do something like that to his wife? And no one had guessed for all these years?

"You seem to have a sudden tendency to think men guilty of killing their wives," said Kurt. "Even if there's no real evidence of foul play. Is there something wrong? Something you want to tell me about how you feel for me?" He smiled, trying to make it into a joke. He'd used that trick on the boys more than once, and they were all in stitches moments after being in the midst of a fight.

It wasn't going to work on me. "Don't talk to me like that," I said, and stood up. "Don't patronize me. I'm not making things up here. I'm not leaping to conclusions. I didn't call the police to trample through Tobias's garden while he is on his deathbed. I'm talking to you." I didn't move to the door, but I wasn't going to let him treat me like a child. I hadn't made up what I'd seen in the garden. Or the hammer. Or the headstone. It was all there, and it had to mean something.

"He's an old man, Linda. What do you possibly think we could get out of him at this late date? From a man who is dying?" asked Kurt. He had his hands templed on his desk. I knew that move, too. It was the "calm down" motion that he used when couples were arguing with each other in front of him. "Even if he is a murderer — which I don't for one minute believe — what is the point of trying to punish him when God has already taken care of it?"

What about Anna? Didn't she deserve to know the truth about her husband?

"I think you may want to consider that this is really about something else," said Kurt.

"And what's that?" I asked him.

"I think you're letting your guilt over not noticing Carrie Helm's unhappiness make you see abusive men everywhere. You're angry. At God, at my entire sex, and at yourself, for not stopping what happened to her."

Maybe I was angry, but if that was true, I had a right to be. And if Carrie Helm was fine, Tobias Torstensen's first wife wasn't.

But I put the anger aside, and sat back on the couch and tried to speak to Kurt the way he could hear me. Without emotion. "Look, I don't think Tobias's mental state is that much in question. And if he did this, he'll want to confess to you before he dies.

Asking about his wife's grave, and the whole show yesterday in the garden — it means some part of him wants to let his sons know before he's gone. It might be his last chance. So you could hint to him that you know. You could make it easier for him to tell you the truth, when you're in private. That's all I'm saying. Give him a chance. Don't accuse him, but listen if it comes up. Will you do that for me?"

"I wish I felt something from the Spirit about this. I'll go pray about it," he said. And he did. I left his office, but he didn't. He was in there all through dinner. Samuel and I ate alone.

Late that night, he went to visit Tobias Torstensen again, but whatever he found out, he didn't tell me. And the call came early Tuesday morning that Tobias Torstensen had passed away in the night.

CHAPTER 16

Tuesday night, I couldn't sleep. I had this fantasy playing in my head of going out to Tobias's garden while Anna and her sons were at the funeral. The whole ward would be at the church; no one would know what I was doing. The service would take several hours, including the eulogies and the luncheon afterward. Plenty of time for me to dig in the backyard and find if there was a body under there.

If there wasn't, well, then, I would have missed a funeral and would make my excuses. I'd come home, take a shower, and tell myself never to jump to conclusions with insufficient evidence. What did I really know about anything here? I was acting as if I were some kind of Sherlock Holmes, but I had no experience at this sort of thing. I'd watched people's expressions before, listened to them talking, decided that I could read people pretty well. But sniffing out a murder? That was for the police.

"The funeral is supposed to be on Friday, right?" I asked Kurt in the morning. The funeral home had known to expect Tobias's body, so a lot of the decisions had already been made and the process could be expedited. Tobias's body had been taken by the mortician within hours of his death.

Anna and Tobias had picked a reasonably priced coffin together, and Tobias had even talked a little about what he would like at his funeral. But he knew as well as anyone that it isn't the place of the dead to choose a funeral service. Ultimately, Kurt, the bishop, is the one who decides what is appropriate and what isn't. After any speakers he chose, Kurt would speak himself, the final word on Tobias's life and what his death would mean. I knew Kurt took the job of speaking at a funeral seriously, even more than he did all of his other jobs as a bishop. And he had genuinely liked Tobias, which would make it more difficult in some ways. He was dealing with his own grief and at the same time trying to ease the grief of others.

Anna had asked me to help her dress her husband in his temple clothes on the morning of the funeral. I wasn't looking forward to it. I had helped my mother do the same for my father when he died of cancer the year that I was pregnant with Zachary, but it had been a long time since I had performed this service.

"You've gotten very close to Anna in the last several weeks, haven't you?" said Kurt on Thursday evening, after he got back from church meetings and we were lying in bed.

"Yes, I have."

"I always thought you were the kind of woman who had a very small intimate circle with her family, that you didn't need close female friends."

"Well, there were always women in the callings I worked in, in the church."

"But I have the sense it's different with Anna. This isn't just about you bonding with her over a joint purpose. Or is it?"

"I don't think so," I said. I suppose I had spent all of the time since Kurt and I were married focusing on my own children, and my only relationships had grown out of that primary one. I looked back on my life before I had married, though, and I hadn't had many female friends then, either. I had grown up with three brothers, and had learned to talk as bluntly as they did. That didn't seem to endear me to other women. But it was also true that my personality was prickly, and that I tended to offend people easily. "Anna is different. She's — like who I might have been," I said. "If I hadn't — if I'd gone through her life instead of mine." I didn't know if that was the right way to put it, but it was as close as I could come. I didn't have any sisters, but I imagined the way I felt about Anna was how I might have felt for a sister.

"I'm glad," said Kurt.

"Why?" I asked.

He shrugged. "I don't know. I think it makes you stronger somehow. Like you're linked to someone else strong."

"Oh. Well, yes," I said, plumping a pillow behind me so that I could sit up better. Kurt had a wide field of friends to call on, both from work and from the church. He might not go shopping with them or call them on the phone just to chat, but they were always there for him when he needed them for anything.

"You've lived in a household of all men for a long time. I thought that was what made you different from other women. You don't do a lot of the feminine stuff. And I guess there was a part of me that wondered if it was my fault — mine and the boys' — that you were like that. I thought maybe you were missing something."

I *was* missing something. I had been for

over twenty years. What if I'd had a daughter who wanted frills and pink and lacy dresses? Who pouted and manipulated the way that girls are often taught to, to get their own way? Would that have changed the kind of woman I was? Maybe it would have.

But what if I'd had a daughter who was like a younger version of Anna, who could have been a friend and a confidante? What if that was what I had been missing all this time?

"She doesn't make me feel like I have to hide who I am," I said.

I thought about hiding, about secrets. What was going to happen to my relationship with Anna if I pressed her to have the garden dug up so that Tobias's secret came out?

I needed to talk to Anna about that, but it would have to wait. If there was a body there, the timing of its discovery wouldn't make a difference, after all. Here was my chance to prove I'd learned patience.

Kurt knew me too well, because he said, "You know, I'm going to have to talk to Tomas and Liam about their father's life history for the funeral."

"Yes, I know," I said.

"Maybe something will come out then," said Kurt. "And you won't have any more questions about Tobias and his first wife."

"I hope so," I said.

I thought about the two of them. By my calculations, Tomas had been only two years old when his mother had died, but Liam had been six or seven. Liam might remember, if he were asked the right questions. Maybe being back in the family house would trigger memories.

"I don't suppose — do you think it's possible the first wife ran off somewhere?" I said, the idea suddenly occurring to me. It had been Carrie Helm's disappearance that had first made me wonder about Tobias's dead wife, but what if the two stories were even more similar than I imagined?

Kurt chewed on his lower lip, then said, "I suppose it's possible. Tobias might have lied to his boys, thinking that telling them the truth would hurt them more."

Unlike Jared Helm. I thought again, cringing, of how he'd told Kelly that Carrie had taken her daughter's favorite book because she hadn't wanted Kelly to have it anymore.

"And then after so many years of lying, he couldn't tell his sons the truth," Kurt was saying. "Maybe that was what he really wanted when he said he needed to see his wife's grave. He wanted to tell them the truth, but his mind had gotten too confused to know how to do it."

But that still didn't explain the hammer with the hair and dried blood on it, did it? Or the strange stone in the garden.

Maybe there was no explanation for those things. There are mysteries that they say we will just have to ask God to answer when we are on the other side. I always wondered if we would just stop caring about them then.

Thursday morning, when Kurt and Samuel were gone, I sat down on the computer to do some investigating on my own. I'd had to do genealogy work for the church, and I knew how to find out birth dates, death dates, and other important information. After looking on FamilySearch.com, Ancestry.com, and Genealogy.com, I found several death certificates for Torstensens who had died in Utah in the five-year period I estimated was right, but none of them were listed for Draper. All the death certificates from that period were supposed to be available online, but I wondered if I should send in an official form just to be sure. But I didn't even know the woman's first name. Tobias had never mentioned it, nor had Anna.

As I worked on the computer, there was

another knock on the front door. It was Brad Ferris, Gwen's husband.

"Oh," I said. "I'm sorry, but Kurt's at work. Do you want me to call his cell phone? Is there an emergency?"

"I — she isn't — I came alone this time — because —" Brad was nervous. He took a deep breath. "I was hoping to talk to you, Sister Wallheim," he got out. "About something private."

"Me?" I said, surprised. I had thought nothing could surprise me anymore.

"If you don't mind," Brad said. "It's about Gwen, but it's woman stuff. I thought you might be able to help me understand it better than the bishop."

I looked around the front room, but decided we were too likely to be interrupted there, either by Samuel, who would be home from school soon, or by someone else coming to see me. So, feeling a little odd, I led Brad Ferris into Kurt's office and hoped that Kurt wouldn't feel I'd invaded his private space.

I sat behind Kurt's desk and Brad sat in the couch, as before. I didn't close the door all the way, which was ridiculous, since no one else was in the house. But Kurt was so cautious about being alone with other women, even when he was counseling them, that some of the same nervousness had rubbed off on me. Kurt's chair made me feel strangely small, but I tried to suppress that thought and sit up as tall as I could.

"What can I do for you?" I asked Brad Ferris.

"I feel like I've made too big a deal of this," he said. His voice was shaky and I realized that was because his whole body was shaking. Small-boned and hardly five foot six, he couldn't be more than twenty-six years old, Adam's age. His hands looked like they had been rubbed raw with wringing. Was he getting ready to confess something to me?

"I was hoping that you could give me some advice," he said finally. "About Gwen."

"What kind of advice?" I hoped suddenly that this wasn't a question about female sex organs. For all I wished that Mormons talked more openly about sex, I didn't want to give Brad advice about pleasing his wife in bed. I could direct him to a few books, however, if that was what he needed. I scanned the room for Kurt's laptop. Good, he'd left it to the side of the desk, and I was pretty sure I knew the password. I could print out a list of suggestions and then Brad Ferris would be on his way.

"I want to know how to make her feel as special as she really is."

Relief. This was not about sex, then. "Special in what way?" I asked, feeling a sudden sympathy for Kurt.

His hands flew all over the place. "She has had such a hard life and I want to make her feel how happy I am that she got through all of it, that she made it to me. I want to make her feel wonderful. I want her to wake up in the morning and stop thinking about all the mistakes she made, and think instead of all the possibilities." He captured his hands, and then his head started bobbing. "I — I want her to think about how much better a place the world is because she's in it. I want her to see how happy she makes me and to believe that matters."

I stared at him, shrinking back in Kurt's chair. I could feel tears rising in my eyes. All he wanted was to do what I thought all men should want to do for their wives, and which few managed to do, even once in a while. He wanted to counteract the message so many women heard "the world" telling them, that they were worthless, and that they should just be content to be no more than vessels to please men.

"What's the thing that is causing Gwen

the most pain right now?" I asked.

His hands were free again, and made wide, sweeping ovals. "I think sometimes that it feels to her like her whole life is weighing on her, like everything that has happened to her, and everything she has done wrong . . . like it's all happening right now."

"That sounds like depression. Or possibly anxiety," I said. "Is she seeing a therapist?"

"She was seeing a therapist before, but not now. And yes, she is still on medication. But sometimes the medication isn't enough. Sometimes — she feels like this is all her own fault, and she doesn't even deserve to have medication. Or me. Or happiness. So she pushes it away."

"I see," I said, not sure I saw at all. Was this a clinical matter, about Gwen's mental health? Or was he asking me for tools to manage his own relationship? I wasn't an expert on medications for depression and I was sure Kurt wouldn't appreciate me dispensing medical advice in any case. He sent members of the ward to doctors if he sensed they needed that kind of care. So I decided I would deal with relationship issues. That was what I was good at. "Have you tried writing her notes telling her how much you love her? Sometimes writing something down makes it feel more real, more permanent than just saying it. And then she would have it to look at even when you're not there."

His face lit up. I had never seen anyone look at me like that before, certainly not my children, not even Kurt. "Thank you! I'll do that. Write her letters." He nodded to himself, as if etching these words into his head. "Anything else?"

I felt a sense of power. I knew the downsides to being the bishop, but now I began to understand the upsides, too. Not only did people look at you like you were an angel of God, but you could actually help them to be happy. So long as you didn't give them really stupid advice. How well did I know Gwen Ferris, anyway? How much did I know about what was really going on between her and her husband? I could give general advice, though. And I knew that when I felt overwhelmed, sometimes Kurt putting a hand on my back or shoulder did wonders.

"Touch her," I said. "Not just kisses, and not necessarily sexually. But just casually, remind her that you are there. Touch the back of her neck or her back. Touch her legs while she is sitting next to you. Reassure her. Remind her that you love her. Make her feel surrounded by love, protected by it."

"Sometimes she doesn't like to be touched," said Brad. "She doesn't like to be surprised. She jumps."

What was this? It shouldn't be surprising to be touched by your husband of five years. "Maybe you should just make sure she knows it's coming," I said. "Let her come to expect it." As soon as I said it, I wondered if I was off the mark. Did she have personal space issues? Or was there something darker going on here?

"Okay. I'll do that. Thank you so much. And maybe I can talk to you again later?" he asked.

"Sure. If you'd like to." Although I was thinking that I would very much like to talk to Gwen Ferris again myself. I needed to know if I had given her husband the worst possible advice or not. I needed to know more about everything here.

Brad Ferris stood up and moved to the door.

I got out of Kurt's chair more slowly.

I had to wait until Kurt got home and we'd had dinner to tell him what had happened with Brad Ferris and what advice I had given him.

"Was I completely wrong?"

240

"No," said Kurt. "But —"

"But what?"

He just shook his head. "I don't know. They haven't told me everything yet. I can see how they are with each other. I can see they are good for each other. And you know about how they've wanted to have children?"

I nodded.

"But there's something else there that they're not ready to talk about yet."

"You could send them to a therapist, you know." Why hadn't he already done that?

"I know, but I don't think that's the right thing in this case. I've prayed and prayed about it, and I think that for whatever reason, they need me personally to sit and listen to them."

I nodded again and hoped he and I had both done the right things by the Ferrises. There were times when you hoped that God really did use you as His tool to help others, because you were pretty sure you couldn't do it yourself.

CHAPTER 17

In the midst of getting ready for Tobias Tor-stensen's funeral Friday morning, Kurt had a visitor. It was Jared Helm's father, Alex, who looked as angry when I opened the door as Carrie's parents, the Westons, had looked when they came to see Kurt.

Kurt had hoped to spend several hours reviewing his notes on Tobias's life. Samuel was outside dealing with a few things in the yard that needed taking care of. A fallen tree that had to be cut down. A dam of leaves that hadn't been raked up before it started to snow. And as always, putting out salt on the ice so that it melted quickly and no one slipped.

I knocked on Kurt's door and told him Alex was here to see him. But he said, "Just a minute." I showed Alex Helm into the kitchen, where he sat at a stool and looked around. His expression made me think he was making a snap judgment of me based on the dust on my cabinets and the scuff marks on the wall by the outside door. I immediately disliked the man.

But I was struck by how much Alex looked like his son. Or rather, the reverse. It wasn't just in his features; they had the same mannerisms, the same useless hand motions when talking. And they had the same frozen look in their eyes when they were angry. The first time I'd seen it in Jared, I'd thought it was fear. But now that I'd seen it in his father, who was more voluble, I knew it was just banked anger, simmering not far below the surface.

Kurt came in after we'd made a few aborted attempts at small talk, and he took Alex Helm into his office.

I sat on a chair in the kitchen, thinking about Tobias Torstensen and whatever was in his garden. Occasionally, the sound of the voices in the other room was loud enough to disturb my thoughts. I didn't hear much, but what I did hear made it clear that Alex Helm thought that his son had been wronged, that his daughter-in-law was crazy, and that the whole ward had a debt to pay for not seeing Jared's needs earlier and helping him. He seemed to think we all should have taken Carrie Helm out of the home and sent her to a mental institution, that we should be giving interviews to the press about how wonderful his son was.

I guess every father has a right to defend his son, but I felt for Kurt. I would have told Alex Helm to get out and never come back. But Kurt had always been more diplomatic. I suppose that's why he's the bishop and I'm not, although the fact that I'm a woman doesn't help, either.

When Alex Helm came out of Kurt's office at last, I looked up from my book, checked my watch and realized he had been in there almost two hours.

Kurt gestured to me, and I came over. Alex Helm seemed to have calmed down a little. Another one of Kurt's talents.

"Mr. Helm will be staying with Jared and Kelly for the next few weeks," said Kurt. "With the press camped outside his house day after day, Jared needs someone to give him a break from childcare."

"Wouldn't it be good for Kelly to get out, too?" I asked. I had ached every time I'd thought of her in the week since I saw her last, and yet it seemed wrong that I felt so much for this child who wasn't mine. "Kelly is such a wonderful little girl," I said, the word catching in my throat.

I caught Kurt staring at me in surprise. I

guess he hadn't realized how much I felt for Kelly. Maybe I hadn't, either.

"She's a wonderful child because her father has made an effort to teach her right from wrong. Her mother never did any of that. She would let that child do whatever she wanted. Indulged her too much, like she indulged herself. And Jared put up with it because he loved her. I always warned him that nothing good would come of it, and now I'm proven right. Indulgence and evil always go hand in hand." Alex Helm was only a couple of inches taller than I was, but he lifted his head and had taken several steps toward me before Kurt stepped forward and the older man backed off.

"Children do need to be corrected," said Kurt. "And in this day and age, sometimes parents forget that." I knew what he was doing, agreeing verbally with Alex Helm to lessen the tension of the conversation, but it still frustrated me to hear him take that man's side.

"But not physically hurt," I said. "Using the right tone and showing love is all that most children need."

"You have no right to tell my son how to raise his daughter, so long as his method of discipline is reasonable and timely," said Alex Helm. "That's what the state law says.

245

So long as he doesn't use a belt or any other weapon but his own hand and he isn't excessive."

Reasonable and timely? What was this awful man's idea of reasonable? The idea of Kelly being struck made me ill. I had to put a hand up to the wall to steady myself. She was the kind of child who spoke what she thought when she thought it, and she believed she would be listened to. If she was around this man for very long, what would happen to that open part of her?

"Of course we don't mean to overstep our bounds," Kurt was saying. "And of course Jared is doing a good job as a father. We don't question that. Only that he might be stressed."

I knew Kurt was trying to be conciliatory, but I was not in the mood for it at the moment. I burst out with, "Well, I think Christ taught clearly that children were to be lovingly corrected, gently and kindly, and that those who hurt children would regret it." With millstones round their necks, no less.

"It isn't hurting a child to grab her as she runs into the street into oncoming traffic, or to slap her hand when she reaches for a hot plate on the stove," said Alex Helm. He looked at me with barely concealed disgust.

"As long as you give her a hug afterward

so she knows that you still love her, even if she makes mistakes," I said.

"Giving love too soon after correction can lead children to forget the correction," said Alex Helm. "And little girls in particular have a tendency to believe that they can avoid the consequences of anything by sweet-talking the men around them."

Little girls? I'd met plenty of Mormons who thought girls were less capable than boys at doing certain tasks, and that girls — and women — should be restricted to a certain sphere. But this sexism was so blatant and unapologetic that it shook me.

"I'm sure both little girls and little boys feel that way," said Kurt, who seemed to have recovered more quickly than I had. Why shouldn't he? His entire sex wasn't being attacked.

"Little girls face a harsh world," I said. Kurt must have heard the danger in my voice, though Alex Helm might not have. "They need to know that there is someone always on their side."

"So long as they do right, there is someone always on their side," said Alex Helm. "But if they do wrong, then they will be dragged down to hell and become servants of the devil, who will use their pretty looks and their manipulating ways for his own work."

He made a strangling motion with his hands and jerked an invisible woman to the floor. Quite the performance, I had to admit. He would be an excellent Lucifer in the temple film. Very real.

I tried for a moment to dial back my revulsion for Alex Helm, to feel sympathy for him. Maybe his childhood had been terrible. Maybe his mother had been manipulative and selfish, as he seemed to think all women were. But here he was now, a grown man, a father and a grandfather. And he was looking at me like I was dancing with seven veils in front of him, ready to seduce him and then suffocate him while he struggled to escape from the hell of my clutches.

"With her mother gone, Kelly needs more love than ever," I said. "Or she will grow up thinking that her mother left because she herself wasn't good enough."

"Her mother left because she is one of the whores of the earth," said Alex Helm bluntly. Scripture or not, his tone chilled me. I looked to Kurt. Let him be diplomatic about that.

"I'm sure all of us have an equal chance at repentance," said Kurt, putting out an arm in an attempt to guide Alex Helm toward the front door. "God always wants us to come to Him, and the Atonement is available to any who want it."

Alex Helm didn't budge. I saw a smile spread across his face. "Except those who are sons and daughters of perdition, who have known the full truth of the gospel, have had the Holy Ghost testify to them, and have rejected it. Those who reject Christ in His fullness have no second chance," said Alex Helm. His voice boomed authoritatively, though his words were not precisely authoritative.

The doctrine of the sons of perdition I knew, although I had never heard of daughters of perdition. Mormon scriptures said there were those who would not end up in any of the three kingdoms of glory that were Mormon heaven, but the number was supposed to be tiny. Fewer than a dozen was what I had always thought, because there were so very few who truly had the full knowledge of Christ in their hearts and then rejected it.

All the rest ended up in one of the three degrees of glory: the telestial kingdom, where murderers went; the terrestrial kingdom, where the honest people of the world who denied Christ went; and the celestial kingdom, where only those who were righteous and had had all necessary Mormon temple ordinances could go.

But as I stared at Alex Helm, I rather hoped that if I went to a heaven, it was one of the two he wasn't in. Or maybe he would be one of the sons of perdition himself.

"We can't condemn others. Only God judges us, at the end of our lives," said Kurt. He had stopped trying to push Alex Helm to the door and instead was blocking my path to the man. I'd always told the boys that they should avoid physical violence at all costs, but Alex Helm was the kind of man who inspired extraordinary measures.

"That doesn't mean we are absolved of the responsibility of calling evil evil." Alex Helm shook his head. "If Kelly isn't taught her place now, before she grows too old to learn properly, there will be no hope that she will turn out differently than her mother. And I won't be the grandfather to a little whore."

That was all I could bear to hear. I raised a hand and slapped him hard across the face.

Kurt flinched at the sound, then sighed and shook his head. "Now, Linda, I think you need to apologize for that."

Alex Helm had a hand to his cheek, and he seemed to be gloating. "I think that you have some work to do in your own house," he said to Kurt. "You might have your own whore of the earth, Bishop."

Strangely, this had no effect on my anger, because I didn't care what he called me.

But Kurt did. He put a hand directly on the smaller man's shoulder and pushed him toward the door. "Please tell Jared that he is welcome to come to me for counseling whenever he feels in need of it. And that he and Kelly are both in our prayers."

The door opened and closed, and then we were free of Alex Helm. God, what a noxious man! I hated the thought that he and I shared the same religion, at least ostensibly.

"Do you need to scream now?" asked Kurt. "Or hit someone else? You can hit me if you want." He pointed to his cheek.

I was plenty angry, but Kurt wasn't going to get out of this with just a punch to the jaw. "How dare you?" I said to him. "How dare you agree with him like that?"

"I didn't agree with him," said Kurt mildly.

"You told him that we all needed repentance."

"We do," said Kurt.

"And then you told me to apologize for hitting him."

"Yeah, that was stupid, wasn't it?" said Kurt. He looked a bit sheepish at that. "But mostly, I was just trying to get rid of him. Aren't you glad about that part?"

Yes, I was. I took a breath and let go of the idea that Kurt had in any way agreed with Alex Helm. "Fine," I said.

Kurt moved to the door and glanced out the peephole. I assumed he must have seen Alex Helm in the distance, retreating to his son's house. "What a horrible man. I actually feel sorry for Jared. Can you imagine having a father like that?"

"Can you imagine having a father-in-law like that?" I said. "Poor Carrie. And poor Kelly. What will she think of her possibilities in the future with a man like that whispering in her ear every moment of her life?"

Kurt turned away from the door and looked straight at me. I felt as if he could see to my soul. They say that bishops can do that. "About Kelly Helm. Linda, be careful, please. She isn't yours. If you become too attached, you will only end up hurting yourself."

"And what about Kelly? I'm more worried about her hurts than my own. She's the child. I'm a grown woman."

Kurt stared at me for a long moment, and then he gave up trying to talk me out of my feelings for Kelly Helm. "Well, no wonder their marriage had so many problems," he said. "Knowing Alex Helm is here certainly won't help Carrie want to come back."

But the real question was why Carrie had ever let herself marry into such a family in the first place. Her parents, it seemed, were right about everything.

"By blood and by right." Those were the words that Carrie had used in her letter to her parents to describe Jared's claim to his daughter. And his promise that she would not be remembered, except as a crazy woman — I hoped desperately that wasn't true, and that it was Jared's own craziness that would eventually come out, now that his father had arrived to fan it into flames.

CHAPTER 18

Still shaken by my conversation with Alex Helm, I went over to the Torstensen house at about ten to check on Anna before we were due at the mortuary for the dressing of the body. I knocked on the door and waited for an answer. It took several minutes and another knock before Anna Torstensen came to the door.

I was shocked by her appearance. To my eyes, she looked like she was the one who had died. Her skin seemed thin and papery over the bones of her skull, which stood out clearly in the yellow artificial light. Every movement seemed slow and deliberate and distant, as if she were a puppet of herself, and there was an absence in her eyes.

"I thought we could drive down to the mortuary together," I said. She didn't look like she could drive herself.

"Thank you," said Anna. "I just — I think

I need a few more minutes to prepare myself."

"Have you had anything to eat today?" I asked.

She shook her head again.

"Let me make you some toast and then we'll go," I said. "All right?"

She stepped away from the door, and I led her into the kitchen. I looked through her cupboards, wishing there were some forbidden coffee to perk her up and settling for herbal tea. I warmed some bread in a pan, then spread it with butter and jam. I had to tell Anna to sit down.

"Eat this," I said.

She took tiny bites, showing no reaction of either distaste or enjoyment. When she was finished, she stared down at the crumbs on her hand.

I brushed them off for her and handed her the herbal tea.

She took a sip and made a face, the first reaction I'd seen.

"Too hot?" I asked, taking it back and touching the mug myself. It didn't seem too hot.

"Too sweet," she said. That was a good sign, wasn't it? After a long moment, she got up and poured herself a glass of tap water.

"Is there anything I can do for you now? Anything you can't face doing?"

"Cheri Tate will be here tomorrow. She's going to help me go through his clothes and send them to Goodwill. Or throw them out." She said the words calmly, but afterwards, her eyes were shiny and wet.

"Well, I'm glad to hear that she has things under control."

"She is very organized. She's making sure the funeral luncheon will go smoothly, too."

"I'm so sorry," I said, feeling again how useless the words were.

"I should have been ready, you know," she said. She was standing up, and I pulled her down to sit next to me. We were still in the kitchen, on the hard chairs, but I couldn't see how to move into the more comfortable couch in the living room now that she had started.

"I'm sure you never really can be," I said.

"I keep feeling like there are things we didn't finish. All these things that still had to be done." Her hands flexed, dropped. "I know that he was seventy-three. I had so many years with him, more than most people have. More than he had with his first wife, certainly. But it still feels incomplete. It feels like I've been cheated." There were spots of red on her cheeks.

Good, I thought. Be angry. Shout at God or at me or at anyone, if that helps you come back to life.

She began to talk in a nostalgic tone and I let her, though I was keeping an eye on the clock: 10:15. The funeral was at 2:00 P.M. We still had a little time.

Anna was saying, "We had a summer vacation planned this year, do you know that? All the years we've been married, and we had never taken a vacation in the summer. He was too attached to that garden. We only went on winter vacations, and those were only for a few days because of work and school schedules. We couldn't afford to go very far away, so the weather was always an issue, as well." She looked up at me, and I nodded encouragement. Better she talk about this than about the death.

"We were going to go to Mexico. A long drive down, so we could enjoy time together talking and listening to books on tape and music. I have lists of things that I wanted to get to. And then the hotel reservations and all the sites we were going to see. I wanted to try real Mexican food and see the ocean. I've never seen the ocean, do you know that?"

"No," I said. Apparently, there was a lot about her life I didn't know.

Her eyes flickered as if she were about to start weeping. But I sensed a grand effort and she went back to the brittle happiness pasted on top of her pain. "Tomas's wife is expecting her first child, did you know that?"

"Really?" He had to be in his late thirties. That was late to start a family, at least in Utah. But he didn't live in Utah, and sometimes it seemed like Mormons outside of Utah were part of an entirely different church.

"Yes. In late spring. Tobias was so excited when he heard it was a boy. He didn't want them to name the child after him, but Tomas told me this morning that it's what he and his wife want. What do I say to that? Now that Tobias is gone, do I tell them it's all right? Even though I know it was what he wouldn't have wanted?"

Again, I had the sense she was on the edge of losing control. Should I let her weep on my shoulder or should I encourage her to be strong? This was not the Anna Torstensen I had met at first. "They might have called the boy Tobias even if Tobias were still alive," I said calmly. "He wouldn't have had control over what name they chose." When my sons started having children, I would have to deal with the same thing. Being a

258

grandmother would be wonderful, but letting go might take work. And the more time I spent thinking about Kelly Helm, the more I thought it was going to be a lot of work.

"Oh, you'd be surprised," said Anna, a faint smile peeking out for the first time since she'd opened the door to me. "Tobias had control over many things. He told you how things were, and gave his reasons for why no one could disagree with him. And no one did. He never raised his voice, just spoke rationally and clearly until the rest of us gave way."

He had always been a quiet man, but I suppose I hadn't seen what was underneath that quiet until now. "I feel lost without him," said Anna. She met my eyes, and I saw the piercing clarity that had drawn me to her from the first. "But there is a part of me that is relieved. I hate that it's true, but I feel like a burden has lifted."

"There's no reason to feel guilty about that," I said, though she didn't look guilty. "I think that is very common when someone dies after a long illness."

"Yes, but shouldn't I feel more sad about it? Shouldn't I be crying and having fits because he is gone?" If she had, it would have surprised me, considering the kind of self-contained woman I had always seen her as. But was there something else she was saying to me? I thought of Carrie Helm and wondered if she would have been happy if Jared had died.

"Anna, did Tobias ever hurt you?" I blurted out.

Anna stood up suddenly, her hands fluttering. She was framed in the morning sun coming in the kitchen window behind her, and it made her look like she had a halo all around her. "No. Whatever makes you say that? How could you think that?"

"I didn't mean to offend you," I said. She wasn't like Carrie Helm, I told myself. And Tobias had nothing in common with Jared Helm.

"When I said I felt relief he was gone, it wasn't because of that. He would never have hit me. He wasn't like that." Anna sat back down, and I could hear her harsh breathing. I had upset her and I shouldn't have done that, not today of all days.

"I know you loved him deeply," I said neutrally.

"I loved him so much," she echoed. "I wondered sometimes if he could ever really love me as much as I loved him. And at the end, when he talked about his first wife so often, I thought that was why. I was always

260

second-best in his eyes. The one he lived with because she was dead." She sounded ashamed.

We are never good enough for those we love, are we? Not in our own eyes. "Did he ever say that to you, Anna?"

"No! Of course he wouldn't. He wasn't cruel." Her eyes darted toward mine, and then shifted away again.

"Tell me what you know about his first wife," I said, before I realized that I was asking that more for my own sake than for hers. "Did he talk about her often?" But surely this wouldn't hurt her. It might even help.

At last, her breathing seemed to slow down to normal. "She was very beautiful. Fragile, I think." She gestured to the half-size china cupboard with its gold-filigreed teacups and plates in pastel colors. "I am much taller than she was." She looked down at her feet. I realized they were rather large, a size ten or eleven, and her hands matched. Why had I not noticed that before? "Liam says she was like an old-fashioned movie star, so careful about her makeup, her hair, her clothes. I think she spent hours in the morning getting ready for the day, from the stories he tells about sitting and watching her at the bathroom mirror." Anna wore no more makeup than I did, which was a rarity in Utah these days. Women of every age here wore makeup, even to the gym.

She shrugged. "I didn't do that, and the boys seemed to like it. I was more rough and tumble with them. But it made me wonder — did Tobias marry me for their sake? Because he thought I would be good for them, and not because he loved me?" She tapped her feet on the floor.

"Even if he did marry you for their sake at first, he certainly loved you later," I assured her.

"Was it only gratitude, though? You know, I fell in love with the boys the first time I saw them. It was the strangest thing. Before that moment, I had never thought of myself as the motherly sort. At that age, I'd given up having children of my own and I thought I'd reconciled myself to that. But as soon as I saw them, I felt a lurch inside my chest, and I thought I could never let them go."

Kelly Helm, I thought. Oh, yes. That was how I felt, as well.

Her eyes seemed distant, but not in the unfocused way that had worried me before. "I touched Tomas's little hands, and I felt as if his blood was my blood. And Liam, he tried to kick me at first when I held him up, but I lost hold of him and he slid right underneath me and started to cry. His father was going to shout at him, but I picked him up — his big eight-year-old body — and gave him a kiss on the cheek." She held her hands to her chest as if little Liam was still nestled there. "He looked like a startled bird, unsure where his nest was. I wondered if he was going to be one of those boys who pretended he didn't want to be cuddled or touched at all. But no, he snuggled right into me, his tears absorbed into my skin. I wanted them. No, it was more than that. I was part of them, and I didn't know why it was true."

"As if God had meant you to be there for them," I said, and I knew I was not talking only about her.

"Yes," said Anna fiercely.

"What was her name?" I asked, just wanting one more bit of information for myself. "Do you know?"

Anna looked at me, a little startled. "Oh. It was Helena. I thought you knew that."

I shook my head. "No one ever mentioned it. It was like she was an ideal. Not a real person." That part was true.

Anna nodded. "It felt like that to me sometimes, too. An impossible ideal. On a pedestal, and she died before she fell off of it." She stood up and held up a finger. "Just

263

a moment."

She hurried up the stairs, and when she came back down, she was holding a wedding photo, of Tobias as a very young man and a strikingly beautiful woman at his side, very petite, with long, dark curls and fine features. She was wearing a knee-length wedding dress that hugged her curves and made her look even more like a doll next to tall Tobias. He was holding her in his arms and carrying her as if she weighed nothing.

"That is how they looked on their wedding day." Anna seemed wistful; it wasn't quite full-blown jealousy, but there was a trace of it.

"Did he keep this photograph of her up in your bedroom?" I asked. I was standing now, and I thought again of Jared Helm, and his reminders to Carrie that she wasn't the woman he wanted her to be. Did this photograph serve the same purpose for Anna?

But she shook her head. "It was in his drawer. He didn't want me to know it was there, I think. He never showed it to me. And he always put away his own clothes. But I found it one day, and I put it back right where it had been."

So, it wasn't the same. "Did he have other photos of her?" I asked.

Anna shook her head again. "There was a family album, but he must have gone through it. I never saw another photo of Helena in the house."

That seemed odd. "What did he do with them?"

"I don't know. I only know they were gone. The boys asked him about the photos once, but he said he didn't remember what had happened to them. I think he did it for them, because it was easier for them not to be reminded of what they had lost."

Or easier for him? I handed the photograph back.

"Did you ever have the feeling that Tobias felt guilty about his wife's death?" I asked. The question felt wrong as I asked it, but I couldn't suppress my curiosity.

But if Anna felt the same, she didn't mention it. "Guilty? No, not really. He always spoke of her death as a terrible tragedy, but he didn't blame himself, if that's what you think. At least, I never heard him say anything that would make me think so until this last week."

"And what did he say then?"

"It was only a passing comment. He said that he wished she had been able to see all of this, everything he had. It was a proud moment for him. He felt his life was full."

I let go of my questions about Helena Torstensen with a soft sigh. I had already pushed too far there. I checked my watch. It was getting close to the time we needed to leave. "Where is Tobias to be buried, then?" I asked.

"At the Draper City Cemetery. He bought a double plot some years ago. I think it's a little morbid, knowing there's a place waiting for me."

"I don't think it's morbid at all," I said. I had my own plot waiting for me in the same cemetery, right next to Kurt's. The baby had hardly taken up any space at all, and they had put her in Kurt's plot. Why his and not mine? I never knew the answer to that, and at the time, I hadn't been in any state to ask.

"Tobias said it was comforting, knowing where he would end up, and that I wouldn't have to worry about the money. He had it all paid for in advance. My funeral, too, when that happens. He used to imagine us having a double funeral together, but obviously, that's not the way it turned out."

A double funeral? "But you've years left to live," I said. She was only just past sixty. She could remarry, have a whole new life. Just because Tobias's heart had given out didn't mean Anna had to think of herself as nearly dead.

"I suppose so," said Anna. "I don't know what to do with the house, or the garden. I can't bear the thought of turning it all back to lawn, but I can't take care of it the way he did, either."

Anna was staring at the door, but she wasn't making a move to leave. Should I mention the time? No. She knew. Let her do this at her own pace. This was a difficult moment for her, becoming a widow.

I tried for something less sad. "He loved his tools and his garden, didn't he?"

Anna let out a small laugh. "He did at that. He kept a brand new hammer by his bedside, do you know that? I used to wonder if he got up in the middle of the night and worked on projects inside the house, but the hammer was never used. It looked as new the day he died as when we were first married."

"He had a hammer by the bed when you were married?" I said, feeling the hairs rise on the back of my scalp.

"The boys kept stuffed animals by their beds when they were younger. And Tobias had that hammer," said Anna. "I used to think he needed it for the same comfort that they did."

"Where is it now?"

"Still there, probably," said Anna.

"You should put it back in the shed," I said, the words sounding like they had been spoken by someone else. "With the other tools."

"I will, eventually."

I walked to the door, opened it and stepped outside. "Are you ready to go?" I asked, hearing the brusqueness in my voice.

She nodded and we drove toward the mortuary while I tried to convince myself that no man would have kept a hammer by his bed in order to make sure that he could kill his wife when he decided it was time for them to die together.

CHAPTER 19

A woman in a pencil skirt with her hair up in a severe knot showed us the way to the back of the mortuary, past the viewing rooms with chairs set up in neat rows, to a room where Tobias's body lay on a metal table.

"Oh!" said Anna, and she stepped back at the sight of him.

I stood behind her and put a hand on her shoulder. "Are you all right?"

The woman who had brought us here had already disappeared.

"Yes. It just gave me such a start. I thought for a moment —" She shook her head. "It's like him, and not like him at the same time. How very strange." She stepped closer to the body and looked it over carefully without touching it. There was a white sheet over the chest and the lower half of the body.

I was carrying the grey temple bag Anna had given me at the house. Inside it were all

269

the things we would need for this; I had checked before we left. The smell was strongly floral.

Anna pulled the sheet down a little. "His scar there," she said, pointing to a spot on his lower stomach.

I glanced at it and saw a long, puckered scar. "Do you know how he got it?" I asked.

Anna shook her head, then let out a long sigh. "We should get started," she said.

They had asked us to be finished by one o'clock so that they could make sure the body was transported to the chapel by two, when the funeral was supposed to start.

I put the temple bag on a chair near the body, opened the zipper and pulled out the garments. They were snowy white and soft cotton. Brand new, most likely, and not the threadbare, greying kind Kurt tended to wear, no matter how many times I suggested gently to him that it was time to buy new ones. Kurt seemed to think garments lasted forever, as if that were some kind of bonus blessing for those who wore them regularly and served God in them.

"Top first?" said Anna practically.

I bunched the top up around the neck and she lifted up Tobias's head as we pulled the fabric over it. Then it was my turn to lift up his arms. They felt so heavy and limp that I had a momentary flashback to my daughter's birth/death. They had handed her to me as soon as she was born, as they would have handed me a live child. She was small, but she felt heavy because she was not moving. Her limbs had felt like rubbery weights and her skin tone had been dark. I remember her fingernails in particular, and how dead and black they looked.

I got one of Tobias's arms through an armhole, then the other. Anna tugged down the shirt over Tobias's stomach. I had to help her lift his body so we could smooth down the back. I was breathing heavily with effort, but I nodded, glad we'd managed it by ourselves.

Anna got out the bottoms and pulled off the sheet that covered his lower half. I was happy to discover it wasn't embarrassing at all to see Tobias nude. It wasn't him anymore. It was just a shape of human flesh.

Anna wiped at her sweat and then we pulled the bottoms up to meet the top. Somehow that felt like half the battle. Tobias looked more himself now. She tucked the top in all around the waist.

I glanced at the nearly invisible white thread embroidery, a reminder of specific promises in the temple to follow God. There were three marks, two on the top and one on one leg. People make fun of Mormons' special underwear, and I could see why, although the underwear itself isn't so strange — there are new styles every few years to keep up with the expectations of each generation. We don't wear the ankle- and wrist-length garments our great-grandparents wore, and we don't have slits in the back for bathroom stops the way our parents and grandparents did.

There are stories about the mystical power of garments to keep people safe. I had heard about a man who was caught in a house fire. He went to the hospital to be treated and when they cut off his clothes, they found his skin under his garments untouched. There is a specific promise in the temple that protection to various body parts would be offered to those who keep their promises, signified by the marks in the garments. I had always believed it was a metaphorical protection, rather than a physical one. But who am I to tell other people their faith is wrong and foolish? If I believe in God even a little, I've already passed into the area of the unscientific.

I got out the rest of the clothes. We put on the white shirt, Anna carefully smoothing out the collar and buttoning each of the tiny buttons, even the ones on the wrist. We put on the white slacks, white socks and slippers. And then at last, the final temple garments: the green apron, white robe, hat, and sash.

When it was finished, Anna and I both leaned over the table and caught our breath.

"He looks handsome, doesn't he?" said Anna, stepping back.

He still looked dead, I thought.

"Thank you for coming with me and doing this with me."

"Of course," I said automatically.

"No." Anna grabbed my hand and pressed it to her face. "You are a true friend. To do this with me — of all things. I can't ever thank you enough." Her eyes glistened.

Startled by her sudden gesture, I said, "I'm glad that you were able to share it with me."

Anna looked at Tobias one last time, and then we walked out of the mortuary, stopping at the desk to tell the woman that Tobias was dressed for an open casket.

I drove Anna back to her house. "Do you want me to come in and stay until the funeral?" I asked.

She shook her head. "It's only a couple of hours. And Tomas and Liam wanted to talk to me privately, I think."

So I dropped her off and went home to

find Kurt was already there, dressing in his Sunday best. I changed and put on my own black funeral dress. I hadn't had one before I became the bishop's wife, but I attended every funeral in the ward now.

Since we had enough time, Kurt and I walked over to the church. I held his arm and I was glad to be with him, but we didn't talk. We never talked before or after funerals.

The church was open and we could hear the music coming from the organ in the chapel as we stepped in the back door. The chapel was nearly full, which meant there were over a hundred people here. I was surprised. I hadn't realized so many people cared for Tobias, especially since a Friday funeral required people to take time off work. Kurt went to the podium and I sat down in one of the front rows. In a few minutes, Anna came to sit by me, along with Tomas and Liam and their wives, who had flown in just that morning.

It was a nice service. Tomas and Liam both spoke. Tomas emphasized his father's love of order and how it emerged in the garden and in the way he disciplined his sons. He simply told them what he expected, and then told them he was disappointed if they didn't achieve it. Apparently,

Tomas felt that he frequently disappointed his father. He didn't say a word about his mother, Helena. He did mention a few tender moments he had seen between Tobias and Anna, and talked about how he aspired to have that kind of marriage with his own wife.

There was a short musical number, which someone else must have arranged, because it had nothing to do with the family. Two young women and two young men from our ward sang "How Great Thou Art" in four-part harmony. I wished I had less musical training when I heard them. I was jolted by some bad notes. But it was soon over, and it was Liam's turn to speak.

Liam began with, "I know that at a funeral, it's traditional to talk only about the best parts of the deceased's life. But I am not going to do that here. I am going to tell you all the worst parts of my father."

I turned to Anna, who had gone a little pale. I reached for her hand and patted it. "Kurt is up there. Kurt is in charge, as the bishop," I whispered to her. But to myself, I wondered what in God's name Liam thought he was doing. If he had a grievance with his father, now was not the time to air it in public.

"My father was a fierce man with a temper," said Liam.

The hammer, I thought, and squeezed Anna's hand more tightly. I could see Kurt edging forward on his seat.

"He got angry about many things. He was angry about evil in the world. He read the newspaper every morning and sometimes he would slam his fist down over injustice, or people being hurt." Liam looked down at Anna. "He would remind Tomas and me that he had better never hear of us hurting anyone, or we would regret it."

I was very tense.

"And then he would go out into the garden and he would attack the dirt as if it were those bad men he had read about. And he would water it, weed it, smooth out the dirt and make it perfect again."

I stared at the strength in Liam's hands as he mimed hacking into and then smoothing the dirt, and I thought again of the photo of the beautiful woman Anna had shown me. I thought of how gentle the Tobias I had known had always been, and how people are often different when they are alone. I also thought of the guilt that came from doing the wrong thing, and how it could transform an entire life.

"And then he would come back inside and be my father again," said Liam, "until he read the newspaper the next day, and he had to go out to his garden." He paused for a long moment. "Many people thought my father spent too much time in the garden. They might have wondered if he was neglecting us. But Tomas and I always knew. The garden was his place to be angry. And when he came back to us, he was finished with that. When the flowers grew, and when we picked the tomatoes fresh, they were what my father did with his anger. He felt more than most men, and he didn't try to stop feeling. But he found a way to use even his anger to make the world a more beautiful place."

Liam took a long, shuddering breath.

I realized that Anna's hand was trembling in mine, and my reservations about Liam's speech melted away.

"Another of my father's worst qualities was his way of forgetting. He had a terrible memory. Sometimes he forgot important things. Like the time he forgot to come in and spank me the way he said he would. He let me sit and wait for him for two hours, until I fell asleep. And in the morning, when I asked him if he was ever going to do it, he said he had forgotten.

"He forgot his anniversary with Anna one year, and he forgot her birthday. But for

Christmas that year, he bought her a new car because he was worried her old car might stall on the freeway and put her in danger." Liam was clearly struggling with his emotions. He kept wiping at his eyes, but never broke down completely. He had learned control from his father, I thought.

"He forgot once why he had started a lawsuit with an old friend and told the lawyer that he couldn't pursue in court a case he had forgotten everything about, could he?

"He forgot that he'd told me that I wouldn't get my driver's license until I finished my Eagle Scout project, and let me get it anyway; and he forgot that I was the one who had dented his door the first time I took his car out, and he always told everyone he had done it himself."

Anna was openly weeping at my side. I could see that Kurt was using a tissue on his eyes and nose, too.

"And the last flaw of my father was that he kept secrets. Terrible secrets. Every night when he tucked me into bed, he whispered into my ear that I was his favorite. He told me that I couldn't tell Tomas because it wasn't fair, that he wasn't supposed to pick favorites." He looked over at his brother and shared a tremulous smile.

"It wasn't until I was nearly a teenager that I realized that he told Tomas the same thing every night, that Tomas was his favorite. So I suppose that's another of my father's worst parts that I wasn't counting. He was a liar. He told me once that he would never leave me, and now he's a liar about that, too." He began to sob and Kurt had to help him back to his seat.

The room was utterly silent, except for sniffling sounds and the rustling of tissues.

Then it was Kurt's turn to speak. He read from the Book of Mormon about where the righteous go after death, which was to either immediate resurrection or a place of rest where they could be with God. Then he, too, spoke of Tobias's garden: "I have no doubt that Tobias will find some way to garden in heaven. Only there the plants he grows will be souls, because Tobias was always good at seeing the soul behind any action. He knew that gardens weren't about dirt any more than people were about sin. You have to touch the dirt to work in it, but you clean yourself afterward and you watch what grows from your work." He mimed washing his hands and held them up to the audience. I felt enormously proud of Kurt at that moment. My husband and my bishop, both.

279

Kurt finished with some words about how glad he was that he'd had a chance to know Tobias and that he was honored to be his bishop. Then he closed the service and invited people to stay for the luncheon.

Anna and Tomas and Liam would drive to the cemetery and Kurt would do a simple grave dedication there, then they would all come back and try to enjoy the company of the ward members who loved them while sharing a late luncheon prepared by the Relief Society.

I helped Anna to the car waiting for her, and then went into the kitchen to find Cheri Tate hard at work. She was supervising the warming of funeral potatoes and counting out cups with punch in them to be taken on a dolly to the cultural hall and distributed around the tables that had already been put up.

"What can I do to help?" I asked her.

She assigned me to organize the dessert table and make sure everything had been cut up properly so people could serve themselves.

I went out to the cultural hall and found Gwen Ferris was there.

"I didn't know you knew Tobias," I said.

"I didn't," said Gwen. "But I know Anna. She and I worked on the homemaking committee together last year. She is such a wonderful person, I had to come and show my support for her here."

"That's kind of you," I said, thinking that Gwen had her own problems to deal with, whatever they were. But they say service helps you forget yourself.

Forgetting, I thought. Secrets and anger. What did Liam's talk about Tobias really mean? At the time, I had been mostly concerned about Anna's feelings and the funeral itself, but as I went over his points about his father, it worried me more than it comforted me.

"I wish I had known Tobias better. He sounds like a wonderful father," said Gwen, helping me set out serving utensils and then small plates at each dessert.

"Mmm," I said.

"Do you think that Brad would ever be like that?" asked Gwen.

I had to shake myself to process the question. "Brad seems like a wonderful man," I said, remembering my conversation with him in Kurt's office. I should be focusing on Gwen here, not my own wandering thoughts about Tobias. Tobias was gone, but Gwen was here. "How are things between you?"

"Fine. Good," said Gwen. "I mean, we

have our problems, but Brad is such a good man. I'm so lucky to have found him." She looked away, focusing on the dessert plates.

"He loves you very much," I said.

She nodded. "I love him, too. I wish —" She cut herself off, though I wanted very much to know what she wished.

"Things are going to be all right," I told her.

She jerked her head up to look at me. "How do you know?" she asked.

"I don't know anything about the details," I said, meeting her eyes. "I just mean that I believe God loves us and that whatever He asks us to suffer, we can find meaning in it. I hope that doesn't sound glib."

"I'll think about that," Gwen said slowly. "I've heard people say that God never gives us more than we can handle, but there are days —"

I interrupted her. "I hate that saying, as if God is playing some game with us, or as if we are making too much out of little things. I believe that God weeps with us, the way that a parent weeps with a child over a lost friend. He may know that we will recover, but that doesn't make our losses any less."

After a moment, I realized my words had affected Gwen deeply. She was staring at me as if there was light streaming around me. What a thought. I wasn't any holier than anyone else. If anything, less so. But once again, there was a marvelous sense of power in helping others, in being the tool in God's hands.

"I never thought of Him weeping with us," she said.

"Most important scripture of all time: Jesus wept," I said.

"Sometimes I feel so selfish, getting upset over little stupid things," Gwen said, her gaze dropping again. "They aren't the things Jesus should have to weep with me about."

"If we're weeping over it, then it's not little to us," I said.

Cheri Tate called me from the kitchen, and I went to her. I ended up spending most of the rest of the afternoon running back and forth and I didn't have a chance to see Gwen Ferris again. She must have left as soon as the luncheon was served.

Cheri and I stayed late cleaning up. Kurt made sure Anna got home with her sons and then had to go back to the office to get some things done. I called Samuel at seven to make sure he was all right and could find himself dinner with leftovers in the fridge, then I helped Cheri until we locked up at about nine.

We had to get all the garbage out to the

dumpster, turn off every light, vacuum all the floors, and clean the bathrooms. And that was after we had finished in the kitchen, washing every dish by hand because there was no dishwasher, and then drying them and placing them back in the cupboards. Wiping down every counter, and then mopping the floors, cleaning out the refrigerator, scrubbing the stove tops and inside the oven. There was a long list laminated on the back door of the kitchen that detailed every chore to be done before we could lock up.

"How are Perdita and Jonathan?" I asked Cheri as we walked out to her car.

"They seem very happy," said Cheri, as if she were surprised.

"I'm glad," I said, and walked home despite Cheri's offer of a ride. I was glad to breathe the fresh spring air and I didn't even mind the hill that led to the Torstensen house. The lights were on inside and I was tempted to stop in, but Anna and I had both had a long day. I'd talk to her tomorrow, and I'd get out of my head all thoughts of hammers, blood, and bodies buried in gardens.

CHAPTER 20

On the Monday after Tobias Torstensen's funeral, the brief thaw ended and snow began to fall again. In the midst of it, Jared Helm went in to talk to the police in a formal interview. His father went with him, along with a lawyer his father had hired. To my delight, I was asked to watch Kelly while Jared and his father were gone.

It was nearly lunchtime, so I made Kelly peanut butter sandwiches and apple slices, which she ate eagerly.

"Grandpa Alex says I should eat grown-up food," said Kelly, when I cut off the crust of her sandwiches. "He said Mommy treated me like a baby."

How dare that man say such a thing to such a vulnerable, hurting child? "I see," I said, trying to speak with care and not frighten her. "It sounds like your grandpa, Alex, and your mother didn't get along very well."

Kelly shook her head solemnly. "Mommy and Grandpa Alex used to shout at each other."

"Did they frighten you?" I asked.

She shrugged. "Daddy kept me safe."

"Good, I'm glad." Jared Helm was good for something, it seemed.

I got Kelly a glass of lemonade and watched her make a face each time she took a sip.

"Sour," she said when I asked her if she didn't like it.

"Do you want me to make you something else instead?" I asked, thinking I should have made grape juice.

She looked at me steadily. "I like sour," she said, but she kept making the same face and shivering when she took a sip. It was adorable and a little heartbreaking, to see a little girl who seemed to think shivering like that meant she liked it.

But when I told her it was time to clean up lunch, she spilled lemonade on her shirt hurrying to drink it down. So I took her upstairs and asked her to show me what she wanted to change into. "Grandpa Alex will be mad," she said softly.

"Why?"

"He does the laundry. He doesn't like to do extra laundry," she said.

"Oh, then I'll do a load before he gets back. He'll never know."

She took off her shirt and opened one of her drawers. It was carefully stacked with folded shirts. Even her sock drawer, which I opened, was divided with plastic bins into white socks, dark socks, and socks with stripes. Her underwear was similarly divided. And her closet was organized by color of dresses, from yellow to red to blue and purple.

"Did Grandpa Alex arrange your closet, too?" I asked.

She nodded. "He likes things neat," she said.

Neat was one word for it. "All right. I'm going to go put in that load of laundry. Why don't you sit here and read a book for a few minutes, okay?" I settled her next to me on her bed with several books. At the touch of her warm body, I felt another surge of that emotion I'd felt when she played the piano with me. It felt like the whisper of the Spirit was saying, She is yours. She belongs with you.

I hugged Kelly tightly and I felt her arms wrap around me and hug me just as tightly. Did she imagine for just a moment that I was her mother, as I was imagining for just a moment that she was my daughter? I was a great deal rounder than her mother, and old enough to be her grandmother. And she was too young to be my daughter, if my daughter had lived. But I had missed the small arm years, and maybe those were the parts I wished to have back the most.

Maybe that is why other women like the idea of having their children back to raise again at the age they lost them. It never works that way, though, does it? We can't have any children back, no matter how much we miss them. Time marches on, even for the eternal. We have to find new children to love, grandchildren or other replacements, if we want to continue to be mothers.

"Mommy likes books," said Kelly, pulling back and looking at me curiously. "She reads lots of books to me. But sometimes she cries when she reads them."

"Oh? Did she read you sad books?" I asked.

"No. Books her daddy read to her when she was little."

Was Carrie so unstable that she often cried in front of Kelly, or was she just nostalgic for her own childhood?

"Which do you want me to read to you first?" I asked Kelly.

"I will read it to you," said Kelly. "So I

can show you the right way to do it."

I didn't know if she had already learned to read so well or if she had simply memorized the stories, but she read with a great deal of emotion. She read through *Pig Pigger Piggest* and even did voices for each of the pigs and witches. I was impressed. "Did your mother teach you how to do that?" I asked.

"Yes," Kelly said.

"Well, I think those voices you did are so cute."

Kelly looked at me as if I was crazy. "You *have* to do voices, to make the story fun."

She was a special child. She had a light in her, a talent for life and for learning. It was electric, and it sparked on me whenever I was with her.

Kelly fell asleep on the last page, and I had to tug the book away from her. I tiptoed out of the room to leave her undisturbed, then went upstairs into the master bedroom on the top of the split-level house, nervous and determined. I opened the door and saw a room that was magazine perfect. The bed was made, decorative pillows and all. The curtains had been pulled back to let in the light. There wasn't a hint of dust anywhere. There was one double dresser on the near side of the wall, and on top of it was a photograph, not of Carrie and Jared Helm, but of Grandpa Alex and Kelly.

The police had searched the car and the house already, but they weren't looking for the same things that I was. They wanted evidence that Carrie might have been killed. I wanted evidence that she'd ever lived here. I wanted to know Carrie Helm's story.

I opened a drawer and found nothing but male clothing on the right hand side. The left hand side of all the drawers was empty.

Where had it all gone? Had I missed the chance to find anything useful about Carrie? Surely, her father-in-law could not have erased all trace of her.

I went into the master bathroom and looked in the left cabinet for Carrie's makeup, but that, too, was gone. There was a toothbrush and a man's razor — presumably Grandpa Alex's, because Jared's were in the right cabinet. Was Alex staying in this room with his son now? That seemed a little strange, to say the least.

I looked for laundry, which was the reason I was supposed to be here, making up a load. But I couldn't find any dirty clothes, either.

I backed out of the room and put Kelly's things in the dryer. Then I went downstairs and searched through the lower levels of the house. There was a family room off the garage, then below that an unfinished basement, and that was where I found garbage bags full of Carrie's things. The clothing I was less interested in, but there was a bag of her photos and other memorabilia, a wedding album that, strangely enough, had not a single photo of Alex Helm in it that I could see, and a cheap, flip-top cell phone.

There was also a stack of picture books, including a well-worn copy of *Harry the Dirty Dog,* which made me feel a pang of sadness at Kelly's loss. I couldn't bring it up to her now. Her grandfather would just put it away again, and likely be angry at Kelly, even if it was my fault. I held the book for a long moment. But the cell phone was far more important.

I tucked it into my pocket and left everything else as I had found it, or at least as close as I could manage. After seeing the rest of the house so carefully organized, I wondered if Alex Helm would notice someone had been down here.

The cell phone was out of battery, but when I got home, I would ask Samuel if he could find the right connector to charge it. Samuel was good at that sort of thing, and he wouldn't tell Kurt about it if I asked him not to. I had no idea what Kurt would say if

I told him about any of this, but I didn't regret what I had done.

A few minutes later, I heard the sounds of Kelly stirring in her room. I went up and gave her a hug.

"I don't like taking naps," she said. She frowned at me as if to prove it. "I'm getting too old for so much sleeping."

"I like naps whenever I get enough time to take them, and I'm a lot older than you are."

"Really?" said Kelly.

I nodded and took her downstairs to the kitchen. I got her a glass of water and then we sat together on the couch. "Kelly, tell me about Grandpa Alex," I said.

"He is Daddy's daddy," she said. She put a thumb close to her mouth, and then pulled it away with a guilty expression.

"Yes, I know that, sweetheart. What else can you tell me about him? You said that he shouted at your mother sometimes. Do you remember anything else?"

"Once I saw him hit Daddy," said Kelly quietly.

"What?" I went very still. "When did that happen?"

"When he first came, after Mommy left. He said that Daddy had to learn to be strong." She wrapped her arms around herself and tucked her head into them.

"Kelly, has he ever hit you?" I asked, ready to take her into my arms and haul her to my own house immediately. I would take her to DCFS and report Alex Helm to them as an abuser and he would never *ever* see Kelly again.

But Kelly shook her head.

"What about your mother? Did you ever see Grandpa Alex hit her?" Could his father have killed Carrie without Jared's colluding in it? Could Alex have been behind the phone call I still thought might be fake?

It was horrible to think about. Maybe Jared Helm was as much a victim in all of this as Carrie had been.

"She didn't let him come over unless Daddy was here," said Kelly.

But Carrie had left Kelly behind for Alex now.

And what about me? Was I going to leave Kelly with her grandfather when he returned?

I had no legal right to her. I was not her mother, no matter how much I wished I were. I had a family of my own, and I belonged to them, not to her. It was crazy for me to think of doing anything to save Kelly when it would cost my own family dearly.

With those depressing thoughts in my mind, I heard a car drive up outside. Then there were voices, reporters calling out questions to Jared Helm. The only voice I heard respond was his father's, harsh and low.

Then the door from the garage to the family room opened on the half-level below us.

"Kelly?" said Jared Helm.

"Daddy!" She jumped up off the couch, then hesitated, looking at her grandfather.

"Come give your father a hug," said Alex Helm.

Kelly moved down the half set of stairs obediently and hugged her father. There was a possessiveness in Alex's eyes that made me twinge.

"How did it go?" I asked.

"Fine," said Alex Helm.

Jared Helm met my eyes. "They asked about me dropping her off at the bus station and why we went so early."

"I told you, they're trying to get proof you killed her," said Alex Helm.

Jared flinched at that and stared at Kelly, whose eyes had gone wide. "Don't say things like that around Kelly," he said softly.

"She needs to hear the truth, too," said Alex Helm. "No point in raising a girl who can't hear the truth."

294

The moment I heard his voice, I was ready to slap him again. Did the man have no softer side at all? Was he always a bombastic asshole? "She's five years old," I said. "Maybe some truths could be softened a little for her."

Alex Helm glared at me. "You are not her parent," he said.

"And neither are you," I snipped back.

"I am her grandparent," he said. "And I think that gives me the power to tell you it is time you were gone."

I looked at Jared, thinking he must see his father truly now. But Alex had come to help him when the rest of the world had written him off.

"Of course, Dad. You're right," Jared muttered, not meeting my eyes. "Thank you for watching Kelly while I was gone, Sister Wallheim. We'll take care of things from here on out."

I could make a fuss and confuse Kelly or I could go cleanly. I chose the latter. "Goodbye, sweetie," I said.

She blew me a kiss. As I walked out, I felt the weight of the cell phone in my pocket, the prize I had wrested from Alex Helm without his knowing about it.

As soon as I was away from the news vans, I started to run, partly in fear and partly in excitement at my successful theft. It has been years since I ran. It felt awkward, and I could feel my breasts thumping against my chest, and my flesh jiggling around me. I should have better shoes to do this, I thought. I should have a better body. But I only had the body that I had worked to get, and it was all the fresh cinnamon rolls that had brought me to this. The cell phone felt heavier than it should have. I slid on one icy patch of sidewalk and nearly fell, but caught myself, took a couple of walking steps, and started running again. I didn't turn back to see if Alex Helm was watching me from his living-room window.

When I got home, my fingers were trembling. I checked that the bolt on the front door was locked three times over and then went into my bedroom and locked that door, too. At every sound I worried Alex Helm had come to my house to demand the phone back. My anxiety fed my imagination, and I kept thinking that a creak of the floor meant he had somehow come inside, that he would be brandishing a hammer.

Finally, Samuel came home. I showed him the phone and asked him if he had an adapter for it. He went to his room and poked around for a while, then returned with a cable. For the next several minutes, I waited anxiously as Samuel plugged it in. "Are you sure it will turn back on?"

"Just give it a minute," said Samuel.

Then the phone beeped and I jumped.

"Mom, what's on that phone?" he asked. "It isn't yours, is it?"

"It's Carrie Helm's," I said. "Please don't tell your father."

Samuel's eyes went wide. "Are you sure you know what you're doing?"

I nodded. "A woman's life is at stake here," I said.

He stared at me, then shook his head. "I don't want to know anything more about it, then."

He was right. I had been unfair to put him between me and Kurt.

I checked the phone anxiously for several minutes, until it had charged enough for me to thumb through old calls . . . Mostly calls to Jared Helm's cell phone, and to the family home phone. I was surprised at how few numbers were listed. There was Alex Helm's number, but I couldn't find it in Carrie's outgoing call record; she had never called it, though she had missed multiple calls from him.

But there were also three phone calls to a Nevada area code.

I punched in the number and waited for

an answer. A male voice picked up, and I was startled for a moment until I realized it had gone to voicemail. The voice said that the man's name was Will. The same Will who had picked up the now-dumped cell phone? It sounded like him, but I wasn't sure. I would have to try back later.

CHAPTER 21

That night, the news revealed that Carrie Helm had purchased a bus ticket from Salt Lake City to Las Vegas early on the morning of her disappearance. There was grainy security camera footage of her buying the ticket, and the clear image of her family car in the background. And her husband, Jared, standing behind her, wearing a thick coat with the hood thrown back so his face was visible.

Jared had given a brief interview to reporters outside the police station as he left, and I could see his father hovering in the background as if to make sure he stayed on script.

"Yes, I took my wife to the bus station. And yes, I lied about not knowing where she had gone." His words were dull and emotionless, not what you would expect of someone who was truly remorseful about concealing the truth.

"Why did you lie?" a reporter asked.

"I lied because I was embarrassed that she was leaving me." He didn't look embarrassed. There was a flicker of something — possibly anger — in his eyes. But it was quickly tamped down. "I also thought it would be more difficult for Kelly if she knew her mother had gone willingly."

"And what about the cost of the investigation for the police?"

Jared glanced back at his father, and seemed to swallow hard. "I never wanted the police involved in this. It was her parents who did that. They are the ones who are at fault for making this more than it might have been."

Their fault and mine, I thought. Carrie Helm had apparently wanted to disappear quietly.

And what about Carrie Helm herself? Why hadn't she contacted the police herself? Or her parents? Or her daughter? Or Kurt? She could have done any number of things to save us all this anxiety and pain, and she hadn't. She hadn't looked back.

Maybe she was truly as selfish as Jared and Alex Helm claimed. All the anger I felt for them was now directed at Carrie instead.

"But you could have told the police the truth from the start," said a reporter. "Are you going to face charges for misleading an official investigation?"

"I did what Carrie asked me to do," said Jared. "And I never lied to the police. Not directly." He glanced back at his father again.

"And why did she leave without taking anything? Not her purse or phone or even some extra clothes?" another reporter asked, this one a woman.

That was the right question, I thought. I stared more closely at Jared on the screen, and found that my anger was dissipating. Maybe I was just too tired to feel it anymore. "She felt that she didn't deserve to take anything away from the marriage if she was leaving it," said Jared.

"You didn't make it a condition of her leaving peacefully that she give up everything?"

Jared shook his head. "Of course not. I wouldn't have done that. She said she wanted a new start. She said she didn't want any reminders of her old life."

"What about her young daughter? She didn't ask for a custody arrangement?" asked the female reporter.

"She trusted me to take care of Kelly," said Jared. "She knows I love our daughter very much."

"And what about her parents, who say that you abused her and that she wanted to escape from you because of that abuse?"

I saw a flash of Alex Helm in Jared as he turned angrily and stepped toward the reporter. But he stopped himself and took a breath, then said through gritted teeth, "I loved Carrie. She chose to leave despite my wishes. But it wasn't because I threatened her. And it wasn't because she feared for her life or for Kelly's. That's the end of this conference. Thank you," he said, and got into his car.

I turned off the television and thought about what I had seen in those garbage bags in the basement. Would any woman really leave that much of her life behind?

I had to find out the truth. I called the Nevada number I'd found on her cell phone over and over again that day and the next, always getting the voicemail. Then, at last, Will answered. Just my luck that it was Wednesday night and Kurt wasn't involved in something at the church. He came into the front room just as I was saying, "Hello. Is this Will?" I was hoping the man wouldn't immediately hang up and get rid of this phone, the way someone had gotten rid of the cell phone Carrie had called Kelly on.

"Yeah. Who's this?"

"Linda Wallheim. I'm a friend of Carrie Helm's," I said, staring at Kurt. So much for keeping secrets.

"Carrie Helm?" he said. "Um, I don't think I know anyone by that name." His tone was defensive.

And it should be. This was the same voice I'd said all this to before. "Well, that's interesting, because she has this number on her cell phone. She's been missing for over a month now. She's a wife and mother from Draper, Utah. You may have seen her on the news." I didn't know if anything about her disappearance had gone on national news, but it might have. "And also you and I talked on the phone just a few days ago."

"Hmmm. Well," he said.

This had to mean Carrie really had called Kelly that day, that she was in Las Vegas just as Jared had claimed. "Can I talk to Carrie, please?" I asked.

"Sorry, but she's not here right now."

"Are you just saying that to get me off the phone? Because I'm going to keep calling back if I have to, and you may end up with a visit from the police if they can trace this phone to your address. Is that what you want?"

Kurt had seated himself on the couch. I

303

was acutely aware of him there, watching me work my way into more secrets. Other people's secrets.

"Look, she was here, but she's not anymore. You've got to believe me."

"Why should I believe you?" I asked.

I was just a middle-aged woman a state away, but somehow I'd frightened him. "I swear, it's the truth," he said. "Please, don't keep calling me. I can't take it anymore."

"Then you need to get Carrie to come home and answer some questions. Make sure she appears on TV so that people know that she hasn't been harmed." Kurt was trying to tell me something in sign language. I turned away. He was distracting me and I needed my focus.

"Harmed?" asked Will. "You mean by me? But that's the whole reason she came here, so that she would feel safe."

"Was her husband threatening her life?" I asked.

"Was she still married? She told me he was her ex."

Ex-husband? My suspicions about Jared Helm cooled and my suspicions of Carrie rose to boiling. "They're still married," I said. "Legally, anyway."

Will swore.

"And she has a daughter. A five-year-old.

Kelly. Did she tell you that?"

He swore again. "No," he said. "She didn't tell me that either."

"So you can see that Carrie needs to come back. If she wants a divorce, she needs to get one legally. And she needs to deal with custody issues. Even if she doesn't want to see her daughter, she should legally give over her rights so that there are no questions."

He sighed. "Well, good riddance to the bitch."

The disdain in his voice seemed to echo Alex Helm's, and I cringed. Had Carrie gone from the frying pan into the fire? "What do you mean by good riddance?" He'd said she was gone, but I'd thought he was prevaricating.

"All her crazy — it's nothing to do with me anymore. She's gone. She left last night, while I was asleep. She didn't tell me she was leaving. She didn't leave a note or nothing. She just disappeared. So good riddance, like I said."

She had disappeared again, I thought. This was starting to sound like Carrie Helm's M.O.

"Did she say anything about why she was leaving?" I asked. Was it because of the television news coverage? "Or where she was going?"

"I didn't ask her to come here in the first place, you know. She just showed up, and it wasn't a fun time. But I was trying to be the good guy. And then she just disappeared like that. Proves she never cared about anyone but herself."

The more he talked, the less he sounded like the kind of person Carrie should have expected to help her. What had she been thinking? Was this proof of desperation or real mental illness?

"Did you call the police?" I asked. "Are you at all concerned that something might have happened to her?" She hadn't come back home, as far as I knew. Maybe she would appear any moment and the news vans would get the story of the day. Or maybe she had moved on to another man, another cell phone, another city where she could get lost.

"Why would I call the police?" he said. "It isn't as if we were married. I don't even know that much about her."

Clearly. I was getting the sense that sex with a random woman who needed a place to stay was par for the course for this guy.

"Now, I've got to go —" he began.

How was I going to keep him talking? I

could see Kurt giving me a baleful look, but I wasn't finished yet. He was just going to have to wait his turn to yell at me.

"You don't want anyone to think that you had something to do with whatever happens to her next, do you?" I asked.

"I didn't do anything!" he said, his tone strained.

"Of course you didn't. But that's not how it might look to others, especially if she gets into trouble. Do you know if she was involved with drugs? Or if she had financial problems?" I was racking my brain, trying to think of reasons that Carrie was behaving this way, and at the same time trying to make sure Will didn't hang up.

"I didn't see any drugs while she was here, but she claimed she didn't have a credit card and she didn't bring any money. Like I said, she was all about what she needed from me."

"Did she tell you anything that might be useful in trying to track her down and make sure she isn't hurt?"

"She didn't tell me anything that wasn't a lie, or so it sounds like from what you're saying. She wasn't anything like she seemed online. She was always wanting to stay inside, keeping blinds closed, and refusing to talk."

"You met her online? How long have you known her?"

"About two years, I guess," he said.

And how much of that did Jared Helm know about? Did that affect the way he'd reacted when she asked him to drop her off at the bus station? Was that the reason he hadn't let her take anything with him? Had he forced her to cut herself off from her daughter?

I kept hearing Alex Helm's voice in my ears, the word "whore" echoing. If she'd had a relationship with another man while she was married, it might not matter to him whether or not it involved actual physical sex.

"Did you meet in person before she came to stay with you?" I asked.

"A few times," he said.

So. There it was. This was who Carrie had become, or maybe who she had always been. I wouldn't call her a whore, but I hated the thought that Alex Helm might have seen some truth about her that I had not.

She was alive, I kept telling myself. That was the important thing. But it seemed that Jared was more and more the wronged husband here, just as he had always claimed.

"And she left recently?" I asked.

"Last night. And I really don't want to talk to the police about this. Or her husband."

Of course he didn't.

I thanked him briefly, made no promises, and hung up. The cell phone beeped at me that its battery was low again, and I went upstairs to plug it in.

When I came back down, Kurt was waiting for me in the kitchen with some lemonade. "You know we have to tell the police what you found out. They need to know where she's been all this time," he said. "And that she's not in danger. Her parents need to know."

"It will only make it look worse for Carrie," I said.

"You mean like Jared looks right now?" said Kurt.

I thought about it, but in the end, it was the image of Kelly's face that decided me. It was Kelly who was the most vulnerable. Carrie was an adult, or at least she ought to be one. After what I'd found out, I couldn't see her as the victim.

"She isn't there anymore," I said. "In Las Vegas."

"But she was there? Since she disappeared?" said Kurt.

I nodded. "It sounded like she went to

him as soon as she got off the bus." Though I hadn't asked Will that directly.

"Then we have to tell the police. We have to give them the cell phone you found. Where did you find it, by the way?" said Kurt. His eyes narrowed.

"In the basement of the Helm home when I went over there yesterday. All her things have been bagged up," I said. And somehow the police hadn't found it. Had they not been looking very hard?

"Hmm," said Kurt. "That makes it trickier. The police might not be able to use it as evidence if it was stolen."

Irrationally, I was annoyed with Kurt. Why did he have to take my victory away from me? "I'll take it back," I said. "And after that video footage of Carrie getting on the bus, no one thinks she is dead anymore."

"What about her parents?"

"I'll call them," I said. "Just give me a little time."

"All right, Linda. You know I trust you," he said, and I was glad he didn't add the proviso, "most of the time," which I was sure he must be thinking.

He went to bed, and seemed to expect that I'd do what he said on Thursday. But I didn't. I kept the phone and I didn't call the Westons. Not yet. I just felt this niggling sense that things weren't quite what they seemed to be. Or maybe it was that I wanted Carrie to be better than she was. She'd been a good mother, I thought, and she'd been an interesting thinker. I hated to imagine that I had been so duped, and it was worse somehow to be duped by another woman than by a man.

Friday morning, while Kurt was at work, I watched the news. It was a rather lurid report, late-breaking, with innuendos and nasty laughter from the reporters. Jared Helm had been cleared of any wrongdoing in his wife's disappearance, and Carrie Helm had been with a lover in Las Vegas. After this revelation, which had had nothing to do with me or Carrie's cell phone, the police were no longer actively searching for her or information about her.

The news vans slowly pulled away from the Helm house and by afternoon, when we came home from church, Jared, Kelly, and Alex were free.

By the time Kurt came home that night, I found that my annoyance toward him had dissipated considerably. I kissed him good-night and let him hold me for a long time in bed. Then I turned over and thought about what I had to do now. Did I give up and let Carrie live with the consequences of her own bad behavior? I might have been tempted by the thought, except that there was still Kelly. And for all that Jared Helm might have reason to complain about his wife, I did not think that Alex Helm was a hero here. He had called Carrie a whore and I wondered how much he had pushed her into it with his attitude about women. What I wanted most now was the assurance that Kelly was safe.

CHAPTER 22

Anna Torstensen called me Monday afternoon to ask me if she could come over. A few minutes later, I opened the door and let her into the front room. She seemed full of energy, which I rather envied after the exhausting time I'd had dealing with the Helms. She was carrying a manila file folder and spread it out in front of me on the coffee table.

"I found these papers," she said, tapping at them vigorously, "after I talked to Tobias's lawyer. He claimed that Tobias had never revised his will from before we were married. But he has an address listed on some of Tobias's correspondence that he thinks is Tobias's first wife."

"What?" I said.

She nodded, and I realized that I had misinterpreted her energy. She was shaking with anger and fear, not joy. "He says that half of the money could potentially go to

313

her, if she is still alive." Her voice was moving all over, up and down. "He also said that it's possible that if she is still alive, Tobias's marriage to me is illegal and that she could claim that all of his money is hers. That my marriage to him was bigamous because there was never any divorce."

I was stunned. "She can't be alive, surely." The hammer with hair on it. The dress with blood on it. The odd gravestone in the garden. Had I misunderstood all of it?

"The lawyer had photos of her, and several letters. It sounds like she talked about coming back home at some point, when the boys were older and she could explain where she had been."

"Where had she been?" I asked.

She pushed one of the pages at me, neatly written in nice school-teacher loops. "She was in California, I guess."

"But why?" Why any of this? Why would she leave her sons so mysteriously? I scanned the letter, but there was no answer there. It was just kind words about coming home and how much she missed Tobias and the boys, and how sorry she was. Was that what a woman who felt guilty about leaving would write? Was it what Carrie Helm would write if she had to explain herself to Kelly?

"Even if she's dead now, my marriage to Tobias wouldn't have been legal at the time. I can't inherit because there's no common law wife statute in Utah."

"I'm so sorry," I said. I knew she didn't care about money or even the house. The boys would let her stay in it anyway. But the humiliation and disrespect she must feel — and she had to deal with it at the same time as her grief. So unfair.

Anna was pacing in a short line, up and down the small space of my front room. "He was even corresponding with her two years after he and I were married. And yet he never said a word to me about her being alive or coming back into his life. He didn't say anything about needing to get a divorce." She stopped pacing and threw up her arms. "What kind of man does that?"

I took the moment to draw her down to sit on the couch. "I don't know. I'm sure you feel very confused." Though in a way, this made more sense out of the fact that Tobias hadn't wanted to be sealed to Anna. He must have known that the more scrutiny he brought to himself and his marriages, the more likelihood there was that his deception would be discovered.

In order for a couple to be granted a temple divorce, a lot of paperwork has to be filled out, and often the couple has to wait a year. The First Presidency of the church has to approve it officially, and while I don't know exactly how much personal supervision that entails, it isn't a rubber-stamping process. The Mormon church wants to make sure people take marriage seriously, both before and after making their covenants.

"I feel so betrayed." Anna stared out the window, as if she couldn't bear to look me in the face.

"Of course you do. You were betrayed."

"Do you think he was planning to divorce me and remarry her all along?" she asked desperately.

I patted her hands. "No, I'm sure he wouldn't have done that. He was in love with you. And besides, she had left him once. Why would he give her a chance to do it again?" I paused, thinking. "It must have been for the boys. Were they having a particularly hard time when all this happened? Can you remember?"

I must have said the right thing because Anna turned back to me, her eyes glistening. "Oh, yes," she said. "How could I have forgotten? The first year Tobias and I were married, Tomas and Liam got along very well with me. But the second year — Liam was so angry with me. He would try to push me out of the room when we were all together. He refused to call me Mom or even Anna. I was 'her' or 'the lady.' " She was smiling at this old memory, instead of feeling hurt. That said a lot about her and how she was capable of moving past hurt. I hoped it would serve her well in this.

"He wouldn't eat any food that I made for him," Anna went on nostalgically. "If I served him dinner, he would get up and make himself a peanut butter sandwich, or just starve. And then he started to spit in my food, or put dirt in my side of the bed. He poured honey in between the keys of the new piano Tobias bought for my birthday. He was such a terror. Every time I turned my head, he was off doing something naughty."

"And that's when Tobias was writing to Helena?" I asked.

She looked down at the letters and held up one of them, underlining the date, November 1985. "Maybe he was just trying to find her for the boys. Poor Liam. I don't think it would have helped him at all if his mother had returned. He would have hated her just as much as he hated me. Possibly more. But I can see how Tobias might have thought differently."

317

I couldn't help but think of Kelly Helm. If Carrie came back, how would it affect her? Carrie had been gone too long for there to be no changes in their relationship. When a mother abandons you, you can't simply take her back like that. You can't forget that she left and go on like you weren't afraid she would go away again.

But Anna's expression had darkened again. "What about all those years I spent with Tobias? I was his mistress, not his wife. We were living in sin all that time."

"You didn't know," I said. "I'm sure no one could hold you responsible." But that didn't mean their family wouldn't be torn apart by the truth.

"But what will happen to Tobias?" asked Anna.

"You mean, will he face excommunication posthumously?" That wasn't something the church bothered with much, though there were occasions when people's records were reinstated posthumously.

"And how will I tell the boys?" Anna went on.

Anna wasn't at fault for any of this. But that didn't mean her sons wouldn't blame her. How could Tobias leave this for her to deal with after he was gone?

And then a thought occurred to me. "Can

318

I see the photos of this woman the lawyer showed you? I'm curious."

Anna looked through the piles and handed me some of the photos, all of a woman alone, on the beach or next to a building with blue skies overhead. I compared them to the wedding photo, which Anna had also tucked into the envelope, whether in anger or because she had also compared the faces.

The women were superficially quite similar: dark-haired, petite, with slightly pointed chins. But the eyes did not look at all the same to me. And the nose was certainly not the same. The Helena in the wedding photograph had a tiny, button nose. The other woman's nose was rather large for her face and it had a bump on it, as if it had been broken at some point.

I let out a long breath and tapped the photo of the other woman. This wasn't about bigamy.

"What is it?" said Anna.

I held out the two most distinct photographs. "Do you really think that's the same woman?"

"I already looked at them. I thought it was." She stared down at them again. "I don't know," she said softly. "She would have gotten older. Life might have been hard on her." She touched the second

319

picture, her fingertip landing on the bump. "It looks like her nose was broken."

"But the nose is too big. Your nose doesn't get bigger as you age. Not that much bigger, anyway."

"Hmm," said Anna. "I see what you mean." She looked at the photo more closely. "Maybe she had plastic surgery or something."

"To make her nose larger?" It certainly wasn't what most women wanted.

"Maybe she was trying to hide her identity. Make sure that Tobias and the boys couldn't find her." I could tell even she didn't believe what she was saying.

"It doesn't sound in the letter like she was trying to hide."

"What do you think it all means?" asked Anna.

I was making an enormous leap, but what if sometime soon after his marriage to Anna, Tobias had in a moment of doubt found a woman who looked like his deceased wife and had tried to use her to pretend that Helena was still alive? Then Anna and Tobias had been legally married all along, and the only sin here had been Tobias's wishful thinking. Cautiously, I laid out this theory for Anna.

"So, she would have to prove she is actually Helena in order to get anything," I said, nodding at the newer photograph of the woman with the big nose.

"I suppose. The lawyer is going to send a private detective out."

"But if she isn't Helena, then Tobias didn't deceive you, right?"

"I don't know," said Anna. "It seems so far-fetched." She had her hands balled up now.

"More than Tobias lying to you all these years and pretending his wife was dead?" Or my imagined history of him killing his own wife and burying her in the backyard? Surely this was the least difficult version of his life to believe in.

"Do you need anything while the will is in probate? The church might be able to help if you have bills to pay." She'd said that Tobias had already paid for his own funeral, but I didn't know about other funds. Did she have anything for groceries? For gas?

Anna took a breath and shook out her hands. She seemed more herself. "Thank you, but I'm sure I'll be fine. In fact, I'm thinking of going back to work full-time. And there's enough in our checking account for me to get by for a few months even if the will is contested."

"Well, then I just hope it doesn't drag on

for much longer than that."

She collected the papers and put them back in the manila envelope. I expected her to leave then, but she remained seated and her feet tapped the carpet.

"Can I get you some tea?" I asked.

"No, that's not why I'm still here. I wanted to know — Linda, tell me what you think about the house. Should I keep it?"

"You're thinking of selling it? Where would you go?" The thought of her leaving the ward just after I had found a deep friendship with her was sudden and sour, like the taste of vinegar if I'd been expecting juice.

"The whole idea that Tobias could have lied to me, that my whole life might have been a lie — it has made me feel differently about myself. Or maybe it has made me see myself truly for the first time. I was always the dutiful wife, doing whatever Tobias needed me to do. I didn't argue with him. I gave up my job and never complained about it, never thought of going back while the boys were young. When I did go back, I always worked my hours around the family. I always made sure he had what he wanted, what he and the boys needed. But if I hadn't given up so much, maybe I wouldn't be so upset. Maybe I wouldn't have wanted so much to believe that my life with him was real."

"But you didn't give up yourself. Anna, you were always independent," I said.

"Then how did this happen? I must have done something wrong. And even if I didn't, I've been considering starting over again. Now that Tobias is gone, it just feels like I should be waiting to die, too. I don't want to do that. I want to move on. I don't want to sit and feel obligated to keep up Tobias's garden. I want to have my own life. I want to see the world. I want to go on a cruise. I want to go on dates with other men." She was blushing furiously. "Do you think that's wrong of me? Selfish?"

Tobias had died only ten days before, but maybe this was what she needed to do. "No, of course not. I mean, it may be a little self-ish, but there is nothing wrong with taking care of yourself, Anna. Tobias is dead. The boys are raised. If you don't want to stay in that house, I don't see why you should have to." Though I hated the idea of her not be-ing in the ward for my own selfish reasons.

"I suggested it to the boys and they were very angry. Maybe it was too soon after To-bias died. Liam told me that selling the fam-ily home would be like his father dying all over again. All our memories are there."

Liam and Anna hadn't ever loved each other easily, had they? I couldn't say the same was true for me and any of my boys, but sometimes I thought that Kenneth and Kurt were always butting heads in this same way, always misunderstanding each other, always being hurt by misinterpretations. But in this case, I was on Anna's side. "If he wants it, then he can buy it back from you. He's inheriting money from Tobias's death, isn't he?"

"Yes, a good deal of it. And I noticed he didn't suggest that. He already has his own plans for that money, I suspect."

"Then there's no reason that you can't have plans for your own life, too," I said tartly. I felt a little jealous, strangely. I had never traveled the world. I had never even planned to do that. I just had the view out my window and kept my sights on visiting my kids when I had time. "I'm glad, Anna. You should have some happiness. I hope you do remarry and have a wonderful life."

Anna met my eyes and I could see sadness combined with enthusiasm in them. I was surprised that after the double blow she'd suffered, she could bounce back so well. The news about the other Helena (or whoever she was) might have paralyzed Anna. But she seemed as strong as on that first day when I went to visit her after Kurt put her name on the refrigerator.

"I will miss you, Linda. And your husband. You've been so kind to me. I will miss the whole ward." She stood up.

I stood up, too, reluctantly. "Of course you will. But there's a time to move on." I was trying to be calm about this, though I had never felt as close to a friend as I did to Anna. I had thought we would have more time. I tried to smile. "More happiness in the world is what we're here for, isn't it? Man is that he might have joy? And woman, too?" I changed the scripture delicately.

Anna let out a funny squawking sound, half laugh, half sob. "I'm glad you said that. Thank you. And it's not that I don't want to be with Tobias forever. I always wanted that, even if he didn't. But now that he's gone, it feels like I have other things I need to do. Maybe that means finding another man. Maybe not. But there are other things out there to do than just finding another man, don't you think?"

I followed her toward the door. "I wish I could go on the cruise with you," I said. "Or see Europe. I've always wanted to go traveling."

"You still have Samuel at home. But soon enough you'll be able to do the same thing," said Anna.

Maybe, I thought. When Kurt was released as bishop, could I talk him into going on a cruise? Or going on a world tour to all the sites I was itching to see? Or would he just end up in another church calling that took more time and energy than this one did? And what about Kelly Helm?

Strange that she was the first on my list of responsibilities, and not my own sons.

"Too bad your husband is so young and healthy, eh?" said Anna with a smile.

As I closed the door behind her, I thought about how her mood had swung over the course of the hour or less she had been here. She had been distraught, and was now cracking jokes. Maybe none of her decisions now would last. After all, she was still grieving. I remembered that first month when people told me that I would never get over my daughter's loss. It hadn't been what I wanted to hear. I thought I was too strong to be in pain forever. I just had to get through this day, and the next, and eventually, I would heal.

I never had, and didn't expect to anymore. But that didn't mean that either Anna or I couldn't have joy left in our lives, whatever form that came in.

CHAPTER 23

I went down to Provo for a couple of days midweek because Adam and Marie both had a terrible case of the flu. I left Samuel and Kurt well supplied with casseroles in the freezer (though I doubted they would ever get them out — Cheri Tate had heard I would be gone and likely the Relief Society would bring in meals). For two days I did laundry and made soup and cleaned up dishes and drove Adam and Marie to the doctor's. When they were starting to get up and around again, I left Adam with the warning that next year they'd better make sure to get their flu shots.

I drove home just in time for the ten o'clock news on Friday night. Kurt was eating a late dinner so we were watching together in our room when the channel ran a teaser about a new, dark twist in the Carrie Helm case. I felt sick waiting through the commercials, and then the news came back on.

There was live footage of a body being bagged and carried away from what looked like a long stretch of empty, still frozen road.

"A body that has since been identified as missing Draper woman Carrie Helm was found this evening by a motorist near Wendover, Utah," the reporter said.

"No, no, no, no," I moaned. I felt physically assaulted, as if someone had dragged me through dirt. I'd known it — I should have known it — nothing I'd done had helped her. Kurt tried to hold me, but I batted him away. This was his fault somehow. He was a man, a surrogate for Jared and Alex Helm, for Tobias Torstensen. I wanted to scratch his eyes out, and kick him in the balls again and again. But I didn't have strength for any of that.

Kurt moved across the bed to switch the television off, but I growled at him, and he slid back to his side of the bed, his hands up in surrender.

Poor Carrie. Carrie, who wasn't my daughter.

Poor Kelly, who wasn't mine, either. She was five years old. How could she possibly accept this and have a normal life? How could she ever trust God again?

I listened as the reporter recapped the

missing person case that had now turned to a murder case. "No statement has been given by Jared Helm about his wife's death," she was saying. "The case is under the jurisdiction of Utah state."

Had Jared Helm done this, after all? Had I been fooled into thinking Carrie was alive and with this man Will? Had Carrie been somehow forced to buy that bus ticket and then taken to just across the border and killed, her body left like so much garbage?

I felt sick at the thought that I had felt sorry for him even for a moment, that I had blamed Carrie for any of this. I put my arms around myself and tried to imagine that my body was a shell of protection for my soul, because my soul felt pierced and bleeding.

The television immediately cut to live footage of the police walking up to the Helm house. I jumped up and moved to the bedroom window, Kurt behind me. From our vantage point on the second floor, we could see the police were handcuffing Jared Helm on the street below us, and taking him away. His father was shouting at the police. I could guess at what he was saying; he would be accusing them of incompetence and threatening that they would regret taking his son in.

The figure of little Kelly stood in the big

doorway of the house, watching her father being taken away by the police — that was the worst sight of all. Now all she would have was her grandfather to look after her. Had anyone told her that her mother was dead? Would someone do it gently enough for her to sleep tonight? Would anyone read her a story and hold her close? Would anyone make her brownies when she needed them most?

"We have to do something," I said aloud.

"What do you suggest?" said Kurt. He still didn't dare to touch me, after my reaction before.

"Get Kelly out of that house. She should be with a loving family in the ward. She needs to be safe." I couldn't turn away from the scene down the street. Kelly was still outside, watching everything. She was wearing a thin pink nightgown, frills all over, and she was barefoot despite the cold weather. But it was the look on her face — I was sure I could see it from where I was, and that it was blank terror.

"And you don't think she's safe with her grandfather? Physically safe? You think we have any reason to call DCFS? You would have to prove legally that he's incompetent or abusive," he reminded me. "Being a neat freak isn't enough. Nor is hating Kelly's mother. Or religious extremism."

I was exhausted after spending the last two days as a full-time caretaker for Adam and Marie, and Kurt was just making me angry at him again. I pushed away from the window, and away from him. "You're just going to stand by and watch her spirit crushed," I said. I started pulling the blankets, pillows, and sheets off the bed.

"What are you doing?" he asked, his face alarmed.

"We need clean sheets." It made no sense to wash them at this time of night, but it had to be done.

"Linda, think carefully about this," said Kurt. He still didn't touch me, but he helped me extricate the sheets from the quilt. He folded the quilt methodically and put it to the side, which made me angrier still with him. He could stay calm about all this while I wept because he didn't care.

"You've gotten too caught up in this," Kurt went on. "You're not thinking clearly about it."

Of course *he* was thinking clearly. He always thought clearly. And that was supposed to be the right thing to do. Not feel emotion. Not thrash around in anger. Be rational. Be a man. Well, I wasn't a man.

"Linda, we have to let people make their

own choices. We can't help until we're asked to help. It's one of the frustrating things I've learned about being a bishop, but it's true. If I try to intervene before people are ready to listen, I inevitably ruin their ability to see the problem themselves and set them back months, possibly years."

How could he say this to me? He was playing the authority card. He was the bishop. He had the experience. He had the mantle of being God's voice in my ears.

Well, I didn't care what God had to say about this. God was a man, too, and as far as I was concerned, until I heard Heavenly Mother tell me how to deal with a little girl in shock and fear, I wasn't going to listen.

I threw the sheets into the machine, pulled out the drawer for soap, shoved it back in full, then jammed the START button. I didn't even look at the water temperature or the cycle. I didn't care. I couldn't see the Helm house from the laundry room window, but I heard a car driving away as I stood there, waiting for the washing machine to fill.

"I'm going to talk to him," I said. I was glad I hadn't changed into pajamas yet. I thundered down the stairs and could hear Kurt chasing me.

"Linda, you should at least wait until the

cameras aren't on. He's going to be grand-standing about his son being taken away." He got around me and stood at the door like a guard.

I could have pushed past him, or slapped him. Instead, I took a breath and tried my best to find the rational words that would make Kurt listen to me, whether I felt rational or not. My whole body seemed to have turned to lead, my brain most of all. "And that is exactly why I need to be there for Kelly. He isn't paying any attention to her. And she has just lost her mother and her father in the same day."

"Her mother has been missing for some time," Kurt reminded me. He seemed relieved that I was finally looking him in the eye.

"You know what I mean," I said.

"Linda." He put a hand on my shoulder and I didn't shrug him off. I could feel the warmth of his body spread to mine. "You need to think about how you're going to approach him." I noticed he had stopped trying to convince me not to go. "He's a proud, stubborn man. You've got to appeal to that. Don't tell him he can't take care of his granddaughter. Make him feel like you are on his side."

"How do I do that?" I asked, staring past

333

Kurt at the doorknob.

"I don't know. If I knew that, I'd do it myself. I'm just telling you that you need to think this through before you head over or you'll make it worse."

I thought it through. For about two more minutes. Then I slipped around Kurt and flung the door open. Kurt didn't come after me, and I didn't know if that meant he trusted me or that he didn't want to witness his wife on a rampage. Either one was fine with me.

When I walked up the driveway, Alex Helm was so busy talking to the cameras that he hardly noticed me. They didn't seem to notice me, either, though I had been prepared to say "friend of the family" if anyone asked.

I stepped up to the porch and caught Kelly under one arm, pulling her inside the house.

"Let me get you warm, sweetie," I said as I put her down. I reached for a hand to guide her up the stairs. Her hands were like icicles. "Would you like to take a bath?" I asked. That would warm her up and make her sleepy, I hoped.

She nodded. "Can I have bubbles?" she asked, her voice high-pitched and shaky.

Damn Alex Helm, I thought, for leaving

her out there while he basked in the lime-light.

"Of course, sweetie." I ran a bath for her, listening to Alex Helm's bombastic voice outside, reporters asking questions when-ever he paused. I was relieved to find that there were numerous bottles of bath bubbles under the sink, color-organized from clear to purple. I let Kelly choose one. She played until the water started to get tepid. Then I found the thickest towel I could and wrapped Kelly up in it completely. I carried her into her bedroom and tucked her under the covers for a few minutes to dry before I tried to get her dressed.

"Is Daddy going to come back?" asked Kelly as she pulled on a warm pair of flan-nel pajamas more appropriate to the weather than the nightgown that lay on the floor.

"Of course he is," I said. I was saying that too much. And my voice was too bright, an attempt to cover the real anger I felt. I wasn't sure who I was angriest at right now. Kurt? The police? The reporters on the lawn? Jared Helm? Carrie Helm? Or Alex Helm? Maybe I was most angry at myself.

"When is he coming back?"

"I don't know." I couldn't tell her I hoped it was soon. I didn't. I hoped that Jared Helm would be in jail for the rest of his life.

I'd hope for eternity, but I knew that God had mercy that I couldn't feel at the moment, even for murderers.

"Daddy said he would read me a story tonight. He always says that, but then he forgets."

"I can read you a story," I said. So I did. I read *We're Going on a Bear Hunt,* and then despite the late hour, I brought her down to the kitchen. I didn't think there was any chance she would be able to sleep with Alex Helm making so much noise outside, even if her father hadn't just been taken by the police under suspicion of murdering her mother.

We made hot chocolate and homemade butter cookies and put them in the oven to bake. It was close to midnight by then, and Alex Helm was still out front, enjoying the cameras flashing. The smell of butter cookies filled the kitchen when he finally stepped inside and closed the door behind him sometime after twelve thirty.

"What's going on?" he asked. Apparently, he hadn't noticed me taking Kelly inside, or thought once about where she'd been during his interviews. "Sister Wallheim, what are you doing here?"

I thought about what Kurt had told me. I had to make Alex Helm think I was on his side. "I just thought I would come help out. Keep Kelly company while you were busy, and make some cookies. I hope you don't mind the mess I've made. I'll clean it up when I'm done." Playing to his neat freak.

Kelly was yawning, and I had placed myself between her and him so that her head was tucked against my side.

Alex Helm stared at me for a moment, then nodded. "All right. Kelly and I need to talk privately for a few minutes, though."

"She really should go to bed. It's late," I said, putting a hand on her head.

"I think you should go now," he said. He reached for Kelly.

"But the cookies aren't done yet. And I should clean up upstairs first. Kelly left some clothes on the room of her floor. And the bathroom is a mess." I had to stop myself from listing anything else in that false, cheerful tone I was using. "I'll just take care of that and then I'll be out of your way."

"All right, then. I'll sit here with Kelly and we'll wait for the cookies." He reached around me and pulled Kelly toward him. She was limp, sleepy, and I hoped to keep her that way. Arguing with Alex Helm wouldn't help her, so I let go of my antagonism, for the moment, and left the kitchen.

337

I hurriedly picked up Kelly's bedroom, and then went into the bathroom. I cleaned out the tub, and then returned the thick towel to the upstairs master bath. Only then did I dare go back down the stairs to the main level. "Hello?" I called as respectfully as I could. The timer was still going off, and I hoped the cookies hadn't burned.

"Come on in and have some cookies," said Alex Helm's voice.

I saw that the cookies had been taken out of the oven and were cooling on the stove top. It was strange that Alex Helm hadn't turned off the timer. Did he not know how?

I touched the off button on the stove, then found a spatula and put the cookies on a plate.

That was when I saw that Kelly was snoring away on Alex Helm's shoulder.

I wanted to snatch her away from him and take her home with me. But that wouldn't help. Despite my anger at Kurt, he had been right. I had to be logical about this. I had to do what I could for Kelly, in the circumstances she was in. "Can I help you get her to bed?" I asked.

"No, I think I can manage it," Alex Helm said, lifting her up and putting an arm under her bottom.

"Well, maybe I can come back and help

again tomorrow? I'm sure there will be a lot to do with Jared — and lawyers." I was trying to avoid saying the words "jail" and "murder." For my own sanity as much as for Alex Helm's. "I could come by in the morning as early as you want and just stay here until you come back."

Alex Helm thought a moment, jiggled Kelly as she stirred a bit and then settled. That one moment told me a lot about him as a grandparent, and I wasn't sure that I wanted to see him this way. Indulgent, loving, and well attuned to her patterns. "Thank you, that would be a great help," he said.

I went home and Kurt asked me what had happened. He nodded when I told him I'd be going back tomorrow. "And you think that you are going to find something over there that will help the police? Or are you just there for Kelly's sake?"

I didn't know the answer anymore, and I think Kurt could see I was conflicted.

"Just be careful, all right?" he said, and sighed.

"Be careful? Does that mean you think the Helm men are actually dangerous?" I asked. I guess I was still in an argumentative mood, despite the hour and how tired I was.

339

Kurt put up his hands. "I don't know what it means except that I think you have been finding yourself in more and more dangerous situations lately. I thought you had grown out of that phase when I married you, but apparently not."

We went to bed and kept mostly to our own sides. I woke up several times during the night and found myself snuggled up next to him, and pulled away.

Saturday morning, I woke before him and hurried over to the Helms' a little before seven.

Alex opened the door. He was already dressed, though he looked bleary-eyed. He was buttoning the top button on a dress shirt and I leaned forward to help him cinch up his tie, surprising myself with the domestic reflex.

He told me Kelly was in the kitchen, and he went upstairs to get his suit coat.

In fact, Kelly had decided that the butter cookies we'd made last night would make an excellent breakfast. I didn't argue with her, but I did get out a glass of milk to try to counter the effects of the sugar.

Alex Helm came back downstairs and told me he didn't know when he would be back.

He said he would call me when he knew more about Jared, but I didn't press him.

After her late night, Kelly fell asleep on the couch next to me while I was reading her another book. I gently slipped out from under her and began to go through the house methodically — again. Here was the answer to the question Kurt had asked, I suppose. I couldn't stop myself from trying to find out more. And Kelly was fine, safe and secure on the couch.

In the master bedroom, I found that Alex Helm had left his cell phone behind in his hurry to leave, and I thumbed through the phone history. I was getting used to doing things like this.

He had called the Las Vegas number I had seen on Carrie Helm's phone, the one belonging to Will, several times over the last few days. Had he talked to Carrie directly? Maybe he was the reason Carrie had left Will. Or was he part of the whole scam about Carrie being in Las Vegas? I still didn't know when exactly she had died. It was when I checked Alex Helm's messages that I had to sit down in shock. He had been texting Carrie right up until a few days ago, and she had been texting back. There was no reason for Alex Helm to fake these.

KELLY NEEDS HER MOTHER. I EXPECT

YOU HOME IN THE NEXT DAY, Alex had written imperiously.

I AM NOT READY TO COME HOME. AND I SUSPECT JARED DOESN'T WANT ME THERE, ANYWAY, Carrie had written back.

Alex had texted in reply, JARED WANTS HIS WIFE HOME WITH HIM, WHERE SHE BELONGS. YOU ARE CAUSING A TERRIBLE SCENE, EXPOSING YOUR FAMILY TO CONSTANT NEWS COVERAGE.

Then, HOW DO YOU THINK THAT WILL AFFECT YOUR DAUGHTER?

Carrie responded, SHE'S TOO LITTLE TO REMEMBER ANY OF THIS. Then, almost immediately afterward, she followed up with, SHE'LL BE BETTER OFF WITHOUT ME. ISN'T THAT WHAT YOU TOLD ME?

My neck prickled at this.

IF YOU DON'T COME HOME RIGHT NOW, I WILL COME AND GET YOU.

I WOULD LIKE TO SEE YOU TRY THAT.

YOU WILL REGRET HUMILIATING ME AND JARED. YOU CAN BE SURE THAT IT WILL NEVER HAPPEN AGAIN. WHEN YOU GET BACK, THINGS ARE GOING TO CHANGE.

WHEN I GET BACK? I'M ALREADY MOVING ON.

YOU ARE A MOTHER. YOU CAN'T MOVE ON FROM YOUR DAUGHTER. SHE IS YOURS FOREVER. AND YOU ARE JARED'S FOREVER.

342

You married him in the temple.

You won't ever see me again. I'm dumping this phone. I'll miss Kelly, but not as much as I will be glad to be away from you and your son, Carrie returned.

Alex continued to text her, but got no response.

You can't hide from me. I will find you.

Do you want your parents to know what you've done? I can tell them everything.

And the last one, God will take his vengeance on you if I can't. Wickedness never was happiness. When you are dead, you will see the eternal consequences.

When she was dead?

I realized that my breathing was heavy. I tried to calm down but was overcome with panic when I heard the door open downstairs. Alex Helm had come back — now of all moments.

"I forgot my phone!" he called out.

And I had no reason to be in the master bedroom.

I put the phone down shakily, and then called out, "I'm up here, just doing some cleaning," I said. I tried to step out of the room, but Alex Helm caught me.

"What are you doing here?" he demanded.

I put up my hands in an attempt to prove my innocent intentions. "My husband and sons are terrible at cleaning the bathroom. I just thought I would help."

"I don't need your help with cleaning in here," he said roughly.

"Oh, are you sure? Usually when I come in and help with children, I try to clean up, as well." Meek, subservient, keeping my head down.

"Well, that isn't necessary here."

"Kelly fell asleep and I wanted something to do," I added with a shrug.

"You could go watch a soap opera on television," said Alex Helm. "Or read one of those romance novels women like."

"I didn't bring any," I said, trying to act cowed. "Next time I'll think of that."

Alex Helm simply nodded, and turned back to the phone, as if I was no longer important. "If you can stay for a few more hours, until I can get Jared out on bail, that would be useful," he said, not bothering to look me in the eye.

"Sure. Whatever you need," I said.

He took the phone, and I swallowed hard as the door shuddered closed behind him.

The rest of the day, I stayed close to Kelly

and let my mind run over the messages Alex Helm had sent Carrie. What did they mean? What had Alex Helm done?

I had to leave Kelly with Alex when he came home, and it was one of the hardest things I have ever done.

CHAPTER 24

For the next several days, the whole ward had to deal with the reality of the Helm situation. Jared Helm was in jail on charges of spouse abuse, presumably to be followed by murder charges. In the meantime, Kurt was dealing with Jared's father. Alex Helm was demanding that the ward send character witnesses to Jared's bail hearing. He also wanted the names of all the lawyers in the ward so he could ask them to donate their services to help the lawyer he had hired.

Meanwhile, I stewed over thoughts of Kelly alone with her grandfather. I'd seen a good moment between them, but that was no guarantee that there were many such moments. And just because Kelly Helm was physically cared for did not mean her grandfather's misogyny wouldn't have far-reaching effects.

On Wednesday God sent me a distraction from my worries about Kelly. Anna Torstensen called to tell me that the woman in the photos had been found.

"Her name is Ellie Vasquez. She claims that Tobias offered her a thousand dollars all those years ago to pretend to correspond with him as his wife and to dress up in some clothes that he sent her and have photographs taken. She thought it was a little creepy, but she needed the money."

So, I had guessed right — or had been guided in that leap of intuition. "So how did Tobias find her, did she say?"

"Apparently it was on a business trip to California. He happened to see her and told her that she looked like his wife. He asked for her name and address and wrote to her when he returned home. She felt sorry for him at first, she said."

"And why did Tobias do it? Did she have any guesses?"

"She said that she thought it was because he was lonely. He wanted to imagine his wife was still alive, that she might come home. Ellie Vasquez took advantage of that, tried to get more money from him. But at some point, she worried that the fantasy had become too real. She moved to a different location and never had contact with him again."

Somehow, this sounded more like the Tobias I had known. Emotionally unstable, perhaps, but not a bigamist. "Well, you must be so relieved." But if his wife was dead, then I had to go back to the question of whether or not Tobias had killed her.

"I feel guilty, too," said Anna. "I should have known that Tobias would never have done any of those things to me. I lived with the man for thirty years. I should have known him better."

"You are still in shock over losing him," I said to Anna.

"Maybe," she said.

At that, I decided it was time to change the subject. "What about the house? Have you made any decisions on that?"

"The boys are very upset, and I feel terrible about selling it, so we've reached a compromise. Liam wants me to rent it out for a year instead of selling it outright. That way, I can go on my cruise and still have some money from rental, but I can also come back to it if I want to. I even got a promise of more time off from my job, if I want it."

It sounded like a sensible solution. "Do you have enough money otherwise?"

"Liam agreed to give me a loan against the value of the house at no interest. He's not even making me sign a contract." Anna chuckled at that. "If you knew Liam, you'd see why that seems so out of character."

"He loves you," I said.

She let out a long breath. "And I do love him and Liam. So much. I wondered when I first married Tobias if I could love them as much as they needed to be loved. I still wonder that sometimes."

"Anna, you gave those boys more love than most women give to their blood children," I said. We say that mothering is "natural," but it isn't really. Animals in the wild feed their children and carry them around — most of the time. They also sometimes eat them. That is just as natural, as far as I could see.

"Do you really think so?" asked Anna. "I always worry I was too strict with them. And that I was too much of a marshmallow."

"Which is exactly what any mother who had given birth to children would wonder, Anna. It's the way I feel about my own boys."

"You seem so sure of yourself. I always thought I had missed that sense of certainty. That if they were born to me, I would somehow know what I was doing was right," said Anna.

I let out a laugh at that. "I'm glad I fooled you, Anna, but no, I am never sure of myself as a mother. Well, only of one thing. I love them, and I want what is best for them. But it is always a struggle, figuring out who they are now and what is best."

"I thought that God granted mothers some special power."

"Well, all I think he granted me was the gift of loving them. And on some days, not even that." There had been times when I wanted to throw all of the boys out of the house. Come to think of it, I had done that once. Sent them to sit out in the snow to wait for Kurt to come home, because I had had enough of them all.

"But your boys are at least like you," said Anna. "I look at Tomas and Liam and think that there is nothing of me in them." Her laugh was breathy. "I can't even see anything of their mother in them. They're all Tobias."

"It's the testosterone. It kills anything female in them," I suggested, thinking about my own grown sons. They had been such sweethearts until they hit the age of about fourteen. And then there were all those years when the hormones were going wild. It was almost as if they needed to beat their chests to get the testosterone out or to find out what their place in the pecking order was. Kurt had had to step in so often to parent them then.

Anna said, "Thank you, Linda. You have made me feel so much better."

"And don't you feel a bit guilty about going off on this cruise of yours. You deserve it. Those last few weeks with Tobias were difficult."

"You don't think it makes me, well, weak?" asked Anna.

"Because you want some time to yourself after giving and giving to a dying man? Anna, it makes you smart and independent, which is the opposite of weak."

"It feels a bit like I am running away."

"You're running toward something, Anna. A new life. I think that takes a lot of courage." I was a little jealous of her, in fact, and wondered what new life I should be running after. I felt as if I had been running in circles around my old life instead. I needed to go back to school or get a job or do something other than poke around in other people's problems. Being the bishop's wife wasn't an excuse for having no life of my own.

Anna asked if there had been anything new with Jared Helm.

"He's in limbo, I think. He's been arrested for abuse. Apparently, Carrie Helm went to the hospital just days before she disappeared and was treated for bruises and cuts — all

351

carefully placed so they were hidden by her clothes." The hospital had taken pictures and documented the injuries and the police were able to subpoena those records now that she was dead. "But a trial date hasn't been set yet because the police want to charge him with murder as soon as they can prove he strangled Carrie and dumped her body on the road where she was found."

"But she did leave him," said Anna. "And her daughter. Maybe she was killed by someone she connected with after she left. A new boyfriend or a man she thought she was safe with."

"It could be that," I said. But from my conversation with Will, I couldn't suspect him. Even if Jared had paid him to lie about Carrie, he hadn't seemed smart or determined enough to do something like murder her. He hadn't sounded like he cared about her at all, and I didn't think he was that good of an actor. "In any case, the funeral is tomorrow. They've released the body to her parents for burial, and I assume that means they've gathered all the evidence from it they could." I hoped it meant they had found something they could use against Jared Helm. If he was the one who killed her.

"How terrible for her parents," said Anna

sincerely. "I'm going to be gone tomorrow morning to take some time sightseeing in California before my cruise, but give her family my best wishes, will you?"

"Of course," I said. I was supposed to go over to babysit Kelly in a couple of hours, so that Jared, out on bail for now, and Alex Helm could go shopping for appropriate funeral attire for themselves and Kelly. I had offered to take her shopping myself, but Alex Helm had said he and Jared felt it was their responsibility. I translated this as Alex Helm's not wanting to relinquish even that tiniest bit of control over Kelly.

The doorbell rang and I guessed it would be Alex Helm come to tell me he didn't need me this afternoon, after all.

But it wasn't Alex Helm at all. It was the Westons.

"Hello. Come in, come in," I said, and folded Judy into an awkward embrace. "I am so sorry for your loss." I turned to Aaron, and he put out his hand for me to shake instead. I was happy enough with the compromise, and shook his cold, surprisingly dry hands. My eye caught a splash of color behind the Westons, and I realized the tulips in Tobias Torstensen's garden were already blooming beautifully across the way. They would make it that much easier for

Anna to find a renter.

I ushered the Westons into the front room and then sat down on the couch across from them. "What can I do to help? Tell me anything and I will gladly do it." I knew the Relief Society had the funeral luncheon already in hand. They had chosen to do it in our ward rather than in the Westons' home ward, where Carrie had grown up. I felt it was the right choice, but it must have been a hard decision. There were plenty of people in the ward who did not think well of Carrie now. The truth might reveal her to be a victim, but the rumors were still pretty damning.

"I'm glad you asked that," said Aaron Weston. "Actually, I was hoping that you would speak at the funeral." He was standing very upright, his eyes steely and unavoidable.

It was a shock, and I could feel my jaw drop.

"I know that it is a lot to ask, but there aren't many other choices. And you seem to have the right spirit about you when it comes to seeing Carrie fairly," he added, still staring directly at me.

"I didn't know her very well," I said, and felt again that I had failed Carrie when she was in need. Was this my only hope at penance?

"I know that. But I thought you could speak about Kelly and what a good mother Carrie was to her."

"I —" I did not feel comfortable standing in judgment over another woman's mothering.

"Unless you think she wasn't a good mother?" said Judy. She was holding tightly to her husband's hand and it was obvious she was fighting back tears. He was her rock, as Kurt had so often been mine.

"Of course not. She loved her daughter. I can see that in everything about Kelly. She's a strong little girl who is only doing as well as she is now because she grew up with a mother's love in everything," I said fiercely.

"That's precisely the sort of thing we're hoping you will say at the funeral. Kelly will be there, you see," said Aaron. "We'd like her to hear that from you. Sadly, she isn't going to hear much good about her mother in the next few years."

"I'm so sorry," I said. "About Carrie's death, and about Jared and his father. I hate how they have made this all out to be her fault." Certainly, Carrie had made some of the choices that led to this, but it was clear to me that those choices were influenced by a deep, desperate unhappiness caused by her husband and his father. And even if they

355

hadn't murdered her, it seemed to me that they were culpable for putting her in that vulnerable position in the first place.

"Thank you," Judy whispered. Her head went down, and it seemed as if whatever strength she had mustered up to ask me for this favor was gone now.

"We're going to try to get custody of Kelly," said Aaron. "It's a long shot, according to our lawyers, but at the very least, we want Kelly to know that we love her. And if we don't get custody, we're going to try for mandated visitation as grandparents. We don't want Kelly to hear only from her father and grandfather about her mother. Or about anything else, for that matter. I don't like how either of them think about the world."

"Well, I hope you do get custody," I said honestly.

His eyes widened and I had the sense that he was taking note of this in his mind, which had the capacity to remember everything. He was a formidable opponent, I thought, and wondered who would win if he and Alex Helm were set against each other. It made me happy to think that Aaron Weston was the stronger of the two. He was more self-possessed and he would certainly sound better, more reasonable, to the average person in Utah.

"Would you be willing to give that opinion of the situation in court?" Aaron asked.

I considered for a long moment, then nodded. The danger was that I would fail and become an enemy of Jared and Alex Helm, and then I would have no access to Kelly at all, but I had to take a chance to get her into a better situation.

"That is more than we had hoped for," said Aaron. The warmth of emotion in his voice surprised me. "But I still have to ask about the funeral. We need to get the programs printed and there aren't very many speakers as it is."

"Kurt is speaking, isn't he?" I said.

Aaron nodded. "But I thought a woman's perspective would be . . . kinder."

I thought again about Jared and Alex Helm, and I shook my head. "I think it's best if I don't speak at the funeral at this point. I'd like to make sure I can see Kelly until the trial. They've been asking me to come in and take care of her when they have to go out. It's been my one way of making sure she is well."

Aaron's hopeful smile disappeared, but he patted Judy's shoulder. "We can't fault her for that."

"No," she said softly.

"We believe Carrie was coming home to Kelly that night. That had to be why she was in Wendover," said Aaron.

"Have the police said when she was killed?" I asked.

"Yes. They told us it was just hours before they found the body," said Aaron. "I know it hasn't been reported on the news, but I think it will all come out soon enough."

So if Jared Helm had killed Carrie, he must have cold-bloodedly driven out to meet her somewhere and planned to do it. I wasn't sure it fit with the image I had of Jared in my mind. I believed he could have killed her in anger, but this? Maybe it was someone else, after all. "I am so sorry." What else could I say to her parents?

"Jared claims he never left the house that night. He claims that the reporters have footage of the whole night. He couldn't have gotten out of the house without being seen," said Aaron. His face was dark with anger. "But somehow, he is responsible even so. He is the one who drove her to do what she did," Aaron continued. "And it doesn't matter whose hand was on her neck when she died. It was his fault for forcing her to it."

"Well, God doesn't see responsibility the same way that the law does," I admitted.

Aaron took a deep breath, gave me a

searching look, and nodded. "We'll see you tomorrow, then?" said Aaron.

I nodded and stood, then showed them out. I felt a headache coming on, and went to take some Advil before I headed over to babysit Kelly, all the while feeling a knot in my stomach over my promise to testify against her father in a custody dispute with the Westons. Was I right or wrong? I had been wrong so many times in this case that I couldn't trust my instincts anymore. All I knew was that I loved Kelly and wanted the best for her.

We spent several hours playing with Barbies, something I had never done with my boys. They had scorned dolls, though they had played with action figures plenty. Kelly's Barbies had lots of fancy dresses, but Kelly wasn't very interested in changing their outfits. She preferred acting out different escape-from-jail story lines. We played them over and over again as I tried to guide her away from shootouts and other violent scenarios, but my heart went colder and colder as I thought of what this house had become for her.

When Jared and Alex came home, they called for Kelly and she jumped. Her face went expressionless and she hurriedly put her Barbies into their box. "Grandpa doesn't like Barbies," she told me. "He says their clothes are too small and too tight."

She scurried downstairs while I put the Barbie box under her bed. I went down after her, in time to see Alex Helm showing Kelly the black dress that had been purchased for her to wear for her mother's funeral. She put it on dutifully in the bathroom, then came down to show it off. It looked too big for her, boxy at the top, and went down to her ankles, but it was modest, at the very least. There wasn't a hint of lace or any feminine detailing on it. I supposed Kelly would never wear it again after this, but still, it seemed a strange dress for a little girl.

"Perfect," said Alex. "You look like an angel. Now go take it off and wash your hands for dinner." He turned to me and dismissed me. "Thank you, Sister Wallheim. We'll see you at the funeral."

I had no interest in arguing with the man at this point, so I walked home in the rain.

Joseph called me that night to tell me that Willow was expecting in early September. I should have been over the moon. I tried to act it, enthusiastically offering congratulations and all the help I could. Was she sick? Did they need meals? Did they need any help with housework while she was in the early stages? Could I help take her to doctor's appointments?

Joseph declined all my offers and said that they were just fine for now.

"Do you know if it's a boy or a girl?" I asked.

"Not yet, Mom. We're going in for an ultrasound in about three weeks and they think they will be able to tell."

In three weeks, I would find out if I was going to have a granddaughter. The thought terrified me. How could I protect a girl in this world? Somehow it didn't seem the right time for the next generation to start being born. We hadn't figured out this generation yet.

CHAPTER 25

Kurt was as proud of the coming baby as if he were the father. Samuel was thrilled at the idea of being an uncle. Unlike me, neither of them seemed to worry about whether it was a boy or a girl. But we still had to deal with the funeral for Carrie Helm. I am sure that people all over the world have already noticed that births and deaths happen at the same time, but it still seems like a strange thing to me. In the end, I focused on the list of things to get done. Despite the funeral in the afternoon, I spent the morning shopping for a gender-neutral gift for Joseph and Willow and the grandbaby-to-be.

I wrapped the present and put it on the sideboard in the kitchen, so that it would be visible when we had our next family dinner. That was when Kurt came over and put a hand on my shoulder. "Are you sure that's a good idea?" he asked.

"A present? How could that be a bad idea?" I asked.

"It just seems a little soon. Willow is only — what — three months along? A lot of things could happen between now and six months from now."

Was he suggesting that the baby wouldn't survive? "Kurt, that is the last thought that I should be having right now."

"I just want to make sure you don't get hurt," said Kurt with a sad little shrug.

He was always trying to protect me when I wouldn't protect myself. "The only way to not get hurt would be never to hope for anything and never to love. Is that what you really want?" I asked him.

"No," he admitted. Then he put on his tie, kissed me, and went to the church to prepare for Carrie Weston Helm's funeral.

I came a little afterward, dressed in a wool skirt and sensible shoes. I hadn't volunteered to help Cheri Tate with this one, though maybe I should have, considering the fraught circumstances.

The funeral was more than a bit schizophrenic. There were flowers everywhere, but they seemed like two completely different sets: one loudly pink and big and feminine, the other more matronly and subdued in color and size. The chapel was also divided clearly. The center section and the right were for the ward. The left was for Carrie's high school friends, women who were her age, some struggling with young children, others standing alone in clothing that seemed not quite appropriate for a funeral, a little too revealing and not nearly black enough. I hated that I thought that, but I did. I shuddered to think it was what Alex Helm would have said.

Kurt had insisted that the news cameras stay outdoors, but that didn't mean there weren't reporters there, in disguise. Or some not so much in disguise. I saw several notebooks flip out when Kurt began his talk. I don't know what they were scribbling down so feverishly. Kurt's talk was largely standard funeral fare. He talked about Christ's atonement covering all sins, even the sins that we think are the worst. Pedophiles, murderers, and adulteresses. He read Christ's response to the Pharisees about the woman caught in adultery. He didn't specifically talk about Carrie being an adulteress but he did look out at the audience and ask quite directly who here was so clean of sin that they could cast the first stone.

I felt a little chill run down my spine at that, and was sure everyone else felt something similar. I thought how good Kurt had become at speaking in just a year. His first week as bishop, he could never have imagined this kind of emotional response from the audience.

After Kurt finished, Judy Weston got up. She had brought props with her for her speech. Normally, Kurt might have disapproved, but I was glad to see that he had no reaction to this. Judy showed the mourners a photo of Carrie's high school graduation. She had also brought one of Carrie's favorite books, *Bridge to Terabithia,* and read a passage.

Then Judy brought out Carrie's prom dress, which was pale pink with just a little lace at the bodice. She talked about Carrie's love of laughter and comedies, and her piano playing, for which she had won awards in high school. I was shocked to realize I'd had no idea Carrie Helm played the piano. No wonder Kelly had seemed to sit so naturally when she sat on my lap. There was no piano in the Helm house, but Carrie must have taught her daughter about music.

"Carrie loved her daughter beyond anything," Judy went on. "I'm going to read from a letter that Carrie wrote about Kelly, a letter I did not see until recently."

I went stiff at this. Was this one of the letters that was to be used in the trial against Jared Helm for abuse? I looked at Kurt and saw that he was holding tightly to the arms of the chair. He didn't want to ask Judy Weston to sit down, but he might have to.

I looked at Aaron Weston and saw a muted smile of satisfaction on his face, and wondered how much of this was his doing. From the first time I'd met him, I'd thought that Judy was manipulated by him. But I should have trusted Judy more.

The paragraph she read was simply Carrie saying that she would do anything to be with her daughter, that there was no threat that would keep her away, that there was no hurt she would not endure to be at her daughter's side and keep her from harm. Then she sat down and it was Aaron's turn.

The smile was gone from Aaron Weston's face when he stood, and I wondered if I had misread it. Except for a niggling feeling on that first day, everything Aaron Weston had done had made me believe him to be a deeply caring father and a devout, humble Mormon. His talk was one of the best I had ever heard. It was obvious he had spoken at many funerals before, and knew exactly how to engage the grieving family members in the audience. He looked directly at Kelly below him and told her that her mother would be waiting for her, in heaven. He described a scene of a beautiful young woman waiting in a garden for the one thing that would make her heart complete.

"Heaven is a place of peace. No one there feels any degree of pain. They may wish for things. They may hope. But there is no impatience there, no sense of a long passage of time. They wait easily and happily. And I know that Carrie is waiting to see Kelly again. It may be a hundred years, but she will wait there still, and she will be as beautiful as she was the last day that she saw you."

I felt a sting of pain at the thought of my daughter, waiting. But in Aaron Weston's garden, it did not seem such a terrible thing.

Aaron Weston continued, speaking to his granddaughter in the first row, sandwiched between Jared and Alex Helm. "She will kneel to greet you, Kelly, and she will open her arms and she will tell you that you are her little girl, just as you are now. And at that moment, you will not remember any of the sadness that you feel today. It will all be forgotten. There will only be forgiveness between you. She will be cleaned from all her sins and so will you and you will be two shining daughters of God forever."

If Kurt was good at speechmaking, Aaron

Weston was ten times better. I was wiping at my face and wishing that I had brought more tissues. People sometimes said they'd had a feeling about a man who would turn out to be a prophet, that the Holy Spirit had whispered that this man would be the leader of the Mormon church someday. I felt like that about Aaron Weston at that moment. He was the man who should raise his granddaughter. I had no doubt of that.

Finally, he read some scriptures about heaven from Revelation that supported his vision, but it was that beautiful vision of a garden that stayed with me, long after the songs were over and the funeral luncheon was cleaned up. It made me think of Tobias Torstensen's garden, so carefully kept and so beautiful, even after his death. After the service, there were two distinct lines where people waited to give their respects, one to Jared and Alex Helm — and Kelly — the other to the Westons. Some people only went to offer their respects to one line. Some went to both.

I tried to force myself to go to the Westons first, and then maybe I could manage the other, but I found my legs would not move forward. I was caught at the door of the chapel, reliving my own daughter's funeral, where I had had to stand in a line very like that one, and had struggled to say a single word to the few mourners who were there with us. What words could possibly be adequate, on either side? I had come. I was mourning with them. That was the most I could do.

I noticed that Gwen Ferris and her husband, Brad, were here together. I saw them greeting the Helms, but noticed they left immediately after that without saying anything to the Westons. I suppose they hadn't known Carrie's parents. There was something in Gwen Ferris's expression that struck me. I was trying to figure out what it was when I was startled by a familiar voice.

"Mom, how are you doing?"

I turned around and found my middle son, Kenneth, was there in the hallway by the back door. I realized my hand had flown to my throat. "I didn't know you were coming."

He looked thin. He hadn't been taking care of himself. I wondered if he thought to eat more than once a day. He was wearing the suit I had bought for him when he was eighteen, just starting to think about a mission. It was too small for him across the shoulders and in the sleeves.

I stared at him and was surprised that he looked more like my own father than like

Kurt. He had my father's hawkish nose, and my father's lean face, as well as my father's ears poking out of slicked-back dark hair. When had that happened?

"Dad told me it was today and I didn't know if I could make it. But I did. It was lovely."

"But you didn't know Carrie Helm, did you?" I tried to think back on the timeline. When had Kenneth last lived at home?

"No, I didn't know her. I just knew that you were upset by her death and I wanted to come and support you."

I teared up again. "Thank you so much. That means a lot to me." I wouldn't have thought Kenneth, of all my sons, would have thought of my feelings. He seemed so distant of late, coming rarely to family dinners because he was busy with his own life in the city.

"I know you'll be fine. But I wanted you to know that I'm here for you. If you need someone to talk to. Dad is great and all that, but I know he is sometimes really well — orthodox."

I stared at Kenneth for a long moment. "Are you trying to tell me something?" I asked. I had known he hadn't been attending church for a while, but I'd hoped it was just a stage.

"Don't get that look on your face, Mom," he said.

"What look?"

"The grieving parent of a wayward child look," said Kenneth.

I put a hand on his arm. "Kenneth, there are many paths to truth," I said.

"You mean, so long as I stay in the church," he said sourly.

I looked around. I knew this was not the right place for us to have this discussion. I kept thinking that Kurt would be coming by, or that someone else in the ward would overhear something and pass it around. "Kenneth, I love you. Just as you are, even your doubting parts."

He cleared his throat and I had no idea if I had said the right thing or not. "Well, I have to go. I've got to get back to work."

"Sure," I said. "I'll see you later." He managed a series of laundromats, and Kurt had always thought he could do better, another source of tension between the two of them. But I was so glad he had come to be with me for just this moment, and I couldn't help but reflect on how people are always surprising us. Carrie Helm must have surprised her parents, but in the end, they had loved her and given this beautiful funeral service for her. We can't make our children do anything, but we can always love them.

After Kenneth left, I went into the kitchen to help Cheri Tate with serving the luncheon — the least I could do, since I hadn't helped with anything else.

"So here we are again." How many funerals had she done this for? And how many weddings? "You've had a lot to do the last couple of months."

"You can say that again," she said wearily. "I think I'm going to need a vacation from all callings when I'm finished with this one. If I ever finish with this one." She eyed me speculatively.

"You don't think the blessings far outweigh all the responsibilities?" Wasn't that what everyone said?

"Blessings don't give me more time. And I need sleep," said Cheri. She said it with a smile, as if it was a joke, but I thought maybe it wasn't.

It might be wise for me to talk to Kurt about it, but I had no doubt what he would say. That Cheri Tate did not have to do everything herself. She needed to learn to let go and delegate and accept that what other people did was their best, and what was good enough for God should be good enough for her.

Four hours later, on a final pass through

the chapel, Cheri found something near the podium and brought it to me.

"I think this must be Carrie's mother's," she said.

It was the photo of Carrie at her high school graduation.

"Do you think you could get it back to her? I'd hate to just put this in lost and found."

"Of course," I said. I had the Westons' address at home. I would send it to her in the mail, or possibly drive by next week to return it to her.

But as I walked home with the frame under my arm, it occurred to me that Judy might have left it on purpose. Did she hope that someone would give it to Kelly? I walked by the Helm house, thinking there was no way Jared or Alex would allow it in their home. I could sneak it into Kelly's bedroom, perhaps if I had a smaller copy of it. There were no other photographs of Carrie in the house, as I well knew.

When I got home, it was past time to start dinner, but Kurt and Samuel could fend for themselves. I needed to get out of the house to feel like I was doing something to help this terrible tragedy. I drove to a nearby copy store and got a small color copy of the photo, then went back over to the Helm house. I was feeling more stubborn than courageous. And I kept thinking about Kenneth and his strange conversation with me after the funeral. Had Carrie left her family because she had decided that they couldn't love her the way she really was? Had she been trying to leave the Mormon church, as well?

The news vans were gone now, though I still felt strangely watched as I walked to the door and rang the bell. I wanted to see Kelly and make sure she was all right. If I did end up testifying for the Westons at the custody trial, I might not have many more chances.

Alex Helm answered the door — of course.

"I wanted to come by and see how you are doing," I said. "I didn't make it to the graveside service and I'm sorry. I was busy helping with the funeral luncheon."

"It was very brief," said Alex. "Your husband said a few words and that was all."

I nodded. "How is Kelly?"

"She's a strong little personality. She'll move on with her life as soon as she can. I don't know if you heard, but we had news late last night that the police have decided to drop the charges against Jared. Without Carrie to explain how she got the bruises,

374

which were not Jared's doing, by the way, they have no real evidence against him and are finally admitting it. We are considering a lawsuit against the city for harassment, but it may be best to let it go."

"Yes, an eye for an eye only makes everyone blind," I said blandly. But my heart sank at the thought that Jared would get away with what he had done. What message would that send to Kelly about justice?

"I told Jared that Kelly needs a mother, and that is his next responsibility. He needs to find a woman who is more appropriate who can take over the role and make Kelly forget that all of this happened."

I struggled not to goggle at him. "So soon?" I got out. Carrie had only been dead for a little over a week. And he thought Kelly should forget her mother?

"If she has a good role model, she won't think about this part of her life and the pain in it. If you have any suggestions of single women in the ward who might appreciate a good man's attention, I'm sure Jared would be interested in a phone number or two."

"I don't think I know anyone who would fit that description," I said as calmly as I could manage. My heart felt swollen and tender in my chest. "But I would like to see Kelly, if you don't mind."

He glanced upstairs and his expression seemed genuinely loving. "Poor little girl. She hasn't had a nap all day. We sent her to her room early to sleep for the night, but I can hear she hasn't drifted off yet. Maybe if you went up to tell her she needs to sleep?"

"I will do that," I said. I was glad I'd had the idea to bring the photo with me.

Upstairs, I found Kelly Helm kicking at her wall. I could see the smudge marks. Poor Kelly. What would Alex Helm do if he saw?

I gently brought Kelly's legs down and then rubbed at the wall with spit and my finger. Mother's spit cleans everything, haven't you heard?

"How are you doing?" I asked Kelly.

"Fine," she said, not looking me in the eye.

"Sweetie, no one is fine on the day of her mother's funeral. When my father died, I cried all day," I said. "And I was thirty-three. You're only five."

"I don't feel like crying," said Kelly, her tone defiant. "She's been gone for a long time. I don't miss her anymore."

I wasn't sure if I believed this or not. If it was true, it was something to be worried about even more than her mother's loss. "Kelly, you can tell me the truth. Your mother loved you and you must be sad that she is gone."

"Grandpa says that she isn't worth being sad about."

I realized I was chewing at my lower lip and had almost broken through the skin. "Kelly, I brought you a special picture," I said and tried not to look around suspiciously to see if anyone was watching.

"Is it a picture of Jesus?" she asked.

"No," I said. "It's a picture of your mother." I held it out and smoothed it so she could see it. "This is the photo your grandmother showed at the funeral, when your mom graduated from high school. I noticed that you didn't have any photos of her up anywhere in the house and thought you might like to keep this." I was preparing myself to talk to her about putting it away whenever her father or grandfather came in, realizing that I was going to ask a five-year-old to lie.

But she shook her head. "I don't want it. She's not my mother anymore."

"Of course she is, Kelly. She will always be your mother." What in the world had Alex Helm said to her?

"No, she's not. Daddy's going to find me a better mother."

I was outraged. "Kelly, I hope your dad

377

does marry again and finds some kind of happiness." If, as it seemed now, he was not a murderer, then he had the right to marry again — in due time and maybe after some therapy. "I hope that you have someone in your life who can be your mother, but you can't just erase who your mother is."

"Grandpa says that God won't make me stay with Mommy. She left us, so she doesn't deserve to have us. She won't have anyone. She'll be all alone in heaven, and I'll be with him and daddy and his new wife."

"Kelly, please don't say that." I slowly folded the photo and put it back in my jacket pocket. Maybe she would want it later. Maybe when she was old enough to understand . . .

"Grandpa says that God killed Mommy," said Kelly. "Because she wasn't good enough for us. He says that God makes sure people die who don't deserve to live and who only make other people sad."

I wanted to slap Alex Helm again. And then I wanted to cut out his lying, blasphemous tongue. And then Jared Helm could get in line for doing nothing to counter his poisonous father.

It all sounded so much like the letter the Westons had read from at the first press conference. It made me shiver now, thinking how clearly Carrie had foretold what would happen after her own death.

I read Kelly some "new" stories her grandfather had brought — all of them moral homilies with no fun at all. And then I made my way back downstairs.

Alex Helm was in the kitchen and simply waved to me. Lucky for him he didn't come close enough for me to touch.

I walked home and put the photograph of Carrie Helm in a safe place in my bedroom.

The day after the funeral, the Westons called me to update me on custody proceedings. It seemed that the laws in Utah were not favorable to grandparents in terms of custody, and their lawyer had advised them to drop the case. Aaron Weston was still fasting and praying about it, determined that he would not give up on his granddaughter, but they didn't leave me with much hope for getting Kelly away from the Helms.

CHAPTER 26

In late March, the renters of Anna and To-bias Torstensen's house had a pipe burst. As usual in Utah, it wasn't spring so much as alternating summer and winter. A danger-ous time of year for pipes.

A crew came out to fix the pipes and they ended up having to dig up a considerable section of Tobias's garden. And that was when they found the body of Tobias's first wife. At least, they found a human skeleton deep under the dirt and called the police. They weren't sure yet who it was.

As soon as the renters called Kurt, he called me.

"I think all they know at this point is that the body is between twenty and forty years dead, and that it's a woman who was in her twenties."

"Has anyone called Tomas and Liam?" I asked. I wasn't so sure about Anna. She had begun her cruise and this would only ruin it. And why should she have to come home to deal with this?

"Could you do that?" asked Kurt.

I still had their numbers from before. I had an emergency number for the cruise, too, but I didn't want to use that and interrupt Anna's first chance to get away from problems with Tobias and his first wife. If the police decided to call her to come home, they could do it themselves. Her sons could deal with the rest of the issues here, including the renters' rights.

I tried to call Liam, but he didn't pick up. Then I tried Tomas, and when he answered, I recited the facts as I knew them: the skeleton of a woman had been found in the garden of his father's house.

Tomas was understandably upset. "Well, someone else must have put it there. Though I don't know how Dad never found it, considering the time he spent in that dirt."

I let him think that through himself. "I just wanted you to know what had happened. Do you want me to call Liam, as well?"

Tomas assured me that he would call Liam.

I felt rather morbid walking over to the house, but I did just that. There were nearly a dozen people in protective suits in the backyard, and yellow police tape had been wrapped around the perimeter. I craned my neck and caught a glimpse of soil samples being taken. The skeleton was already gone, and I was glad about that.

The new renter, Sister Brenda Geary, came out and hurried over to me. She was in her late thirties and her bleached blonde hair stood out all over her head. She looked a little lost.

"They've said we're going to have to find a hotel for the next several nights while they work here. Until they've identified her and what happened, we can't be here. But we spent all our money getting into this place. We thought it would be such a great change for the kids to come to a nice neighborhood." She and her husband had moved from downtown Salt Lake City, trying to get their teenage son away from a gang. "Don't worry about that," I assured her. "The ward will pay for a condo for a few nights." In fact, Kurt was likely to pay for it out of his own pocket, which meant out of my own pocket. When Kurt could not justify using church funds to help people, this was what we did.

I spent some time helping Brenda go through the house and pack a few days' worth of clothes for each child and herself and her husband. Then the police asked her for the key and locked up the place.

I called Kurt and he asked me to arrange things, so I drove her to a condo complex where Kurt sometimes sent women who needed to be away from their husbands for a while before they decided on what their next step would be. It wasn't far from the neighborhood, just down off the highest ridge of the mountain, and I spent most of the afternoon ferrying each child separately, since all three were at different schools and got out at different times.

Finally, I got home myself and found Samuel there, waiting for me in that quiet way of his.

"Mom, can I ask you some questions?"

I sat down next to him at the kitchen counter, staring at the bag of potato chips that he had nearly finished off. "Is this about the body in the Torstensen's yard? I don't think they have an identification on it yet."

"It's about Kenneth. And the church."

"Oh," I said. "When did you two talk?" I felt a pang that I hadn't followed up with Kenneth since Carrie Helm's funeral.

"A little bit last weekend, on the phone," Samuel said. "But it's not just that one phone call. It's a lot of little comments he's made."

"Apparently Kenneth is struggling with the church," I said. I didn't want Samuel to think I was endorsing Kenneth's complaints about the church, but I didn't want to ignore them, either.

"Yeah, I got that already," said Samuel. "But last week, Dad pulled me aside and told me to be careful not to get too wrapped up with Kenneth's ideas, that it could be dangerous for me. He wants me to focus on preparing for a mission in August."

Samuel would turn eighteen then, and while he didn't have to go right away, the church encouraged young people to go as early as possible, and not to put off a mission for college or work. The church had even begun to encourage those who hadn't saved enough for their own missions to go anyway, because there were always wealthy donors who would reimburse the church for the monthly $400 bill. Not that Kurt would let that happen with our son.

"Is there anything in particular that Kenneth said that's bothering you?"

Samuel hesitated. "It was about temple marriage. He said that he wasn't sure he wanted to marry someone for eternity. He made a joke about it, but he said that it was hard enough to commit to 'till death do you part.' "

"He isn't dating anyone seriously, is he?" I knew that sometimes the parents were the last to know, but I'd always hoped my sons would communicate better with me.

Samuel shrugged. "He dated a few girls a couple of years ago, but I think he's serious about not wanting to get married. He says that there are almost no girls who are interested in dating someone who doesn't want to get married. At least in Utah."

Suddenly, I worried that Kenneth had other reasons for not dating. I'd always assumed he was just busy. But what if he had concerns about his sexuality? Kurt would be devastated by that, regardless of the new church policy that God ordained some of his children to be born homosexual. The idea that one of his sons might never be allowed to marry in the temple and never have children to be sealed to him eternally would be very hard for him. And no wonder it was confusing to Samuel. "Are you worried about something specific with Kenneth and marriage?" I asked.

"I guess I'm more wondering about people who don't get married and what their place is in the church. I mean, it's all about happy families and families are forever. The singles wards that Kenneth is assigned to right now is all about activities to get people dating, so they can get married, so they can leave the singles ward. But that's not how it works for everyone, is it?"

I could tell that Samuel was genuinely upset about this. His face was flushed and his voice was squeaking like it hadn't since he was fifteen. "I guess we have to figure that everyone has a family of one kind or another."

Samuel blew out a disgusted breath. "But that's not what I'm talking about. I'm talking about the fact that you have to be married to be a bishop. Or to have any role of leadership in the church. If you're not, you're always a kind of second-class citizen."

He was only seventeen, but he saw this so clearly. "I need to talk to Kenneth," I said. I really did need to. I didn't want to give Samuel the wrong kind of comfort. If Kenneth didn't want to get married right now, that was one thing. If he was gay, that was something else again. I had no trouble with a gay son, but it wasn't an easy situation in the church right now. Proposition 8 in California and the specter of same-sex marriage laws here in Utah had made for some militant anti-gay sentiments even among people who claimed to love everyone.

There was a long silence. Then Samuel said, "I hate the way that people are so judgmental in the church. Do you know that there are some people saying that Carrie Helm was punished for leaving her family?"

I was relieved that we were changing the topic, even though the Helms weren't easy to talk about, either. "I think we might be less judgmental if we understand what Carrie Helm's life was like, how difficult it was for her. She left her daughter, yes." I still struggled with this myself. "But we don't know all the reasons for that. We don't know what she thought she was doing, in her heart. Maybe she thought she was saving her daughter somehow."

"Have you ever thought about leaving us?" asked Samuel.

He was on a roll with the hard questions today. "A long time ago," I said honestly. "When you were all little and I was still inexperienced with the mothering thing." I watched Samuel to see what his reaction would be, but he seemed only thoughtful.

"So you don't think about it now?" he asked.

I shook my head. "Being a mother is the most important thing in my life," I said. I

387

was good at what I did as a mother. It was what I had spent my whole life doing. I suppose that was the real reason that I hadn't gone back to school or found a job yet. It felt like it would be saying that being a mother wasn't enough.

"That's why you're so bothered about the Carrie Helm disappearance, right? You're worried about her little girl," said Samuel.

"It's definitely part of it."

"She's cute. I've seen her at church," said Samuel. Then, after a moment, he added, "It seems like it's hard being a mom. Harder than being a dad. You have to be perfect all the time. You're always supposed to be looking out for your kids. You never get a break."

"Ha!" There was truth in it, especially in Mormon culture. On Mother's Day, the entire sacrament meeting in most wards is devoted to talking about how perfect someone's mother is. It was almost always sickly sweet, with tears but rarely laughter. I had once been in a ward where the bishop bought orchid corsages for the oldest mother, newest mother, and mother with the most children (the winning mother had fourteen children). I wondered sometimes if we would expand the categories to the longest delivery, the worst episiotomy, or the ugliest baby, just for fun.

"Even moms have their own lives. We have to try to juggle things. We just do the best we can. We're not perfect. We're not angels," I said softly. "No matter what some people say."

A week later, I was outside, bringing groceries in from the car when I heard a scream from down the street. I let go of the bag I was carrying and turned instinctively. I was running before I thought about where I was going, and then I saw Kelly Helm trying to pull away from Alex Helm, who was dragging her off of the front lawn of their house and back inside. I could have stopped right then and gone back to my groceries. I could have reminded myself of Kurt's advice about people needing space to figure things out on their own. But this was a little girl who was being manhandled by someone who ought to have been protecting her.

And it was Kelly. My Kelly.

I caught up to Alex Helm just as he reached the door. "Who do you think you are?" I demanded, breathless. I really was going to have to do more exercise if I got this angry this often.

"I'm sorry to have disturbed your day," Alex Helm said, his eyes glinting, "but I am simply disciplining a disobedient child. I am sure you have done the same in your day, Sister Wallheim."

God, I wished that I wasn't just "Sister Wallheim." I wished that being the bishop's wife granted me some title of authority.

"Disobedient child? What in the world was she doing that was so terrible?"

"I told her not to go outside. It was a simple rule, designed to keep her safe," he said. He was holding her, and she was struggling.

How I wanted to yank her away from him and call the police. But I knew very well that it would only end with her being sent back home. What I had seen did not constitute child abuse. It probably wouldn't even warrant a follow-up call with DCFS.

"There aren't any news vans out here. What is the danger you are trying to protect her from, then?" I asked.

"That is none of your concern. I told her to follow a rule, and she refused to do it. She needs to learn that she can't do that."

Was this just about power? "It's a nice day. The sun is out. It's not even that cold," I said. It was April at last. "The snow is gone. She must be itching for a chance to feel the grass under her feet." As I looked over at her, I could see that Kelly had bare feet. The ground was still wet, and there were brown splotches from mud that had gotten between her toes, but it made me feel even more sorry for her. What was wrong with a little girl getting mud between her toes?

"Thank you for your opinion, but Kelly is my granddaughter and I am the one who will face the bar of God for her one day for how she is raised," said Alex Helm.

"Yes, you definitely will," I muttered. The heat I had felt when I came running over was gone now. I just wanted to hold Kelly's hand in mine, and tell her that everything was going to be all right, but that would be a lie, wouldn't it?

"Now, please get off my porch, Sister Wallheim, and let me get back to teaching my granddaughter the way that a proper young woman acts." He swept past me and slammed the door.

I was left with the realization that I had gained nothing, and might possibly have lost all the good will I had so carefully built up. False good will, but even so. And now? Alex Helm wasn't going to be asking me to come over and babysit Kelly for him, that was for sure.

CHAPTER 27

The police took two weeks to determine that the body in the Torstensens' backyard, killed by blunt-force trauma to the head, was "likely Helena Torstensen." The problem with an actual identification was that there were no dental records that anyone could find for Helena Torstensen, and they had no DNA from her. They could do a mitochondrial test with her two sons, but that would take months to finish and it would be expensive.

There was no evidence that she had had cancer, which was what Liam Torstensen now insisted. The stories Tobias had told about a heart condition and a car accident were both clearly out. But Liam seemed to believe that his father might have worked some kind of "mercy killing" on his young wife, and suffered for it for the rest of his life, concealing the guilt he felt, but still being enough in love with her that he did crazy things like trying to find women who looked like her to pretend with him for a while that she was still alive.

The only thing that made me consider Liam's version was that it helped explain how Tobias Torstensen could have remarried a woman like Anna and then lived happily with for thirty more years without a hint of a criminal personality. If a man was a wife murderer, how had he changed so completely? How could a man who killed be such a kind and loving father?

The police had called Anna back from her cruise, and it had taken her ten days to find a port and book a flight home. She'd only been back since the weekend, and she, too, had not been allowed in the house.

Anna had called to ask me to go with her to meet the police. I met her at the walk leading up to her house and was delighted to see her. I hugged her briefly, then stepped back to look at her. She looked tanned and tense.

"How are you doing?" I asked.

"As well as can be expected," she said.

She already knew the news about Joseph and Willow's baby coming, which I'd shared in a short email, excited that she and I were going to be grandmothers within a span of months. I suppose we could have emailed more, but I've never learned how to do real sharing via a computer screen.

"Thank you so much for coming," Anna said.

"I'm glad you called to ask me." I desperately wanted to find an answer here. The case with Carrie Helm seemed to have ground to a halt, and the police were not following any new leads. It seemed that her murder would go unsolved, and I found myself waking up in the middle of the night, unsettled by the thought.

"I feel like I'm reeling, like I haven't been able to sit down since I heard about the body," said Anna. "At first I thought it was the cruise, but even when I was on solid ground, I felt the same disorientation. The whole world keeps moving around me, and I have to keep looking at my feet or I will fall."

"I know," I said.

"It isn't just that he killed someone. It's that I never guessed. I always saw him as such a gentle man, incapable of violence for any reason." At least she wasn't spouting a theory like Tomas's about Tobias's innocence. "We all believed him," I said. I didn't like to think that I was gullible, but they say Utah is the con capital of the world. People who are strong adherents to a miracle-based religion are more likely to believe in other miracles. And we tend to believe the best of others, never guessing that a scam might be perpetrated on us by someone claiming to be a member of our own church.

"Thirty years," whispered Anna. "Why did he do it?"

"Kill her, you mean? Maybe there was some terrible argument, and then he panicked and buried her? I suspect he must have thought about her every day since then, and felt guilty about it."

"But that doesn't mean I have to forgive him, does it? He killed his wife and then hid it. He escaped all the consequences."

I felt more sympathy for him than she could in that moment, perhaps. Tobias had been so young at the time, and he had two sons to care for. He must have wondered what would happen to them if their mother was killed and their father was in prison for life.

"Everything was a lie. Every word that he ever said to me," said Anna, her whole body slumped as I had never seen it before, even when Tobias was on his deathbed. This wasn't just physical exhaustion. It was emotional dissolution.

"Surely not. He loved you, Anna. He truly did."

"He loved her, too," said Anna. "And look what he did to her."

I thought again of the brand new hammer Tobias had kept by the bedside, a twin to the ruined one in the garden, and quailed.

"What's in that?" asked Anna, nodding to the bag I was carrying.

It held the old hammer and the dress I had found in the shed. I had delayed taking it into the police several times during the last two weeks, not wanting to deal with questions about why I hadn't called them in the first place, back in February, when Tobias had still been alive. But now I wished I had made a separate visit so that Anna didn't have to deal with so much all at once.

I showed Anna the dress again, reminding her that I had found it in the shed. This time she saw the bloodstains immediately.

"How did I miss this? I was so blind," she said. Then her head jerked up. "You think that it was the dress she was wearing when she died?"

"It might be."

"And the hammer?"

I told her I'd found it in the garden.

"A hammer," she whispered. "Like the

one on his side of the bed, always within reach."

I put a hand on her shoulder. "It might be a coincidence."

She stared at me. "You don't believe that."

"I believe that people can change," I said truthfully. And Tobias might be one of them. Wasn't that what religion was all about?

But it was also true that if people changed, part of the evidence of the change was the willingness to face consequences for their past sins. And Tobias had not shown that. He had done everything he could to obscure the truth about his wife's death, until he himself had been too far gone to tell any more.

A police car drove up and a detective got out. He introduced himself to us as "Detective Eric Dun," then motioned to us to follow him into the house, so we did. He was younger than I would have imagined, and he had startlingly blue eyes. He smelled faintly of motor oil, though I could only guess at why.

As we stepped through the front door, I felt surprise rinse through me like cold water. The house seemed completely changed. It wasn't just the plastic on the carpet and the stale smell. The furniture had all changed. I had seen it when the

Gearys moved in, but it was strange to be here now with Anna at my side. It made the change feel more permanent. The house had died, too, not just Tobias.

"Can you think of anything that your husband might have told you about his first wife that would tell us why he killed her?" asked the detective, when we were all sitting in the front room.

"He never spoke of her to my recollection," said Anna.

"Never? Did that strike you as odd?" asked Detective Dun. He was sitting across from us on an upholstered chair the Gearys must have brought in.

Anna looked at me, and I smiled at her reassuringly.

"It was a painful topic and it didn't seem to have immediate relevance to our lives. She was dead and he was married to me," said Anna.

"Well, what about your life with him? Was there anything about it that made you suspicious about the kind of man you had married?" He took notes on a small pad of paper spread over his lap.

Anna told him about an argument over checking accounts, when she had wanted to have hers separate from Tobias's. She claimed it was the only time she had ever heard Tobias raise his voice to her. "It was right here. In this room," she added, pointing at the space between us, and I could see that she was imagining it in her mind.

"And what about his sons? Was he ever angry or violent with them?"

Anna shook her head. "He sometimes shouted at them to get their attention, but I never worried he would hurt them. He was a very good father and loved his sons devotedly."

"Hmm. So if his wife had threatened to take the boys away with her?" Detective Dun asked.

This wasn't what I had expected. I hadn't realized the police took this case so seriously. I thought this was only a formality.

"I don't know," said Anna. She looked at me again.

If someone had threatened to take my boys away when they were that age, I might have been capable of murder. But then again, I might have been capable of murder on any day of the week. I didn't have grand notions about some people being born killers and others not.

"This is hard for her to take in, of course. We all thought of Tobias as a wonderful man," I said as tears started to drip down Anna's face. I handed over the dress and the hammer and explained where I had found them.

"Damn," said the detective as he opened the bag and held up each piece in the light streaming in from the front window.

"Can you still test the blood on the dress?" I asked. "Or whatever is on the hammer? Could it be the murder weapon?"

"It could be. The problem is the chain of custody. You took the hammer from the garden and to your garage, where it has been for months now. And as for the dress, we don't know anything about how the blood got to be on it. If you'd called us immediately, we might have been able to question Tobias about it while he was still alive." Detective Dun was staring at me accusingly.

"But there was no body at the time," I said. "You would have thought I was crazy, thinking a dying old man had killed his first wife some thirty-odd years ago."

"I wouldn't have," he said.

I rolled my eyes at him.

He let out a breath and seemed to sink into himself a bit. "I'll tell you a story about why I would have listened to you, all right?"

"Okay," I said. I looked at Anna and she nodded.

"My sister was killed by her husband. Three years ago. She called me the day it happened, asking me for help. I thought I could wait to get to her. I thought she was exaggerating."

I bristled at that.

"That evening, when I finally got to her house, she was dead. So I take women more seriously now. I listen, and try to step in when I can still save a life."

He was breathing heavily, and it looked like he felt a little ill. I knew what that was like, giving away too much of yourself when you hadn't expected to and then waiting to see how it was received.

"I find myself telling that story more and more often now. I wish it wasn't applicable in so many of the cases I investigate, but it is."

"Even here in Utah?" said Anna.

"Maybe especially here in Utah," said Detective Dun.

It humanized the detective for me, seeing why he felt called to his profession. I'd never faced a tragedy like that in my own life — before this. "But it's not as if Tobias could be prosecuted now," I said. "I don't see what the point is in making a fuss over all of this."

Detective Dun straightened his shoulders, back in his authority role, his head rising above the line of the chair. "The point is

401

that people like you think they have seen enough detective shows on TV to do things on their own. But they shouldn't. If there were a possibility of a real case here, you would have jeopardized it to the point of making the D.A. wonder if he should even try to go to trial. Any defense lawyer would have a field day with the possibilities of what might have happened to the dress and hammer in the time it was in your garage."

He was right, of course. After the fact, I could see that I had taken too much on myself. It stung to hear him treat me like a child who had stepped into the street without looking both ways.

"Promise me you won't ever do something like this again. Call the police if you find something. Immediately," said Detective Dun. There was just a hint of pleading in his voice now, underneath the demand. He stood up, putting everything back in the bag. "I will tell you what I am most afraid of, Mrs. Torstensen," he said, towering above her now, since she was still on the couch.

"What's that?" asked Anna, her hands shaking until she put them flat on her knees.

"If your husband was able to fool you and all your neighbors, and keep this body buried right under your noses, it makes us

concerned that we may yet find other bodies," said the detective. "It could be years
before we figure out the extent of what he
did."

This struck me as both far-fetched and
insensitive to Anna's emotional state. Surely
the police didn't assume that there were serial killers behind every body found buried
in a garden. Although, I suppose a body
having gone undiscovered for so long was a
sign of careful planning. Sociopathic serial
killers are good at covering up their crimes,
because their strategy is never compromised
by remorse.

Not that I was any expert on serial killers.
As Detective Dun had said, I was relying on
what I'd seen on TV and what I'd read
about Ted Bundy and Arthur Gary Bishop,
both Mormons, in the days when I'd been
an atheist and looking for reasons to stop
believing in the church.

I stood up and tried to meet the detective's
eyes. "What makes you think that there are
any other bodies?" Had they found something in the garden that we hadn't heard
about yet? Were there unclaimed murder
victims in Draper from the last thirty years
they think could be linked to Tobias?

"We don't know if there are, but a man
who has killed once and gotten away with it

is more likely to try again," said Detective Dun.

"Now aren't you the one who is making assumptions?" How pompous that sounded. He was the detective here. I was just a stay-at-home mother and a bishop's wife. That was my life. It just so happened that this one murder had impinged on my world. Well, two murders, I suppose.

The detective reopened his notebook and wrote a few scrawled words. I imagined they were warnings about not talking to me again.

"He wasn't a dangerous man," said Anna. "If you'd known him, you'd have seen how carefully he controlled his temper."

"Then he had a temper? You saw that?" asked Detective Dun.

"Well, we all have feelings that we can't control," Anna said. She was still seated on the couch and had to look up to talk to him. I wished she'd stand up and not let him intimidate her like that. "But we control how we act on those feelings."

"So you're saying he often suppressed his feelings?" said Detective Dun. "He was a very controlled person?"

"Tobias was a good man. A good husband and father," said Anna.

"Have you considered the fact that you

were in danger every day of your life with him?" asked Detective Dun.

Anna put a hand to her throat and shook her head.

Detective Dun seemed to realize finally he had gone too far. But the burden his sister's death had left on him was heavy. I could understand that.

"If you could guide me through the rest of the house," he said.

Anna stood at last, and led him through the house then, showing him every little corner or cubbyhole she could think of. She insisted she had cleaned them all when she moved, but then the detective pointed out a wall that was strangely placed, considering the footprint of the rooms overhead. While Anna and I waited in uncomfortable silence, Detective Dun went up to Tobias's shed and got a pry bar. Then he came back and used it to break through the wall with a few well-placed taps. There was only sheetrock there, no studs.

"What do you think you're going to find?" I asked.

He shrugged. "You never know. But sometimes people keep things they shouldn't. They don't want to let go."

Then the space was open, dust flying all around, and I saw him lean in and pull out

405

a book and some papers. The book, when he opened it, was clearly a diary written by Helena Torstensen, more than thirty years ago, beginning the day of her wedding. The papers were her wedding certificate and other legal documents and photos.

Detective Dun turned to the last entry in the diary.

"Does it say something about being afraid of Tobias killing her?" I asked after watching him try to read it in the dimly lit basement.

He shook his head. "Not that I saw. But I'll read through all of it." Then he leaned into the space again and pulled out some clothes. I didn't know why Tobias had kept the other dress in the shed when he'd kept all these clothes here.

The detective packed everything up, keeping notes on it all. "What happens now?" I asked.

"We still have to prove the identity of the woman. And then the autopsy will have to show us conclusively how she died. But even after all that, I don't know if we'll ever be absolutely certain about who killed her at this stage. We may leave the case open," he said.

"And what about the body?" I asked.

"After we've finished the investigation we

can release her remains to the family to bury." He nodded to Anna. "That would be your sons, I assume."

"Yes," said Anna quietly. She looked at me.

"I'll make sure the arrangements are made for that, Anna. If it happens." Another funeral for the Relief Society to put on. I could make sure this part was done right for the long-dead woman, even if we had done so much else wrong.

CHAPTER 28

We had a big celebration for Joseph and Willow at the family dinner in late April. We'd skipped the March family dinner. Kurt had slept through his non-meeting times because of the pressure of the tax season, even on family Sabbath.

I made a cake and everyone brought presents to go with the one I'd already bought.

"We're having a girl!" Joseph announced.

My stomach dropped and I did my best to conceal this reaction. Why wasn't I happy? We needed a girl in the family. This should feel like my real chance to fill the hole that my daughter had left in my life. I should be able to let go of Kelly and Carrie Helm now, shouldn't I?

Kurt was listing everyone's guesses about the birth date, and promising a "significant" prize to the person who guessed it right. He looked like the father of the bride, the way he was strutting around. Too bad he couldn't hand out cigars.

"They're so happy about this, maybe you should start having kids, too," Zachary said, nudging Kenneth.

"I think your mother and I would prefer that you were married first, Kenneth," said Kurt.

Kurt still hadn't talked to Kenneth about his problems with the church, and I hadn't talked to him about my suspicions that he might be gay. How do you ask your son that? By the way, are you gay? If he's not, does he ever get over your asking him? Maybe it was best for me to wait for Kenneth to come out of the closet in his own good time. If he was even in a closet.

"Prefer?" I said sternly. "If any of my sons has a child without marrying the mother first, I will make sure you suffer significant pain," I said sternly, looking at Samuel and Zachary more than Kenneth.

"Oooh, we're scared!" said Zachary.

"Don't mock a mother with a thirst for vengeance," said Kurt.

"I thought Mom was all about forgiveness," said Samuel.

"I'm about making sure that I get to know my grandchildren. And if there is any chance that I will end up missing out on the life of one my grandchildren, you will all pay for it," I said.

We ate the cake and then the boys had a wrestling contest, which ended with me losing one glass vase I didn't care much about and two plates I did. Apparently, what was most important about this was that they had proven their masculinity to their own satisfaction, and to the satisfaction of everyone else. Including Kurt, who joined in at the very end, and lost to Kenneth, which I could see made him grin fiercely.

Finally, they all went home, leaving the house very quiet. Samuel went upstairs to get ready for Monday classes, and Kurt put on an apron and helped me do the dishes.

"Do you want to talk about the baby?" he asked.

Which one did he mean? Joseph and Willow's or ours? I sighed. "What is there to say?" What had there ever been to say?

"That is what I always thought before now, that talking would only cause pain and heartache, Linda, but I don't know. The grief seems to be affecting you more and more lately, instead of less and less."

"It was an important moment in my life. In some ways, it defines me and what I have become since then."

"Then why don't you want to talk about it?" asked Kurt.

"Because you and I think so differently about it. I think we'd just argue over it."

"We're both hurt by what happened. Why can't we find similarity in that?"

I handed him a dish to hand wash. "I think you want answers more than I do. I think the questions are more soothing to me."

"Questions aren't soothing. By definition, they demand answers."

I pressed my lips tightly together. There it was, the difference between us, the reason that we never talked about this together.

We got through the rest of the week as usual. Kurt had his meetings. I was on autopilot mostly, dishes and laundry and making sure that Samuel had what he needed for the last term of his senior year.

He'd been accepted to the University of Utah and BYU. He and Kurt would soon have to talk about whether he needed to defer his acceptance for a mission or if he planned to go to a semester or two of college first — if he went on a mission at all. Joseph's not going on a mission had nearly destroyed his relationship with Kurt, and that was back before Kurt was a bishop.

On Friday afternoon the first week in May, Kurt called to tell me that the police had more information on the Carrie Helm case.

"Do they know who did it?"

"It doesn't sound like they're much closer to that, but they wanted me to warn the two families involved that they will be releasing the information that she was found naked and it appears that she had sexual intercourse within an hour of her death. There is no physical evidence that it was rape."

Why had they taken so long to release this information? Why hadn't they done anything to find her killer since her death? Was it because they, too, thought she'd deserved what she got? "Do they think it was this Will she was staying with in Las Vegas?" I asked.

"Apparently, Will has an alibi for the time of her death and he was hundreds of miles away in Las Vegas. But they claim they are still looking for the man involved and they're hoping this press release will bring a witness forward who might identify the killer. The reason they called me was because they don't know how the information is going to affect the Westons in particular. It seems that Carrie was soliciting sexual partners for money on this Will's computer while she was staying with him. She posted photos of herself that aren't very, shall we say, tasteful?"

I felt my throat constrict. What experience

with sex would have made her treat her own body so badly? Was this yet further evidence of how terrible her marriage to Jared had been?

"I thought you might be the best person to talk to the Westons about this," Kurt was saying. "Make sure they're not blindsided. I don't know if there's anything you can really do to make it hurt less, but you can try."

"All right, I'll call them," I said. I couldn't even blame this chore on his being bishop. I had kept on with this even when he'd told me not to.

"Maybe you should go over and talk to them in person," said Kurt.

"Obviously. Kurt, I meant I would call and ask them if I could come over to visit. I just want to make sure they're both home."

"Oh, yes. Good," said Kurt. "Thank you. I'll see you tonight?"

"Or maybe not, if I end up spending a lot of time with them."

"Right, of course. Then I'll call Samuel on his cell and see what he wants to eat."

I thought about asking him to get something somewhat healthy, but didn't. Kurt was proud of his refusal to eat rabbit food.

The last time I had talked to the Westons had been when they had told me that they were giving up the custody battle. After a minute of prayer that I would say the right thing, I called the number the Westons had left with me. A male voice answered immediately.

"This is Linda Wallheim," I said. "Is this Aaron?" I was surprised that he was home during the day.

"Yes, Linda, it's me."

"I was wondering if I could come over and talk to you," I said. "You and Judy both. Would you be home in about thirty minutes?" It would take me twenty minutes to drive north to Sandy.

"Yes, we'll be home. We don't do much these days, either of us." There was a short silence. "I lost my job when Carrie disappeared, and I couldn't go into work for several weeks. I haven't started looking for a new one yet. I can't find the heart for it and there's no guarantee that I would be able to get anything like the same level of position in management at another company."

"I'm so sorry," I said. "I didn't realize that." What kind of company would fire a man for having trouble working after his daughter disappeared?

"This is about Carrie, isn't it?" asked Aaron.

"Yes, yes it is," I said.

I left a note for Samuel atop a plate of

fruit suggesting that any of these would be an excellent choice for an after school snack. Then I got into the car.

As I drove by the Helm home, I could see Alex Helm through the front living room window. I cringed at the sight of him. Jared and Alex seemed to be sharing childcare responsibilities for Kelly now that the press had disappeared. I didn't think Kelly had gone back to school, and I hadn't seen her at all since the argument Alex and I had had back in March on his front lawn. How much of what her mother had done would Kelly ever understand? I didn't know. But for now, I had to deal with her grandparents, and the reality of her mother's death.

The drive did not take long enough. I tried to make myself appreciate the beautiful mountains on either side and the outline of the Great Salt Lake in the distance. Whenever friends from other parts of the country come to Utah, the first thing they mention is the feeling they get from the mountains. Some people feel oppressed by them. Others feel safe, like they are wrapped in a cocoon. But I am so used to them I take them for granted. If I go elsewhere, somewhere without mountains, that's when I realize how much I miss them. I don't know how anyone can tell what direction they're headed without mountains around to help.

I was dreading the conversation I would have to have with the Westons, who had already been forced by the law to virtually walk away from their granddaughter. Their lawyer claimed that even demanding a monthly visitation would be impossible unless they could prove that they had had frequent contact with their granddaughter before Carrie's death — which they hadn't. I arrived at the large house in a tract of large houses, and turned off the engine. I took a moment to gather my thoughts and stared out at the immaculate lawn. The flowers weren't as spectacular as Tobias Torstensen's, but it was clear that the lawn was treated with chemicals often and never allowed to go brown.

The three-car garage was dwarfed by the rest of the house. It was grey stucco and the columns in front rose to the third story. Inside, there were marble floors in the foyer, stained-glass windows in the dining room, and the kind of carpet so thick you can feel it even through your shoes.

With hardly a word, Aaron Weston led me to a small office that seemed completely unused, despite the huge oak desk in the center and the leather chairs. Judy was waiting for me there, as well.

I kept thinking about Carrie Helm. She'd come from this. How did any of her subsequent choices make sense, knowing that? Why would a woman who realized her marriage had failed run away to Las Vegas with a lover, and then feel forced to sell her body online, when she could have come home to this? Why hadn't she made frequent visits with Kelly to her parents? I knew she was afraid of her husband and likely her father-in-law, but to go from this to that — there was something I was missing.

"I'm so sorry," I said, my mind whirling.

"Oh, dear," said Judy. "That doesn't sound like a good beginning."

Aaron held her hand. "She's gone now. There's nothing more that can hurt us," he said, but there was a catch in his voice.

"It's going to be on the news tonight or tomorrow, but Kurt learned from the police that she was found naked and that she had had sex — most likely consensual — within an hour of her death." Putting it so baldly made me want to cringe. I wished I had thought of a better way, but really, what was going to make it sound better? I wanted to get the facts out quickly, so that I could get on to comforting them.

417

Kurt would really be better at this than I would. He would be able to tell them with far more confidence that they would see their daughter again, that she would rise again in the resurrection to her perfect form. All I knew was that these parents must be feeling the same way I had felt after my daughter died, and there was a part of me that was cowardly enough that I wanted to shrink away from them.

Judy let out a long breath, and I stared at her. For that one moment, I thought that she was faking her sadness. I don't know what it was about her, but something seemed false to me. Too many tears. Too much ultra-feminine hand-wringing and weakness.

But what right had I to judge other women for their unique responses to their own situations? I shook myself. Judy Weston had the right to act as over-the-top as she needed to. A mother wasn't supposed to outlive her children. She was supposed to lay herself down and take the blow instead. But we didn't always get that choice.

"Is it this man Will?" asked Aaron. "Do they think he did it? Are you telling us there will be an arrest soon?" There was a fierce look in his eyes.

"No," I said. "It isn't Will. He was far

away at the time." I took a breath and steeled myself for the rest. "There's more, I'm afraid."

"Oh," said Judy, gripping her husband's arm more tightly.

"She apparently met a stranger near to where she was found, to trade sex for payment."

There was no sound from either parent.

"She had put photos of herself online. Asking for men who wanted to meet her," I said. "For money."

"Oh, my poor Carrie," said Judy. She put a hand to her heart.

There it was again. My sense that she wasn't really feeling the emotions she was putting on. What was going on here?

"So the police are following up on this lead? This man she met for sex? They think he's the killer?" asked Aaron, who was pale but composed, his hands resting gently in his lap. He was very well dressed for someone who didn't have a job. He was wearing a full suit and a white shirt that had probably been professionally cleaned and starched. His tie was expensive silk, better than anything Kurt had ever worn. I realized, thinking back, that he'd always been dressed well — I just hadn't noticed before, because of the context of our meetings.

Why had Carrie left Jared Helm and not come home? Why had she been virtually estranged from her parents?

I had been silent for too long. I had to focus to remember Aaron Weston's question. "The man she met for sex? Yes, I suspect they will try to find him. I don't know anything about that part." It was hard to speak. Words demanded a certain distance from pain, and I felt as if the pain — the pain of Carrie's death, of continually being reminded how little I knew about her, of how I'd failed her, of her daughter's suffering, the pain of my own loss, so distant and yet so fresh — had come crashing down over my head, drowning me. They said that you eventually conquered grief, but it didn't feel like that to me. It felt like grief conquered me again and again, and I never knew when it would strike.

"But they aren't going to give up on the case, just because of how she was killed, are they?" asked Aaron.

I took a deep breath and cleared my throat. Then I took another breath. "It's been given a lot of publicity. That's thanks to you two, so I think you can take some comfort in that. You did help, in the end."

"Do they know who he is? Do they have any information about him?" asked Aaron.

He wasn't looking at me. He was looking at his hands, and the words sounded sad and almost rote.

"I don't know. I'm sure they're doing all they can," I said.

"But do they have a name? A face? Anything?" Aaron's questions were rapid-fire. "Do they know where she met him, if it was so close to where she died? Was it in a car? Did they have an argument? Did she change her mind about having sex with him and he got angry with her?"

I shook my head. "We'll have to wait and see. I just wanted to make sure that you knew about this before it came out publicly."

"But why?" said Judy. Her face was dripping makeup now.

"I don't know," I said softly. "Maybe someday we will find out the answer. Maybe we won't. We'll have to live with it anyway."

"I think Judy meant why would the police put out this information publicly?" Aaron asked. "They don't have to tell all the details. It would only tarnish Carrie's memory."

"Oh. Of course." I scrambled to think logically rather than emotionally. "They must think it will help them find the killer, if people know more about the circumstances of her death." That was my own conclusion, anyway.

"Or maybe they're doing it because we pressured them and made them look bad," said Aaron darkly. "Maybe this is their revenge. We look bad in return. Carrie's name is forever ruined. And what about Kelly? What will this do to that little girl?"

"I'm sure she won't understand it," I said. "She's too young, really. That will protect her, in a way." I felt a sensation like scissors in my stomach at the thought of Kelly Helm hearing this about her mother. I could imagine Jared and Alex Helm sitting her down and forcing her to listen to the details. They would want to pound into Kelly that her mother had been a bad woman, that Kelly should forget about her.

"And what about how it makes us look to our friends and neighbors, in the church? It will make everyone question the way that we raised our daughters. How will anyone trust me in a business situation? I used to have control over millions of dollars." Aaron looked angry, but there was a thread of panic in his anger. It sounded like he cared more about his own vanity than his daughter's death — or his granddaughter.

But I tried to be sympathetic. He had probably not slept for days, I reminded myself. And he had just buried his daughter.

He had lost his job. He had this huge house to pay for. The pressure on him must be enormous. But even as his wife was reacting too dramatically, I could not help but think that he was taking this all in too coldly. Instead of feeling anguish, he seemed to be planning, thinking about his future business empires and his reputation. And that made me wonder about his lost job, and his choice to give up pursuit of custody of Kelly legally.

"There's no need to make assumptions about what will happen in the future. One day at a time," I said. I had thought that Kelly would be better off with the Westons, but suddenly I was not so sure.

I had seen real love, however twisted, between Alex Helm and Kelly. He was protective of her, and seemed to see her as more than an extension of himself. I wasn't so sure about the Westons. I realized I had never seen them interact with Kelly, unless you counted Aaron Weston's addressing his granddaughter from the funeral podium. Did the Westons love Kelly? It was humbling to realize how quickly I had jumped to the conclusion that they would feel for the little girl as I did.

I stayed a few minutes longer, then drove home in a daze, wondering if I had been a party to bringing Carrie Helm home from

Las Vegas, and if that had ultimately led to her death. Was I part of her betrayal, too?

CHAPTER 29

On Sunday night, Kurt told me there had been an argument in priesthood between Alex Helm and Brother Rhodes over the subject of black people and the priesthood. Brother Rhodes had loudly insisted on the historical facts, which were that black men had been ordained in the early days of the church, but then the practice stopped and certain General Authorities said that it was because black skin was the "mark of Cain." Others said that it was because blacks had been "less valiant" in the preexistence. Those General Authorities had gone silent when the 1978 revelation restored universal priesthood.

I smiled a little. "I almost wish I had been there," I said.

"No, you don't. When Alex Helm suggested that God had His own reasons for denying blacks the priesthood, Brother Rhodes insisted that there had never been any revelation to take priesthood from black men, that it was all just racism within the church and that Joseph Smith would have been appalled. Alex Helm nearly burst into flame, he was so incensed. He declared that he could not stay in the building with such a person, and walked out."

"Hmm. Am I supposed to be unhappy about that result?" I asked.

"He marched into Primary and yanked Kelly out of her class. He gave a piece of his mind to the Primary Presidency while he was on his way."

"He didn't," I said, my heart sinking. The Primary Presidency was a thankless job. I'd been one of the two counselors a few years ago, and in addition to the long hours spent planning programs, visiting children at home, and preparing lessons, there was also the reality that the most capable members were often used in positions other than as Primary teachers, which made staffing a constant problem.

"The three of them came to talk to me this evening, and we discussed what could be done for Kelly. But if Alex Helm stays in the home, they are going to find it difficult to contact her."

Where was the best place for Kelly? I didn't know anymore. Home with me? But that wasn't even an option.

"Is there anything you would recommend the Primary Presidency try? Would you be willing to talk to them about how to work around him?"

I sighed. "I'll think about it."

I was still thinking when Anna Torstensen called me Wednesday of that week. She was staying in a nearby condo since the Gearys had moved back into the house, now that the police were finished with it.

"It's definitely Helena's body," she said.

"Did they find dental records?"

"Yes. And a lot more than that. I don't want to talk about it over the phone, though."

"No, I can understand that. Do you want me to come over?"

"I'll make some lunch," said Anna. "We can pretend we're just two friends having tea together."

When I arrived, she gave me a choice between a raspberry-vanilla tea and an orange-chamomile tea. I chose the former because I was afraid the latter would make me too sleepy. I wanted to be alert for all of this.

She brought out sandwiches, tuna with cucumber on the top. They looked very fancy, and when I took a bite, I realized they tasted even better. Crisp and delicate. Even the bread was amazing. I hadn't remembered Anna doing anything this elaborate before. The kitchen was smaller in this condo, but it had very nice equipment and was set up efficiently.

"I realized when I got back from the cruise that the last thing I wanted to do was go back to work at the bank. Full- or part-time, I had the revelation that I have a limited amount of time left in my life and since I don't need the money anymore, I want to use it doing things that are fun. So I've taken up gourmet baking as a hobby. That's homemade bread. I'm working on a few different recipes, to perfect them. And I've started to write a cookbook to share my secrets."

"It's incredible," I said. Anna smiled at the compliment.

"So, this is what I know about her," she said. "Helena was a convert to the church from Catholicism. Apparently her parents were very opposed to her joining what they saw as a cult. This was in the seventies, and a lot of people thought that about Mormons then. Polygamy, horns, and all that," said Anna.

"A lot of people still think that," I said.

And I could understand it. There are things Mormons still do to make it seem like we are a cult. Secrecy about the temple. The fanatically positive view of Joseph Smith and Brigham Young. Forced tithing. Talk about preparing for the end of the world. And the way we make it difficult to leave the church, even when people want to.

"Well, the police have found her brother. Her father has been dead for years." She tapped her teacup to the table. "But the brother apparently did not want to hear anything about her, said that she was dead to the family and had been since she joined the church and married Tobias."

"Oh, how awful," I said. That no one cared that this woman was dead seemed worse to me almost than what Tobias had done to her.

"So when she disappeared, they didn't notice. That was part of the reason that Tobias got away with it."

She was assuming that Tobias had murdered his first wife now. "Didn't she have any friends?"

"No one has come forward to talk about her. She seems to have been very quiet." Anna sighed, and then took a sip of tea. "I suspect that was what Tobias liked about her. And apparently, it was what he looked for in me, as well."

I was taken aback at this. "There's nothing wrong with being quiet," I said. I knew Anna to be more thoughtful than quiet. And not at all the kind of woman who could be easily deceived or manipulated.

She shook herself. "Maybe not."

"Are they certain it was Tobias who killed her, then?" I asked.

"Who else could it have been?" she said, then shrugged. "Since he's dead and there's no one to charge, they're not working particularly swiftly. I haven't heard the specifics about cause of death."

"What about how she was killed or why? Is there any hint in the papers she left?"

"A little," said Anna. "The police say that she came into some money shortly before she disappeared. An uncle had died and left it to her. Her father took his sweet time telling the lawyers where she was living, and she was surprised about it, coming so late like that. There's also an entry in her diary where she talks about what she wants to do with the money. She wanted to see the world on a cruise ship." Anna gave me a pained, ironic smile.

"Ah," I said.

"It made me wonder, when I read the entry, if Tobias had planted the idea of a

430

cruise in my head. I don't remember him ever talking about it, but I couldn't help but feel —"

"Violated?" I said.

She nodded and looked down. She took a sandwich from the plate. "It might have been only a coincidence," she said. "But I didn't want to be the woman she should have been, just because Tobias wanted that. As expiation of some kind."

She had been the woman Helena Torstensen might have been, as a mother for Tomas and Liam. I hoped Anna wasn't going to pull away from them, as well. But how could she not? She would need time to recover and find her own way back to them, if she could. I hoped they would give her that time.

And then I thought of Kelly Helm, who was being molded by her grandfather into the woman he thought she should become. If she had no other women in her life but the ones who agreed with him, how would she avoid the destiny he saw for her? Someone was going to have to try to talk to Alex Helm about her, and I wasn't sure sending in the Primary Presidency would work.

Anna looked up at me. "I feel so strange, as if I'm reinventing myself suddenly. I thought I was done with that sort of self-searching."

I wasn't finished with it myself. Maybe it was something that mothers had to do later in life, because we spent so much time not being ourselves, taking care of others. Or maybe it was because we were women and had worried too much about fitting the expectations of others.

"So what are Tomas and Liam saying now? Surely they can't still believe their father is completely innocent."

"They won't talk about it at all," said Anna with a small, tight smile.

"I'm sorry. I can only imagine how difficult it must be for all of you."

"They want him to be the gentle father they loved and nothing else. Not that I blame them. I don't know how to deal with the double image in my mind, either. It gives me a constant headache," said Anna, touching a spot right between her eyes. "He was a good man in many ways. A part of me wants to think that he changed, rather than just believing that he fooled me for so long. But maybe that part of me just doesn't want to deal with the truth because it's so painful."

"Did Helena ever write in her journal about him hurting her? Arguments? Abuse?"

Anna shook her head. "By her account, he

was a marvelous husband. Attentive, kind, the same Tobias I knew. The only thing that bothered her was that he hated her family and would spend hours raving about how they would all burn in hell. He thought the Catholic church was the 'great and abominable church' from the Book of Mormon."

Anna started cleaning up the tea, and I stood up to help her, though she tried to wave me back down. "According to her diary," she went on as she worked, "Helena used to beg Tobias to pray for her family. She still loved them, even after they kicked her out of the house and refused to speak to her. She went to the temple often and prayed for them. She did work for all her ancestors she could and she wrote about feeling like a vulture, waiting for her mother and father to die so that she could seal them in the temple together, and herself and her brothers to them."

Anna stopped for a moment, and I thought she might become tearful about the reality that she and Tobias wouldn't be able to be sealed like this. But she must have thought better of it, because she only shook herself and went back to the dishes.

"The police gave me a copy of the diary because they thought I might be able to see things in it that they didn't. I've been through it several times now."

Only because she was looking for proof that Tobias had killed Helena? "It sounds almost as if you've come to like her." Her rival, or precursor, or whatever it was that Helena was to Anna.

Anna let out a breath, nodding. "She was a good woman. I like to imagine we would have been friends. Does that sound very odd?"

"I've heard of stranger things," I said. A woman in the ward was best friends with her husband's ex, and they had met after the second marriage. "Friendships should be taken wherever they work, I think. They are rare enough things, real friendships." It made me think about Anna and how much I wanted her to stay near.

Anna closed the dishwasher and sat back down, her visage thoughtful. "I still have a hard time understanding how he could have been so different from how he appeared. Wouldn't he have shown some sign of violence before he killed her?"

"Maybe they argued suddenly about her family. Maybe Tobias didn't want her to take the money," I said. Mormon men could be very prickly about that. I had once suggested to Kurt, early on in our marriage, that I could work nights and he could watch the kids. He had objected strenuously. At first I thought it was because he was afraid of being left alone with them. It was only after weeks of teasing the truth out of him that I realized it was a blow to his pride for me to admit I thought he wasn't earning enough money to provide well for his family.

"She loved her boys so much. She poured everything into them, and into that diary," said Anna, her voice tight.

"Well, I'm glad there is something of her still left, after all this time. She didn't disappear. She has been found."

"Mmm," said Anna. She looked out the window of the small foyer. Its only view was of the dumpster in the back of the row of condos. "And what about me? What do I leave behind? How am I to avoid disappearing in the same way she did?"

"Oh, Anna." I reached over and put my hand over hers. "I didn't mean it like that. Tomas and Liam are your sons, too. They are your legacy."

"They can barely speak to me." She sounded faded, far away.

"That's right now. But in a year or so, you'll figure things out." I wanted to believe it as much as I wanted her to believe it.

Anna pulled away from me. "I wonder if

that's the only reason I want to write this cookbook. So that I leave something behind of myself. Without children, it feels like it doesn't matter, though. It's a poor substitute to leaving behind genes."

I wondered how many women who had families would think that leaving behind a book would matter more, because a book was something that you shaped consciously. Children, as I had learned like all women before me, were an accidental art. The more you tried to shape them, the less shape they took. Or at least it seemed that way some days.

"In any case, I may be coming home soon. To the ward." She tried to smile about it. "The Gearys have asked to be let out of the lease and I'm inclined to let them."

"Well, I can't complain about that," I said.

"I wanted to get away from it to prove who I was, that I wasn't just Tobias's wife. But now that I know Helena died there, I don't know. I feel like I want to go back. I want to be where she was," said Anna. "I want to understand her, and me. And him."

"Her diary has really affected you," I said.

She raised her eyebrows. "Oh, yes. Enormously. She was a fine writer. She has a way of making me feel like even the details of life are delicious. Every dirty sock in the laundry, every burned pot that has to be scrubbed, every burned out light bulb. They all mean something to her. They are all part of her being. She really lived life, in that diary. It makes me feel even worse that her life was so short. She made so much of it."

"You're not doing this out of obligation to her? Because you think that you owe her because you got her sons and her husband?" I said.

"No, it's not like that. I want to honor her for her own sake, not for her sons or for Tobias. I've already done everything I could to honor her in that way."

"You don't think God's asking you to stay?" I asked.

She shook her head. "I'm not going to put this decision on God. I prayed about marrying Tobias, and always thought it was the right thing to do. But was it, in the end? Or was I the one who wanted to marry him so badly I didn't listen? Or was there enough good in it that God let me make the decision I wanted? I don't think I can trust myself on what God directs me to do anymore."

I knew that place. Sometimes I was still in that lonely place where nothing made sense except in the most obvious way. It was hard to see anything luminous in the everyday world of pain and purpose. "Well, for purely selfish reasons, I'm glad you're moving back closer to me," I said.

Anna laughed. "That's why you're the bishop's wife, isn't it? You make us all feel welcome, no matter what our problems are."

If that was true, she had just offered me the best compliment of my life. Being welcome was a good feeling, and definitely one to share.

CHAPTER 30

All that night, I stewed about how to approach Alex Helm. After my experience with the Westons, I told myself that maybe he wasn't so bad. Maybe no parents were really as good as I imagined they were. Maybe Kurt and I were only just beginning to see our own flaws as parents as our children grew up and started becoming parents themselves. I had always thought I was teaching my children what was right, and not what was a "foolish tradition of their fathers," to use Book of Mormon lingo. But it was almost impossible to tell the difference. Just because I thought the Westons and the Helms were broken in terrible ways didn't mean that I was better, or that God couldn't love them as they were.

I wished I hadn't reacted so impulsively the last time I saw Alex Helm. I'd been able to act calmer around the Westons; I didn't think they had noticed that I left their house with a bad taste in my mouth. What was it about Alex Helm that brought out the worst in me? And what was it about the Westons that had made me so determined in the first place to be on their side? I wasn't sure I liked looking at that reality. Was it because the Westons were rich and I had been reacting to a mantle of privilege? Was Alex Helm more open about his flaws? I'd always taught the boys that honesty was more important than how you looked, but was it true?

When Kurt kissed me awake in the morning, I'd managed a total of twenty minutes of sleep. "You're thinking about Alex Helm, aren't you?" he said.

I nodded. He wasn't the only one, but he was top of the list.

"You just need to see how to find the man behind the monster. You're usually so good at that," asked Kurt.

Kurt left for work, which was still crazy with people who had filed extensions now needing to figure out their taxes. Soon after, Samuel came downstairs to get ready for school. He still hadn't talked to Kurt about the question of when he would go on his mission and if he should apply for a deferral from his first year of college. In fact, Samuel was avoiding his father as much as

Kenneth had done for a couple of years now, and that wasn't a good thing. Kurt hadn't noticed yet. He was too busy. He would, though. I trusted that.

With Kenneth, Kurt had simply let it go, thinking that eventually Kenneth would work out his post-mission problems. Plenty of missionaries had difficulty returning to normal life. It should have been a relief to return to life without the pressure to convert others, but for some, it was a letdown and they began to question everything that had gone before. I'd thought at the time that was what Kenneth had been struggling with. Now I was sure it wasn't.

When Samuel was out of the house, either on a mission or at college, what was my life going to be like? What about when Kurt was released as bishop? I had fantasized about going to see church history sites in Nauvoo, Kirtland, and Palmyra, which we'd never had a chance to go to with all the boys. Or even Europe — Paris and the Eiffel Tower or the remains of the Berlin Wall in Germany. We had the money to do almost anything we wanted. But would that be enough for me? Would I feel happy in a life that wasn't about filling someone else's needs?

But for now, there was plenty of work to

do for others. For instance, the laundry pile had become enormous, and I worked through that as I turned on the television news to discover that the police had found the man Carrie Helm had "met" an hour before her death at a hotel on the Nevada side of the border. He had told the police that she had been alive when he left her, though she had said something about being afraid of what would happen next in her life.

It seemed no one would ever find out what had happened to Carrie Helm. Each lead the police followed led them to a dead end. Unless the police had only let this man go temporarily, and were waiting for him to prove his guilt by fleeing? I knew it wasn't likely, but I had to cling to anything at this point.

The doorbell rang late that morning. I opened it and found Gwen Ferris waiting, staring at the ground.

"I need to talk to you," she said.

"Come in." I pulled her inside to the front room, but she was jumpy. The sound of the dryer beeping upstairs to alert me it was finished made her jump two feet.

"Is anyone else here?" she asked. She was wearing elaborate makeup, but with it yoga pants and a worn T-shirt.

"Kurt's at work and Samuel is at school," I said.

Gwen relaxed a little and nodded. Clearly she did not want to talk to Kurt. It was one of the tricky things in the church: men were always in positions of authority with the priesthood, but there were certain times when women needed to confide in other women.

Once I'd gotten her settled on the couch, Gwen said, "I have something I need to tell you. It's been on my mind for a long time, but I didn't know what to do. I should have said something earlier. I should have been braver." She finally looked into my eyes.

"You can tell me anything, you know," I said.

She took a long, shuddering breath. And then another one.

"Is this what you've been talking to Kurt about?" I asked,

She shook her head. "Or at least, I've only told him part of it. That I can't get pregnant. Brad and I have been trying for years, and the doctors say there's really no chance of it now."

"Oh, I'm so sorry." I was tempted to offer suggestions of alternatives or hope for the future, but stopped myself. My place was to listen for now.

"We've been talking about adoption, and that's what Brad wants. That's why we've been to talk to the bishop."

I thought she and Brad had been going in for counseling with Kurt. But it was this instead, though it might not have been entirely separate from counseling.

"We'd like his recommendation on our application to several local adoption agencies now that the church isn't doing adoptions anymore through LDS Family Services. But I can't go through it just yet. It feels like announcing to everyone what the problem is."

Did she mean infertility? Or did she mean whatever it was she hadn't told Kurt? "What is the problem?" I asked as gently as I could.

"I've only ever talked to one person apart from Brad. But after what happened —" She paused, and said nothing. Her eyes were all over the room, darting from the bookshelves to the piano to the window and then back to the books.

"What happened?" I asked.

She shook her head. "You have to understand," she said, then fell silent again.

I waited, trying to imagine what she was about to say. I remembered our conversation in the women's bathroom and her distress at the glorification of motherhood

444

— could it be that she didn't want children at all and didn't want to go through with the adoption process? Or was it possible her husband was abusing her after all?

"It's so hard —"

"Take your time," I said, although this might have been the most frustrating conversation I'd ever had. I reminded myself that whatever she was trying to tell me was something she had shared with almost no one.

"Carrie and I —" she started again, but her voice broke.

I remembered Gwen Ferris at Carrie Helm's funeral, and wondered if this young woman had been grieving more deeply than I'd been able to see then. "You were close," I said, hoping to lead her easily.

"Yes. We'd had a lot of the same experiences."

I thought about the abuse charges against Jared Helm that had been dropped because Carrie wasn't alive to testify against him anymore. But Brad Ferris? I felt about him the same way I'd felt about Tobias Torstensen. He was so quiet, such a good guy.

I needed to listen to Gwen. I hadn't listened to Carrie Helm. I hadn't had chance enough.

Finally, Gwen said, "After Carrie was

gone, I knew I should say something. But Brad said it was up to me. He said that it had to be my choice. So I waited to feel strong enough. Only I don't know if I ever really will be."

I reached out to put a comforting hand on her, but she flinched before it touched her and I remember suddenly what Brad had said about not knowing how to touch her. Was that what an abusive husband would be worried about?

"It's so hard for me to get the words out," she said. Her voice was surprisingly clear. "I can see everything in my head, bright and sharp as color. That's part of the problem, actually. I can't get it out of my head sometimes. But it's always there."

I still had no idea what she was talking about. "Maybe it would help to write it down?" I asked. "I could get some paper and a pen. Or a computer, if you think you can type it."

She shook her head so hard at that I was worried for a moment she'd get sick from the motion. "I just need to say it. For Carrie. And for me. But I can't do it just for me. It has to be for Carrie."

"For Carrie," I echoed. That would be my conversational tactic — just echo what she said, help her get through this.

She took in little breaths, and her whole body seemed to be so fragile, like her skin was about to melt away and reveal everything underneath. "Brad gets so angry when I try to talk to him about it. I haven't told him many of the details because he just starts smashing things around the house. He scares me a little, making threats."

"Are you afraid of him?" I asked. "Has he hurt you?" We needed to be clear on this.

Her eyes flew to my face, wide with surprise. "What? No, of course not. No, he's angry at my father."

I was taken aback. "Your father. Oh." The pieces clicked together in my head, and I felt sick.

She looked down at her hands, knotting around each other like an intricate knitting pattern. "I — I had an abortion when I was thirteen. And when I was fourteen. And two when I was fifteen," she said.

I found I couldn't say a word. I felt as if I'd fallen off a cliff and no one could hear my final scream. But it wasn't even my horror. I was only listening to it. This woman was living it. And I'd thought an abusive husband was bad. This was far, far worse.

"And after all that, it seems that there are consequences. I've lost one ovary and my cervix is damaged." Somehow, I could see

447

the delicate lace she was knitting with her fingers, like a gift from God, the life she had made, with so many holes, so fragile but so incredibly beautiful — so good. She was good.

And I had to put words to it that would make it so ordinary. "Your father sexually abused you?" I said.

"Yes, he . . ." She trembled and I wished again, desperately, that I could touch her and soothe her fears.

But this was about what she needed, not what I needed. "I'm here," was all I said, though I knew she knew it.

"It started when I was very young. He did it with both of my sisters, too."

"What else?" I asked. "You can tell me."

More knitting. I could see the veins in her hands, blue lines on white. "My mother claimed that she didn't see any of it. She said that it wasn't true, that we were liars. She is still with him. My father was in the bishopric of the ward for a while. No one would believe that he could do such a thing. He was . . . very beloved. And he did good things, he really did. He just had this one flaw."

One flaw? That was one way to put it. A terrible, wrong way. That one flaw had been devastating for this woman. No wonder she

448

was depressed and on medication, as Brad had told me. No wonder she didn't like to be touched. And he had asked me for advice without being able to reveal his wife's secrets to me. I hoped what I had said had been useful; though if it had, it was likely because God had intervened and given me the right words.

"He sounds like a monster," I said, discovering that my voice was raw and my throat hurt as if I'd been rubbing it with sandpaper. "Gwen, you must realize that you are innocent of all of this. You are a victim of a terrible crime, and your father will have a lot to answer for on Judgment Day." God had better make sure the man paid for this. I sent the thoughts heavenward. Was it wrong that my prayers could sometimes be vengeful? Maybe I wasn't doing this right.

"You're saying all the same things that Brad says. That my therapist has said. I guess I need to hear it again and again," said Gwen. "I — it's hard for me not to think of this as God's judgment on me. My father used to say that it was my fault he did it. He said that I was too pretty, that I tempted him. He said that I was born of sin, that Satan inhabited me."

I cringed. Her father sounded so much like Alex Helm. Alex Helm, who was alone with a little girl. I had no reason to believe he was abusing her that way, but I didn't know if Kelly Helm would be any less damaged in the end.

Gwen's eyes were bright as she said, "I never thought I would get married, really. Getting away from my father was my highest ambition. But then I met Brad — and everything changed. I started to believe I could be happy, have a normal life. You know, I didn't tell him about my past before we got married. I think that was wrong of me. But I just wanted to forget it had ever been. I thought that if I forgot about it, it would actually disappear as if it never was."

I could only imagine how her wedding must have been, with her parents at her side. Or had they not come? I suspected they would have, if only for show. They would have wanted her to keep her secret as much as she had, I suppose. And Brad knew nothing of what he was getting into, poor boy.

"I'm glad you came to see me, Gwen. I'm glad you felt able to confide in me. I wish I could give you something in return. Is there anything I can do to help make things easier for you at church?" It seemed like such a small gift, but it was all I had to offer.

She smiled faintly. "I'm grateful for the

offer," she said. "I know you are such a fierce protector. That's part of the reason I came to see you."

I was flattered and overwhelmed with emotion for a moment.

"I had another protector, for a little while. But now she's gone."

"Carrie Helm," I said, feeling inspired that I could see the connection.

"Yes," she said. "She and I got to talking one night after a Relief Society meeting. We were in the parking lot. It was summer, and it was warm, but it was pitch black by the time I told her the whole truth. I think it had to be that dark for me to be able to tell her. Just me saying words into the darkness, almost as if she wasn't there."

I had thought of Carrie Helm as a victim so often, it hadn't occurred to me to think of her as a savior at the same time. She must have been stronger than I thought, if with all her own problems she had been able to help Gwen with hers.

"That's why I had to come," Gwen said. "Because of what Carrie told me, when we talked. I don't think she told anyone else, either. Though maybe Jared knew some of it. But when I saw her parents on television, talking about how she had been mistreated and abused by her husband, and that they wanted her real story out there, it made me sick."

I put a hand to my stomach to hold back the nausea. I had been to the Weston home. I had felt strange there, known something was wrong. But I hadn't guessed at this. How could I have been so blind — again?

"He abused Carrie sexually, just like my father. For years, from when she was very small until she was a teenager." Gwen sounded more angry about what had happened to Carrie than she had sounded about her own abuse.

"I think he was trying to still abuse her, after she got married. It was one of the reasons that Carrie clung to Jared so fiercely." Gwen looked down at her hands and tried to lay them flat in her lap again, but they kept moving. "She knew that there were problems with Jared, but he was strong enough to fight her father, in her mind and in real life."

She looked me in the eye at that, and I felt like I was seeing to her soul. Kurt talked about this happening sometimes, that he was given the chance to see people directly as God saw them, with good and bad combined, past hurts and future, and that it was always a glorious moment. I felt like that now, like after all of the horror Gwen Ferris had experienced, she had come out of it somehow and made beauty. She made herself beautiful, even if she didn't know it. God did. And now I did, too.

But what about Carrie? I had never had the chance to see her like this. I regretted that as much as anything else. All those missed opportunities. And of course, now I knew why a woman like Carrie would stay with a man like Jared Helm. It was the missing piece in the puzzle of her life.

"She told you about her father?" I said. I was trying to think how this would work, legally. Jared Helm hadn't been prosecuted because Carrie couldn't testify against him and the charges were so old. What about her father? Could Gwen testify in Carrie's place somehow? Please, God, there had to be some way to make Aaron Weston pay for what he had done, to make people see that he wasn't the man he seemed to be that day he had stood up in front of the cameras on the TV news.

"Carrie showed me some of her scars." Her hand drifted to her right side, though if that was where Carrie's scars or her own were, I couldn't tell. "She was really careful about keeping them hidden. He didn't just sexually abuse her. He hurt her physically, in every way he could. He tortured her."

"And Jared?" I asked. "Did she tell you about him abusing her, too?" Or were the wounds she had gone to have documented at the hospital all from her father? Had I been wrong about Jared? Had he been Carrie's Captain America after all?

Gwen sighed and waved one of those delicate hands. "Oh, I think she knew that Jared was a little crazy. Too gung ho, too rigid about the church and about all the extra doctrines he and his father believe in. But he never hurt her physically. He might have made her feel like she wasn't good enough, but I think she wanted him to do that. I think she was punishing herself the way her father punished her." She drew a line across her wrist, and I could see faint lines on the skin of her arm. So she understood Carrie perfectly there, too. "As if she had become so used to the pain that she had to have it. A craving, like an addiction." She looked me in the eye again and I could see suddenly a little-girl version of her not so very hidden inside, a little girl who was also used to pain.

So much hurt. So much pain. It was easy to brush it off as something that happened everywhere, say that the church dealt with such crimes harshly and that God could never look on sin with the least degree of allowance. But the disguise had worked within our church. And the vulnerability was made possible by the hierarchy as it stood now. Could that possibly be God's purpose?

Gwen's hands kept curling and uncurling. Her frenetic movements seemed to echo my own whirling thoughts. "It's taken me all this time to work up the courage. Not just to tell you about Carrie, but to tell you about myself, and why it matters so much to me. I'm so worried about Carrie's parents. She warned me that if anything ever happened to her, they would try to take Kelly. I can't bear to see that happen. I came today to hope that you will make sure that they are stopped. It was the one thing that Carrie was proud of, that Kelly was going to grow up with a better life than she had."

"Why did Carrie leave her, though?" I asked. "If she loved Kelly so much, how could she go off to Las Vegas like that?" To take the chance that Kelly would be unprotected — surely that was the greatest crime of all?

Gwen stopped moving and looked out the window, speaking to the world itself, as if she could trust it more than me. "You don't know what it's like. The demons that talk in your head. I think maybe Carrie decided it was better for Kelly for her to be gone. Or maybe she just had to punish herself more. I don't know."

"And the letter her parents have, about Jared's abuse? Was it real at all?"

"I don't know." She shook her head and turned back to me. She seemed out of energy now, and I felt the same. All the time I'd spent awake thinking last night, and it had been so useless. I had never come to this, the final, most important truth.

"Carrie told me sometimes about weird things Jared or his father did. But she also loved him. Maybe she wrote to her parents just to scare them away."

It had all been so complicated. Why had I ever thought it would be simple? There were monsters here, but they weren't the ones I had seen first and foremost. No wonder Carrie had fled her life here. None of us was willing to see the truth, and if we couldn't do that, how could we help her?

CHAPTER 31

As soon as Gwen Ferris left, I walked over to the Helms' and rang the doorbell. Alex Helm met me at the door. He looked me up and down. "Can I help you, Sister Wallheim?"

It felt as if I was literally swallowing my pride, which was a hot and heavy stone. It kept rising back up, and I would have to swallow it down again. "I wanted to ask if you needed any babysitting help," I got out at last.

He sneered. "Help from you?"

"I know that we did not part on the best of terms and you must think that I — that I am not on your side. But I came to apologize for that. I realize now that I was wrong."

"Wrong about what, Sister Wallheim?" he asked.

"About Carrie," I said softly. "And her parents." I would have to deal with them soon, but somehow I felt like I needed to make this right first.

"Someone has told you something," he said, leaning in enough to stare me in the eye.

I had to work hard not to lean away from him. I wasn't going to give him any names. I might have been wrong about him, but that didn't give me the right to expose Gwen Ferris's secrets.

"So," he said when I didn't reply. "You've realized that my son married a troubled young woman and spent a good deal of time trying to figure out the truth."

"I know that she loved him," I said. At least, she must have for a few years, until she left. I was trying to make it easy for him to open the door wider and invite me in.

"Do you know that she called him, before she left Las Vegas?" he asked. "Told him that she loved him and that she missed him? At three in the morning, when Kelly was asleep? The morning of the day she died?"

My mouth was dry, and I wished I had a drink of water. I was struggling not to lick my lips in front of this man. "I didn't know that," I said. Could I believe him? So far, I could not think of anything that Alex Helm had directly lied about. He might be an odious man, but he was a truthful odious man. "Did she say she was coming home?"

458

"Not directly, but that was the gist of it," said Alex Helm. "She said she was sorry for the havoc she'd caused and that she knew she'd been searching for something that only Jared could give her."

I felt a chill run through me at that. Did she mean love? Had only Jared been able to give it to her? Surely people who are sick can hope for better healing than that even in this broken, mortal world. "Has he told the police about this phone call?"

"The police no longer consider Jared to be a suspect, and they have not asked him about the details of the day Carrie died."

"And he hasn't volunteered it? It might be useful for them, in trying to get a timeline of her movements." But what did I know about detective work? I had stuck my nose into two murder cases in the last five months. I had thought I knew what I was doing. I thought I knew more about the underside of my ward than anyone else, and especially about the women's world.

"Why should he volunteer anything to the police after the way they've treated him?"

"So they will be able to catch her killer," I said. "Surely Jared wants that as much as anyone." I couldn't see Kelly anywhere behind him. Was she sleeping? Or was she too afraid to come near the door? Had her

459

grandfather forbidden that, like so much else?

He glanced behind him, then closed the door and stepped out onto the porch with me. He sat on one of the steps and nodded for me to follow suit. I suppose this was a kind of reconciliation between us. I wasn't worth the couch, but I could be seated here.

"I think Jared believes that it will only make Carrie look worse for the press," he said. "After all this, he still cares about her name. After all that she did to him, and the way she left him, he wants to protect her. I don't understand it, but I think my son loves her still." He didn't seem admiring, but neither was he disgusted.

I felt a strange peace at this moment. Love didn't conquer all, but it endured through many things you'd think would kill it. Real love, which I had to admit I saw in Jared and Carrie's marriage, despite all their problems.

I tried to remember the expression on Jared's face when he had first appeared on our doorstep with Kelly in his arms that January morning. He'd been distraught. Whatever his relationship with Carrie had been, however odd and unlike any healthy marriage I had seen, he had loved her. And I couldn't help but think, now, that she had loved him.

"And then there is Kelly and how it will affect her, all of this," he added, nodding behind him.

"How is Kelly?" I asked. I wanted to see her so much. Just a glimpse of her messy hair, a hint of her fresh washed little girl smell, a shared smile over a brownie.

"We don't need you to keep checking on us like some kind of Mormon child services. Jared and I are perfectly capable of taking care of her," said Alex Helm. "She's been sick the last couple of weeks. Last cold of the season, I guess, and I've kept her indoors for her own safety." He glared at me, waiting for me to contradict his style of caregiving.

I didn't. "I know you care about her. But it's not the same as — well, as a mother."

"I agree. She does need a mother. A better mother than the confused creature who gave birth to her. That is something Jared agrees on, and he is working on it. He has a new woman in mind to be Kelly's mother, and his wife."

I knew he had told Kelly he would find her a new mother, but it seemed crazy to think that Jared would marry so soon after Carrie's funeral. Hadn't we just been talking about how much he'd loved her? "So

461

he's dating again?" I asked, trying to find a way to make it sound more normal.

He let out a brief laugh. "Not dating. He's courting. She's met Kelly already and she has fallen in love with her. Now all Jared has to do is convince her that he will be a decent husband and he's won. Women marry for children. Men marry for —" He didn't finish, but made a crude hand gesture that it took me a moment to recognize meant the sex act. But I refused to blush. I was too old for that. "Well, who is she?" I asked.

Alex Helm shook his head. "So you can call her and tell her all the sordid details you think you know about Carrie and Jared? She's heard enough on the news. But she met Jared herself and realized how wrong it all was. She is a lovely person and I won't have you ruin what could be a perfect ending to this tragedy."

There was no perfect ending to this tragedy. "Well, I hope Jared is happy. I think he deserves some happiness," I said, the words grating, but not untrue. I was still trying to salvage things. I still needed Alex Helm to let Kelly come back to Primary at church.

He began to pick at the bits of debris on the steps, which were already nearly clean enough to eat off of. A bit of an aspen leaf.

A pebble. A wrapper probably carried from the street to here, or possibly tossed by a child on the way home from school.

"Do you know, I told Jared not to marry Carrie?" he said as he collected the bits into his hand. "I knew about her past problems. I thought he could do better. But he insisted. He wanted so much to save her. And then she turned back to it. Whoring again." He looked me in the eye, and I knew that he knew what Aaron Weston was, and what he had done. I wouldn't have called it whoring, but I knew what he meant.

Alex Helm did a strange thing then, and put the pebble into his mouth, chewing at it like it was a bit of gum. There was a long, uncomfortable moment of sympathy between us. I hated that he seemed to be the one person who saw this picture the same way that I did. I did not like to think that I had so much in common with someone like him.

"I appreciate what you and Jared did for Carrie, giving her a safe haven," I said, even if it hadn't lasted long. I could see him moving the pebble around inside his mouth, which was distracting. "Jared was a good husband," I admitted.

Alex Helm nodded. "He was a good husband. If he ever hurt her, it was for her own good. She knew that, too. It was why she loved him so much."

For her own good? No, I thought. I could go a certain distance to see another person's point of view, but not that far. I stood up and brushed off my pants. "Well, thank you for your time," I said, though I hadn't even begun to ask him about Kelly and Primary. Perhaps the Presidency would have to do that on their own. I couldn't do everything.

"Do you know," Alex Helm said suddenly, "when she called him, she begged him for forgiveness. She said that she had always been looking for a place where she belonged. As if a whore like that could ever belong anywhere."

I tamped down my emotional response to his word choice. "And what did Jared tell her?"

"He told her the truth, that he couldn't take her back into the house with Kelly. He couldn't let her contaminate their daughter anymore." He spat out the pebble into his hand and examined it.

I had tried. I really had.

My heart felt as if it were beating outside of my chest, I could hear it so clearly. I couldn't fix this.

There was a sound behind Alex Helm, and I caught a quick glimpse of messy blonde curls before the door flew open.

"Sister Wallheim!" Kelly shouted, and ran barefoot toward me.

Alex Helm caught her and moved swiftly back to the door without a word to me. As if I didn't deserve even a farewell. He closed the door in my face, and the last I saw of Kelly were her feet kicking over her grandfather's shoulder.

I finished the laundry at home, then started on dinner. I had to do something about what I'd found out about Carrie Helm and her father, but what? Drive down to his house and smash into it? Take a chainsaw with me and see if I could get close enough to take off some body parts? I felt wrung out after my conversation with Alex Helm, as if nothing I did was ever going to matter, and what was the point? Why was I pretending that I could change the world?

I had originally planned to make some chicken stew for dinner, which required two stalks of celery, an onion and a carrot. I had taken out a whole five-pound bag of carrots, a triple bag of celery stalks, and a whole ten-pound Costco bag of onions. And then I had peeled and chopped my way through all of them, telling myself that I would freeze them, that it wasn't a waste. It was a useful therapeutic exercise.

But then I got out the potatoes. The fifty-pound bag we'd gotten in November when, in a parking lot on the way home from work, Kurt had seen a truck advertising fresh potatoes, straight from the ground in neighboring Idaho. We had barely made a dent in it, in part because the potatoes were so dirty it took more effort to peel them.

I rinsed, scrubbed, and peeled every potato. I diced them, cubed them, and shredded them. I packed them into the gallon-size Ziploc bags (also from Costco) and then put them in the freezer. And when I was done with that, I got out chicken. I boiled it, froze the stock, and then shredded the chicken. My hands had tiny cuts all over them by then, and there were probably flecks of blood all over the food. My wrists ached and my feet were on fire from standing for so long. But it all felt good. Anything felt good. It reminded me I was alive.

"Um, Mom?" asked Samuel when he got home from school. "Is there something wrong?"

"I'm just doing some prep work," I said, as if it was no big deal.

"For the next millennium?" he asked.

"Nothing wrong with that," I said.

"Mom — do you know something I don't

know? Did Dad tell you about a letter he got?" asked Samuel.

I took a moment to look at him. My beautiful son, scared because I was too caught up in my attempts to mother people I couldn't mother. Why couldn't it be enough for me to mother him?

Because he didn't need me anymore. Not really.

"You think the apocalypse will be announced by the First Presidency in a letter?" I said.

"I was thinking more along the lines of the Second Coming," said Samuel, smiling faintly.

Yes, let's make this into a joke. A very, very funny joke. "There has to be all that other stuff first. Gog and Magog. The prophets lying in the streets. Blood on the moon."

"The blood on the moon thing already happened. Didn't you hear? Neil Armstrong got into a fight with some Russian astronauts."

I raised my eyebrows. "And we never heard about it?"

"The Russians didn't want to admit they'd lost the fight, so there's been a cover-up for years."

"But you found out about it — ?" I asked.

"On the Internet," said Samuel. "Of course."

"Yeah. Of course," I said. He had gotten me out of myself enough that I could see what the kitchen looked like. The sink was filled to the top with potato peelings. The kitchen garbage was overflowing onto the floor. There was pink from blood mingled with vegetable juice all over the counter-tops, and the handle of one of the knives had come off. I'd stuck the knife into the wooden cutting board before ignoring it and moving on.

"This isn't what it looks like," I said.

"It looks like someone got you really mad," said Samuel.

"Then it is what it looks like," I said. I started to clean up then. Samuel helped me. And then I got some actual stew cooking, though it was a bit after Kurt got home that it was ready to eat.

I was a mess. My kitchen was a mess. My house was a mess. My family was a mess. My whole world was a mess.

I had tried to help Kelly Helm, and I had failed and I was never going to make up for the daughter I had let die. She was always going to be dead and there would never be anyone to fill the hole in my heart.

We ate in near silence, though I could see

Kurt and Samuel sharing meaningful glances over the table. As soon as Samuel had cleared his place, he skedaddled, leaving Kurt and me at the dinner table. I stood up, swayed with exhaustion, and broke into tears.

He eased me back down, moving his chair close enough to mine that I was half sitting on him. I wished I didn't feel so squished against him. But the reality was that when you got to be our age, it seemed like things didn't fit the way they used to.

"You're allowed to cry, you know," he said.

Which only made me cry louder. "Thanks."

"Bad day?" he asked.

"You could say that," I said, though I didn't elaborate.

"You know, it makes me feel like there is something wrong with me, that you almost never let me see you cry. About anything."

I realized we were actually talking about what was wrong, the deep wrong that had been put away. "You know, you haven't cried about it in ages, either," I pointed out.

"I cried about it at the time. For weeks, if you recall. And I kept waiting to see you break down. Other women would have spent days at home alone. But you didn't. You just got right back up and moved on with your life, as if nothing had happened. As if there was nothing wrong." He had pulled away from me and was examining me. It reminded me of nothing so much as when Alex Helm had looked down at the pebble in his hand after he'd cleaned it in his mouth.

That was the problem between us. It had always been the problem. I was worried that Kurt was judging me and finding me wanting. It had become even worse since he was called to the bishopric. He was the one who was superior. He had better access to God. He had the priesthood and could use it to give blessings, to call down God's voice with his own words. What did I have? I was a mother, and I had lost my way and wasn't sure I was ever going to find it again.

"Say something," Kurt begged. "I always know you're all right if you're talking."

I sighed. He wanted words. Fine. I would let them out. "It was just that I couldn't see how it would ever be right again. And saying that out loud — it felt like I was being unfaithful. Like you would tell me I wasn't allowed to be so broken." I looked up to search his face, but he turned away.

"I don't know what I would have said then, Linda. I can't say I would have known the right thing. But I wish we hadn't gotten

470

into the habit of silence."

"People always try to talk about the compensations. That you get blessings from trials. That you have little angels watching over you if you have lost children. But I don't feel like she is here with us. I never feel it. It makes me wonder why. If there is something wrong with her. Or with me. With us."

"I don't know. I don't feel her, either. But maybe we're keeping her away somehow. Maybe it still hurts too much to feel her."

"So it's my fault?" I said softly. "Because I'm still sad?"

"No. I didn't mean that." Kurt tried to move the chairs closer, gave up, and let me slide away from him onto my own chair. But he grabbed my hand and held it tightly. As if he and I were crossing the busiest street in the world together. "If it's anyone's fault, it's mine. And I'm sorry. I wasn't there for you, when you needed me. How you needed me. I've always wondered how it is that I could be called to be bishop, to be there for other people, when I wasn't there for you."

"And now?" I asked.

He let out a short, barking laugh. "Now I know that being bishop is just God's way of letting you see all your flaws. It's not just you I haven't been there for. I try to do what I can, but afterward, it always seems like it wasn't enough, or it was at the wrong moment, or that I said the wrong words to the wrong people."

"So you discovered that you're not enough for anyone?" I asked.

"Yeah." Kurt let out a low breath.

"Join the club," I said. I told him about what had happened with Alex Helm. Kurt was my bishop, as well as my husband, and at times that felt awkward. But at the moment it felt good, like we could connect on even more points than before.

"And Gwen Ferris came to visit," I added after a moment's hesitation. Was it my secret to share? She hadn't sworn me to silence. I wasn't her bishop. There was no expectation of confidence. But she had trusted me, and I couldn't share lightly.

"Did she tell you what she would never tell me?"

"You knew?" I said.

Kurt shook his head. "I don't know what it is. But I know she's held something back. Some heavy burden. I wasn't even sure that Brad knew about it."

"He knew," I said, and then I explained it. All about Gwen Ferris's father, and about Carrie Helm's, as well. Aaron Weston, the

472

man I had felt for a moment as he spoke at the funeral would be an apostle or possibly a prophet. How was it that we could ever believe that we had real inspiration after an experience like that? But I couldn't give up the hope that next time, I would have learned better to tell the difference between a good liar and God's truth.

"Something has to be done to stop him," I said, sometime long past midnight, still sitting in the kitchen amidst the dishes of dinner that I had yet to put into the dishwasher.

"Yes, but what?" said Kurt.

"Can't you call a church trial or something? He should be excommunicated at the very least. A man like that in the same church with us — it makes me want to run away like Carrie Helm did."

"Hmm," said Kurt. And he guided me upstairs, tucked me in bed with a kiss on the forehead, and then went back down the stairs. He was on the phone most of the night in his bishop's office.

CHAPTER 32

"It's done," said Kurt when he came home from work that Friday evening. He looked terrible. The last time I had seen him like this was when he went on a high adventure with the Varsity Scouts for a full week in the Uintas, a backpacking trip where he claimed to have gotten no sleep at all and had to cook food over a fire for fifteen boys ages sixteen and seventeen — two of them our oldest sons, Adam and Joseph.

I touched his beard. "You forgot to shave this morning," I said, rubbing at it. I hadn't seen him before he left for work. I'd slept in, feeling good. I trusted that Kurt would do something. It might be that I didn't agree that men should hold all the offices in the church, but I trusted Kurt that if he had power, he would use it well.

Kurt put a hand to his face. "Oh, damn," he said, which said a lot to me. Kurt didn't curse easily, and I didn't think he was cursing about his beard.

"So, what happens now?"

He shook his head. "I can't tell you anything about it. It's too personal, and I don't really know any of the details. I've just set something in motion. I don't know how it will turn out."

I looked him in the eye. "Don't tell me there's a possibility that he will go scot-free." Church discipline wasn't exactly a legal system. There was no "evidence" to be offered, no experts to testify. Some witnesses might be called, and then the "jury" of priesthood holders deliberated, allowing the accused to speak for himself if he wished. And they all prayed.

The idea was that God would tell the truth of the matter, and it was supposed to be far better than a regular court system, where you had to rely on things like reason and logic. But those men who would be deliberating were all likely to be men who knew Aaron Weston, who admired him, and served with him. If he denied everything, which I was sure he would, would they be able to see past the shiny sticker of perfection he wore so well?

"If he's innocent, then he will face no punishment," said Kurt.

I pressed my lips tightly together. Kurt

had to know that wasn't an outcome I could accept. Would it simply be a matter of Gwen Ferris's word against Aaron Weston's? A woman who had mental-health issues, who wasn't a mother, and who didn't always come to church, against a Melchizedek priesthood holder and leader in Zion?

"And if he's not, which I'm confident God will show to all who are deliberating, there will be harsh consequences," Kurt finished.

"Can you tell me what they might be, say, hypothetically?" I asked. I had an idea, but I didn't know the particulars. I hadn't seen a church court in action before, except for returned missionaries who had admitted to breaking the law of chastity. That happened fairly regularly, and they were often disfellowshipped, which meant they had to serve a certain number of months without all of the blessings of the church like going to the temple or taking the Sacrament.

"Well, for a man who has been in the high positions he has been in, to be seen as guilty of sexual abuse in a church court would mean almost certain excommunication, cancelation of sealing to his wife and daughter, and revocation of any temple blessings."

I let out a long breath. It wasn't much. It wasn't a jail sentence. But it was something to show that the Mormon church took a crime like this seriously and didn't blithely go on as if the most important thing was how a man looked, how well he managed paperwork, and how much the other men around him liked him. And it separated him from Carrie, who could only be helped in the hereafter. At least she wouldn't be bound to her father forever there.

"And how hard would it be for him to be rebaptized?" I asked. Was that vengeful of me?

Kurt shook his head. "Part of getting repentance for something like this would be confessing the truth and showing remorse. It would be accepting the consequences of a legal admission, which would mean confessing to the police and serving time for his crimes. In addition, he would have to do whatever is possible to make it up to those who were sinned against. In this case, I don't know how a man could ever gain forgiveness from his dead daughter. Or how he could ever make it up to her. But I won't say it's impossible. God forgives even the most heinous sins, so it would behoove us not to deny forgiveness ourselves."

"I don't suppose ritual castration is one of the options?" I asked Kurt.

He choked a little at that. "Not that I've heard of."

■ ■ ■ ■

Saturday afternoon, Anna and I went on a walk. She had given up the condo and moved back into her old home. That made it easier for us to get together often, and we had begun to go on long walks together around the ward. It is surprising how much you can learn about people just by looking at their houses. The car that hasn't moved for days. The windows with blinds that are never opened. The porch with more and more boxes piled up around it, the sagging fascia or the unpainted garage. The brick that has been painted, yellow or blue, over and over again, year after year, until it doesn't appear to be brick anymore. I should have been noticing things like this years ago.

We usually had tea at her house after our walks. Sometimes I stayed for lunch, if we talked for a long time. It depended on what we had to say.

This time, Anna was just starting tea when then there was a loud knock on the door.

"Maybe it's the mailman dropping something off?" she guessed.

But it was Liam.

"Liam, what are you doing here?" asked Anna.

"I had to come," he said. He glanced up at me, and I thought he would ask me to leave, but he didn't. "I have to tell you something."

"All right, but come in and sit down. Did you fly here?"

He shook his head. "Drove."

"From Tacoma?" said Anna. "Did you stop?"

He shook his head again. "I should have told you this before. At the funeral. Maybe before that. I don't know. I didn't want anything to happen to Dad and I was afraid —" He gasped in air and shook his head.

"Sit, sit," said Anna, gesturing to the front room. It didn't look the same as it had when Tobias had been alive. There were a few more feminine touches than before, and some of the furniture she had gotten rid of completely. She had also painted one of the walls a deep maroon with texturing. I liked it a lot.

Liam looked around and finally sat on the couch gingerly, as if he wasn't sure it would hold him. The couch had a floral pattern that matched the wall, one of the new pieces Anna had put in.

"Tea?" asked Anna. She brought some in from the kitchen, but he only seemed to pretend to sip at it. "You know, your father is gone now, but nothing you say about him will change the man he was, the husband and father we both know he was," said Anna. She seemed relaxed and her tone was calm.

"Yes. He was a good man," said Liam. Then the words started pouring out of him. "I remember now. What happened all those years ago."

"When? What do you mean?" asked Anna. Her voice was a little strained now.

Liam set down the tea and waved his hands. "Dad. And Helena. My mother. The day she disappeared."

"Oh," said Anna. She sat down abruptly on the couch next to Liam.

Then I could see Liam's face clearly, and it was alight as if with revelation. "I heard them arguing that night. I was supposed to be asleep in bed, and I knew Dad would get mad at me if I came out of my room. But I heard them shouting and I was scared." His voice became more high-pitched and less clearly pronounced, like a child's. "I don't remember what they were arguing about. I don't think I understood it then. But she threw something at him. I heard it shatter against the wall." He shuddered as if it were happening now instead of thirty years ago.

Was Liam trying to argue that Tobias

might have had some excuse for what he had done? That it had been self-defense?

"Did you hear Tobias — hurt her?" asked Anna. Her voice sounded stuffy, as if she had a cold, but I didn't see any tears on her face.

"No. You don't understand. Dad didn't kill her." He sucked in a huge breath.

"I know you don't want to believe that, Liam. Neither of us does. Tobias was a good man, but we have to accept that something happened between them that changed that. Maybe for only one moment. I don't know how he could have changed back so quickly, but he did. The evil closed over him and then he broke free of it again. He was a good man, but he also hurt your mother, Liam," said Anna. She wasn't looking at him. She was looking at a point just past my head, on the other side of the room, as if that was the only way she could keep herself calm enough to speak about her husband this way.

"No! I saw — I heard what happened," said Liam, standing up. His teacup fell to the carpet. None of us moved to pick it up, despite the stain it was spreading on the tan threads. "There was someone else there. I heard the door open, and I heard another voice. It was deeper than Dad's, and it spoke to her. To Helena, my mother."

He moved to the door, and gestured as if opening it. "I heard her say Daddy. Like she was calling the other man Daddy. He was angry with her and she was begging him not to hurt them. They're babies, she said. I think she was talking about me and Tomas. I was mad, then, that she called me a baby. Tomas was a baby, not me. And then he said that they were — we were — little bastards, little demons sent from hell. And then I heard Dad say that he loved his wife and his sons as much as any man ever had."

Anna was stiff with tension, leaning out of her seat on the couch, her neck stretched as far as it would go.

Liam let out a small gagging sound, but nothing came up with it. "And then," he said hoarsely, "I heard a scream, and a thump. After that, I didn't hear anything except the door closing again. I fell asleep." He looked as innocent as a little boy at that moment, a boy whose life had been devastated and who had heard it happen, and did not understand it in the least, who only knew that something was terribly, terribly wrong.

Could Helena's father have been the one who killed her? Had I been as wrong about Tobias as I had been about Jared Helm?

And in the same way? Two murders in our ward, but neither of them the kind of murder I had imagined, a husband killing his wife. But fathers had so much power over their daughters, even when they were grown. Sometimes in our world, we forget that. A father is like a god. Thus we call God "Father in Heaven."

"You think your grandfather killed your mother?" I asked cautiously. I could see Anna struggling to process Liam's story. "But if that is what really happened, then why would Tobias bury her body? Why didn't he report her father to the police?"

"I don't know," said Liam. He seemed himself again, weak and pale, but his adult voice had returned.

I stared at him and tried to calculate whether Liam had been old enough when his mother died to remember a scene like this. The fact that he had never spoken about it in the intervening thirty years said something about the trauma of the memory. Was it real? He could have invented it to fit the facts. On the other hand, it was clear that he believed it. And the way he spoke, in that child's voice, was eerie.

"Why didn't you say anything about this? All this time, Liam," said Anna. "When your father was asking about Helena's gravesite?

When we were asking you if she died of a heart problem or in a car accident? Why did you never confide in me, all those years?"

"It felt like a nightmare. I didn't know if it was real, and then as I grew older, I remembered it less and less because it wasn't a part of my life. You were my life then. You were my mother."

For a moment, Anna's head bowed with this heartfelt return of all her love. I stared at her and swallowed hard. Then she lifted her head.

"You didn't see him bury her, then?" she asked.

"No," said Liam. "I didn't know she was in the backyard. Maybe if I'd thought about it more, I would have seen the connection, but I didn't." He sagged back to the couch, and after a moment, Anna put a hand to his back and patted him.

"So what do we do now?" asked Anna. She had turned to me.

She thought I knew the answers here? "We could call the police and have Liam give them a statement." But I had no idea if they would believe him. And what did it matter? Helena's father was dead now. They couldn't prosecute him any more than they could Tobias.

"Why wouldn't Tobias have reported it?" I

asked. "I don't understand. He should have had the man convicted for murder. And then his wife could have been buried properly, in a cemetery," I said. Why would he cover up for a man who wasn't even his own father? A man he had, it seemed, hated?

Anna sighed. "Tobias was always a quiet man. The kind of notoriety that would have come with a murder trial would have destroyed him. And the boys, too."

"But it doesn't make sense. He buried her himself so there wouldn't be a trial? Does an innocent man do that?" I asked.

"Maybe it was more than the trial. Maybe he wanted to keep her to himself," said Anna. She looked at peace again at last, an expression of relaxation that I hadn't seen for a long time spreading across her face. "Keep her here, with him, in the garden."

"She was already dead," said Liam. "It wasn't as if a trial would have brought her back. And she loved her father, too. Maybe that was the real reason he said nothing, because he knew he would be ruining her father's life if he reported her death, and he thought Helena wouldn't have wanted that."

I still thought it was very odd, all of it. I didn't know if I believed Liam's story, but it made a sense of all the strangeness in our ward these past months in a way nothing else had.

"And the hammer by our bedside all those years?" said Anna. "Do you think he might have worried it would happen again, and if it did, he wanted to be the one with the weapon?"

"I'll talk to the police if you want me to," said Liam. "If you think that will clear Dad's name in some way."

"Write me a statement," said Anna after a long moment. "Then I can decide if I want to talk to them and show it to them if I need to."

"Thank you," said Liam with great relief. He stared around the house as if realizing for the first time where he was. "I should go. I need to get back home, to work."

"Not right now. You need to sleep first," said Anna. "I'll call your wife and tell her where you are."

Liam nodded and followed Anna to his old bedroom.

Anna came back down and got a towel from the kitchen to wipe at the tea stain. When that didn't suffice, she worked on the color with a spray bottle and a hard brush.

When she was finished, she looked at me and held my gaze. She spoke with determination: "Liam was never a child to lie. Tomas, yes. He could lie with the best of them, but not Liam."

If she believed it, then I supposed I had to, unless the police wanted to investigate the case more thoroughly. It was Anna's husband's reputation we were talking about here. She had every reason to want to think he wasn't a killer. "It feels unfinished somehow," I said. "There are still so many questions I wish we could have answered."

"And you hate having it end so abruptly, don't you?" said Anna, smiling like a mother watching a child make a familiar mistake.

She knew me too well.

Chapter 33

I knew as much of the truth about Tobias and Helena Torstensen as I was ever likely to get. I knew the truth about Carrie Helm, too, and I knew that God would mete out justice far better than the Mormon church ever could. But it wasn't enough for me. I had to do more. I had to do it for Carrie. And for my own daughter.

Kurt was still at work, so that evening I drove to Sandy and marched to the Westons' fine-looking front door. Judy Weston answered, though for a moment I thought I had seen a ghost. She looked so much like Carrie it was truly startling. She had her hair down instead of up and it had been lightened. It was carefully curled and she had far more makeup on than I had ever seen on her before. She wore sandals instead of heels and a pair of jeans that fit her figure nicely.

I had no idea if the transformation was on

purpose or not, but it was eerie and it stopped me in my tracks. I had been ready to demand, to scream, to make a ruckus. Now I was tongue-tied.

"Sister Wallheim, what a relief to see a friendly face. Come in," she said, looking behind me as she reached for the door, checking one direction and the other.

For news vans? Or for neighbors? A church court wouldn't be public, but it wouldn't be private, either. And even if people aren't supposed to talk about what goes on behind closed doors, the results would likely be immediately obvious to anyone who was in the church itself.

"How are you?" I asked her, trying to play along with her warmth. She clearly didn't know I had anything to do with instigating the church court all the way over here in Sandy, and I wanted to keep it that way as long as I could.

"It's been difficult," she said, her expression strained.

"You look — different," I said. She looked like a woman who was trying to be a teenager again. Did she know that made her look even older? If I were truly her friend, I would pull her aside and gently tell her that she didn't have to compete, that her wisdom and experience were of far more value than jiggly boobs or a clear complexion.

She held out her hands and looked at the cotton-candy-colored fingernail polish. "I'm trying to be my best," she said. "I'm trying, even if no one notices." She caught her breath on a sob, and then she sat down abruptly and covered her face with her hands.

How could I not have seen that something was wrong with her before? So deeply, deeply wrong. Gwen Ferris had said that her mother had been complicit in the rape of her daughters, but this went beyond complicity.

I stepped closer and put a hand on Judy Weston's shoulder. "You can get out of this situation," I said, each word clear as cut glass. "You don't have to stay here, no matter what he has said to you, no matter how many years you have put up with things you knew were wrong. You can start over. There are people who would be willing to help you." I was done playing roles here. I had to see who she was.

She threw off my hand immediately and looked up at me frostily. "I don't know what you are suggesting. I will stand at my husband's side no matter what terrible accusations are thrown at him. We are married eternally, and that's what those vows

490

mean to me and every other woman who loves the church and God."

But I still didn't know. Was she a monster who had sacrificed her own daughter to the god of a terrible, fiery pit? Or was she simply sick?

I tried to speak calmly to her, let her take her time to see the truth. "I'm sure this has all been very difficult for you. It must make it hard to see what the right choice is."

"It hasn't made it hard to see the right choice at all," she said, playing with her hair like a child. She looked up at me. "But it has put a great deal of pressure on my husband. It makes him angry at times, though he is normally such a calm and peaceful man. You know that. You saw him before." Her childlike tone made me want to shake her, and I had to clench my hands to keep them at my sides.

"I saw him," I said. I had seen him in a fervor about Carrie's disappearance. I wouldn't have called him calm. He had been a force even then. I just hadn't realized what kind of a force.

"But someone is spreading a terrible rumor about him and now Aaron has been called to a church court. This very morning he spoke to our stake president."

I said nothing to this.

491

"And he blames me," she went on. "He thinks that I had something to do with it, that I told the Relief Society president in our ward or one of the other leaders. No one will give him a name, but he is sure that it was me, and he will not speak to me. Maybe you could talk to him and explain that I would never do something like that."

If only it had been her who had told the truth about him. I felt a heaviness settle on my chest and shoulders. Here it was, the revelation I had been waiting for. She wasn't unaware of what had happened to her daughter. She wasn't afraid of her husband hurting her if she told the truth. She was just afraid of it upsetting her perfect life.

"He blames me for the other girls, too. He says that it is my fault they won't speak to him anymore." She was literally wringing her hands over this.

"How many other daughters do you have?" I asked. I had never had the chance to ask Gwen Ferris if she knew. Gwen had sisters, but I hadn't realized Carrie did. Strange that her father hadn't mentioned that in any of his numerous television interviews. The sisters had never been interviewed. They hadn't been at the funeral, either. And as far as I knew, Carrie hadn't been in touch with them.

"Three," said Judy. She looked cautious now of my questions, and I knew I would have to tread carefully.

"I hope they fared better than Carrie did. Did they marry well?" I asked.

"Yes, indeed they did. He was very proud of their marriages. It reflected well on him to have his daughters make such good matches."

"Was that all he cared about?" I said.

"No, of course not!" She shot me a sharp look. "He only wanted them to be happy."

Staring her in the eye, I asked, "And are they happy?"

I could see her struggling to hold my gaze, but she didn't look away. "When they first left, he had a good relationship with them. They would call him two or three times a week. Sometimes they would not talk to me at all. They wanted their daddy, and he spoiled them. He gave them money for clothes and to go out to dinner. When they were in college. It wasn't right. I told him that they needed to grow up, but he wouldn't listen to me. He said that they would always be his little girls." She kept looking at me, as if waiting for me to give her some kind of approval.

I withheld it. It seemed the only piece I had to play in this game. I didn't accuse her, just let her talk and try to get me to nod and smile at her, as everyone else seemed to.

"You said the relationship was good when they first left," I said. "Does that mean it's not so good anymore?"

"It wasn't his fault they stopped calling for him. They didn't ask him for money anymore, either. I thought it was a good thing. They needed their independence, and all children will go through stages, won't they?"

"Will they?" I said.

"Yes, of course they will. But it was a trial for both of us. One of our daughters wouldn't even let him come to her first baby's blessing. We didn't even know she was pregnant. She just sent us a card in the mail after it was done. Can you imagine how that hurt us both?"

Good for her, I thought, but all I said was, "Mmm."

I felt sorry for Judy Weston. I felt sickened for what she had accepted, as a wife and mother. But I could not like her. And my desire to try to help her escape was gone.

Carrie's choice in marriage had been dictated by her mother's example of submission, blindness, utter loyalty no matter what her husband's flaws, and she had only realized years later how limiting that kind of marriage was. Though perhaps she had still wanted to come back to it, for the comfort it offered her.

"What about that letter that Aaron had from her?" I asked finally. "The one you shared at the press conference? About Jared abusing her? Where did you get that?"

The red spots on her cheeks spread so that all but her lips seemed suffused in color. It was a strange thing to see, her lips pale against her darkened face, as if she had become a digital image with coloration reversed, not a human being.

"Aaron said that Carrie sent it to him," she insisted.

As I stood staring at her, trying to suppress my disgust, she burst out defensively, "We were good parents to her! We gave her everything she needed. And we would have done anything for her. She should have known that."

"Oh?" I said. Direct questions appeared to be less effective than nudging and letting her talk.

"Of course. We sent her Christmas gifts every year, and birthday gifts. We both wrote to her every month, and sent her scriptures to help her along in daily life. We were concerned about her, but we never pushed her. We only wanted the best for her. We wanted her to be happy, and she wasn't happy with Jared. Anyone could see that."

"But she was happy with you?" I said.

"Well, she was when she was younger. When she got older, she was confused. She started dressing provocatively. You must know what that's like with a teenage daughter." She made a dismissive hand gesture, completely unaware of the searing pain she had just caused me.

No, I did not know what that was like. And I never would.

"She started dating just about any boy she could. And Aaron would catch them together, practically naked, here at the house. But he never got angry with her. He disciplined her, but he didn't shout and he didn't hurt her. He loved her too much to do that."

He loved her indeed.

"He was always looking out for her online. He found out how to see her Facebook posts, even though she wouldn't friend us. He needed to know how she was doing."

He had stalked her via the Internet. That did not surprise me. "Of course he did," I murmured.

"And when Aaron saw that she had posted photographs of herself online — photographs like that — he had to go see her and talk to her. He had to stop her."

I felt the world shimmering around me. "He saw the photographs she had posted online from Las Vegas?" I said. This was too obvious, wasn't it? She couldn't have just told me the last clue in the puzzle of her daughter's murder.

"That wasn't from Facebook," said Judy. There was a strange pride in her demeanor now. "He watches certain sites. He does it to check on the girls in the ward, and the women. He wants to make sure that they are safe. Sometimes photos are posted as a cruel joke, or by a woman who is in a fury and changes her mind later. He is only looking for people he recognizes, so he can help them."

"I have to go," I said to Judy Weston. I needed to tell the police this. Then they could arrest Aaron Weston for the murder of his daughter at last. They could trace him on the Internet, surely. Then I could go home to my own family, where I was safe, and where the whole world wasn't upside down and inside out.

CHAPTER 34

I left the Westons' house, not bothering with any social niceties and leaving Judy gawping behind me. I drove home and called the police while I was still buzzing from the adrenaline rush.

After that, things moved quickly. Late Saturday night, Aaron Weston was announced as a suspect in the case of his daughter's murder. The police served a warrant on his house and took possession of his computers and his car. According to the Sunday morning news, they were looking for proof that he had driven to Wendover and that he had killed his daughter in his own car. I was not happy with the ending of this sad story, but at least it was an ending. I had done something for Carrie Helm at last, even if it wasn't nearly what I'd wanted to do. And Kelly Helm would be as safe as I could make her, though I might not see her often.

"It seems the best ending I can hope for," I told Kurt when he got home from church meetings after ten.

"But who will his daughters be sealed to, then?" asked Kurt. "I know I should simply trust in God, and I do. But I wonder even so."

It was one thing to think of a woman with children sealed to someone besides their father in the eternities, but it was another again to try to imagine a way out of this mess. Would the daughters all be sealed to different families? Then what about their connection to each other? I could not imagine that God would bind them forever to a mother like Judy Weston. They say He forgives all and that we will all be changed beyond recognition, once the work of redemption is complete. But could those daughters ever have happy marriages and relationships with their own families after this? All I could see was generation to generation, daughters and mothers set adrift from sealings. More questions that had no answers.

Monday I had the television on to watch the news, as I usually did during lunch. I didn't expect to hear anything about the Westons, but around noon, their house appeared on the screen, surrounded by SWAT vans. People in uniforms were converging on the house with guns.

"Breaking news. Aaron Weston, father and suspected murderer of young Draper mother Carrie Helm, has locked himself and his wife in their house and threatened to kill her and then himself rather than surrender to police, as he was supposed to earlier this morning. Police say that Aaron Weston has a weapon and that he has spoken to them on the phone. He claims that he is innocent and that his daughters, who have made statements against their father to the police, have been subject to brainwashing worked on them by his wife."

He had turned on her, and I couldn't feel sorry for her. But I felt no satisfaction. I might think Judy deserved to lose her daughters in the hereafter, but I didn't think she deserved to die. Not at her husband's hands.

I turned the television off immediately and got in the car. I called Kurt and told him about the news as I drove south.

"What are you doing? Why? No. Linda, this is none of your business. They're not in our ward. They're not your responsibility."

"Yes, they are," I said. "You know they are. This is what I have to do. I started all of this and now I have to finish it."

"Is this about Georgia?" said Kurt.

It was the first time he had said her name in years. It jolted me a little, and I had to work harder to focus on the road. "Not really," I said. "Not in any direct way."

"Then why are you doing this? Why put yourself in danger?"

I could see the Draper temple in my rearview mirror, the Oquirrh temple to my left behind the South Jordan temple. The Salt Lake temple was less visible ahead of me. So many temples, where only good thoughts and godliness were supposed to be, and so much horror in the real world around them.

"Kurt, you knew who I was when you married me. I need to be doing something. I need to make a difference."

"You are making a difference already. At home. In the ward."

Where he was in control of my influence. "Maybe that's true and maybe it isn't. But I should have done more. I should have seen things more clearly. If I'd been doing what I was meant to do from the beginning, this might have turned out differently. I've been running away from myself. And now, for the first time, I feel like I'm running forward, not hiding myself." I should have been scared to death, but I wasn't. I felt like I was flying. I felt like I had lost fifty pounds and twenty years. "Firm as the mountains around us." The powerful line from one my favorite old hymns, and that was how it felt. The mountains were firm around me, so I could fly.

"Linda, there's a SWAT team there. You don't want to get caught in the cross fire."

"I'll be as careful as I can," I promised him, and hung up. I needed to talk to Aaron and Judy Weston. I could convince him to turn himself in. I could save Judy's pitiful life. And I was the only one who could do it. I was the bridge from faith to truth here, and I wasn't going to step aside while other people told me that they could do it better. Even if those people were Kurt or the police, people who had more supposed authority than I did. Authority was given by God, and He was surely telling me to do this now.

After twenty minutes of driving I was pulling into the cul-de-sac of the wealthy neighborhood in Sandy. No one was watching for me. I parked a block away and then tucked myself into my coat. I had always had the gift of being invisible. It would serve me well again.

I was parked by the garage, near the

bushes that divided this property from the next. I could see the SWAT team near the van at the front of the house was on the phone with someone inside, most likely Aaron. I wanted to see Judy. And there she was, her face peeking out of the curtain of the sliding back doors.

I didn't look back. I simply moved forward. By the time the SWAT team saw me, I was already knocking on the glass door and Judy Weston was opening it.

She didn't look particularly glad to see me, but she was trembling and I think she was glad to see anyone who wasn't her husband.

"What are you doing?" said Aaron loudly, as he came into the vast living room. He was carrying a butcher knife casually, and he was holding a phone to his ear. As soon as he saw me, he smiled at me and pointed at me with the butcher knife.

I hadn't imagined I would get him to turn himself in without facing him like this. But somehow when the moment came, it was more terrifying than I had anticipated.

Aaron Weston spoke into the phone: "I have a second hostage now. Her name is Linda Wallheim." He hung up the phone, and motioned for Judy to close the sliding doors.

My stomach seemed to drop to my knees.

I hadn't said a word of prayer, the whole time I'd been on my way here. Not out loud and not in my heart, either. Maybe I should have, but somehow I had thought in this case God was counting on me instead of the reverse.

Why had I wanted to come in here again? What in the world had I thought I could do that a SWAT team couldn't? I had had no training in this, no matter how much I told myself it was what I was "meant" to do. I felt a sudden cold sweat of fear at the realization that I had just placed myself into the power of a man who had killed his own daughter. I was now in the same situation Carrie Helm had been in for so long. Was I going to be able to effect an escape any better than she had?

"You," said Aaron. "You whore."

The fact that he used the same word as Alex Helm had to make me slap him was strange. I didn't feel the same anger at all. Possibly because Aaron Weston was speaking so calmly, wearing a fine suit like he had the first time I met him.

My failure to react physically seemed to enrage him, because he lunged at me with the knife. Then I shrieked involuntarily and he pulled back.

"This is the fault of people like you," he spat out. "My daughters would never —"

"You can stop trying to tell me your excuses. How they seduced you or lied to you or anything else. I'm not interested."

He stared at me. "I'll kill you, too. Don't think I won't. I've gone this far. I killed Carrie, and I'm glad that I did. She needed to die. She didn't know how to be a mother anymore, or a wife. Her husband will thank me, too, in time."

At last, I had the impression that I was seeing the real Aaron Weston. There is a legend among Mormons that if you meet a spirit, you should ask to shake hands. An evil spirit will agree to shake, and you will feel no substance. A good spirit will refuse to shake your hand. I wished I had had such a simple test for evil men and good men when I had met Aaron.

"What about Carrie's daughter?" I asked. "Will Kelly thank you for killing her mother?"

Aaron Weston shrugged. "She is a girl. She belongs to her father, not to me."

This wasn't Mormonism, I thought. This had nothing to do with my Mormonism. Only with Aaron Weston's, and his was wrong.

The phone rang again, but Aaron ignored

it. He looked up at me smugly. He nodded out the glass doors to the SWAT team in the driveway and on the street. "They think they are building a relationship with me. They think that they are doing something other than delaying the inevitable."

But he hadn't killed himself or Judy yet. Or me. That meant something, didn't it? "You don't want to die," I said. That was, I hoped, where his goal and mine coincided.

"Don't I? My life is over. Everything I've built, my reputation, my family," he said, his expression dark.

Good. If he saw that clearly, then maybe he could see the rest. "And when you die, what do you think will happen? Aaron, what kind of a God do you believe in?" I asked him.

This was the biggest gamble I had taken in my life. I assumed that after all of his years in the Mormon church, he actually believed some part of it, that it wasn't all part of a pretense to abuse power. I felt my fear fading and a strange calm envelop me. Maybe I had gone beyond fear, or maybe it was the Holy Spirit. I don't know.

He stared down at the knife as if talking to his face in a mirror. "God will justify me," he said. "I have done a lot of good. If I have made mistakes, well, so have others."

"Aaron," I said, to make him look at me. He wasn't alone in this house. He wasn't in some dreamworld of his own making. "It's not just a mistake to kill your daughter. You planned it."

He waved a hand. "Look at Joseph Smith. He had affairs with women long before he instituted the so-called doctrine of polygamy. He was a man with certain lusts, and he found a way to make them palatable to others. He declared a new doctrine."

"You are not Joseph Smith," I said. I wasn't here to defend the founder of Mormonism and the polygamy that had long since been repudiated. Joseph Smith had not been a perfect man, but I believed in the church he had built, and in the Book of Mormon he had translated.

"That is how people outside the church see him. As a lecher. A despoiler of young girls," said Aaron Weston. "But he was a holy man even so."

So was that his excuse? That another man had done what he had done and still been praised for his life? "Joseph Smith did not abuse his own daughters," I pointed out.

"Are you so sure of that?" said Aaron. "He could have made it holy if he had. A holy man makes everything holy that he touches."

I had seen him as a prophet for a moment at the funeral. Did he see himself that way? How often had that excused him in his own mind?

"No one wants to see the underside of the church anymore, the bloody truth behind glory. If the Mormon church has lost its way, and I think it has, then it is because the leaders don't understand that there is a danger and a madness to true holiness." He waved the knife, shiny blade glinting, to punctuate his speech.

I thought of the afternoon I had spent hours chopping those vegetables in my kitchen, until I'd ruined one knife and had to reach for another. I didn't even remember doing that. I shuddered at the thought that I was like Aaron Weston in some way.

"This new group of apostles, old men who are used to comfortable lives — they want to stay on the side of the law. They want to be accepted by society in general. They don't want to be seen as a cult. And they have abandoned everything about Mormonism that made it difficult to live. They will make us all men who choose what is easiest, not what is right."

This was a doctrine I had heard before, in different forms. If the "world" believed something, then you had to believe its opposite to be righteous. It made people rage against everything from a global economy to public schooling and immunizations, but mostly I thought it was just an excuse not to have to do the work that seeing shades of grey requires.

"So you believe that when you die, you will go to the celestial kingdom because you are doing terrible, illegal things? That's why you're so eager for death?" I asked, staring the man straight in the face.

I felt like I was right on the edge of a fragile rock bridge in Zion National Park. We had been there with all the boys once, and I had never felt anything like the sensation of standing there, on such a thin piece of rock, with the wind blowing all around. That was the valley of the shadow of death. And here I was again.

The knife turned again in his hand, and I wondered how many times he had handled it like this before, as a weapon rather than a tool.

I glanced at Judy Weston. She was still shaking, but there was no expression on her face. She was blank, as much a puppet as Aaron Weston had always seemed to think that she was.

"I believe — there may be a time of waiting," he said, the knife moving so casually

509

from hand to hand. "But yes, ultimately, I believe God will agree with what I have done. He will see that in the moral dilemma in which he placed us, this was the only choice. Like the forbidden fruit in the Garden of Eden."

I tried not to look at the knife. I didn't want him to think that it was what mattered here. This had to be a conversation between two equals or it would never work. I tried to lower my voice, and I widened my stance, like a man might. "A period of waiting?" I asked him, seizing on this one hint of doubt. "You mean spirit prison, don't you? And who do you think will be there with you, waiting?"

He didn't answer me. He looked out the front window, visible through the kitchen, at the SWAT teams surrounding the house, the knife turning and turning. The phone rang again. He looked at the number, but he didn't answer it.

He was on the precipice too, I thought. But he was completely alone, staring into the abyss.

"I won't be there long, so I hardly think it matters. But if I have to endure the company of the wicked there, it will be no different from what I endure here." He gestured at the front door of the house with the knife, and then at his wife.

She stared at the knife and seemed unable to look away.

"And what about Carrie, your daughter? Do you think she will be waiting for you in spirit prison?"

"Carrie — well, maybe she will be there."

"Then what do you think she will say to you when you see her in spirit? Before you die, you should consider that, don't you think?" I could see him rubbing his thumb across the edge of the knife now, making friends with it. "If you give yourself up, you will have to face a trial. But you think that anyone who hears your story will believe you, right?" I asked.

Judy Weston was silent, as she had been all her life. I was glad this once; it meant she didn't get in my way.

"Think about this choice. If you killed yourself now, or goaded others into killing you, wouldn't that be a crime in itself? To give up on what you could teach here? Do you think God would approve of you giving up so easily, when there are so many things you need to change in the church itself?"

He looked at me. "What do you know about the priesthood? About the heavens and the place of gods there? You are a woman," he said.

Damn. I'd been hoping he wouldn't think in that direction. "My husband sent me here," I said. It was pure inspiration. "He thought I would get in more easily. But he gave me the words to say."

"Ah," he said, nodding. "Your husband is a good man."

"Good" and "man" being synonymous, it seemed. Just as it was with Alex Helm. Carrie must have thought the Helms were different at first, but the more she lived with Jared, the more she realized she had simply traded one kind of misogynist for another.

I held up my hands, playing on the woman card now that it was out there. "Aaron, I just want to get Judy out of here. She and I will leave and you can stay and do whatever you want." I really did not care if he lived or died, except for the trouble and danger it would cause the SWAT team outside. I was quite confident that God would deal with him justly, once he was gone. The punishment he would get there would surely be worse than anything he could suffer here. And I wanted him to suffer badly. I wanted Carrie Helm to know that he was suffering.

"Please, Aaron," said Judy, her voice breaking as tears streamed down her face. She was good at tears.

"Go, then. Both of you," he said at last.

He turned his back on me, and threw the knife in the air.

I didn't wait to see where it landed. I grabbed hold of Judy's wrist, yanked on the sliding glass doors, and threw Judy out of them. Then I jumped on top of her and rolled, taking her with me down the lawn and toward the street.

The SWAT team came in immediately after that. With an open door, and the hostages out, they seized the opportunity.

Long minutes later, I heard gunfire inside the house. Judy flinched with each shot as I prayed my thanks that I was still alive. An EMT came over to us and helped us to our feet, then led us to an ambulance that was waiting nearby.

I was bleeding and hadn't noticed it. Aaron Weston had cut me with that knife of his, after all. I stared at my bleeding left arm and wondered why he hadn't dug deeper, or simply killed me.

They say God looks after fools. Maybe this was the proof of it.

We saw Aaron being carried out of the house on a stretcher while we were still waiting for transport to the hospital. I couldn't see his face because it was covered with an oxygen mask. He looked as if he'd been shot in the chest, but they had a separate ambulance for him.

Kurt came to see me at Lone Peak Hospital. They insisted that I go to have the cut on my left arm checked out, even though I thought I was fine.

He didn't chastise me. He simply sat and held my hand and told me loved me.

When I was finally discharged late that night, he kissed me gently on the cheek.

"We'll have to talk about this," Kurt said.

"I know."

We had a lot to talk about.

CHAPTER 35

Samuel wouldn't speak to me Monday night when I got home. There was no pretense of Family Home Evening.

"He's mad you could have gotten hurt. He'll come around," said Kurt, as he helped me up the stairs to our bedroom.

I hoped Kurt was right about Samuel. I couldn't bear for my youngest son, the one most like me, to hold a grudge.

When I woke up the next day, I felt as if my skin had been filled with sand while I slept. There were no muscles inside me, and I felt very heavy.

Kurt brought me breakfast in bed, and I spent the morning on the phone with the older boys, who were apparently still talking to me. Samuel had gone off to school without a word, and he hadn't answered either of the two text messages I had sent him.

Kurt had taken time off work, despite the

clients who insisted they had "emergencies." I was touched by that. We also had a visit from Cheri Tate, who said she had arranged for meals to come for the next week.

Kurt didn't hover, but went down to his office and got to some church paperwork he'd been putting off for a while. About noon, I got up and coaxed myself into taking a careful bath. The heat seemed to melt away the sandy feeling. My left arm still hurt where they had put in stitches, but if I put on a long-sleeved shirt, I could almost forget about it. No one else could see it, either, and when I looked at myself critically in the mirror, I did not think any of the events of the day before showed. I looked tired and my eyes were a little red, but there was no more proof that I had nearly been killed than that. But the change was inside me, even so.

I thought of going for a short walk, and I stepped outside without knocking on Kurt's door.

The first thing I saw was a FOR SALE sign in front of the Helm house. It hit me hard and I could feel my legs falling out from under me. I went down on my knees on the sidewalk and then knelt there for a long minute. My ears rang, but I didn't appear to have broken anything. I tried to laugh at

516

myself. This was literalizing the metaphor, wasn't it?

A car drove by, and I saw the kind face of a ward member poking out from a window.

I lifted a hand and waved them on. "I'm fine," I called out. Just wanted to kneel on the ground for a few minutes. They probably thought I was being super devout and had decided in the middle of my walk to kneel down and pray. Or maybe they just thought I was crazy. That would be closer to the mark.

I pushed off the sidewalk with the palms of my hands and got to my feet. I took a few small, steadying steps before deciding that I was fine, that I could do this walk, so long as I didn't have to face any more bad news about Kelly Helm.

I went back inside and told Kurt I was going to Anna's. He asked me if I was sure, but he didn't try to stop me.

"I'll be here if you need anything. Make sure you have your phone," he said.

In case I fell again and needed help getting up, yes.

I walked over to Anna's house and we went around the neighborhood. When we passed the Helm home, Anna's hand tightened on mine.

"Don't look," she said to me.

"I already saw it," I said, and looked again. It still hurt to see it. I found myself holding my breath, unable to keep walking. The pain in my left arm suddenly flared up and I felt almost as if I were back in the house with Aaron Weston and his knife.

No, I was home. I was free of him. Kelly was free of him, too.

But not of Jared and Alex Helm.

"She will be fine," said Anna. "She will go to another ward and she'll be taken care of there. You have to depend on that. There are good ward members all over the world."

I stood there, staring at the window. Kelly's window. She was not my daughter, my Georgia. She hadn't come into my life to be a substitute for me. But she had come for a reason. She had come to bring me to myself.

"Have you seen her at all since the funeral?"

"A couple of times," I said.

"It's not your fault, you know. That Jared is taking her away. He would likely have done it anyway. He needs a new start, and maybe Kelly does, too."

Maybe.

I caught a glimpse of a face out the window, and then there was a small hand waving at me. I smiled and waved back.

Then she was gone.

"We should keep going," said Anna. She rubbed her shoulders as if it were still winter. "It's cold."

She was doing it for my sake, I knew, pretending that I should do it for hers.

We had headed back up the street when suddenly something hit me from behind, at about thigh height. It was soft and warm and I thought at first it must be one of the neighborhood dogs that sometimes get out. I would probably recognize it when I turned around and could help it find its way home.

But it wasn't a dog.

It was Kelly Helm, and she was alone. I looked back at her house. How long until either Jared or Alex came running after her and snatched her up? A matter of seconds, most likely.

So I turned around and wrapped my arms around her, lifting her into the air. "How are you, sweetie?" I asked. She wasn't my daughter, but that didn't mean I couldn't enjoy her little-girl softness and her little-girl smile.

She started babbling at that pace young children have, so fast a lot of the words got lost in the mix. "Daddy bought a new house, and it has a little house in the backyard just for me. He says I can have sleepovers in it and I can have a kitty. And he says my new mommy will be there for me. And I'm going to go to school there. The school is just across the street and I will be able to walk there. When the summer is done I'm going to meet my new teacher and my new friends and I'll get a new backpack and new shoes and maybe even a new hat and mittens. And my new mommy will make me a lunch to put in a sack and I already went to church there. And they sing the same songs that we sing here, except they also sing one about snow and rain and sunshine." She began to sing in a sweet, clear soprano.

Tears stung my eyes, thinking of the musical ability in her that I would never be able to nurture. Not my daughter, I reminded myself again.

"Do you want to come see my room? It's all packed up in boxes. It looks funny."

"I don't think that's a good idea," I said, looking up at the house again. Where were Jared and Alex? Who was looking out for Kelly? "Let's take you back home. I'm sure they're wondering where you are."

"Grandpa is on the phone," said Kelly. "He's talking to the movers."

Ah, that explained it. And Kelly had

slipped out while he had his back turned. Again.

And she would be punished again if he noticed she was gone.

"You go on, Linda," said Anna. "I'll see you tomorrow. I'm going to get home now."

I watched Anna's receding back and felt a little lost. A part of me wished she had stayed, but another part of me had an impulse to pick Kelly into my arms again and run to my own house with her. I could put her in the car and take her out for ice cream and then? There was no "and then." She had her family and I had mine. We were sealed to them, and not to each other.

"You can walk in," said Kelly. "The door isn't locked."

"You go in and when I ring the doorbell, you can open it," I told her, thinking that the confusion of me at the door might make Alex or Jared not notice that Kelly had been coming in, not coming down the stairs to the door.

After Kelly let me in, it was a minute or two before Alex Helm appeared with a cell phone to his ear. He said, "Look, I'll call you back, all right?" He put the cell phone away and then looked up at me again, as if he expected I might have disappeared in the meantime.

"Hello," I said.

"Kelly, are you finished in your room?" he said to get rid of her. "Are you ready for your father to come get you and take you to the motel for the night?"

"Yes," said Kelly. "It's going to be an adventure!" She smiled up at me brightly.

Would she remember her mother at all? I had tried to give her that photograph, but it was still at home where I had tucked it away. Maybe it was better for Kelly this way, to forget the mother who was dead now. Her father was getting remarried and she would have a new mother, and she could keep smiling like that for the rest of her life.

I thought of Helena Torstensen, and Tobias. And Liam, who had tried to forget his mother's last moment of life.

"I'm very happy for you, Kelly," I said. "I wish the very best things for you."

"Now up to your room," her grandfather said, pushing her away and up the stairs.

"But I want Sister Wallheim to see our new house," said Kelly. "Can she come with us when we go today? Or tomorrow? Please, she could bring us some food."

"No," said Alex Helm. "That's not appropriate. She lives here. And you will live there." Alex Helm looked acutely uncomfortable.

"I'm very busy this afternoon and tomorrow anyway," I said, though the last word was thready. I didn't want to say those words at all. I wanted Alex Helm to say no to Kelly. I wanted him to be the bad guy. But he was going to be in Kelly's new happy life, and I wasn't. So I did what I did for her sake, not his. Not mine.

"Oh," said Kelly. Her lips turned downward for just a moment.

"But remember, after we see the new house, we're going to McDonald's," said Alex Helm.

"McDonald's! Yay!" said Kelly. She looked at me, and for a moment, I thought she was going to ask me to meet her there, too, and I would have to tell her no again.

"Go on and check your room one more time. Make sure that your dolls are all safe," said Alex Helm.

Kelly trotted up the stairs obediently, and I was left alone with Alex Helm.

"They are marrying in the temple next Friday," he said. There were no rules about waiting to be married in the temple for a certain period of time after a death, like there were with divorce. You just had to get a special temple recommend from your bishop to do living ordinances for yourself. And Kurt hadn't told me that Jared Helm had come to him in the last week. Maybe it had been even earlier.

"If you would like to come —" Alex Helm added.

It was an olive branch, but I shook my head. It wasn't as if Kelly would be there, and I didn't feel that comfortable with Jared or Alex Helm in any case. "But thank you. Give him my best, if you will."

"He's at the office today. He's leaving the moving to me and Ginny."

Ginny was to be Kelly's new mother, it seemed. I nodded.

There was a honk, and I looked over my shoulder. A woman with short dark hair had pulled into the driveway.

"There she is. Ginny," said Alex Helm.

I had a few moments to stare at her. She seemed completely different from Carrie Helm, who had been beautiful and so very feminine. Ginny seemed more no-nonsense, capable. She was small, but sturdy. I liked her immediately, and that surprised me. I hadn't expected Jared Helm to choose a woman like that. Except — she was different from Carrie. It made a kind of sense that he would want that.

"I told him not to pick someone who needed rescuing this time," said Alex Helm in my ear, the intimate understanding of my thoughts uncanny enough to make me shiver. Then he moved around me and went to speak to Ginny.

She turned off the car and came in.

"This is Linda Wallheim, Jared's bishop's wife," Alex Helm introduced us. But not his? He lived here now, didn't he? But if he owned another home, that would count on church records.

Ginny held out a hand, and I shook it, impressed with her firm grip. She had an unabashed way of looking at me, straight in the eye. "Thank you for taking care of my family until I could find them," she said. I had the feeling it wasn't just words to her, that she meant it.

Alex stepped into the house and called for Kelly, who bounded down the steps and threw herself into Ginny's arms.

"I've got your car seat already buckled in, so you can do the rest yourself," said Ginny.

Kelly ran to the car and got inside.

Ginny turned to me. "So nice to meet you and thank you for all you've done."

"I'm not sure it was much, but I am glad to meet you. Take care of Kelly for me, will you?" I asked.

"Of course," she said. "And Jared and Alex, too."

Of course, Jared and Alex, too. Later that

afternoon, I heard the moving van and let myself look out the window just once. Six men in worn clothes were packing the last of the Helms' belongings into a huge truck. Then the house would be empty. It was time to move on.

I went home and began planning a special family dinner. Because they were my family, and that was the only reason I needed for a celebration.

CHAPTER 36

By June, a new family quickly moved in to the Helm house. They had three young children and the mother seemed very frazzled.

Later that summer, I knocked on Anna's door for our daily walk, but she held car keys in her hand.

"It's Helena's birthday today," she said. "I thought we would go visit her grave. And Tobias's. Do you mind?"

I knew she hadn't been to the cemetery since Tobias was buried.

We drove down to the city cemetery. Helena's remains had finally been released to her family, and then buried beside Tobias, in the plot where Anna had always imagined she would be.

"Have you decided what to do yet?" There wasn't a plot directly next to Tobias's on the other side, but she could buy another plot nearby.

"The cemetery said that I could be buried on top of her. They'd be willing to rebury her further down."

"And do you feel good about that?"

"I don't know," said Anna. "Maybe that's another reason why I'm here today. And why I wanted you to come with me." She leaned over and gripped my hand tightly. She had already turned off the engine and was staring at the expanse of green grass.

It was a beautiful day in Utah, one of those summer days when the sky seems endlessly blue and you can't imagine that winter will ever come again. There is no hint of cold in the air. It is all dry, scorching heat trying to turn you into a desert stone.

Anna took a deep breath and reached for the door. I stepped out with her into the shimmering heat.

We walked in silence over to the left, where Tobias was buried. The last time we were here, there had been no headstone. Now there were two.

BELOVED WIFE AND MOTHER was carved under the name Helena Torstensen. I pointed at it. "Did you choose that?" I asked Anna.

"The boys and I chose it together."

We stood over the two graves, the final

date for Helena thirty-two years before Tobias's.

"What do you think?" Anna asked. "About
me being buried with her?"

"I think you're going to live for a long
time yet," I said. "Maybe you will get remarried and you'll decide you want to be buried
with your new husband."

"You are such a romantic," said Anna.

"Me? I'm practical. You're young and at-
tractive."

"Young?" sputtered Anna. "I'm sixty-two."

"Which is still young," I said. It was only
a few years older than me, and she looked
younger still, or at least she looked beautiful
and strong, the kind of woman men should
want to marry. "Besides, it's hard to live
alone when you're used to living with
someone else."

Anna shook her head. "You know, women
who are happy in marriage are a lot less
likely to marry again than men who are
happy in marriage," she said. "It's a statistic
I heard somewhere."

"And you think that's because of what?
Women don't need men as much as men
need women?" I asked.

"That would be one explanation. Or it
could be that the good men are already
taken by the time you'd have a second

chance."

"I can't believe that. There have to be good men out there who have lost their wives." The words came out before I realized what I was saying.

"Exactly," said Anna. "And then I would have to choose again, if I wanted to be buried on his other side. If I wanted to share him. Again."

"It might not be like that," I said. But it was too late to take it back. She was right. At her age, she was most likely to find someone who was either widowed or divorced. She would have to deal with being second all over again.

"And besides, I believe that Tobias and I were a miracle, really. That he found me and that I found him. I'm not sure that I could expect that ever again. He needed me and I wanted to be needed like that."

"Do you still wonder who he will be with, afterward?" I asked her.

She shook her head. "Somehow it just doesn't seem to matter anymore."

We walked quietly around the cemetery for another hour. Then we got back into the car and she drove home. We went inside her house, and she got out tea. We talked about Carrie and Kelly Helm, and about Georgia. I cried in Anna's arms, and then I went

530

home, to figure out the rest of my life, whatever I was going to make of it.

ACKNOWLEDGMENTS

I'd like to thank Juliet Grames for taking a chance on this book. We met serendipitously at Sirens Conference in Vail, Colorado, in October of 2010 and she asked me to send her something if I ever wrote something she could publish. Over the next few years, I sent her several things, but none of them were right for Soho. Even when I sent her *The Bishop's Wife* in January of 2013, I was merely asking for her opinion, not imagining she could publish the book. After all, Soho Crime mostly specialized in international crime stories. When she offered publication on that first read, I was stunned, happy, confused, nervous, and a whole host of other emotions. When I asked her how she could publish a book set in small-town Utah that was *not* international, she said, "It's like Mormons are a different country. They speak a different language, and you're

533

the interpreter."* I've never worked so easily with an editor before. I found myself anticipating her suggestions, and having fun with them. Thanks also to Briony Everroad for a final tightening of this book.

Barry Goldblatt has been my agent from the first, and by that, I mean the first book I ever published, *The Monster in Me,* a contemporary realistic young adult that was my first attempt to get at this world I live in. Natalie Wills's foster family was also Mormon, but I felt constrained in my ability to talk about their Mormonism at that time. Barry has guided me through the confusing maze of the publishing world and he has made it possible for me to try out this new form of storytelling. At his yearly client retreats, he often talks about "the book of your heart." It has taken me ten years of retreats to realize what that even meant. After I figured it out, it was actually very easy to write it. To all his other clients, and to other writers out there, this is a real thing. There are actually books that only

* Editor's note: Juliet remembers a different version of this original story, wherein Mette pitched the book to her by saying, "I know Utah isn't international, but it's like Mormons are a different country."

you can write. You will do yourself and the world a service by figuring out what they are.

Thanks to my book group, which was at first officially sponsored by our ward's Relief Society, and has now become its own independent entity. Thank you for letting me be loud when I needed to be loud, and for reading my suggestions even when I forgot all the bad words and other naughty things. Thanks for making me feel like I was welcome again, when I felt I had lost myself and my place in the world. Thanks in particular to Sylvia Pack and to Jen Koldewyn, who have been fine examples of real bishop's wives in my life. Thanks to the non-Mormon women who have joined our group rather daringly, and shown me the rest of us from their perspective.

To my own Mormon community, I sincerely hope that this book makes you laugh in parts, cry in parts, and that you feel I have done justice to the complexity of our doctrine and our culture. As Linda says, this is my Mormonism. It may not be yours exactly, but I hope it is close enough. I hope there are many Mormon women out there who read this book and see parts of themselves in Linda. I hope that there are many non-Mormons who read this book and see how smart, thoughtful, kind, and powerful Mormon women can be, even if they seem to be following a traditionally feminine path, and even if you do not see them in the church leadership. In that way, I think Linda is actually very ordinary, and that I, a stay-at-home mother of five who finds the power of motherhood overwhelming at times, am ordinary, as well.

ABOUT THE AUTHOR

Mette Ivie Harrison is the author of numerous books for young adults, including her critically acclaimed The Princess and the Hound series. She holds a Ph.D. in German literature from Princeton University and is a nationally ranked triathlete. A member of the Church of Jesus Christ of Latter-Day Saints, she lives in Utah with her husband and four children.